MURDERS AT THE BLACK ABBEY TOWERS

A PRUNELLA PEARCE MYSTERY

BOOK FIVE

GINA KIRKHAM

BLOODHOUND
— BOOKS —

First published in 2025 by Bloodhound Books.

www.bloodhoundbooks.com

Print ISBN: 978-1917705431

For my mentor & friend
Tara Lyons

'No beauty shines brighter than that of a good heart'

PROLOGUE

31 OCTOBER 1899

*T*he house stood bleak and brooding against the last rays of the weak October sun as it set behind the imposing bell tower. The red stock brick, crumbling mortar and aerial roots of weathered ivy that gnarled its fingers into every crevice, combined their presence to give credence to the village tales of dark deeds and malevolent spirits that dwelt within. The formidable arched entrance doors, adorned by heavy black hinges, held their place upon the aged wood with large square studs. Each narrow window, arranged in groups of three or four, dug deep into the façade and produced what appeared at first sight, to be an orange glow of welcome from within.

The girl stood before the doors and marvelled at their majesty. Even with the warm velvet cloak wrapped tightly around her, she shivered, unsure if it was in anticipation of a night that promised joviality, high jinks and good food, or because of the sudden and unexpected tingle that crept along her spine. Her fingers traced the deeply etched letters on the wall-mounted sandstone nameplate.

BLACK ABBEY TOWERS

She gave a wry smile. A perfect venue for a perfect All Hallows Eve.

Before she had chance to announce her arrival, the doors suddenly parted company, silently opening inwards. She did not enter but waited with bated breath, mesmerised by the vast expanse of marble flooring that stretched across the grand entrance hall to eagerly join with the rich oak of a bifurcated staircase that swept east and west, showcasing the elaborately stitched red velvet curtains that framed the floor-to-ceiling stained-glass window at the top. A gasp of wonderment caught in her throat as she unfurled the letter held tight between her fingers. She checked again that she had the correct time for the gathering and once she was sure all was in order, she hesitantly placed one foot over the threshold, and then, just as quickly, snatched it back. Tentacles of apprehension had suddenly crept over her, clawing at her, making her hesitate in her desire to enter Black Abbey Towers.

How odd that there was no butler, no maid, no invitation giver or occupant to greet her.

A sudden chill came from within the walls of Black Abbey Towers, flowing towards her through the opening. It swirled around her, picking up dry autumn leaves and debris, turning them into a tiny maelstrom of energy prior to scattering them across the floor. She watched mesmerised as they created an almost perfect pattern. She tilted her head and listened, but before she could consider her position, or her intention to step inside, the energy reformed and encircled her, pushing her from behind like an invisible hand against her back. She half stumbled, half fell, over the worn threshold stone, and throwing her hands out to save herself, she tumbled forwards into his arms.

'Florence my dear, I'm delighted you could make it!'

His presence had appeared from nowhere, like the ghosts from the tales that the village mothers would tell their children to keep them in their beds. The tales of missing daughters who had passed by The Towers and had never returned home, becoming lost spectres of the night when darkness fell. The Myths of Fallow Falls were legendary, added to and embellished over many years to become deeply embedded in local lore.

He stood before her, radiating no warmth, no true welcome and no kindness in his eyes. Bewildered, she pulled away from him. 'Where is everyone?' she whispered as she turned circles searching around her, her emerald-green cloak undulating with the momentum. 'Where are the Hobeddy lanterns, the neeps and candles... the lights I saw from outside?'

Calduggan Wraithe grinned, his demeanour suddenly menacing. 'Who needs them when we have the Devil himself to entertain us?' He roughly grabbed her hand, squeezing it tightly within his own to ensure she could not escape. His laughter was chilling, his movements around the grand hall erratic as he dragged her towards the banqueting room. Florence stumbled and fell to her knees, but that did not stop him in his progress; he continued to drag her by her cloak, pulling her onto her back as he hauled her over the marble flooring she had only moments before admired. Tribal masks hung from the walls either side of a fearsome half-man, half-goat statue that loomed above the great fireplace. She fought him, writhing and screaming for him to release her as her ballet flats squeaked and caught on the polished tiles, her eyes white with terror. The intricate bow cord she had tied and admired at the neck of her cloak only an hour earlier in the tarnished mirror at her cottage, was now acting as a makeshift garrotte. Her fingers scrabbled for purchase at her neck in an attempt to release it, but a surge of blood rushed to her cheeks as the cord tightened with each slithering motion across the expanse of floor. She kicked out, knocking over a tall candelabra. It crashed noisily to the floor, the lit candles scattering and rolling.

He abruptly halted his progression in the middle of the vast room and knelt down beside her, briefly touching her cheek as he allowed her some relief from the tight cord. Florence was unsure if the flickering glow in his eyes was a form of madness or a reflection of something she could not yet see. A wave of fear burned deep in the pit of her stomach as she inhaled a thick, acrid vapour that forced her to cough uncontrollably. She barely knew this man; had only accepted his invitation because he himself was the want of every young girl in Fallow Falls. The dashingly handsome and very rich Calduggan Wraithe would be a *fine catch for any one of them, not least for nineteen-year-old Florence. A pairing with the Wraithe name would drag her from the poverty she now endured to a life of affluence and comfort. She had expected to be vying with many others for his interest this very evening, whilst dancing and making merry. Instead, she was alone with him in a room, eerily draped in black gossamer fabrics that were...*

... on fire!

This had not been part of the plan; she had failed to heed the warnings and had ignored the ghostly tales, and now the fear was overwhelming her. Had her desire for betterment overshadowed basic common sense? His invitation had promised her simple things associated with the fun and frivolousness of All Hallows Eve, and an introduction to a man who was desired by many. Not what she now knew to be the immorality of black arts and sorcery.

The stories had not been myths or make believe to force children to be good. The Wraithe family madness was real, and she was now very much part of its insanity.

She scrambled to her feet and stumbled backwards, the dense smoke surrounding her as the glow of the flames flickered and ate at the hem of her cloak. Calduggan's hands found their target and tightened around her neck, his nails digging deep into her pale skin as he spat the foulest of words. She fought him with every ounce of strength that remained, but it was a futile fight.

In her short life, Florence had been gifted very few choices, and now at its end, she was starkly aware that nothing had changed for her.

Two choices were all that remained.

An agonising death by fire or a quicker demise at Calduggan's hands.

She wished with all her heart that it would be the latter and he would take her last breath before the flames painfully consumed them both. As the seconds passed, her heart ceased to beat and her eyes became hooded and still, playing host to an ethereal haze and otherworldly stars. For once, Florence Rose Clancy had been granted a wish.

A dying wish.

Not the one she had desired, of wealth, status and a contented future, but of a quick and relatively less painful passing.

Black Abbey Towers had awoken.

The flames playfully leapt from windows and roared along corridors, devouring everything in its path, until sated, they slowly returned to their source. As the dying embers glowed, the Abbey bell, rung by an unseen hand, swung backwards and forwards, striking out a sombre beat until finally when the timbers and ropes had become defeated, it crashed down into the void below.

In the silence that followed, the house returned to its slumber.

It would lie empty and dormant for many decades to come before it would be reclaimed and renewed. And when the work was done, it would once again offer false sanctuary to those who would dare to enter and seek it.

'We can easily forgive a child who is afraid of the dark. The real tragedy of life is when men are afraid of the light...'

— Plato

THE LAST TRIMESTER

PRESENT DAY

'*I*'m a whale! I'm a wobbly blob of... of...' Prunella Barnes paused in her sandwich-making chore and swept her free hand over her huge bump. A mix of motherly pride and despair as she desperately sought the right word to describe her rotund condition.

'... er, blancmange?' Andy, her husband, helpfully obliged. He saw the look on her face and quickly ducked as a wholemeal bap hurtled through the air towards him. He observed the bread knife Pru was wielding with gusto as she berated him for his crass remark. He could almost imagine the newspaper headlines.

'Winterbottom Police Detective Victim of Pregnancy-Related Hormonal Surge in B&Q Budget Kitchen...'

Suitably chastised, he turned on the sympathy. He knew Pru was having a pretty rough time, swollen ankles, backache, sleepless nights and – well, he didn't like to mention *that* particular pregnancy-related manifestation, but, safe to say, he now knew the location of every single toilet in Winterbottom, Nettleton Shrub and Fallow Falls. She was also missing her part-time hours as the librarian in the cosy, converted shop in Winterbottom village, and that had also added to her spasmodic crankiness. It had become her sanctuary ever since the local council had shut down the main library, and under her direction Winterbottom village library had become a warm and welcoming social hub for those who loved books and reading. Her best friend, Bree Richards, had kindly offered to step in and cover some hours for Pru when the going got tough, but Bree's idea of book-filing had left a lot to be desired. Andy shuddered as he remembered the tears and tantrums from Pru when she had discovered Ann Cleeves parked next to Stephen King on the fiction bookshelf.

'D'you think Bree's dyslexic?' He took a slurp of his tea, chuffed that he had quickly managed to steer the conversation away from blancmange and the risk of a second buttered bap coming his way.

'What?' Pru emerged from the fridge, her cheeks bulging like a Siberian hamster. She quickly wiped her mouth with the back of her hand. 'No, absolutely not, Bree's like me; she loves her food.'

Andy was in no doubt of that with Pru's sudden desire for extra picky bits. Lately she seemed to spend more time with her head in the fridge than standing in front of it. He angled himself behind her and gave her a gentle bear hug, resting his chin on her shoulder so that he could place his hands on her stomach. He waited until a little ripple followed by a kick told him that their baby was acknowledging his presence. 'That's anorexic, my little pudding, which judging by the way Bree shovels cheese and onion crisps into her gob, proves she is anything but. I meant her mixing the books up at the library, you know, confusing a "C" and a "K".'

'*Oh…*' Pru giggled. 'And I meant that as an exclamation, not as the missing letter!'

'Prunella Barnes! I do hope you're not being risqué?' Andy gave her a cheeky wink. 'I don't know what's come over you lately.' He budged along the breakfast bar, shifting to make himself comfortable on the stool. Pru frisbeed a plate filled with a bacon batch and two piccolini tomatoes along the counter before heaving herself up onto the stool next to him, offering him his Homer Simpson mug filled to the brim with hot chocolate. She cupped her hands around her own mug and took a welcome slurp. 'Nothing beats a bacon butty and a hot chocolate before bed.' She hunched her shoulders up to her ears in pleasure.

Andy was inclined to agree. 'Yep, definitely beats last week's craving of pilchards and jam on toast!' His stomach gave an obligatory heave at the mere memory of that particular delicacy Pru had crammed in her mouth at bedtime for eight solid nights. Pilchard breath in the marital bed was definitely not something he had signed up for in his wedding vows!

'Have you seen this...' Pru pushed the *Winterbottom News* towards him. 'We've got a film crew descending upon Winterbottom and Fallow Falls in the next few weeks. They've chosen a couple of locations around here for a blockbuster movie. Could be really good for local business. Can't wait to see what big names they've got lined up.' She bit into her batch a little too eagerly, failing to catch the drip of ketchup that plopped down the front of her top. 'Just wait until the WI ladies hear about it; they'll be organising a road trip!'

Interested, he devoured the article. 'No doubt there will be some sort of contact with Winterbridge police station and the local council for road closures and the like. If we get the heads up, particularly on security, I'll let you know who they've got. They always have their own for the filming locations, equipment and the bigger stars, but they sometimes ask for a uniform presence if it's a really busy location.' He looked pensive, biting his bottom lip. 'That's if we've got anyone to spare the way the cuts are hitting.'

Pru knew that the reduction in officers was already having an impact on both uniform and CID. Andy's team had lost two already, taken back from being trainee investigators to uniform. She was pleased that Lucy Harris was still with them. By Andy's own admission she was a good detective, fun to work with and an enthusiastic influence on the rest of the team. She also kept Andy in line when his own enthusiasm and passion for his job overshadowed everything else. Lucy had a happy knack of reminding her sergeant of the work/life balance theory.

'The Curious Curator & Co could help you?' she offered by way of assistance. 'Me and Bree could step in and be a sort of female only security detail.' She adjusted her position, trying to make her baby bump look less noticeable to fit with the narrative.

Andy grinned. 'Oh aye, with your condition and Bree's over-indulgence with Aldi's two-for-one Quality Street tins, you'd be more like Tweedledum and Tweedledee bouncing along our country lanes!' He leant forward and took her hand in his. 'Look, I know you're missing it, but we agreed, once baby is here and you've had time to adjust and rest up, then you can get back in the driving seat with the Curious Curator and all the headaches it brings to our door.'

Doing her best impression of a childish pout, Pru gave him the side eyes in reluctant agreement. In partnership with Bree, The Curious Curator & Co Private Detective Agency had been her first 'baby'. They had both enjoyed some great adventures and investigations over the years, but had also been bored to tears with infidelity cases, mind and bottom-numbing stakeouts, lost cats and budgies. They'd also come very close to being six feet under on a few occasions too, with only pure luck saving them from imminent death when they'd sailed too close to the wind. Still, it had been so much fun, and she couldn't wait to get back in the saddle.

'You always spoil my fun...' she jiggled herself from the stool and attacked the fridge again. The rest of her sentence became muffled as soon as her head disappeared into its depths. Seconds ticked by, then she reappeared slamming the door shut. 'Mmmffph mmmmnnfff...' She swallowed hard, clearing the handful of food she had just shoved into her mouth. 'Don't you think?'

Bemused, Andy nodded in agreement to whatever it was she had said. It was easier to agree rather than disagree and risk a kitchen implement being embedded in the back of his head. 'Come on, up the wooden props, time for you and our little one to get some sleep.' He gently guided her up the stairs and into their bedroom. He sat watching as she brushed her hair, her silhouette against the amber glow of the bedside lamp making her more beautiful than he could ever have imagined.

Pru turned to face him, a serene smile played on her lips as she began her bedtime routine. Maternity leggings off without falling over, barrage balloon blouse flung to the far side of the bedroom, humongous pregnancy support knickers on, and for the pièce de résistance, and as much as her bulk would allow, she added a little coquettish dance for his entertainment, before whipping off her bra and whirling it around her head.

'Ta da...' she trilled, as that sudden action forced her ample boobs to flick upwards and then bounce rhythmically together before flopping onto the curve of her stomach. She looked down at them in despair. 'Great, now I've got bloody spaniel ears too,' she wailed.

'Good grief, my not-so-little sprout...' Andy threw his hands up to protect himself as half a pound of grated cheese, four ounces of wholemeal breadcrumbs and three salted peanuts showered down on him from the reinforced cups of Pru's blush-pink bra as it swirled in the air like a helicopter rotor blade. 'I've heard of keeping what you love close to your heart, but never thought I'd see the day when a pack of *Wookey Hole* mature cheddar was closer to yours than I am! Why don't I get the chance to be wedged between your cleavage, Mrs Barnes?'

Laughing, Pru heaved herself onto the bed. 'Oh, but you did,

Mr Barnes, don't you remember?' she pointed at her tummy. 'What got me in this condition in the first place?' Andy smirked and threw out his hands as a sign of faux ignorance. 'I don't know – maybe too much cheese?' In the split second that followed his quip, his detective skills on observation and personal safety failed him. The pillow whacked him so hard across the head he saw stars. It was quickly followed up with one of her slippers, but now on high alert, he ducked. 'Whoa, tiger…' He playfully grabbed her, taking the opportunity to relieve her of the second slipper.

'I can't help it if I miss my mouth sometimes and stuff sort of drops down there and gets caught.' Pru picked up a peanut between finger and thumb flicked it across the bedroom.

Andy gave her a knowing smile. 'Dropped? Methinks every time your head disappears into that fridge, you're actually stock-piling a bit extra to keep that giant watermelon belly of yours satisfied!'

'Just wait and see! You do know what happened when a mogwai was fed after midnight?'

'What?' Puzzled, he raised himself up on one elbow.

Pru jumped on him, hands like claws. 'It became a gremlin!'

WILLIAM

JUNE 1973

'One o'clock, two o'clock, three o'clock…' William Bennett puffed out his cheeks and held the breath he had just created in check, his lips tightly pursed and almost touching the white feathered stars of the dandelion ball. He could feel his skin stretching with the effort, causing his plump shiny 'crab apples' as his nan called them, to sting when he refused to release the breeze that would disintegrate the small weed he held in his hand.

He thought about that simile. At just eight years old, he was pretty good on comparisons. He had actually seen a crab apple once, but it had been a long, long time ago. It had fallen from a nearby tree and nestled itself in the uncut grass of Abbey Towers and had quickly attracted a variety of insects as it rotted. For the life of him, he couldn't see why his grandmother should liken his own cheeks to a small ball of shrivelled skin full of yucky worm holes and fruit flies. He had always hated it when her gnarly thumb and forefinger had pinched his cheek and jiggled it, making him wince, as though that one action would have elicited something magical to burst forth from him, giving her something new to coo over. He then thought about her passing, an unfortunate accident on the stairs of Abbey Towers. She had plunged down them, headfirst, hitting each step with gusto before finally coming to rest wedged underneath the oak reception table, spreadeagled like a broken doll, those same gnarly fingers clutching at air. The culprit? Her loose dressing gown cord wrapped around her foot. Well, at least that was what his parents believed. A simple misadventure.

But William knew better. William knew lots of things about Abbey Towers, but he had learnt to keep his lips tightly shut and his words locked inside him, unspoken.

'Four o'clock...' he blew heavily, dislodging some, but not all of the seeds. They floated upwards before lazily drifting slowly from side to side, to seek out a safe landing. He sometimes wished he could fly. If he had been gifted with that superpower, he could take himself to faraway lands on unseen thermals, thousands of miles across the sea to mountains and forests full of mythical creatures, mauve mists and marshmallow clouds. He stood up and held his arms out to the side, propelling himself across the grass in circles that began small and then grew bigger. He picked up speed and flapped vigorously like a bird, his hands bending at the wrists to give momentum. He closed his eyes and wished he could be anywhere other than the freakish mausoleum he was forced to call home.

'Come on, William, stop your daydreaming; it's time for dinner...' Peggy Bennett wiped her hands on her apron and beckoned him to the door.

His mother's shrill voice carried on the mild breeze until it reached him and broke the spell. He opened his eyes and looked down; the realisation that his frantic flapping hadn't gifted him so much of an inch of air between his feet and the grass made him want to cry. His bottom lip wobbled as he bit back the tears.

Another day without the magic he so desperately craved.

William smeared his hand across his cheek to eradicate the single tear that had the temerity to escape. His fingers touched the uneven edges of the scar that was his constant reminder of the opposing forces of oscillation from his wooden swing and an immovable object. That immovable object had unfortunately been him, leaving him with the red welt that now graced his face. A sudden chill bit into him as he looked towards the looming bell tower of the red brick Manor House, rather than at his mother. He squinted and shielded his eyes as he focused on the windows. The original cast bell was long since gone, the open vents had become arched windows with metal scroll shutters, and a turned staircase now led to a constructed room that he was not allowed to venture to. If you waited patiently in the early evening, there was a point where those windows became ornate frames for the fiery orange hues of the setting sun as it filled the tower to become a vivid burst of light in four directions.

North, South, East and West.

And then would come the dark, bringing with it the voices.

The black heart of Abbey Towers that William feared above everything else.

He quickly broke his gaze, not wanting to see what he imagined lived there. Only it wasn't his imagination, he knew exactly what whispered and slithered along the corridors of the place. It haunted his dreams and lived with him through his waking moments.

'William George Bennett, do I have to come out there and drag you in myself…?' his exasperated mother chastised as she strode purposefully across the grass towards him. She stopped abruptly when she saw his face, his small hands pressed firmly against his ears. She paused briefly before tenderly placing her hand on his shoulder. 'Oh, my dear boy, again?' she sighed as she pulled him to her. 'There's no such thing as ghosts, spectres, ghouls or monsters, William. It's all in your imagination.' She kissed the top of his head and then ruffled his hair.

'Because Daddy says so?' William wasn't sure if that was a question or a statement. His father, The Reverend Chester

Bennett, vicar of St Barnabas Ealing, advisor, administer of faith and forgiveness, seeker of truth and leader in prayer, could summon his flock every Sunday but still failed to see that the scales that weighed good on one side needed the balance of evil on the other. Without the dark, there would be no light.

Despite his tender years, and because of his life at Abbey Towers, William couldn't help but be aware of the opposing forces. He sighed and searched his mother's face, waiting for her reply.

'Yes, because Daddy knows, that's his job to know. Now, come on, chin up and let's have lunch...' Peggy curled her fingers around William's hand, partly to steer him towards the house, partly to show him comfort.

William hesitated and looked back to the tower room, an upwards glance that was long enough to catch sight of the dark figure looking down at him from the main window. The hooded cowl shadowed its face. He shuddered, feeling his heart miss a beat, the breath catching in his throat.

It had seen him.

'Mummy...'

Peggy turned to give him her full attention. 'What, sweetheart?'

'I think I'm going to die tonight.'

Horrified, Peggy dropped to her knees to comfort him, wrapping her arms around her son, she held him tight. 'Oh, William, whatever makes you say that? Of course you are not going to die tonight, or any other night for that matter. Do you think I would let anything happen to you?'

He held her gaze, his blue eyes welling up with the tears he was struggling to hold back. 'If not me, who else does he want then?' He pointed to the bell tower window.

'The house needs feeding, Mum; and it won't stop until it's full...'

EXTRAS

PRESENT DAY

he little brass bell above the door of the Twisted Currant Café tinkled excitedly as the ladies of the Winterbottom Women's Institute piled through the threshold. A slight breeze settled on the gingham window curtains, causing them to undulate and wave, as though welcoming them. Their jovial chatter and eagerness to partake in the delicious scones, cakes and light bites that the delightfully quaint café provided, filled the cosy room.

'Come on, Brenda, get that well-padded posterior of yours out of the way, I haven't got time to spare, waiting for you to waddle your way around the tables.' Ethel Tytherington, stalwart WI member, sharp of tongue and holder of an even sharper wit when the mood took her, assisted Brenda in her passage by giving her a hefty shove. Poor Brenda staggered forwards and kicked the patterned chamber pot that had been acting as a planter for a giant aspidistra in the corner of the café for more years than anyone cared to remember. It tottered first one way, then the other, shedding a large leaf in the process. Brenda grabbed a nearby chair and half fell, half sat on it with a muffled thud. Completely ignorant of the result of her impatient action,

Ethel raced for the best seat at her friends' regular table. 'I've saved a seat next to me for you, Clarissa!' she hiccupped loudly, and attempted to muffle an ensuing burp with her hand.

'I think you'll find that's *my* seat, Ethel; it's been my seat since... well... since forever.' Hilda Jones folded her arms and waited for Ethel to acknowledge her claim to the floral-patterned seat cushion on the chair nearest to the window. She might be slowly losing her marbles; in fact, she was almost sure she'd lost another one under the sofa this morning, judging by how long it took her to remember whether or not she had a cat. But at this particular moment, she was pretty confident that the chair Ethel had territorially claimed by plonking her handbag on it, belonged to her. She stood her ground, grabbing her best friend, Millie Thomas, by the coat sleeve as a reluctant ally. 'Stand here, Millie, you can be the shield. Don't under any circumstances let 'Rissa sit on that one.' She dropped her own handbag onto the seat next to Ethel's bag and stood her ground. Like gunslingers of the old wild west, they eyed each other with suspicion. Hilda suddenly made a grab for the strap of Ethel's bag at exactly the same time as Ethel's claw-like fingers snatched at Hilda's.

Florrie Patterson, proprietor of The Twisted Currant Café, sandwich-maker and baker, wiped her damp hands on her pinafore apron and rolled her eyes as she watched Ethel and Hilda, chins jutted and fingers clenched around their respective bag straps, in a handbag-to-handbag combat.

'Ladies, please!' The shrill tones of Kitty Hardcastle, past president of the Winterbottom Women's Institute, cut through the melee. 'Decorum at all times, girls! Remember where you are and the foundation that is part of you!'

Ethel was ready with a quick retort. 'The only ruddy foundation that is part of me, Kitty Hardcastle, is this girdle I bought to tempt Albert in 1968. It's practically welded to me!' She laughed heartily as she patted her hips. 'And in all those years he never did quite get the hang of relieving me of it at bedtime!'

Clarissa Montgomery squeezed herself between the chairs that had been left higgledy-piggledy in the rush to secure a decent seat at the tables. She gave a wistful smile, grateful that her best friend had not lost her sense of humour and could recall memories of her husband Albert, without too much sadness. Clarissa, herself the eternal spinster, could only imagine how painful it must be after fifty years of marriage, to lose the love of your life. The last six months had been one of offering a shoulder to cry on whilst delivering home-made soup and copious bottles of sweet sherry to keep Ethel's spirits up, and judging by Ethel's demeanour and second wave of hiccups, she was now beginning to wonder which type of spirit she had indulged in prior to her arrival at the café. She waited for the duel between Hilda and Ethel to abate.

'Right, if you two have quite finished your handbags-at dawn-routine, may I take a seat?' Not waiting for a response, Clarissa sat down in the chair next to the one that had been the subject of their conflict. She unbuttoned her coat and made herself comfortable. 'Just the usual for me, please, Florrie.' Suitably chastised, Ethel sat back down in her chair and allowed Hilda to take up hers next to Millie. 'There you go, that wasn't too difficult, was it?' Clarissa softly chided as she welcomed the new-found calm that had graced their table. 'Now, changing the subject to something a little more exciting than your bickering, have you seen this?' She presented the latest edition of the *Winterbottom News* to her friends, her index finger pointing to a half-page advert.

Ethel, Millie and Hilda, their shoulders hunched in anticipation, gave her their rapt attention as they leant over the crumpled paper. A low hum filled the small café as the ladies chunnered and mouthed the words of the article as they read its contents. Millie was the first to speak coherently. 'Background actors wanted for available filming in September and October, Fallow Falls and Winterbottom locales...'

An audible gasp of excitement gave Clarissa a little shiver of glee. She loved the idea that for once she was the bearer of news that her friends had not previously been privy to. Courtesy of Billie, her hairdresser in Fallow Falls, who knew every ounce of gossip between Winterbottom, Nettleton Shrub and beyond, she now had more to add to the narrative.

'It's a gothic horror and it's being filmed at Abbey Towers, that big old manor house in Fallow Falls. Apparently, the diocese has agreed to it being a film location because of the money that it'll bring in. Towards a new roof for the church, I think.' Clarissa paused in her story to thank Florrie for the pot of tea and a toasted teacake she had placed before her. 'So, no experience needed and they're looking for all ages, but mainly women to play village folk. They pay some expenses, feed and water you whilst on set, but best of all, it would be one hell of an adventure. Anyone up for it?'

Kitty and her table of ladies had stopped their chatter to listen in. 'You mean *Black* Abbey Towers?' Kitty's emphasis on the word 'black' and the heightened tone of her voice, made Clarissa wince. 'You wouldn't get me near that place in a million years; you must have heard the stories?' Kitty looked at her table of companions to validate her feelings on the eerie mausoleum that stood dark and foreboding at the edge of Fallow Falls village. When none was forthcoming, she felt the need to elucidate. 'Murders, arson, witchcraft, spectral sightings – and that's just off the top of my head. Do I need to go on? Nope, I'm sorry, 'Rissa, you won't get any of us putting our names down for it.'

The deafening noise of multiple chairs being scraped across the black and white chequered tiles in eagerness to take up Clarissa's call to arms drowned out the rest of Kitty's nervous outburst, as members of the Winterbottom WI rushed to add their names to the list, completely contradicting her own call to boycott the event.

'Ooh, me, me, me, 'Rissa...' Millie waved her hand in the air like a child wanting to be picked for the school rounders team. 'And Hilda, too, you'll do it, won't you, Hilda?' Hilda, in her own little world and none the wiser for the reason why her friends had suddenly become so animated, nodded her agreement.

Clarrisa was quickly surrounded by several of the Winterbottom WI ladies, all keen to be included. She licked the end of her pencil and began to jot names down in a little notebook. 'Well, Kitty, looks like you've been out-voted; names in the book, ladies and I'll get Pru to email them over to the film company. Black Abbey Towers here we come!'

'Well, I won't be adding mine to your little book, Clarissa Montgomery! Nothing on earth would entice me to spend even one minute at *that* place!' Kitty huffed, clearly irked that her days of speaking for her ladies was waning. 'Don't say I haven't warned you!'

Clarissa gave Ethel a knowing smile. 'Not even for the internationally famous, very delicious Flynn Phoenix and the fabulous Dana Simon?'

Kitty's eyes widened and her telltale lip pucker made an appearance. 'Not interested in her, but what's it got to do with him?'

'He's been cast as the lead...' Clarissa waited; pencil poised. 'With Dana playing his mother.'

Ethel, Millie and Hilda held their breath. Kitty was never one to miss out on the opportunity to rub shoulders with the rich and the famous but would her fear of the supernatural and things that go bump in the night be quelled by the prospect of meeting Flynn Phoenix, the best bit of eye-candy this side of Hollywood? They didn't have to wait long.

'Well, if you *really* need me, maybe I could provisionally put my name forward. As past president of the Winterbottom Women's Institute, I suppose it is my duty.' Daintily buttering her scone, Kitty tilted her head and waited for the gasps of delight and approval from her friends.

But the reaction she had hoped for didn't materialise, just a muffled snigger from Ethel which broke the silence. 'Aye, if you say so, Kitty Bucket.'

Kitty almost choked on her scone in a fit of pique. 'It's pronounced *Bouquet* and I'll have you know I sound nothing like her!'

Their collective laughter bounced from wall to wall and aspidistra to Kentia palm, filling The Twisted Currant Café with the warmth of their friendship. Clarissa, Ethel, Hilda and Millie had enjoyed and endured many adventures together over the years. This new adventure would be no different, but perhaps without the added excitement of murder and mayhem.

Then again, they were The Four Wrinkled Dears!

MURDERS, MYTHS AND MYSTERIES

*a*n excited buzz filled the main office of Colquitt Productions. Annie Baines hopped from desk to desk, dropping files, letters and notes for the imminent filming schedule for their latest predicted blockbuster, *The Haunting of Fallow Falls.*

Annie knew all about Fallow Falls and Abbey Towers, the subject matter for the movie. It was her job as Colquitt's lead researcher to know. She had entered as a set PA six years previously, an entry level position that had given her the chance to work hard and shine. And finally, after climbing what seemed like hundreds of rungs on the ladder to get there, she now had her dream job. She knew she was about to shine even more than usual, the fabulous history and locations she had found that had contributed to the stonkingly good script, had that very morning been singled out as 'excellent work' by her boss, Lucas Sullivan.

'Annie, anything come in yet on the daily background actors from the village?' Daphne Bewley, assistant to the casting director, was eager to get her hands on the list.

Annie chewed at her bottom lip and gave Daffy, as she was affectionately known, an amused one eyebrow up expression.

She had seen the list, along with the small head and shoulders photographs that had been attached. In fact, she had spent the best part of an afternoon in fits of the giggles whilst sifting through them. 'It would appear we're a very popular option for the over seventies this time, and we have a lot of applicants from – er, let me see...' She shuffled a couple of files and found the sheet of paper she was looking for. 'Yep, that's it, the Winterbottom Women's Institute. It's only a couple of miles away from Fallow Falls, so pretty local. It would be handy to have at least some that are already bonded and aware of each other, more likely to work well together.'

Daffy bit into the chunk of chocolate brownie she had been savouring for her tea break and wiped the crumbs from the front of her jumper. 'Well, if they're bringing cake with them, we'll take them all on!' She laughed. 'Pass it over, let's have a look.'

Annie handed her the list along with the photographs. 'There are some amazing faces amongst them, full of character. They'd be perfect for some of the Abbey scenes, particularly the Halloween one.'

'Oh my God, look at these...' Daffy placed four headshots side by side. 'They're the Sanderson Sisters plus one, from Hocus Pocus!' Annie edged her way around the desk to get a better look at the photographs Daffy had chosen. 'Clarissa Montgomery, Hilda Jones, Millie Thomas and what's that one?' she squinted as she pointed at the final headshot. 'Ethel Tyttering, is that what it says?'

'Tytherington, it's Ethel Tytherington. Now *she* looks the part, she's got "naughty" written all over her face.' Daffy chuckled. 'Right, we'll sift through these this afternoon, narrow it down to a short list, and arrange a day at Fallow Falls where we can see them all in the flesh before we make a final decision. What have we got on the location?'

Annie was about to come into her own. She'd spent many hours poring over the archives at the library, and had carried out field research by visiting Fallow Falls to speak to the locals. She shivered slightly, as though someone or something had walked over her grave, as she remembered some of the reactions she had received. Not all of her chats with the villagers of Fallow Falls had been amicable, some had been downright hostile, refusing to discuss Abbey Towers and its long history. They seemed to hold a rather archaic fear that their voices would stir up long-rested demons, bringing evil to the village once again.

'Right, Abbey Towers, or Black Abbey Towers as it was known then, was built in the early 1800s for the Wraithe family as their country retreat. The Wraithes were exceptionally wealthy, their trade as merchants, ship owners and shipbuilders kept them within the top ten richest in the area of that period.' Annie flicked over two pages of what she felt was unnecessary information. 'There's very little on their personal life in the archives; the information's mainly about their wealth, business assets and the occasional soiree they hosted when in the country. But, and here's the biggie, on Halloween in 1899 there was a devastating fire that tore through the house, destroying the huge Mariner's Bell that the tower was specifically built for. According to the reports of the time, fatalities had been kept to the minimum because the then resident of Black Abbey Towers, Calduggan Wraithe, had given every member of staff the night off. He perished in the fire, along with one of the village girls, Florence Clancy. Florence was just nineteen years old, and to this day there has never been any explanation as to why she was at the house on that night – or any other night, for that matter.'

'Ooh how tragic, I wonder if they were secret lovers! Can you imagine dying in each other's arms consumed by both terror and love?' Daffy could be such a romantic.

Annie couldn't imagine being in love with anyone that much to stop her from bolting for the front door, knocking everyone out of her way in search of safety, if a fire ravaged through her basement flat. 'Ah that's where you're wrong, there was plenty of talk amongst the womenfolk of Fallow Falls of girls being spirited away in the dead of night, never to be seen again. One of my contacts said it was like the house fed on them so it's more likely Florence was a victim of the much talked-about and very dark-hearted Calduggan Wraithe, rather than a romantic liaison that went awry. Anyway, after the fire, the house stood derelict for many, many years with some remedial work and renovation carried out on it by the Wraithe family estate to prepare it for sale. In the late 1930s the church diocese purchased it as a rectory attached to St Barnabas Ealing. It was used by the bishop, as well as his rectors, as a residence.'

Annie noticed that Daffy was taking notes. 'So, this Calduggan Wraithe, did you research him?' Daffy tipped her head, eager for a response.

'Yes, he was said to be into the dark arts, satanic worship, smuggling, that sort of thing. But it doesn't stop there. Abbey Towers – they dropped the "Black" to try and dispel some of the rumours attached to it – still played host to many deaths over the following years. The entire estate was requisitioned in the early 1940s by the government as a military hospital. There were many tales of ghostly sightings, particularly in the hours before a patient would die. Those staying there nicknamed the spectre, or whatever it was, the "Death Collector".'

'Now I like the sound of that!' Lucas slumped down in the office chair next to Daffy. 'Pity we didn't include that in the script.'

Daffy tutted and waved a finger at him disapprovingly. 'It's bad enough that we've based a fiction film on real life events – well, supposed real life events. Can you imagine the locals if we'd included their nemesis as well?'

'They do still believe in it, you know...' Annie was quite matter of fact. 'They still attribute that horrific incident in 1973 to the Death Collector.'

Daffy and Lucas, their interest piqued, hunched forward over the desk eager to hear more. 'Come on, spill,' Lucas encouraged.

Annie settled herself into a more comfortable position to relate her findings and to tell the story with as much drama as she could muster. 'Well, it was during the early 1970s when the then residents of Abbey Towers, the Reverend Chester Bennett, his wife Peggy and their eight-year-old son William, became newspaper headlines…'

THE VICAR

31 OCTOBER 1973

'*H*e was dreadfully upset, Chester. Whatever has got into him lately, I just cannot fathom. He's been like this for the last few months.' Peggy Bennett curled the 4-ply wool around her index finger and twisted it over the knitting needle. She stretched her legs, relishing the warm glow from the fire on her slipper-clad feet. That was another thing she couldn't fathom. How dreadfully cold Abbey Towers could be, virtually 365 days of the year. A roaring coal fire in October was one thing, but she had never lived anywhere that called for some form of heating in the middle of summer. She hated Abbey Towers, but as the wife of the village vicar, her choice of abode would always be dictated by the bishop.

Chester broke away from his book and, with much care, placed a bookmark at the appropriate page before closing it and resting it upon his knee. He peered over his spectacles at his wife. He knew she was talking to him, but the words didn't reach his ears. He watched her lips.

Open, close, open, close...

The more he concentrated on them, the more he saw. The red blush of lipstick that bled into the smoker's lines around her mouth, a small crumb of biscuit caught in the rogue hair that sprouted from her chin. How he despised that hair! It quivered in the wind on stormy days and almost waved to him with regular monotony when she spoke. The barely perceptible tic that touched her left eye and the spasmodic sniff she would automatically give each time she reached the end of a row and turned her woollen creation to start again. The *click, click, clickety click* of her needles. Night, after night, after night. They touched every single nerve his body possessed.

Chester could feel the rage building inside him, not from his want but from the want of another. His prayers and devotions had not lessened it, in fact it had grown and was now something he feared most, and something he could no longer control. He furtively tipped his head and listened, not to Peggy but to the voice that would whisper to him when the darkness fell. A voice that had become increasingly more regular and increasingly more demanding.

He placed his book on the little mahogany drinks table next to him and fondly patted the embossed cover. 'I think I'll go and check on William and make sure he's turned his bedside lamp off. The bishop was quite vocal on the running cost of Abbey Towers at our last finance meeting.'

Peggy barely acknowledged him, she silently mouthed *knit one, purl one*, keeping her eyes keenly focused on the knitting pattern that had been carefully laid out on the arm of the ancient, almost threadbare, armchair. Chester paused awhile to watch her.

Click, click, clickety click...

With each in, over and through of the needles and yarn, Peggy's head wobbled slightly, which in turn caused her tight permed curls to bounce. It gave him a reason to revisit his long-held hatred of red hair. Well, she wasn't really red, she was actually ginger, a fiery, vibrant ginger! Chester wondered why he had been attracted to her all those years ago, what on earth had he been thinking? And then he remembered. Contrary to popular belief, not all redheads had temperaments to match. Peggy had been a gentle soul, a perfect wife for a man who had his heart set on climbing the ladder of ecclesiastical heights. She was a fair cook, kept house well, and was an enthusiastic arranger and participant of church activities, particularly the knitting club and flower-arranging classes on the second Tuesday of each month. So he had overlooked the colour of her tresses in favour of her being a suitable presbytera to accompany him in his climb to the top. He now seriously wondered if having a ginger-headed wife had been the root cause of his stagnation and failure to proceed to a higher rank.

The resentment was beginning to fester and grow within him.

She's not giving you her full attention, sir. If you don't mind me saying, that is very disrespectful for a man of your standing...

Chester jutted out his chin, his back ramrod straight. He brushed an imaginary fleck from his cassock. 'I do mind you saying, but it is something I will deal with later.' His voice gruff with emotion filled the room.

It startled Peggy. She dropped her knitting into her lap and looked at him. 'What did you say, love?'

He paid her no heed. Instead he made quick progress across the wide expanse of carpet, his steps making no sound until they reached the woodblock flooring. *Tap, tap, tap.* He paused by the doorway, deep in thought. 'Nothing, dear. I'll be back shortly...'

Chester closed the lounge door with a soft click and slowly made his way across the grand entrance hall. He paused before the gilded portrait of Geneviève Calduggan, the original mistress of Black Abbey Towers. He gave her a cursory bow before making his way up the bifurcated staircase. Turning left, he sought out William's room, passing several doors that led to unused bedchambers as he went. The thick red carpet runner absorbed his footsteps as he progressed along the long, bleak corridor, pausing only to collect a feather cushion encased in an elegant brocade cover from the leather high-back chesterfield chair which sat outside the guest suite. Stuffing it under his arm, he continued until he finally reached his destination. The ceramic plate on the door, etched with the name 'WILLIAM' had a colourful painting of a hot air balloon in red, blue and yellow hues. A little colour in the blackness of Abbey Towers.

Perfect, sir. Now, you know what you need to do, don't you?

Chester nodded and for the first time saw his mentor. The mist that had until now clouded the voice, dissipated. The shadow stood by him, urging him on, giving him the strength that he needed. His fingers touched the oak panel, every nerve and muscle ready as he pushed through the door.

He looked down on his sleeping son, the warm glow from the bedside lamp casting shadows that touched William's face. 'Forgive me, Father…' Chester whispered as the cushion found its mark. Howling like a wounded animal, Chester pressed down hard, and even when the boy fought back, he carried on.

'The Lord is my shepherd, I shall not want, he maketh me to… he maketh me to…' Chester couldn't remember any more; Psalm 23 was deserting him, just as his God had deserted him.

Perfect, sir, absolutely perfect. Now doesn't that feel better?

Exhausted, Chester dropped to his knees and wept. The deed was done.

No rest for the wicked, sir. You still have work to do.

As if in a dream, Chester made his way back to Peggy, his cassock billowing as he almost tumbled down the last three steps of the staircase in his haste to obey. He grabbed the ornately carved lion-head newel post to steady himself, his fingers clawing at the wood. He silently slipped across the marble tiles and pushed open the door.

Peggy was exactly as he had left her.

Head nodding ever so slightly, needles click, click, clickety clicking, her lips silently mouthing words he could not hear, and with the faint glow of the fire's dying embers that were beginning to bring a chill to the room. Her knitting basket was carefully laid out on the sideboard, displaying an array of needles for the choosing. Over the years Chester had listened to her drone on and on about their uses. Number 9s were perfect for sweaters and cardigans; Number 4s for baby garments; circular needles for socks and hats; blah, blah, blah…

His fingers caressed a rather decent single Number 7 needle.

He felt its light but robust structure, the metal cool and smooth against his palm as he crept up behind her.

'Peggy, dear…'

The motion was swift and decisive; poor Peggy didn't know what had hit her. The needle found its mark with such force, her head snapped sideways. Chester drove the metal deep into her neck. He watched her eyes, at first pleading as her hands dropped the jumper she had been so lovingly knitting for him, then slowly clouding to become glassy and still as her life ebbed away.

'So much blood…' he whispered as he watched it merge with the rust-coloured curls around her neck to become one. 'So much red…'

Well done, sir, well done.

Chester allowed a tear to fall for his once-beloved wife, keeper and cleaner of the church vestments, lighter of altar candles, indulgent mother and, until recently, a fairly good egg.

No time to grieve, sir, you still have the final sacrifice to perform.

Weary both in body and soul, the Reverend Chester Bennett left his wife and son and slowly climbed the stairs to his sanctuary, the notorious Black Abbey bell tower. Only now there was no bell, no ropes, and no headstock within the belfry. It was just a room full of artefacts and relics. Each step was painful as the terror within him grew, but he had no will to resist. His heart heavy, the words he had so vainly sought earlier, returned to him. He flung open the ornate metal shutters and then the window beyond.

'Yea, though I walk through the valley of the shadow of death, I will fear no evil…' he roared into the darkness.

Chester wailed and beat at his chest with his fists as he climbed onto the parapet. He marvelled at the stars in the ink black sky, searching for his saviour, the ground below him waiting. With fearful clarity, he accepted that there would be no saviour, no last-minute reprieve. He would fear evil, for he had heard its dark words and had carried out its black deeds. He stepped out into the void, ready to welcome death as a release, his cassock flapping wildly and his mouth fixed in a silent scream as he plummeted into the darkness below.

Black Abbey Towers sighed and now, sated once more, it quickly and silently returned to its slumber.

BELL, BOOK AND SCANDAL

PRESENT DAY

*B*ree Richards checked the time on her ancient Swiss Flik Flak watch. In any other life she would have been embarrassed to be caught at the grand old age of... she paused using her fingers to calculate her age and plumped for 'over forty' to cover all bases rather than admit to advancing years.

The pink watch with alphabet letters and numbers on the strap had been given to her as a gift in 1987 by her dad. It held so many happy memories that she was reluctant to wear anything else on a day-to-day basis. Granted, it did sometimes let her down, but in the main it was pretty reliable, unlike her best friend and until recently, her finest gin-drinking buddy, Pru Barnes. She was late again.

The little bell above the library shop door tinkled, gently heralding her first visitor of the day. When she had offered to help Pru whilst she was lumbering around like an elephant waiting for the chubby tadpole to make an appearance, she hadn't expected the task to be so mind-numbingly boring. She quite enjoyed perusing her monthly edition of *Take A Break*, but drew the line at anything that was encased in a hardback cover or held more than thirty pages. She replaced the book she had been dusting back onto the shelf and turned to give her undivided attention to whoever had crossed the threshold in search of literary enlightenment. As expected, it wasn't Pru.

'Morning, Ethel…' Bree gave her a warm, welcoming smile. 'Have you come for a browse or something in particular?'

Ethel nodded her greeting before rummaging around in her holdall. She whipped out a piece of paper with a flourish. 'This, I need this, please. It's called *You Can Be a Movie Extra*, and it's by Rob Martin.' She held both hands in front of her close to her chest, as though she was holding in a secret that she was desperate to spill.

'Rob Martin!? Blow me down with a feather, Ethel!' *The* Rob Martin?' Bree gave Ethel her best wide-eyed, colour-me-impressed expression, whilst stifling a giggle.

Ethel bristled with importance. 'Yes, *the* Rob Martin. I take it you've heard of him, then?' She gave Bree a smug smile.

'Er, nope. Sorry, Eth, I was just teasing.' Feeling a little guilty at having a laugh at poor Ethel's expense, she tried to make up for her childish behaviour. 'Let me have a look for you. If it's not here on the shelves, I'll do a search on t'internet for you; we might be able to source it at another library or find somewhere that's selling it.'

Ethel looked horrified. 'Bloody hell! Who said I wanted to pay for it? I'm not Elizabeth Taylor; I'm just going to be acting my tights off as an extra in the background.'

'It's socks…'

'What is?'

'When you work at something that exceeds expectation, you say "acting my socks off" – not what you said.' Bree carried on searching along the bookshelf in the 'M' section, her index finger touching the spine of each book as she went.

'I don't wear socks, I wear tights.' Ethel quickly hitched up her skirt and stuck out her leg for Bree to see. 'They're 80 denier American Tan with reinforced gusset, but heaven knows why I need a reinforced gusset at my age – particularly since Albie curled up his toes and departed this life!'

'Oh my goodness, Ethel Frances Tytherington, are you being naughty?' Pru's rounded tummy made its appearance through the shop door with the rest of her following closely behind as the bell tinkled longer than it usually did. 'If I get any bigger, I think I'll burst.' Barely acknowledging Bree, she dropped her shopping bag onto the desk. It tipped over and a large block of cheese fell out.

Bree picked it up and waved it at her. 'This is your problem, missy; after chocolate, cheese is the worst thing for putting on weight.'

Pru bristled. 'Oh don't you start; I've just had a terrible experience coming out of Dylan's Dispensary. Some guy outside has just stared at me for ages and then said, 'Is it crowded in there?' I gave him a piece of my mind, telling him how rude it was to call attention to a pregnant woman, making her feel fat, and that it wasn't a laughing matter being this big. I was so embarrassed...' she broke off to give herself time to catch her breath.

'Quite right; you tell him, dear. And anyway, why should *you* feel embarrassed? He was the one that was being cheeky.' Ethel was full of support.

Pru sheepishly grinned. 'Because he was actually asking me if it was crowded inside the chemist as he didn't have time to queue if it was. I just got the wrong end of the stick!' She chuckled as she eased herself into the nearby chair and checked her ankles for any swelling that was more than usual. She pushed her index finger into the skin on her right foot, leaving a dimple. 'Oh gawd, can this get any worse? I'm supposed to be blooming not festering, I can't even bend down to shave my legs now – look, they're like something out of *The Hobbit*. I'll be able to comb them by next week!'

Sensing a potential meltdown, Bree had already put the kettle on and set out three mugs. 'Cuppa for you too, Ethel? Whilst I make it, why don't you tell Pru all about your exciting news?' She hoped that would be the distraction that was needed; Pru had been so emotionally unpredictable lately. The last thing she wanted was her having a blue fit because she'd managed to cultivate strands of yeti-style leg hair.

Ethel was well up for the challenge. She took the seat next to Pru, unbuttoned her coat, and made herself comfortable. 'We've all applied to be extras in the film they're shooting at Fallow Falls. What do you think of that? And if we get picked, look at this place. It's very atmospheric; we could stay there. Make it a bit of a holiday. It's called the Bell, Book and Candle Inn.' She pushed a leaflet across the table.

Pru had a chunk of cheese wedged in her mouth from the block she had just bought. She chewed vigorously to clear it so she could speak. 'Who are "we", Ethel? Please don't tell me it's the WI ladies!' She could think of nothing more dangerous than to have certain members of Winterbottom Women's Institute running riot around a film set totally unaccompanied and unsupervised. She looked over at Bree, currently raiding the biscuit tin, who shrugged her shoulders and nodded her confirmation.

'Why shouldn't we? We've already sent our applications in, and nearly all of us have had call-backs. They're going to give us the once over next Tuesday and pick a final list.' Ethel was beside herself with delight. 'I'm pretty sure Clarissa and I will get picked, though I'm not sure about Hilda and Millie.' She became thoughtful, sipping from the mug of tea that Bree had put in front of her. 'Although those two could still come for the break.'

They sat in silence, Pru and Bree contemplating the ups, downs and concerns of letting half of Winterbottom WI loose on an unsuspecting film crew. Pru couldn't imagine either Clarissa or Ethel being happy to leave Millie and Hilda behind. After all, they had self-styled themselves as a permanent foursome in all their endeavours, misdemeanours and adventures.

'If Hilda and Millie don't make the cut, I take it you and 'Rissa won't be doing it, then?' Bree was thinking along the same wavelength as Pru. Even if they didn't make the cut, she and Pru would still have to do some form of chaperoning for the other ladies. After all, their presence would represent the Women's Institute and all the values that it held. She looked over at Pru and her ever-expanding belly. There was no way she would be in any fit state as the current WI President to take up the mantle, so it would be down to Bree as vice president to do her bit. She puffed out her cheeks; this was the last thing she needed.

'Not on your life! Would you give up the chance to meet and work with the delicious Flynn Phoenix?' Ethel preened.

'Oh wow! *The* Flynn Phoenix?' Bree's eyes widened as she licked her lips and seductively pouted. 'Maybe there could be hope for me in the romance department after all!' Suddenly the idea of volunteering her chaperoning services seemed very attractive. She could certainly ensure the WI ladies were on their best behaviour whilst simultaneously drooling over Flynn Phoenix as she offered her 'services' to him too. 'Ah well, in that case I'll escort you all to your auditions next week, and of course I'll make sure I'm free for the duration of filming too,' she gushed.

Pru, who was currently using the library ruler to measure the length of the hairs on her legs out of curiosity, snorted loudly. 'Aye, I'm sure you will...' she laughed, 'put me down too. I might not be able to do much, but I could be a mental welfare advisor for the ladies, to help them out a bit if they get a little star-struck and hysterical.'

'So, are we're all going, then?' Ethel finished her mug of tea and sneaked her fingers out for an extra biscuit from the plate. 'It'll be like old times, but without the murders, although if you've read up on the history of Fallow Falls and the ominous Abbey Towers, you might have second thoughts. I've been delving a bit deeper into the reports of ghostly sightings and we'd be fools to ignore the stories.' She took a bite from her biscuit and used the remainder as a pointer to emphasise her concern. 'There's quite a bit we can do to protect ourselves whilst we're there, you know.'

Pru knew all about Abbey Towers, its history and dark tales. She had read a book a few years ago that had documented the dastardly goings on within its walls and in the village too, but she preferred to stick with what had been backed up by newspaper articles and police reports at the time. The 1970s scandal was ruled murder/suicide with no mention of supernatural involvement. 'I think you've got to take the tales of devil worship, ghosts and ghouls with a pinch of salt; all old places have experienced death in some way. In fact, Andy and I only found out last month that there had been a death in our house.'

Bree shivered. 'When, how, and which room? I hope it's not your guest room or I'm never staying at yours again.' She pulled her mouth down at the corners and widened her eyes.

'Kitchen, allegedly, according to Mrs Chegwidden from next door. It was in the 1950s, faulty wooden clothes dryer, by all accounts. It collapsed as some poor pensioner was hanging his Y-fronts on the bottom rung.' Pru made a choking motion with her hand on her throat and stuck out her tongue to mimic lack of oxygen. 'It folded up like an accordion trapping his head in the middle, and the momentum of the drop made the catch snap shut. It was days before he was discovered.'

The little library fell silent as they digested that snippet of information, each musing the pros and cons of a simpler life when tumble driers weren't a household feature, and each trying to think of an appropriate and suitable response to Pru's disclosure.

As expected, the first one to speak was Ethel. She stood up, gathered her belongings and made her way to the door.

'Well, that certainly was the end of an "airer" for him then...' she quipped. 'Must dash, things to do, people to see, and protection spells to research at The Pendle Raven in Chapperton Bliss before next Tuesday!'

The brass bell tinkled for the third time that day proclaiming her departure, leaving Pru and Bree impressed by Ethel's quick wit and shocked by her sudden interest in the dark arts and an imminent visit to the only 'Witchery' shop in the county.

NOW YOU SEE ME, NOW YOU DON'T

*A*lice Moorcroft swung the rotating floor mop across the marbled entrance hall of Abbey Towers, making sure even the most difficult edges were touched, and that the area under the circular flower table was sparkly clean. In her eagerness to complete the task, she inadvertently knocked one of the carved trestle legs. The crystal vase on top containing yellow roses and gypsophila wobbled and tottered. Alice screwed up her eyes and held her breath, her heart pounding, just waiting for the sound of breaking glass. As the seconds ticked by with no sound of disaster, she ventured to open one eye. Geneviève Calduggan, her lips set in a thin smile, looked down upon her in judgement from her ornate gold portrait frame on the wall. Alice shuddered and mouthed the word *sorry* to the picture.

All was well with the table, the vase and the flowers. She breathed a sigh of relief. She wasn't particularly comfortable working at Abbey Towers, but the pay was pretty decent and considering her own circumstances, it was a case of needs must. So, to say she had a choice in the matter, which her elderly mum always insisted she had, was way off the mark. Alice was a maternal carer, a housekeeper and cook at home, all roles unpaid, so her job here was their only source of income. The last thing she needed was to be sacked for clumsiness. She bent down to unplug the machine, and as she did so a dark shadow moved across the landing, just caught in her peripheral vision.

'Hello…' her voice quivered. 'Who's there?'

Alice knew she would not be given the courtesy of a reply; it was always the same. The fleeting vision, the call-out to whoever had appeared, then her tentatively checking with Archdeacon Gregory and his wife to see if they had any actual, real-life visitors. It was always a negative response. No point asking them this time, they were both out at the church coffee morning, so she knew she was currently the sole human occupier of Abbey Towers. She felt the hairs on her arms stand to attention. She couldn't wait for Abbey Towers to be opened up to the film production company. If it was full of people and bustling with activity and action, then just maybe there would be no room for the ghosts of the Towers to roam and wander aimlessly along the corridors whilst terrifying and enthralling her in equal measure.

The starring actors were here now, but she had strict instructions not to allow them entry until her employers had returned, so for now they were just doing a walk-through of the grounds. She had sneaked a quick peek through the library window at them, their fancy limos parked up and their entourage following and fawning around them. She had been gifted a very brief glimpse of Flynn Phoenix and Dana Simon as they swept by in front of the window on the way, she assumed, to the folly. She checked the time on the grandfather clock in the entrance hall. She just had time to put away her cleaning equipment and pop the kettle on ready for the return of the archdeacon and his wife.

Alice coiled the extension lead around the handle of the machine and pushed it along the corridor towards the scullery, the door that led to the bell tower loomed to her right. She had never been up there as it was always kept locked with strict instructions from the archdeacon that it was out of bounds to everyone, a challenge that excited her. She pressed her palm against the warm wood of the panel before taking a furtive look around. Dropping her fingers to the large brass handle, she turned it.

Click.

She quickly pulled her hand away, her fingers tingling. 'Oh my…' she gasped. 'It's not locked!'

And without a second thought or a moment's hesitation, Alice took the opportunity to simultaneously quell her fears and satisfy her curiosity by silently slipping through its threshold.

'Six on a geriatric passport and two paying, please.' Ethel waved her bus pass at the driver of the 164 to Fallow Falls. She beckoned her group of companions on and stood aside so their respective passes could be scrutinised and confirmed as they filed aboard. Bree waited her turn, money in hand to pay for her fare, as did one of the younger members of the Winterbottom Women's Institute who, like herself, hadn't yet reached the age to qualify for free local travel.

'Are we all on, girls?' Bree took her VP role seriously, counting heads and being mindful to include the first group led by Brenda Allinson that had raced ahead of Ethel to monopolise the back seats. After much jostling, huffing and puffing, Brenda and her crew were seated.

Ethel bristled. 'I see Brenda is trying to prove a point!'

'In what way?' Clarissa bumped herself along the double seat to nab the window view.

'That she can squeeze her fat ar…'

'Ethel!' Kitty hastily interrupted. 'That's quite enough, I do hope we're not going to have you hurling insults all afternoon.'

Ethel smirked as she enthusiastically plonked herself down next to Clarissa. 'Fat *arms*, Kitty, I was going to say fat arms!'

Kitty raised one eyebrow and gave Ethel her famous 'side eyes'. 'And you expect me to believe that?'

Not caring if Kitty believed her or if Brenda was insulted, Ethel whipped out a little bag of treacle toffees she had been saving for the journey. She offered one to Clarissa before taking one for herself and passing the bag behind her to Millie and Hilda.

'This is so exciting, isn't it? I can't wait to do my audition; I've memorised a little something from *The Tempest* for mine. I'll do it as a ventriloquy I think.' Hilda happily imparted to her friends whilst chewing on her toffee.

'You're going to talk with your mouth closed and throw your voice? That'll be a first...' Millie chuckled. 'I think you mean soliloquy, it's a sort of monologue, a speech. Honestly, Hilda, no offence meant but you're lucky if you can remember your own name most days.'

Hilda harrumphed. 'Piffle, Joan Crawford had to start somewhere!'

Clarissa took the opportunity to join in the conversation. 'I'm sure she did, dear, but she definitely wasn't travelling on an OAP bus pass to a haunted mansion somewhere in rural England with a touch of dementia to boot.'

Ethel blew on her fingers. 'Brutal!'

'That's what friends are for!' 'Rissa laughed.

As the trees swayed in the October winds, dressed in the reds and golds of the finest of autumnal colours, and the wheels of the 164 to Fallow Falls bumped and rolled along country lanes to deliver a fine selection of soon-to-be thespian ladies to Colquitt Productions, The Four Wrinkled Dears continued to laugh, tease and encourage each other.

Just as good friends always do.

MISSING IN ACTION

'Where is that darned girl?' Untangling her foot from the loose cord of the rotary floor cleaner, Fiona Gregory tutted loudly. 'Clement, have you seen her? She's just left this abandoned in the middle of the corridor, and those actor people will be knocking on the front door any minute now!'

Archdeacon Gregory's head emerged from around the door of his office. His wife, electric plug in one hand, a plate of sandwiches in the other and an indignant expression, glared back at him. 'I don't know, my dear, have you shouted loudly?' He hoped that his small input was enough to quell his wife's pique and assist her in finding their missing housekeeper. 'She's probably upstairs doing the hoovering.'

Fiona marched towards him and thrust the plate of sandwiches into his hand. 'Here you are. Honestly, Clement, why you agreed to this I'll never know. It's our home, for goodness' sake, not a film lot!' She turned heel and marched back down the corridor, ready to tackle the offending machine. 'They'll be everywhere those... those... what are they called? Luvvies? Yes, that's it, luvvies!' She had answered her own question and now no longer had any use of her husband's wisdom on the arts and theatrical world.

Clement, grateful for the respite as she disappeared into the scullery, electric cord dragging behind her, cosseted his plate of cheese and pickle on wholemeal, placing it carefully on his desk. He made himself comfortable, bouncing on the leather captain's chair, until he found the perfect position to enjoy his lunch. He raised the neatly cut triangle and opened his mouth...

'Ooh that looks delicious! Is it from the canteen? Someone said they give you a free lunch here. I couldn't find anyone around when I arrived, so I just let myself in. It looks like you did too.' The mouse-like woman wearing a wool-blend coat topped with a silk scarf, scrunched her nose up and pursed her lips before plonking herself down on the visitor's chair in front of the archdeacon whilst simultaneously slamming her handbag onto her knees. Clement froze, his sandwich mid-mouthful.

'Are you a famous actor? I don't recognise your face...' she clucked. 'Are you playing a vicar? I'm going to be an extra, although I don't quite know what one does, but I'm sure my friends Clarissa and Ethel will help me.'

It was not often that Clement was lost for words; he was a regular one-hour sermon giver at St Barnabas Ealing every Sunday, but this rather enthusiastic beldame with a lilac rinse had floored him. He placed his one-bite sandwich back on the plate. 'Madam, I think you are a little lost. This is my office, and I am the archdeacon of Fallow Falls diocese, not a thespian of the screen.'

Hilda harrumphed loudly. 'Well, you could have said so, and save me wasting my time!' She stood up, hooked her handbag over her arm, straightened her coat, and before Clement could stop her, her gloved hand sneaked out and took the untouched half of his sandwich. She took a nibble and waved it at him. 'Very nice, but it could have done with a bit more butter. They barely touch the edges with it these days.'

The door clicked softly shut behind her, leaving Clement with the uneaten half of his lunch and a bemused look on his face. His stomach took the opportunity to grumble loudly as he settled himself back into his previously comfortable position, rearranged the paperwork on his desk, and sat in contemplative silence. No sooner had his fingers curled around the remaining half of his sandwich when the office door burst open for the second time.

'She's not here, Clement. I've searched the whole house and she's not here!' Fiona's lips pursed closely together; chin jutted, awaiting his response.

'She's probably just knocked off early; nothing to worry about, dear.' Clement dropped his sandwich back down onto the plate and mourned the mouthful he had almost tasted.

His wife was not to be placated. 'Leaving her coat, handbag and outdoor shoes behind? I think not. No, she's missing in action, Clement, and I intend to find out where she's gone when this lot have finished nosing around our home.' Having said her piece, she quickly left him to his peace.

Clement sat watching the back of the door, not daring to pick up his sandwich just yet in case he was treated to yet another unwanted visitor. After giving himself ample recovery time from the old lady's chagrin and his wife's suspicious nature, his hand reached out and reverently picked up his sandwich again. He opened his mouth, his taste buds tingling in anticipation.

A blood-curdling scream suddenly echoed down the corridor, snatching away any chance of a bite to eat.

'Out, out, get out…!'

Recognising his wife's dulcet tones, he dropped his sandwich and ran for the door.

THE SPECTATOR

*C*larissa pushed through the crowd that had gathered in front of the doors to Abbey Towers, with Ethel close on her heels. They had barely been at the auditions five minutes when chaos had found its mark. The loud scream had startled everyone who had been patiently queuing outside, waiting to gain entry to the great hall for their chance to shine.

Bree made a quick head count and immediately knew Hilda was missing. She scanned the crowd to no avail. 'Any of you ladies seen Hilda?'

'Not since they put us in groups. Honestly, that woman will be the death of me,' Clarissa huffed as she strained to look over the mass of heads. 'I turn my back for all of two seconds and she's gone.' The commotion behind the partially ajar arched doors continued, causing more mirth than misgiving from the crowd as they listened in.

'Get that woman out of here, Clement!'

'I'm trying to, dear, but she won't budge…'

'For goodness' sake, just pick her up and carry her out!'

'*What*?! Lay hands on her? I'll get arrested…'

'Is that before or after I find your thick head with this…'

Ethel couldn't help herself. Desperate to know what *this* was, she peered through the gap in the doors. 'Oh my…!' she exclaimed. 'It's Hilda causing havoc, and some woman chasing a man in a cassock around a table whilst brandishing a very large rolling pin. It's like something out of a *Carry On* film!'

Ethel had barely finished her observations before Hilda, totally nonplussed by the uproar she had caused, emerged triumphant through the doors, a plate containing a chocolate muffin and two custard creams in her hand. 'Oh, there you are, girls. I got these to go with our cup of tea. I've already had a sandwich, which wasn't very nice,' she grumbled under her breath whilst smearing chocolate across her pale face. 'I've made a start; what do you think?' She pointed to her sunken eyes, haunted and black, as they searched for approval.

'Night of the Living Dead springs to mind!' Bree snorted as she reined Hilda in, reuniting her with Millie. 'Stay there, don't move, don't go anywhere – in fact, don't even breathe! I'm going to have to sort this out.'

Whilst the film crew had the unenviable task of placating and disarming Mrs Fiona Gregory of her rolling pin whilst reassuring her bemused husband, the archdeacon, that everything was in order, Bree smoothed things over with the casting director, thus providing a perfect opportunity for those assembled to understand the dynamics of a strong-willed wife and a man who not only preached peace but desperately tried to maintain it in his own household.

'I can't believe we all got selected, even Hilda! Just gutted we missed out on a glimpse of Flynn Phoenix and Miss Simon. They were there too, albeit fleetingly.' Clarissa shuffled along the upholstered booth bench in the Dog & Gun, making room for her friends. She removed her gloves and wriggled her fingers in the warm air that came courtesy of the roaring log fire in the inglenook grate. Until today, the weather had been quite mild for the first week of October, but a sudden cold snap that had rushed in from the north had put paid to lightweight jackets and shoes in favour of padded anoraks and boots. 'Bree, can you make that four sweet sherries, please. I've just spotted Ethel coming up the path.' She waved four fingers in the air to support her request.

The door to the pub creaked open, bringing with it a swirl of autumn leaves that scattered across the modular stone floor. Ethel held out her arms to announce her arrival. She stamped her booteed feet and gave a little shudder. 'Blimey, it's blowing a hoolie out there.' She wrapped her gloved hands around her and patted her arms.

Jason Boyd, better known by his nickname of Juicy Jase, manager and head bottle-washer of the quaint pub, placed four schooners on a tray. 'Well, ladies, it's a joy to have you all here, I must say. Florrie Patterson's bloomers at the café not doing it for you today, I take it?' He gave Bree a cheeky wink.

'You're not wrong there, dear. Florrie's bloomers really have seen better days, just ask that husband of hers!' Ethel grinned, knowing full well she had taken the double entendre in the manner Jason had hoped she would. 'Budge up, Pru. You and that inflated bowling ball of yours are taking up more than half the bench.'

Happily accepting Ethel's bon mot in the humorous manner it was intended, Pru took the opportunity to shift sides in the booth, leaving Clarissa, Ethel, Millie and Hilda sitting side by side. She mentally had an image of three monkeys plus one. See no evil, hear no evil, speak no evil – and then there was Hilda, better known as Captain Chaos. She took the lull in conversation to question her. 'So, Hilda, what on earth happened at Abbey

Towers?' Pru had a rough idea of what Hilda had got up to, but she wanted to know if there was anything more she should be concerned about as WI president.

Taking her first sip of sherry, Hilda relished the slight burn in her throat. She waved her hand dismissively. 'Pah, that woman just went hysterical; there was no need, I tell you, absolutely no need. I wasn't to know the place hadn't opened up yet, and there I was helping myself to the biscuit tin and she starts screaming and wailing like a banshee.'

Bree almost choked on her drink. 'Hilda, you scared her half to death! She wasn't expecting anyone to be in her pantry, least of all you looking like a dug-up corpse.' After her tête à tête with the bishop, they had discovered that Hilda had found her way into the ground-floor powder room. Bree's admonishment continued. 'The casting director wasn't too chuffed with you delving into the set make-up cases they'd stored there, either. What on earth possessed you to slap that white stuff on like there's no tomorrow? You left such a mess.'

'Oh come on, Bree! She did do a pretty good job of it. That's why they agreed to take her on. She wouldn't have looked out of place on the set of *The Addams Family*!' Ethel let out a hearty chuckle as she knocked back her sherry. 'Anyway, here's to us…' she held her almost empty glass aloft.

The clinking of drinks glasses gave way to a contented silence, the ladies smug in the knowledge that it had been a highly successful audition for the Winterbottom Women's Institute. Even Kitty had secured herself a place, and some of the ladies that hadn't made the cut had still volunteered their services for teas, coffees and tasty bakes for the cast and crew. All in all, it had been a fruitful day for them, one worth celebrating.

As they ordered a second round of drinks, they were blissfully unaware they were being watched. The stranger, hat tipped just enough to conceal their identity, the heavy serge collar pulled up and a wool scarf holding comfort beneath the chin, kept watch from the table in the corner. A large rum, its amber warmth colouring the glass, sat untouched as overheard conversations were committed to memory.

The opening scene had been set.

CURIOSITY KILLED THE MAID

*E*xcitement tingled from the tips of Alice's fingers, right through to her toes. She stood in awe at the foot of the staircase that cosseted the brick walls of the tower as it wound its way up towards the heavens. She tentatively placed one foot on the first step, her soft house-shoe catching the tread nosing, causing her to stumble slightly.

'Helloo…' She chuckled to herself as her small voice carried upwards. Not expecting a reply, and even though she knew the archdeacon and his wife were out, she still felt the need to show respect by announcing her presence. The fact that she was entering a part of Abbey Towers that was out of bounds and strictly forbidden made her care not one iota. Her fear now gone was replaced by anticipation. 'Anybody there?'

She waited; head cocked, listening. As the seconds ticked by, satisfied she was alone, she began her ascent, counting as she went. 'One, two, three, four…' Her pace, hurried by her eagerness to discover what lay ahead, began to slow the further up she went. 'Ninety-eight, ninety-nine, one hundred…'

Alice stepped out onto solid floorboards, not daring to look back or below her. The room appeared smaller than she had expected, the mullioned windows she had always admired on her daily approach along the driveway to Abbey Towers were set in three walls surrounded by heavy oak panelling with intricate carvings.

And that was it. Nothing more. The floor, four walls and three windows. No hidden treasures, no antiques that had been squirrelled away from historic pillaging of the nearby villages, or dark deeds and secrets. It was just an ordinary, boring and very empty room. Her fingers traced the sill and glass of the window and she checked the tips for dust and grime.

'Mmm… clean as a whistle!' Now in her book, that meant someone had been up here keeping it spic and span – and it most certainly wasn't her. She scanned the ground below, the almost bare trees giving her a better view than she would have received during the summer months. Her index finger tapped her lips as she pondered the layout of the tower. 'Four windows, there's definitely four windows from outside, but only three inside,' she questioned herself. Her eyes travelled up to the ceiling checking its structure. Placing her hands on the panels, she began to press each one systematically, with no effect; they remained solid. Disappointed, she checked her watch, aware that the Gregorys would be returning home very soon.

'Well, Abbey Towers, you've been a massive anticlimax, I must say…' she trilled, as she made her way back to the staircase, hoping that it would be quicker and less taxing on her thigh muscles on the way down. 'You really are all fluff and no substance, a proper damp squib!'

In the split second it took Alice to let her guard down and become distracted by her bitter disappointment, a cord had been deftly looped over her head and tightened at the nape of her neck. Her head snapped sharply back as her slipper-clad feet lost their footing. She desperately scrabbled for purchase with her heels on the wooden boards. Bunching her hands into fists, she flailed and hit out, her elbows becoming weapons as she jabbed backwards, but they barely touched their target. Her assailant was so much stronger. The cord became tighter and tighter, so tight her fingers could only scrape at her skin and the ability to take in air was lost.

Alice had only once before experienced the futility of an elusive breath when as a child she had inadvertently swallowed a massive gobstopper from Miss Madran's Sweetshop in Fallow Falls. It had wedged fast in her small throat. Her bulging eyes, scarlet face and foaming mouth had alerted Joe, the local postie, who had been nonchalantly going about his rounds, that she was in danger of choking to death, and only his prompt intervention and a huge thump to her back had saved her. For his heroic actions he had been presented with an award from the town mayor and Alice had never again consumed a boiled sweet in any shape or form.

But this time there would be no award-winning Joe to save her, no spat-out gobstopper or lifesaving next breath. She had finally used up all of the nine lives that her mum had been convinced her daughter possessed.

Alice would soon be gone from this mortal coil, and probably very much forgotten – if not for one thing…

The rotary floor mop she had left abandoned in the middle of the scullery passage in Abbey Towers and a pair of outdoor shoes.

QUE SERA, SERA

The metal rings rattled against the pole in Frugal Finds as Clarissa swished back the dressing room curtain. 'Ta-da! What do you think, girls?' She paraded out into the middle of the second-hand clothes shop in a particularly snazzy pale blue dress. The hem undulated as she twirled to give her friends the best angle.

'Ooh, very Boris Day,' proffered Hilda.

'Boris Day, who on earth is that when they're at home?' Ethel coughed several crumbs from the biscuit Miriam Howard, the proprietor of the shop, had given her, onto her skirt. She quickly brushed them away with a flick of the hand.

Hilda rolled her eyes and shrugged her shoulders, taking care not to spill her cup of tea in the process. 'You know, her with the blonde hair. She had a bit of a thing with that Rocky actor for years until he fell out of the closet!'

'You mean Rock Hudson, and he *came* out of the closet, Hilda. He was gay.' Clarissa helpfully offered as she checked her reflection in the full-length mirror.

Hilda tutted and took another sip of her tea. 'I don't care how gay and happy he is, I'm gay and happy, so is Millie here. You smile a lot, don't you, Millie?' She prodded her friend, but didn't wait for a response before ploughing ahead. 'I'm just saying, he was an item with Boris for quite some time and she wore a dress like that in *The Man Who Knew Too Much*.'

Ethel puffed out her cheeks in frustration. 'It's a pity it wasn't the woman who knew too much, or we might finally have a conversation that we can understand. It's Doris, *he* liked men and *she* was a public front for him. They were just very good friends!'

Slightly annoyed that her dress reveal was being hijacked by Hilda's misinformation, Clarissa quickly took back control. 'So, Doris Day and Rock Hudson aside, what do you all think of this?' She waited patiently as her three friends scrutinised her choice. 'Well, don't all shout at once; we might as well have tumbleweed blowing through here!'

Miriam quickly handed the ladies a card each. 'Go on, girls, give her a score!'

Like the numbers rung up on an old-fashioned James Ritty cash register, Ethel, Millie and Hilda flicked up their cards.

'Three, five and a seven!! Is that all?' Clarissa laughed. 'I expected at least a nine somewhere amongst that lot.' Deflated she returned to the changing room, ensuring she rattled the curtain with much dramatic gusto. Her muffled voice continued from the depths. 'We don't have to provide our own costumes, so that's something, but apparently there is a bit of a party when filming is over. We should all look to be attired in something a little special as WI representatives, particularly if Flynn Phoenix is attending.'

'That's if it goes ahead as planned; haven't you heard?' Miriam couldn't believe that for once she would be the first to be the bearer of a juicy piece of gossip. 'Rumour has it that the house-keeper at Abbey Towers has gone missing – not been hide nor hair of her seen for two days.'

Hitching her arms to her chest, Ethel was all ears. '*What*? Just vanished into thin air? Oh my! How exciting! The curse of Black Abbey Towers strikes again!'

'I don't think the poor girl's mother is finding it quite so exciting,' Miriam huffed. 'Anyway, that's what I've heard.'

Millie emerged from the next cubicle, totally oblivious to Miriam's revelation and more invested in her chosen creation, which was causing quite a bit of a stir. 'I like this one, and I'm sure Flynn will too!' she jauntily announced.

Clarissa popped her head between the curtains to join her friends in their anticipated mutual admiration of Millie's choice of frock. 'Oh dear...' was all she could muster.

They stared in silence, not wishing to be the friend that would have the unenviable task of speaking the truth as they took in the shiny contours of the black PVC miniskirt and see-through lace blouse that Millie was parading in. Miriam, for all her years of experience in the rag trade, chose to disappear into the store-room rather than face being asked for an opinion. Clarissa could see that Ethel was bursting with her unspoken thoughts. She pressed her index finger to her lips in a 'shushing' motion; the last thing she wanted was for Millie's feelings to be hurt. As usual, Ethel chose to ignore her.

'Bloody hell, Millie, that barely covers your furry fandango...' Ethel slapped her knee and roared with laughter. 'Please tell me you're joking?'

Millie, hand out in a modelling pose, sashayed across the floor and gave her a cheeky wink. 'A couple of sherries and a gin and tonic and I'll wear anything, Eth. You should know that. And besides, who was it who turned up to Beryl's 60th birthday party dressed in fishnet stockings, black stiletto boots, and a spiked dog collar? There was more than a furry fandango on show that night, I can tell you!'

Ethel blushed. 'I read the invite wrong; it was all that fancy printing. It looked like it said "You are invited to Beryl's Goth Party"...'

The four friends chuckled fit to burst, completely forgetting the original mission for their attendance at Frugal Finds. Miriam, hearing their laughter assumed it was safe to return to her station behind the till. 'Have we made our choices then, ladies?' She secretly crossed her fingers behind her back. As much as she adored the foursome, it was easy for a whole morning to be taken up with their antics, and it would cost her dearly in a box of Fox's Classic biscuit selection and several tea bags. She checked the tin and stared forlornly at the only biscuit that remained. Not to be downhearted, she was grateful that they had at least left one for her. She took a sip of her tea and raised the biscuit to her lips, relishing the anticipation of a sugar rush.

'It's got teeth marks in it!!' She retched as she stared at the perfectly shaped indentations left by a rogue set of dentures. Indignant, she challenged them. 'Really, ladies!'

Three index fingers pointed and three pairs of eyes settled on Hilda, her friends ready and willing to give her up at the drop of a hat.

Hilda feigned surprise. 'Thanks for the loyalty, girls! Don't stress, Mim...' she cheerfully clacked her teeth together, '... they've been soaking in a glass of Steradent all night – you won't catch anything!'

THE FIRST SEVENTY-TWO HOURS

'*D*amn...' Andy Barnes jumped up from his chair like a scalded cat, dark splashes rapidly appearing on his grey trousers. The pool of tepid tea spread out from beneath his mug, forcing him to put the staining of his new trousers in second place to saving his paperwork. 'Lucy, do me a favour and chuck a couple of sheets of blue roll over.' His hand, acting as a barrier to the liquid, was in danger of failing as the tea began to seep underneath his palm.

Lucy executed a quick sprint to the brew corner and grabbed the paper towel, ripping off a couple of sheets on the way back to Andy's desk. She draped them across the tea puddle, letting the liquid soak up enough to free Andy's hand.

'Thanks. Now where was I?'

'A Misper in Fallow Falls. The file's right there...' she pointed to the two sheets of A4 in a clear plastic wallet.

He picked it up and read the first section, a frown beginning to furrow his forehead. 'And why is this a CID matter? Is she vulnerable or is foul play suspected?' He rummaged around in the desk drawer and pulled out the MISPER Protocol booklet before bringing up the incident log on the screen. Uniform had updated it with the extensive enquiries they had already carried out.

'Look where she's gone missing from, Sarge…' Lucy pointed to the last location address. 'She's the housekeeper at Abbey Towers.'

'And?'

'Black Abbey Towers! You must have heard the stories. It's never been a happy place, has it? Murders, suicides, suspicious deaths, report after report of intruders, with never any sign of the building being insecure or a forced entry. Rumours have been rife for years that it's haunted.'

Andy smiled and shook his head. 'Oh come on, not you too! I had this with Pru last night; her WI ladies went to an audition at the Towers the other day. They're going to be extras for a spooky film that's being shot on location there, which is a bit bizarre as it's actually a vicarage housing an archdeacon and his wife. As you can imagine for the WI girls, excitement is high, ghost-hunting is top of the list, and knowing that lot, it won't be long before they get themselves embroiled in something they wish they hadn't.'

Lucy jiggled his mug. 'More tea, vicar?' She laughed. 'Well, they won't have Pru to keep an eye on them, she'll be far too busy blossoming and blooming to be chasing spectres of the night!'

Andy grunted. 'More like growing and grumbling. The bigger she gets, the more tetchy she becomes, and, yes, for the record, she definitely won't be gracing Abbey Towers with her presence.'

Lucy brought him a fresh mug of tea and one for herself. She sat down next to him, a second file in front of her. 'Right, her name is Alice Moorcroft, she's a forty-eight-year-old single female, lives with her elderly mother in the village, no other relatives. Mum is in her eighties with very poor health; hence Alice is her sole carer.'

Andy sipped his tea. 'So what are the factors that have flagged this particular case?'

'Number one, she would never leave her mum unattended and alone. That's the biggest factor. She's bedridden and totally dependent, hence we've now had to get social services involved. Two, she left her handbag, coat and outdoor shoes at Abbey Towers, and three, everyone the uniform troops have spoken to have said she is reliable and consistent and would never just willingly disappear. Early enquiries show there's no love life to speak of, no recent relationships, and nothing out of the ordinary to indicate she had anything planned.'

'Does Abbey Towers have CCTV?' Andy was thinking out loud without expecting an answer; he knew whoever had taken the initial report would have checked that as standard practice. 'So, no sighting of Alice from the time she was seen inside Abbey Towers and when she was discovered missing – and since then?'

Lucy shook her head. 'Nope, nothing. She wasn't wearing suitable outdoor clothing for this weather, just jeans, sweatshirt, a cleaner's tabard and the light house slippers that she always wore at the Towers.'

Taking a good slurp of his tea, he used his other hand to swiftly kick the mouse and curser into action. 'Right, so for now we have to assume that she didn't leave Abbey Towers. It's a substantial building. Can you get on to the National Archives for a copy of the architectural drawings and records relating to the property, and include any outbuildings on the land, too.' His fingers flicked over the keyboard as he endorsed the log with his rank and force identity number. 'I want a full, top-to-bottom search of the premises. Every nook and cranny before we spread our search outside. I take it the MPU at National Crime Agency have been updated?'

'Yes, fully briefed. Uniform did search the premises at the time, Sarge; it's noted on the incident log.' She used her pen to point to the relevant entry on the screen. 'It's going to be a nightmare with them filming there, although the main bit with everyone on set doesn't start until next week. From the phone conversation I had this morning with Colquitt Productions, they'll send their lighting, riggers and grips in first, so even that will be a bit chaotic whilst they set up.'

Andy was more than aware that a thorough search of the rooms would have taken place, but he was also mindful that old buildings like Abbey Towers held secret and less obvious hidey-holes. He wanted all avenues explored, and the best place to start would be any plans held on the layout and structure of the manor house since the first foundation brick was laid, right up to how it had evolved over the ensuing years.

He needed his teams to coordinate a well-informed and systematic search on the Towers before the modern take on Alfred Hitchcock with his cast, film crew, the Four Wrinkled Dears and their best WI buddies descended upon it. A dull ache was starting to pulsate behind his eyes.

Andy groaned and reached for the packet of paracetamol as he counted up the potential footfall that would grace the building and grounds with less than seven days to spare.

A CLOSE SHAVE

The office atmosphere of Colquitt Productions was unusually subdued, particularly so close to the start of filming. Gone was the excited chatter of anticipation and the enthusiastic hum of final preparations, replaced instead with a morose feeling of potential failure.

Annie sat at her desk, her left palm propping her chin whilst her right hand artistically produced several doodles on the notepad. 'Are they absolutely sure this woman went missing *inside* the Towers? Could she not have slipped out and gone missing from somewhere else?'

Lucas Sullivan was as keen as Annie to hope that the police investigation might change direction away from his chosen film location. This was all he needed. Time was money in this game, and the massive salary that Flynn Phoenix commanded could be a make or break for Colquitt. A long delay would be a financial disaster. 'They're carrying out a full search now; hopefully, if they find nothing, it's full steam ahead, but if…' he tailed off. The alternative was unthinkable. A dead body, tragic though it would be, could be the end of the project. 'Annie, get me Alan Taylor on the phone, he needs to get moving on sourcing an alternative location with permits if this one goes tits up.' He knew he was being optimistic; it took months, sometimes years, to find perfect film locations, and as the script was loosely based on Abbey Towers' dark history it would be nigh on impossible to find another eerie venue that ticked all the boxes for the storyline.

'He's on line two for you,' Annie passed the call through to him and turned her attention to the file marked 'Background Actors'. Daffy had given her the task of tidying up the groups they had corralled each applicant into. She followed the numbers, stacking the photographs and CV history of each one into the relevant piles. She paused when she came to the ladies they had voted as their favourite four and smiled to herself. 'Remember this one, Daffy?' She held up the photograph of Hilda. 'What an absolute hoot she was. Honestly, the look on everyone's faces when she came bowling through those doors.'

Daffy took the snapshot from her. 'She was rather sweet with a bit of a tart edge to her, wasn't she? Mind you, her friends are full of character too. Have you got the one called Ethel? Now she had me in stitches.' She looked at the photo Annie had pushed across the desk. 'Yep, that's her. I think the four of them are going to be a bit of handful, but if we keep an eye on them, see how they go on their first few days, maybe we can use them for the Halloween scene with Flynn.'

'Are you sure, Daffy? You saw how much of a commotion just one of them caused; can you imagine quadrupling that?' Annie smirked and straightened the edges of the pile marked 'Male A'.

Daffy pondered Annie's observation for all of two seconds. 'Maybe, but they could also liven up some of the more mind-numbingly boring moments of being on location – you never know what they'll pull out of the bag, given a bit of free rein.'

Annie knew only too well that when donkey's had free rein, they rarely led others in an orderly fashion but more often encouraged them with bad behaviour. She just hoped this wouldn't be the case with Daffy's bright idea for the four old ladies.

$$\sim$$

Andy ran his hands through his hair in frustration. He pushed the plans around his desk, turning them in a full circle to view them from every angle. 'Are they absolutely sure?'

Lucy laid out the search log for him to see. 'Yep, they have literally searched every single inch of Abbey Towers and the grounds, and found nothing, not even the smallest of clues as to her whereabouts either inside, outside or anywhere else for that matter.'

'What about here…' his fingers jabbed at the bell tower. 'And here…' a second stabbing motion followed covering the basement and wine cellars.

'Everywhere, Sarge, there's nothing. The bell tower is a series of steps up to a room which is completely empty, it hasn't been used since the murder/suicide in 1973. It was cleared out and the access door locked with strict instructions for it to never be reopened. As far as the diocese is concerned, the only person to have a key now is the archdeacon, and that never leaves the chain on his belt. They've even searched the old folly in the grounds.'

Andy read the entry for the bell tower. A team of two had utilised a four-corner search of the room and the storage cupboard under the bottom flight of stairs. He knew they couldn't have been any more thorough. 'Right, we widen our search. I take it nothing more has come from CCTV enquiries?'

'Nothing. Admittedly there are no cameras at Abbey Towers, and the nearest one is two miles away from the main entrance to the estate. It's been viewed with nothing of value, although uniform are chasing up on vehicles that were in the vicinity at the time of the last sighting of Alice.' Lucy clicked her mouse through a series of tasks on the screen.

'Okay, good work, Luce, and can you pass on my thanks to the teams...' he picked up his mobile phone and car keys. 'Can you carry on allocating the outstanding tasks and, if possible, fix up an appointment with Archdeacon Gregory and his wife? I'd like to speak to them myself. I'm taking an early dart. Pru's got an antenatal appointment and we're going to see the maternity unit.' His face screwed up slightly, evidencing his secret reluctance to skip along the corridors of the local baby eviction ward.

'Have fun.' She grinned.

Andy laughed. 'Yeah! Since when did shaving my wife's legs and cutting her toenails become *fun?*'

'Since you intricately shaved the Winterbottom Wanderers football logo in the hairs on her left leg – she told me all about it, you naughty boy!'

AN INTRODUCTION

If I should die before I wake,
I pray the Lord my soul to take...

*B*ut that's the thing you see.
I don't have a soul.

I am filled with a blackness that comes from pain, fear and shame. And from just merely existing. Although in truth, I should not exist. I am a spawn, an abomination. A carrier of darkness and death. It is in the blood.

My blood.

It's true what they say, that the apple doesn't fall far from the tree.

My days are filled with reading, creating and playing make-believe, and my nights are spent wandering dark corridors and streets. Do I know what day it is, or month or year? Do I follow the seasons as they change, or do I pretend they no longer exist? Do I find comfort in words, the bottle or a pill? Is it warm, is it cold? Does the sun shine or the rain fall?

It matters not.

Not here.

Not in my inner sanctuary.

My mind.

So, how do I choose my sacrifices, I hear you ask?

Over time, my quest has become more fluid. It undulates and shifts position; it changes, just like the seasons I remember from my childhood. The motive has long since died, replaced by a need rather than a want.

If you can keep a secret, I will tell you…

They choose themselves.

THAT SINKING FEELING

*A*ndy waited in the delivery room for Pru to catch up with him. They had enjoyed, if he could use that word, an in-depth tour of the maternity unit, which included things that as a man he really wished he didn't have to know about. There were certain aspects of labour and giving birth that had jumped out at him from posters plastered across the hospital walls, showing it all in full glorious technicolour that had then been subsequently burned onto his retinas.

He dropped his left arm onto a padded sling contraption that was hooked on the end of the bed, giving himself some respite from his aching back. He was pleased to see a second sling on the other side, and with a bit of stretching he made it pivot so he could angle his right arm into it. Leaning forward he transferred his weight onto his forearms and moaned softly, relishing the relief it gave him as he arched his back to elongate his spine.

'Ah there you are!' Pru waddled into the room with the midwife close behind her. She stopped abruptly, her eyes wide in surprise. 'Dear god, Andy, what on *earth* are you doing?'

'Just taking the weight off a bit. I think it's one of those

Japanese shiatsu things for stress and posture. Dead handy, isn't it?'

Pru shook her head in despair. 'Only if you're in labour, on your back with legs-akimbo and in the final ten centimetres of dilation, getting ready to push. They're birthing stirrups for legs, you idiot!'

Andy had been conditioned to move fast in his job, sometimes his life depended on quick reflexes to get himself out of danger, but this time he surpassed himself. 'Good grief, really?' was all he could mutter as he staggered backwards away from the now offending contraption.

Jenny, the midwife, grinned. 'I take it you haven't read the books, then?'

If embarrassment could be summed up by a colour, then Andy's face was the paragon. He visibly squirmed as he shrugged his shoulders. 'What?' He held out his hands in disbelief at the look Pru was giving him. 'Oh come on, Pru. I said I'd be there to hold your hand and support you any way I can, but at the nice end. I'm not good with the messy working bits – that's your domain, isn't it?' No sooner had that observation left his lips, he realised that he'd dropped a massive clanger. It wasn't only Pru who was giving him a look of incredulity, Jenny had added her best googly-eyes to the moment too.

He stood with his hands in his pockets staring at the floor, reminiscent of his schoolboy days when being chastised by the headmaster for running in the corridors. It took a great deal of mental strength to ignore the childish urge to scrub one shoe over the top of the other as a sign of discomfort. 'I'll just go and get some leaflets, shall I?'

'Good idea, Mr Barnes. There's a vending machine in the lounge area. Go and get yourself a nice cup of tea and read them whilst Pru and I discuss her "messy working bits"!' Jenny gave Pru a discreet wink. 'Oh, and while you're there, can you ask at the nurses' station if they'll give you three packets of san...?'

Andy didn't wait to discover what was required of him. He beat a hasty retreat through the door and along the corridor. No way was he going to ask for those, let alone carry them around the hospital. He knew exactly what began with 'san'. He'd seen Pru's stash of them in the bag she had prepared for their eventual hospital dash when baby Barnes was due to make an appearance. Horrified, he ran like the wind, half expecting his old headmaster to jump out from a doorway and grab him by the scruff of the neck.

'Blimey,' Jenny giggled, 'I was only going to ask him to grab a couple of prepacked sandwiches for lunch.' She handed Pru an admission's goodie bag and shrugged. 'Oh well, it's his loss!'

'Are you still not speaking to him?' Bree swung her legs over the end of the sofa and plumped up the cushion behind her. 'I wish I'd been a fly on the wall, though. I bet it was dead funny.'

Slamming the fridge door shut, Pru waved her hands to indicate that she couldn't speak with her mouth full. She chewed vigorously, trying to reduce the size of the chunk of cheese she had just devoured straight from the block, no knife required. 'Aw, I actually felt sorry for him. For the all the things he has to deal with at work, for some reason anything to do with "lady-bits"...' she used her index fingers to air quote the word, '... will make him squirm like a giant earthworm. It was quite awkward for him too when they did the questions part, as his family history is really limited, so some of the stuff they need to know about health and genetics are missing.'

Bree gave a sigh of support. 'Ah, was that because both of Andy's parents are dead?'

'Oh gosh no, it's because he's adopted. Honestly, I thought you knew, please don't say I mentioned anything, though; he doesn't like to talk about it. I think he would probably be keen to know more about his birth parents, but he just considers his adoptive parents as his real family, so he's never taken it any further.' She stroked her tummy. 'This is why our rainbow baby is so important to him; it's his flesh and blood, his family, and after what happened with our first little sprout...' Pru became pensive, chewing her bottom lip as her eyes began to glisten with tears. She quickly caught herself, swallowing hard before she spoke again. 'Well, I'm sure you understand. It means even more for him, and me too.'

Bree was only too aware that the loss of Pru's first pregnancy the previous year at just twelve weeks, had nearly broken her heart. There was no rhyme or reason as to why; it had been 'just one of those things', words that had seemed so matter of fact and unfeeling at the time. In the grieving period that followed, Bree thought she would never see her beautiful friend smile again, but six months later she had been there to toast the delighted couple with their news, tentatively announced but still with much excitement and anticipation, that they were expecting the patter of tiny feet again.

Quickly changing the subject to avoid a mini-blub-fest, Pru grabbed her water bottle and plonked herself down next to Bree. 'Anyway, all is going well, baby Barnes is settling in a nice position, and I can look forward to many more weeks with swollen ankles, loud flatulence – and cramp!'

'You had the flatulence before you got pregnant; don't go blaming that poor unborn child on your inability to fart quietly!' Bree quipped. 'Anyway, moving away from maternity leggings, incontinence, and a useless hubby...'

'I don't have incontinence; my water bottle has got a leak...' she shook it at Bree to prove a point, '... and he's not *that* useless!'

The subject was swiftly changed to the other forthcoming event. The filming of *The Haunting of Fallow Falls* at Abbey Towers. Neither Bree nor Pru could contain their excitement at the prospect of a glimpse of Flynn Phoenix. Pru was bitterly disappointed that her current condition would mean she would have to swerve her involvement with the WI posse this time, as Andy had forbidden her to undertake anything more strenuous than an amble into Winterbottom village for an afternoon tea at the Twisted Currant Café. She just had to hope that maybe Flynn would pop in for a bath bun or two at some point, and she could accidentally bump in to him – with 'bump' being the operative word.

'Anything new on Alice, the missing housekeeper?' Bree nonchalantly flicked through a magazine from the coffee table, as though her enquiry was just an aside to Dr Belladonna Atkins *Intimate Issues* column on page nine, and not her being blatantly nosey. She knew Andy always chatted about work; just how much, she wasn't sure, but if anyone was to know a juicy piece of information, it would be Pru.

'Not much, really, just that there's been no sighting of her at all. Everyone seems stumped by her disappearance. There's been talk that she might have had some sort of a breakdown and just taken off, run away.' Pru felt a twinge of sadness for her. To know that someone not that much older than herself had never had adventures, travelled or found love, was incredibly depressing. 'Can you imagine it? She'd been caring for her mum since she was a teenager, no life of her own, and day after day cleaning up other people's mess and muck to earn enough to keep them afloat.'

The friends were suddenly lost for words. They sat together, thinking about how different their own lives might have been if they had been dealt the hand that Alice had held.

'What happened to her dad?' Not that it made any difference, but Bree was curious.

Pru's face flushed pink. 'Oh my! Talk about having a brain malfunction. Not once did I put two and two together when Andy was talking about her. He was the gardener at Abbey Towers in the 1980s, it was such an awful accident.' She grabbed her phone, thumbs deftly tapping the keys of the search bar on Google.

'Here you go...' She held the screen out in front of her, showing the headlines from the *Winterbottom News* archives. 'I vaguely remember Florrie Patterson talking about it a few years ago, and it was given a bit of a mention in a book called *Tales from the Black Abbey Towers*; there's a copy of it in our library.' Her finger tapped on the screen until she found what she was looking for. 'How awful for Alice's mum. It must bring back so many dreadful memories. Funnily enough, it was hushed up quite a bit. The area was cordoned off as out of bounds, and then the hole was filled in really quickly once his body was recovered. Have a read.' She passed the phone to Bree.

Thursday 31 October 1985: Tragic Accident In Fallow Falls.
Local man, Theodore Moorcroft, discovered deceased after falling into a sink hole in the grounds of the church-owned Abbey Towers.
Mr Moorcroft was employed by the estate as head gardener.

THE MINIATURE MANOR

*a*ndy pulled into the lay-by near to the gates of Abbey Towers. He wanted to get his first view of the building out in the open, not through the windows of his car. He grabbed his jacket from the back seat, the chill October wind finding any available weave in the fabric of his suit to cool his bones. Lucy was already muffled up with gloves and a scarf to complement her Marmot Parka. They stood side by side, with Abbey Towers looming up in front of them. It was bathed in weak autumn sunlight.

'It's spooky, isn't it?' Lucy shivered. 'No wonder they're using it for a horror film; it won't need much improving with CGI!'

Andy had to agree, it was not the type of place you would immediately warm to and want to live in. His eyes scanned every corner of the building before finally settling on the tower itself. 'It's a wonderful bit of architecture and the grounds are stunning, but for once I agree with you, Luce.' He scribbled a quick note in his book before slipping it back into his pocket. Using his pen as a pointer, he indicated to the four windows of the tower. 'See that one there, straight ahead? That's where the vicar chucked himself from in 1973, I was reading the file this morning. No chance of surviving a fall from that height, I can tell you.'

They began the long walk along the driveway to the main doors, taking care not to trip on the expanse of electrical cables that were now littering the tarmac and grass. The high-sided vans, their tailgates down, were a hive of activity with film crews rolling out huge black and silver crates on wheels. The setting up for filming had begun as soon as Andy had given the nod to Colquitt Productions. In truth he hadn't been given much option, because, as the saying goes, money talks. There was a huge budget with many investors tied to this production, and one of those investors just happened to be in a position to have a quiet word in the ear of the chief constable. In turn, he had pushed for Andy's office to wrap up the search if nothing of evidential value had been found, and to open Abbey Towers to the film crews.

'Detective Barnes?' The portly man skipped over two large cables that were draped in his path, his size belying his gracefulness. 'Archdeacon Gregory; pleased to meet you.' He held out his hand. 'But call me Clement, there's no need to be on ceremony here.' He gave a warm, welcoming smile to the two detectives as he ushered them through the large oak doors. 'Apologies for the chaos, just watch your step.'

Andy and Lucy followed him into the grand hall, the marble flooring polished to within an inch of its life, with a fresh display of flowers sat in the middle of a large round table. The archdeacon beckoned them into his office. Lucy held her breath as she entered the room, all around her were examples of antique paintings and fine art displayed on the walls. A glass-fronted cabinet sat majestically in the corner, filled with delicate porcelain ornaments and glassware. Whilst Andy discussed Alice's disappearance with Clement, she took the opportunity to walk around the room admiring them.

'Oh my goodness, what is this?' Momentarily forgetting the purpose for her visit, she stood in front of a huge model that was displayed in the bay window, framed by rich gold and green brocade curtains that had been draped and tied back.

Clement was delighted that a youngster like Lucy had paused to admire such an important piece of Abbey Towers' history. 'It's called a diorama, dear, and very popular in the early nineteenth century, mainly for theatre and entertainment, although it developed over the years into what you see here today.' He gently lifted a small hook and opened out the front in two pieces, the hinges working smoothly and without fault to reveal the inside. 'See, everything is exactly as it should be, it's Abbey Towers in miniature.'

Andy peered inside, clearly impressed by what he was seeing. 'Is it exact in every detail, Clement? What about any updating or changes over the years?'

'All been taken care of, updated as and when needed. It has had many identities over the decades, the biggest being in the 1940s when it was returned to the church as it was no longer required for the war effort as a military hospital. It did need a bit of a makeover after that, I must say. The only thing that has stayed constant is that...' his finger carefully pointed to the tiny wall plaque to the right of the main doors.

'Black Abbey Towers...' Lucy whispered.

'Yes, my dear. It has never been changed on the diorama; it was thought bad luck to do so. How on earth the locals came to that conclusion I will never know, because without a second thought or care, they changed it on the actual house you're standing in now. Purely to appease the locals and to try and dispel all those awful stories of black magic, ghosts and spectres that were attached to it.' Clement gave a little nervous chuckle and furtively looked around the room. 'I've lived here for quite some time, detective, and I can say hand on heart I have not seen or heard anything out of the ordinary. Alice's disappearance is the first upset we've had for many a year.'

Lucy's eyes scanned the model, room to room, and along

corridors and narrow passages. Abbey Towers certainly was a house of many architectural personalities. Looking at it in miniature it teased her mild OCD; there was definitely something 'off' with the whole structure, but she couldn't quite put her finger on it. 'What are these?'

Clement peered over her shoulder. 'They're the inhabitants of Abbey Towers, dear; we have a little box over there, full of past and present residents. That's me…' he pointed to a rather stout-looking figure standing by the fireplace in a room that had floor-to-ceiling shelving and books, which, without a doubt, was the library. 'And that's Fiona, my wife…' The more delicate figure with fair hair was propped up in the kitchen near to the sink. 'And then we have Alice, she's… er…' he paused, his eyes searching the diorama. 'Well, that's strange, Alice should be in the scullery or one of the bedrooms.' He lifted the roof of the adjoining scullery annexe and looked inside. 'No, she's not there either.' He opened the William Morris designed box and looked inside, eventually tipping out its contents onto his desk. His fingers deftly separated the figures as he searched. 'No, not there either.'

'Could your wife have moved it, archdeacon?' Andy was not immediately placing any store by the missing item.

'Fiona would never touch the diorama, Detective Barnes; she has no interest in it whatsoever. Well, it looks as though not only has Alice disappeared from Abbey Towers in real life, but vanished from its replica too!'

DANA

*D*onna Smith slammed her hand down onto the alarm clock with so much force it skittered across the bedside cabinet and knocked the half-empty wine glass onto the floor.

'Damn, damn, damn...' Pulling off her sleep mask she squinted and blinked rapidly, the bright autumn sunlight streaming through the partially opened curtains instantly pushed her headache to the upper limits. She clacked her tongue to the roof of her mouth and pulled a face. 'Bleurgh, talk about a camel's ass in a sandstorm.'

Donna, better known by her stage and screen name of Dana Simon, gingerly sat up and swung her legs over the side of the bed. She let her head droop backwards with her mouth gaping open as she tried to bring her thoughts and energy back on line. 'Come on, girl, get that saggy arse into action,' she chided herself. Her toes touched the damp patch of red wine that had already soaked into the beige carpet. She picked up her phone and pressed the key for her personal assistant. It was answered on the second ring. 'Mark darling, there's been a little bit of a spillage in the bedroom, can you get one of the girls to clean it up?' Without any show of appreciation, she clicked the red circle to end the call and threw her phone onto the bed.

Grabbing a robe, she made her way to the en suite; today was going to be a long one, another read through and then tech rehearsals. She stopped by the floor-to-ceiling mirror. 'Bloody hell!' She stretched her neck and pushed out her chin. 'Wattle, I've developed a neck like a ruddy chicken overnight.' She pulled at the folds of skin and then utilised the back of her hand to slap them into submission.

It was no surprise that her best days were behind her. The film industry didn't welcome or value the ageing process in their female stars. Only the men could get away with silver fox hair and laughter lines whilst still commanding fabulous roles and the salary to go with them. She was now at an age where her feet were no longer the first thing to hit the shagpile rug when she got out of bed in the mornings. She looked down at her pendulous boobs and momentarily thought about slapping them into submission too, but quickly realised it would hurt like hell and would probably only serve to swing them under her armpits anyway.

Donna desperately wanted to cry. Sixty-eight years old and her latest role was as the mother of the star of the film. She'd been signed for *The Haunting of Fallow Falls* by her agent, who had quite brutally informed her that at her age, 'beggars can't be choosers'. Flynn Phoenix was currently enjoying all the perks that she had enjoyed at the start of her own career, whilst the production company had seen fit to downgrade her, the one and only Dana Simon, in both casting and trailer.

'The actual goddam mother of a thirty-five-year-old bloody upstart!' she screamed at her reflection. If she was honest with herself, she knew Flynn had worked hard to get where he was; he had started at the bottom, honed his craft, and had eventually made it. The only difference between him and herself was the casting couch.

She turned the power shower on full and stepped beneath the sharp needles of hot water. They pummelled her skin, bringing about a strange, almost pleasant, pain. Her hands pressed against the tiled wall as she leant her forehead into its smooth coolness, willing the alcohol-induced headache to go away. Closing her eyes, she tried to block out the memories that frequently haunted her when the black moods came to visit, but they always lingered. She could still feel the discomfort of the various button-backed leather sofas of her younger days digging into her thighs, the desperate fumblings, the smell of expensive aftershave, Montecristo Cuban cigars, and the greatest pieces of acting emotion she had ever performed, time and time again.

Pleasure, enjoyment and willing participation.

Only it had never been an enjoyable pleasure, nor had she been willing; it was simply a means to an end. She had sold her virtue and her soul to so many men that held her career in their hands. And for what? To end up playing someone's goddam mother in a horror movie. She had learned the hard way over the years: success had a high price. What followed each of her sordid liaisons was not just the promises of starring roles, fame and fortune. It was something much more than that, it was something that could never be washed away.

Shame.

Her revenge would be a dish served not just cold, but overflowing.

Mark Joynson held the phone out in front of him, the dead air being the only indication that there had actually been a caller on the line. 'Of course, Miss Simon, anything you say, Miss Simon...' He half-heartedly sighed into the disconnected receiver. 'Betty, she's made a mess in the bedroom again.' He pointed to the ceiling. 'It'll probably be the Chateau Lagrange she was quaffing last night, so take a bottle of white up with you. It'll help reduce the staining on the carpet.'

Betty, Dana's housekeeper, grabbed a cheap bottle of white plonk from the fridge. 'I'll use this one, it was a tad vinegary anyway.' She laughed. 'Sounds like she's in one of her moods.'

Mark took a large gulp from his Mickey Mouse mug. Black coffee not only stimulated his ability to discover an extra ounce of mental energy, an energy he would definitely need if Dana was being a diva, but also took him back to his heady days at Harmony Hollows Resort when two mugs and four biscuits would be the start of his day there.

After the grisly murders carried out by a member of the Harmony resort team no less, and the further decline of the holiday camp, his employment as their electrician, sound engineer, mechanic, lifeguard and all-round general dogsbody had come to an end. So 'Mighty Marko' had joined the ranks of the unemployed until this prime position became available through Colquitt Productions. He had started off as Dana's chauffeur, but she had soon spotted his other talents and had taken the opportunity to have his remarkable services around the clock. The pay wasn't bad, the hours were extensive, but the perks were too good to turn down. He just had to bite his tongue several times a day as she was an absolute mare to work for, but as long as he could do that, he thought his life was as good as it gets.

'Afraid so, I thought this film would placate her for a while, but it's made her ten times worse. She found out yesterday that her trailer is on the back sector.' Mark pulled down his mouth in a grimace and lifted up his shoulder, as though he was dodging an imaginary incoming missile.

'Oops, I bet that went down like a lead balloon. She wasn't happy about the film location to start with, and those rumours flying around, but the production company are over the moon. It's all adding to the mystique of the film, and no doubt they'll use it for PR.' Betty was nobody's fool when it came to the workings of the film industry; she had been part of it for over forty years in one role or another. 'She's very bitter, you know, and it's eating her away. I do worry about her mental health, coupled with her ability to polish off a couple of bottles of wine each night.' Betty tucked the microfibre cloth into her apron pocket. 'Keep an eye on her, Mark, I've seen her in action, and when that top lip of hers starts twitching, I guarantee there's going to be trouble ahead...'

FIRST DAY

'Wahoo, here we come...' Ethel stormed along the aisle of Frank's coach, eagerly knocking Kitty back into her seat with her handbag as she aimed for the front, desperate to be first off. The soft hiss of the pneumatic system as the doors opened was the cue for the rest of the Winterbottom Women's Institute ladies to follow suite.

Frank Atkins, owner and driver of Rubber, Springs & Gaskets Coach Tours, took the opportunity to give a discreet wink to Kitty as she drew level with him. Their on/off secret affair – which wasn't really a secret at all – had cooled somewhat over the past six months, but it was obvious that Frank's persistence was a grade up from Kitty's. She swept by him without a care, nose in the air.

Before their little tiff, Frank had been commissioned by Kitty to transport the ladies to and from Abbey Towers when needed. The Four Wrinkled Dears, on the other hand, had made their own arrangements. At Ethel's behest, they had agreed to her idea to turn their adventure into a 'stay and play', so rather than travel in each day, once their filming schedule was known, they had booked two rooms at The Bell, Book and Candle Inn in Fallow

Falls. Ethel's leaflet had shown a cosy, inviting place to stay and therefore the vote had been unanimous.

As the ladies spilled out into the temporary car park at Abbey Towers, they were met by chaperones who quickly, with the minimum of fuss, sorted them into their groups and ushered them to wardrobe and make-up.

The friends, having not yet been corralled, waited for their turn. The minutes ticked by, giving rise to four booteed pairs of feet to shuffle and kick gravel.

'I think they've forgotten us,' whined Hilda.

A warm but tart response from Ethel was to be expected. 'That's rich coming from you! Can you even remember why you're here anyway?' She laughed.

'I hope they've got toilets; I do need a tinkle...' Millie jiggled a little dance.

Clarissa rolled her eyes so far back she thought they'd smack her on the bottom. 'Oh for goodness' sake, girls! We've been here five minutes and you're at it already! They'll get to us, we just have to be patient, and Millie, pelvic floor, dear, pelvic floor! Snatch, grip and hold, that should help. Right, we need to find somewhere to store our suitcases. Check-in at the hotel isn't until after 3pm this afternoon.'

They stood huddled together waiting, whilst taking the time to examine the exterior of Abbey Towers. Ethel, her eyes twinkling with mischief, shuddered with anticipation. 'I think we could have a little dabble into the disappearance of Alice Moorcroft whilst we're here, if we play our cards right.' She sniffed and blotted the end of her nose with the small cotton handkerchief she had retrieved from the sleeve of her coat. 'Just think of the fun we could have!'

Clarissa was riled. 'Oh no you won't! I'll definitely put my foot down this time, Eth. We do *not* want to be getting involved in anything that might endanger us. Wasn't our near-death experience at Harmony Hollows bad enough?'

'And Rookery Grange?' added Millie.

'Or Montgomery Hall Hotel…?' was Hilda's offering.

Ethel stood her ground. 'What's wrong with a few buttock-clenching moments, hey? And what happened to "we can still kick ass when needed; we're the Fearsome Foursome?" Are you lot going all jelly on me?'

Clarissa huffed loudly. 'No, not jelly, but maybe a little blanc-mange! Okay, maybe a brief sniff round, but if it looks like we're poking our rather large noses in too deep, we call it quits.'

Contented they would have a sideline of snooping whilst they were prancing around the set as extras, the ladies treated them-selves to a group hug and a promise to watch each other's backs.

'Hello, ladies, so sorry for keeping you waiting.' The young woman holding a clipboard, gave them a warm greeting. 'I'm Annie Baines, you might remember me from the auditions. If you'd like to come this way, we've got quite a special part for you all to play. It's not a speaking role but I promise it'll be fun…'

'Noo, you're joking!' Pru's hands automatically supported her rounded tummy, allowing her to laugh just that little bit harder than she should have done.

The smile on Bree's face stretched from ear to ear. 'Yep, they spent the whole morning prancing and preening, and when it came to the refreshment period, they couldn't wait to let all the WI ladies know that they'd been personally chosen by the casting director for very important roles in the film.' She took a sip of her tea and offered Pru another biscuit. 'If only they'd waited until they knew exactly what it *was* they'd been cast as!'

'Oh my gawd! Can you imagine them appearing on the credits at the end, "Dead body number one", Ethel Tytherington, "Dead body number two", Clarissa Montgomery – and so on, right up to "dead body number four".' Pru's stomach suddenly took the opportunity to bounce out of shape as a lump rolled from one side to the other.

Bree looked horrified. 'Oh my God, it's like something out of *Alien!*'

'I think baby Barnes is just protesting at the jiggling I'm giving her, that was a foot...' Pru was amazed that her friend could be so surprised at anything to do with pregnancy considering she'd given birth herself, albeit almost seventeen years ago when her son Nathan was born.

'She? You just said "her". Do you know something I don't?' Propping herself up from her slouched position, Bree waited for confirmation.

'No, we still don't know; it's still going to be a surprise, but I have this secret feeling it's going to be a girl, and I've got a bet with Andy; he's convinced it's a boy.' For the second time in as many minutes, Pru cosseted her tummy. 'Anyway, getting back to the Four Wrinkled Dears, how have they taken their dead body roles?'

Bree started to laugh uncontrollably. 'Lying down, probably...'

DOROTHY MAY BARKER

DOTTIE

*I*f there was one thing that Dorothy May Barker hated more than anything else, it was being overlooked. To be overlooked was, in her opinion, on a par with being dead. Lack of respect or recognition gave a person no meaning or value in life.

Since her retirement from the firm, she had secured several interesting, but relatively mundane, positions that had kept the worst of the boredom at bay, but they had also added to her feeling of being insignificant. Her latest as a stunt advisor, with the odd helping hand in craft services for Colquitt Productions, had been the most fun, giving her the opportunity to meet famous film stars in person, whilst secretly allowing her 'specialist training' a bit of leeway when the moment took her. It had also given her the opportunity finally to return home. Financially she didn't have to worry; she'd carried out some pretty decent hits over the years for which she was more than handsomely paid. But when her trigger finger fell victim to arthritis, her replacement kneecap went south on more than one occasion and though she found she could climb walls chasing a target, she couldn't get down again on the other side, Dottie had taken the difficult decision to hang up her Glock 17 and had officially become a pensioner.

Dottie 'the Rottie' Barker as she was known, one of the best female assassins in the last thirty years, had finally left the building.

She forked out the contents from a tin of cat food into a little ceramic bowl and replenished a second bowl with fresh water. 'Here you go, Wick, dinner time.' She gave his ears a little rub and added a coo of affection. Wick, named after her favourite film character, John Wick, was the only companion she had. He had been a scruffy little bundle of fur that nobody wanted because he was black. There was so much superstition surrounding black cats that it often made it impossible for them to be rehomed. But Wick was like her, an outsider, a solo adventurer, so she had scooped him up and carried him home, wrapped up in her sweatshirt.

She made her way into the small lounge of her cottage, her shoes tapping on the woodblock flooring before becoming muffled as she skipped along the carpet runner. Settling herself down in the armchair, the log fire in the inglenook just beginning to bestow her with a warm, orange glow, she cupped her hands around her mug and took a slurp of hot chocolate. Wick followed her, jumped into her lap, and curled up on her knee.

'Blimey, slippers, log fire and hot chocolate! What on earth has happened to me, Wick? Have I become soft in my old age?' The cat purred loudly and pressed his front paws into her jumper, padding and kneading it as a form of comfort.

But Dottie knew nothing could be further from the truth. The fire still burned within her, only this time she didn't need to be paid for her services. Sometimes her targets would make themselves known by their behaviour; they would actually put themselves forward for a little bit of correction. Other times it was simply the way they treated her.

Like that dreadful diva Donna Smith, better known to her fans as Dana Simon or 'The Bitch with the Twitch'.

Dottie squirmed in her chair and involuntarily shuddered with her distaste of the woman. 'She's definitely a fur coat and no knickers type of gal, isn't she, Wick?'

And she was definitely one for Dottie's personal hit list, too.

Dana had shown her true colours during a break in the tech rehearsal at Abbey Towers. As Dottie handed her a drink and a sandwich from catering, Dana had loudly declared with a sneer and a twitch of her top lip to anyone within earshot, that Dottie's very manly thumb was too close to the crust and promptly demanded a fresh one be supplied forthwith. She had then complained bitterly to David Preece, the film director, that Dottie was a liability and should not, under any circumstances, be allowed to serve her again as she lacked the ability to obey instructions.

'Obey!!' Dottie spat out loud, making Wick startle. She had never 'obeyed' anyone in her life, and she sure as hell wasn't going to start now. Just ask that little toe rag from Fallow Falls who had dared to jostle her at the cashpoint machine making his demands.

She smirked and held out the thumb in question in front of her. The glow from the fire cast a shadow on her skin as she turned to view it from various angles. She had to admit it was quite a 'manly' appendage, probably on account of all the years of curving it around the back strap of her trusty Glock. She held her hand up in the shooting position, her pretend gun aiming at the imitation Whistler's Mother painting on the wall, imagining Dana's face, lips pursed tighter than Wick's arse, underneath the lace cap. 'Pow, pow...' she mimicked, before blowing on her two fingers that represented the gun barrel.

'Job done, no charge...'

SUMMARY JUSTICE

The investigation into the disappearance of Alice Moorcroft had become frustratingly static, much to the annoyance of Andy and his team. Every potential lead they followed had produced either a negative result or a complete dead end. She had vanished without a trace and there was very little else to follow up on. He was still waiting for her bank to give them access to her recent transactions and withdrawals, but what they did know was from the day she had disappeared her cards had not been used.

Detective Inspector Murdoch Holmes strode with purpose across the office, making a beeline for Andy's desk. Andy inwardly groaned; he knew he was going to be subjected to the 'Wrath of Holmes' for at least the next ten minutes. He plastered on a smile. 'Good morning, sir,' he tentatively offered.

'Is it? A good one, that is?' Holmes proffered the file that had been tucked under his arm to Andy. 'I need you to drop one of your team from the Moorcroft Misper investigation and put them on this. It's a nasty Section 18 assault that's been handed over by uniform.'

Andy scanned the first line of the crime report. 'Jackson

Rutter is the victim! Well, that's a turn up for the books. He's got a criminal record longer than the Thames. He's actually one of the suspects in our cashpoint robberies; I think he was next on the list for Jack Finnigan to bring in.' Andy was amused but not surprised to see Holmes smiling whilst delivering the news that Rutter would probably be sipping soup through a straw for weeks to come.

'Aye, probably summary justice for something he's either done or was about to do. Anyway, he's still in hospital; they're operating today to pin his jaw. He's as high as a kite on meds and is still insisting it was an OAP that beat him up and stole his watch – a TAG Heuer one, if you can believe that.' Holmes' chuckle gave way to a belly laugh. 'The only thing he can remember as he hit the pavement was the handbag that smacked him in the face and the suede ankle boots she was wearing, only because they reminded him of the ones his beloved granny wears.'

'Rutter has a granny and a TAG Heuer!' Lucy gasped. Considering ninety-nine per cent of Rutter's victims were in the sixty-five plus age bracket, she was shocked to think he would choose a target so close to the age of a vulnerable family member. Then again, he wasn't nicknamed 'Rutter the Nutter' for nothing. 'I'll go with the granny-mugger at a push, but a TAG watch! It's probably as fake as the twenty-quid notes he's been passing around for the last couple of weeks.'

Andy waited until Murdoch had returned to his office and closed the door before he spoke. 'I'll put Jack on this one. He's already got the cashpoint robbery file, so he can kill two birds with one stone. It'll be amusing to see Rutter's statement, though; let me know when he's got it, Lucy.' He checked his phone, reassuring himself that Pru hadn't tried to call him. 'Can you give Alice's mum a call, just to let her know that we're still doing everything we can to find her daughter.' He rubbed his temples, the circular motion only serving to push the impending headache up a level. Just one phone call from Alice to say she was safe and simply needed time out would be a bonus for him. She could be seen and interviewed, wherever she was, and he would then only have to monitor the situation until she returned.

But his gut instinct told him, even though he had no evidence to the contrary, that this job was not going to have a happy ending.

~

'Clement, wake up. Did you hear that?' Fiona Gregory sat up in bed, her eyes trying to adjust to the darkness. 'Clement…'

His gentle snoring continued without interruption. She could just make out his large frame with the duvet tucked over him by the moonlight that penetrated the gap in the bedroom curtains.

Thump, whump…

'Clement!!' This time she called him a little louder, but not loud enough to alert whoever was bumping along the corridor outside their bedroom door. Fiona cursed their single beds. She stretched out one leg from under her duvet and tried to prod him with her foot, hoping a swift kick in the buttocks would rouse him from his slumber, but for all her height and long limbs, she couldn't reach him. Her hand crept out to the bedside cabinet, her fingers spidering across the surface until they found the hard-shell glasses case. She grabbed it and hurled it at the sleeping form. It hit him on the back of the head.

'Urgh, what's the matter?'

'There's someone in the house, that's what's the matter! We've got an intruder…' Fiona quickly pulled her duvet up to her chin in the mistaken belief that it would act as a safety barrier and saviour should the burglar suddenly burst through the door.

Clement swung his legs out of the bed. He grabbed the brass candlestick from the dresser and tested its weight against his hand as he crept to the bedroom door, his blue striped pyjamas making him look more like a deck chair on Brighton beach than a reluctant hero.

'Be careful, it could be that Death Collector thing they all talk about.' Fiona was trembling so much her teeth had begun to chatter.

Clement took the opportunity to sneer at the ridiculousness of her warning, content that she would be unable to see his facial expressions in the dark so no repercussions would be forthcoming. 'Just do something useful, dear, and phone the police…'

He paused at the door, his fingers curled around the brass knob as he pressed his ear to the wood panel and listened. Fearing the sound from his heart would alert whoever it was, he willed it to stop beating so loudly. To his horror, the doorknob suddenly began to twist in his hand, he gripped it, tightening his fingers to stop the motion, but the unseen hand on the other side was bringing brutal force and momentum to its turning. Clement clung onto it whilst pressing his ample body against the door.

Boom, boom, boom…

The door began to bow inwards pushing him backwards with each blow. Accepting he would not be able to hold the fort for much longer, Clement took matters into his own hands as a false bravado washed over him. Raising the candlestick above his head, he turned the knob and flung open the door. 'In the name of God Almighty I command you, drop your weapon…' he screamed at the top of his voice as he stepped out to face his enemy, eager to believe that his heavenly boss hadn't yet deserted him.

'It's not a bloody exorcism, Clement…' Fiona hissed from under her duvet. 'Just smack them over the head with it, for goodness' sake.' Fear getting the better of her, she flung back her bedding and stumbled across the bedroom to find sanctuary.

He bounced onto the landing flailing his candlestick ferociously.

Swish, swish, swish…

The dark passageway was empty except for small dust motes dancing in the shaft of moonlight that stretched along the carpet to reach the restored portrait of Calduggan Wraith. Calduggan's eyes bore down on him, their inky blackness bringing a ferocious chill to his bones as he dropped to his knees to pray.

Unsated and disappointed, Abbey Towers slipped back into its silence, leaving Clement Gregory to his prayers and Fiona to the discomfort of musty mahogany wood against her back, whilst tightly crammed inside their double wardrobe with only her husband's oversized Union Underwear onesies for company that were dangling from the rail like limp marionettes.

CORPSING

'It's embarrassing lying here with my jowls tucked behind my ears!' Ethel, eyes closed, fake blood dripping across her neck, lay on the marble flooring of the ballroom.

'Sh…!'

'What?'

'They've just called "action"; the cameras are rolling,' Clarissa hissed at her from the corner of her mouth. 'Just keep quiet.'

'I've got an itch.' Millie surreptitiously used her thumb to scratch at her thigh through the cheesecloth nightdress that wardrobe had attired her in. 'I think I'm allergic to this material.'

Hilda tried to stifle a giggle, which unfortunately morphed into a loud snort.

'*Cut!*' David Preece, director, visionary and photographic genius for Colquitt Productions, shook his head. 'We have one of our dead bodies having a lambada with her leg in the background, folks, and another one appears to have fallen asleep if her snoring is anything to go by!' He took a sip from the paper cup that had been handed to him. 'Let's take a break. Annie, can you have a gentle word with your four prodigies, please, before we do the actual shoot?'

Ushering the scene background actors to the holding area, Annie took Clarissa to one side. She was the one she felt would be more accepting of advice and words of wisdom. 'You and your friends are going to be our regular corpses for this production, Clarissa, so I do need you to be on the ball with what happens on set, and the same for when we take filming into the village. I know this is a tech run-through, but it still needs to be treated as though it's really being filmed.'

Embarrassed, Clarissa nodded. 'I don't think they realised the director had started, but I'll make sure it doesn't happen again.' She tugged at her costume, pulling the neckline back into place whilst actively avoiding the vivid purple bruises the make-up department had painted on her. 'Are we going to be dead bodies right through the film, or will there be other roles for us?'

Annie smiled. 'You're disappointed, aren't you? There are some crowd scenes where you can be utilised. I'll make sure you get at least one "standing up" gig, but please, once the director shouts "action", you must be completely still. Don't talk on set, even when it's a rehearsal, and keep your enthusiasm to the holding area and the butty bus.'

As if on cue, Ethel excitedly interrupted their conversation. ''Rissa, look who's here; it's Pru's hubby, the Delectable Detective.' She pointed wildly at Andy who was deep in conversation with Clement Gregory. 'I've just heard some juicy gossip in the tent; there was an incident here last night.' Barely pausing for breath or a reply, Ethel was off, hitching up her dress as she ambled across the grass towards her intended target.

'Helloo, detective, yoo-hoo…' she hollered. 'It's me, Ethel! Can we help at all.' Andy broke off his conversation with the archdeacon to take in the vision that was bearing down on him. 'Oh dear Lord!'

'Ask and He shall answer!' Amused at his own witty response, Clement began to laugh. 'I take it you have prior knowledge of the lady?'

'Oh boy, do I?' Andy shook his head in resignation. 'Meet Ethel, one quarter of the Four Wrinkled Dears, also known as the Meddlesome Maidens of Winterbottom Women's Institute!'

FALLOW FALLS

'Well, that was a pretty good first day, wasn't it, girls?' Hilda quickened her pace along the cobbled pavement, her small blue Radley cabin bag bumping and rattling behind her as she led the 'charge of the Winterbottom ladies' with gusto towards their chosen accommodation.

Fallows Falls was such a pretty little village, albeit slightly spooky with its witches' stocks still standing proud next to the pond as an historical relic. It also boasted a small post office-cum-provisions store, a haberdashery shop, a ladies' salon with an ornate candy pink hanging sign, lots of little farmers' cottages dotted around the village square, and there in front of them their final destination, the Bell, Book and Candle Inn.

'Here we are.' Clarissa stood in front of the quaint lopsided building. The sign above the blackened wood door bore the date 1782. 'It's very... er... atmospheric, for want of a better word.'

'I think creepy is a better word, 'Rissa!' Millie visibly shuddered. 'Is there nowhere in Fallow Falls that doesn't look like it's haunted? I shall die of fright if we have any visitations in this place, you mark my words.' Her eyes scanned the ancient entrance porch, taking in the large orange pumpkins that had been carved in all manner of horrific faces before being stacked on the gossip benches either side.

'We're coming up to Halloween; most of the little villages join in the fun. Fallow Falls is no different, although their superstition does have some base if the stories of Black Abbey Towers and the Wraithe family are to go by.' Ethel prided herself on her knowledge of the area, she had spent many hours researching the Towers and the village.

'Creepy or not, it's our home for the next ten days, so get used it!' Clarissa was in no mood for ghost stories or histrionics from her friends. She made the first move, pushing open the door to the inn and beckoning the others to follow her.

A small reception desk greeted them, a tarnished brass bell on the counter, along with several faded leaflets extolling the virtues of Fallows Falls and its surrounding areas as places of natural beauty. Clarissa patiently waited for someone to attend to them whilst Ethel read out the teatime menu board.

'Cheese and onion pie with chips, cheese omelette, cheesy pasta bake, and...' She peered closely at the chalked words. 'Oh, would you believe it, just for a bit of variety they've got cheese sandwiches and cheese on toast too. Our Pru would love it here!' Her eyes scanned the specials board on the wall that was devoid of any words. 'I wonder what the special is?'

Without warning, a head popped up from behind the reception desk. The tiny wizened lady was barely visible above the well-worn counter. Her greying hair piled into an untidy chignon, bobbed and wobbled each time she moved. 'Good evening, ladies, it's cheesy leeks with cheese sauce,' she cackled, her eyes crinkling with the effort. 'I'm Hazel, your host, we've been expecting you.' Her hand trembled as an arthritic finger with a misshapen joint pointed towards each of them in turn, her vivid amber eyes stark against her parchment paper skin. 'One, two, three, four. Oh good, that's what we like to see: you're all here. It's like having all the right ingredients for a...'

'You're not picking me out for the pot!' Hilda squealed whilst slamming her suitcase in front of her as a barrier. 'I don't go very well with cheese. I'll curdle – and I've got sage in my handbag, I'll have you know. Ethel gave it to me just in case we came across any witches!'

'Hilda, really! Don't be so rude.' Clarissa gave their host an apologetic smile as she took the two sets of keys that were offered to her.

Hazel waived her hand to show no offence taken. 'If you go up the stairs, ladies, the first two rooms on the left are yours. Anything you need, please don't be shy to ask.' Her dry lips parted into a wide grin, taking the opportunity to reveal a set of yellowing teeth. 'We like to bring a "spell" of happiness to our guests.'

Ethel gripped Hilda's arm and began to drag her up the stairs, with Millie hot on their heels. Clarissa followed at a more gentle pace, her suitcase being slightly heavier than theirs due to the several bottles of sweet sherry she had brought with her. She handed Millie the key to Room 2. 'Here you go. Ethel, you're with me as usual.' She checked her watch. 'Shall we say an hour to get ourselves settled in, freshened up, and then we'll go down for dinner?'

Hilda harrumphed. 'Just so long as we're not on the menu. Did you see her, she wouldn't have gone amiss in a village production of *Hansel and Gretel*. Those eyes! Honest, 'Rissa. I'll tell you now, that woman is a goddam real life witch!'

As the doors to their respective rooms clicked softly shut and the old-fashioned latch handles fell into place, Hazel made her way into the bar and poured herself a small brandy before taking a seat next to her husband. 'I think I might have taken the Halloween spirit a bit too far this time, Gareth.' She laughed as she spat out the novelty dentures she'd rammed into her mouth whilst hiding under the reception desk. 'I nearly gave one of those old dears a heart attack.'

Gareth squeezed her hand affectionately. 'They are younger than you are, dear, but don't let that spoil a good story!'

ONE FOR ALL

*B*ree watched her charges filing out of the costume and make-up cabins, chattering ten to the dozen with excitement. She felt a little twinge of envy, wishing she had put herself forward as a background actor too. She bit into a fried egg butty and washed it down with a slurp of tea. Then again, it was proving to be testing enough just keeping an eye on them all, without the distraction of her having the opportunity to swan around in a costume as well.

She rustled the sheet of paper that had been given to her on their first day on site, listing all the dos and don'ts of being a background actor on set. The first few had caused several loud groans of disappointment, not least the: 'It is strictly forbidden to talk to the actors, ask for autographs, or take photographs'. That rule had put Flynn Phoenix out of reach for all the WI ladies, including herself. Her dream of finding Mr Right had been ruined at the first hurdle. She was just about to enjoy a second bite of her lunch when she spotted the four WI mischief-makers, huddled together by the catering wagon. She watched their body language and immediately knew trouble was on the horizon.

Dropping her butty back onto the paper plate, she edged her way through the crowd.

'Why are my spider senses tingling, ladies? Are you up to something?' Bree stood in front of them, paper plate balanced in one hand and the fingers of her other hand mimicking spider legs.

'Who, moi?' Ethel dramatically pointed a finger at herself and laughed. 'Now what on earth gave you that idea? We've been wrapped for this session, so we're just deciding on what to do for the rest of the day.'

Releasing a resigned sigh, Bree shook her head. 'I'm just giving you a gentle reminder. Whenever you four get your heads together like that, mischief is always sure to follow. Please, girls, don't do anything I wouldn't do, or you'll get kicked off the production.'

'As if we would! Just chill yer beans, love…'

Clarissa was aghast at Millie's reply and started to laugh. '"Chill yer beans"?! Good grief, Millie, where did that come from?'

Millie pointed to another background actor who was busy tucking into a bacon bap, tomato sauce dribbling down her chin. 'My new friend over there, Olive. She's a right rum one, but quite funny, and she's staying at the same place as us.' Millie excitedly beckoned for Olive to join them. 'She could be in our group; we could be the Five Wrinkled Dears!'

'Doesn't quite have the same ring to it, Millie, but there's no harm in us palling up whilst we're here.' Clarissa looked to the others for approval and was pleased to see two heads nodding in agreement.

Olive gratefully accepted Millie's hand signal to approach. Bacon bap momentarily paused mid-mouthful, she lumbered over to them, her strange gait of feet at ten-to-two 'Charlie Chaplin' style, giving her an awkwardness that was actually quite endearing when it was teamed with her warm smile. 'Delighted to meet you! Olive's the name, Olive Auldwrinkle. Auldwrinkle by name Auldwrinkle by age!' she chuckled as she pointed to her well-lived-in complexion.

Bree watched the ladies embrace a fifth friend to their group as they eagerly got to know each other. She was so taken by this turn of events that she forgot to delve deeper into her suspicions that they were plotting something that neither she nor the production company would approve of.

~

'So you see, Olive, she's been missing for several days now, absolutely no trace of her and what's more…' Ethel paused in her storytelling to allow for an extra bit of tension, '… she was last seen here, in Abbey Towers!'

Olive digested the tale, giving herself time to decide if she wanted to be onboard with these four funny ladies she had only just met. 'Well sweet Felicity Arkwright, that's a turn up for the books!' she exclaimed whilst raising her sparse eyebrows. She exhaled and whistled loudly in surprise. 'What's the plan, then? I take it you've got one.'

Clarissa took the lead. 'They've finished filming inside Abbey Towers for the day and moved on to the folly, and from what I can gather, the archdeacon and his wife are out at some church function, so we can have a little wander around the house, do a little bit of snooping. It's still accessible because the set designers are working in the ballroom. It would be fun to get access to that too…' She pointed to the bell tower.

Five faces turned skywards to take in the looming presence of the edifice.

'I don't like it,' Millie moaned. 'It's far too spooky. Maybe we should wait, she just might turn up like nothing's happened and carry on with her hoovering. And anyway, didn't you say there was an intruder there the other night? They might have security cameras, stuff like that.'

'The police searched the place, there was no sign of anyone, no forced entry to the place, nothing damaged or stolen, so according to Andy it was just er...' Ethel paused trying to think of the term he had used. 'That's it: "sus circs", it was just sus circs, that's all, and, no, the place doesn't have cameras, so don't be such a pansy.'

Olive crammed the last piece of the bacon bap into her mouth and chewed on it whilst contemplating her next move. She really didn't have anything better to do. She had only promised herself to return to her room at the inn and curl up for a few hours with the bundle of knitting magazines and Wednesday's issue of *Woman's Weekly* that she had brought with her, then maybe take a stroll by the river. Other than that, she couldn't really say she was otherwise engaged with anything more riveting.

Ethel prompted her. 'Well, are you up for it, or have you something better to do?'

Olive clucked her throat and chuckled. 'Not unless you count plucking my chin hair and darning socks for the old guy that lives next door to me as something better to do – then no I haven't!'

'In that case...' Ethel shot her arm out in front of her and waited. Four more arms quickly joined her to form a team hand stack.

'One for all and all for one!' they unanimously shouted.

Clarissa held out her walking stick in front of her, cheerleader style. 'This way, ladies, let the fun commence.' She stretched her arm up, pumping the air in time to a beat that only she could hear. 'Onwards, and with a bit of luck...' she glanced at the tower again, '... upwards too!'

THE CHOSEN ONE

The chaos was too much.

He looked down on them, his breath catching in his throat, and his heart pumping so fast his fingertips began to tingle with anticipation.

They reminded him of little black ants, running in so many different directions, traversing each other, giving no heed or care to their peers or their environment. He watched them, taking notes, numbering and naming them before placing them into groups, but only on paper. He knew that in life they were uncontrollable, forming their own clusters, holding them so very briefly, before scattering outwards, breaking the bond.

They had no purpose, no intent, and no goal.

But he did.

Alice was keeping him company. She was an ideal companion, with an ear to listen without talking back. No judgement or criticism. She just sits and waits. Today he had brushed her hair and straightened her a little so that she sat beautifully in her chair, looking very much like a Halloween decoration. Her waxen features showcasing her milky eyes and blue lips set in a rictus grin. She is perfect in every way and the first of many.

It felt so good for him to be back in control. He was exactly what Abbey Towers had been waiting for.

Welcome, sir, we've been expecting you... the nothingness whispered to him. *Are you ready?*

He nodded, excitement surging through his veins. He would willingly accept the offer, without hesitation or regret. It was his destiny. The nothingness had told him so.

He was to be the new Death Collector.

If Clement Gregory and his wife had been in residence, they would have been quite alarmed to see a quintet of pensioners, camel hair coats and furry boots on show, furtively making their way down into the bowels of Abbey Towers, clinging for dear life to the curved iron handrail that snaked against the brick wall. Their initial foray into Abbey Towers had yielded nothing to excite them, until Olive had found the door to the cellar.

Millie, desperate not to be the 'fatty at the back' who was always in danger of being the one to be abducted first, had taken it upon herself to ensure that Olive was now in that prime position rather than herself. 'It's ever so dark down here...' she mumbled.

The stairs finished abruptly, forcing Clarissa to come to a standstill. Her friends, still caught up with the momentum of the descent, failed to adjust their speed, causing a rear-end shunt as they stumbled into each other, pushing Clarissa into the middle of the small entrance chamber. Her walking stick made another appearance as it tapped out, touching the walls around them.

Tap, tap, thunk...

'Here we go, this way, ladies...' Clarissa pushed on the heavy oak door that her stick had pinpointed in the dim light. 'Keep up, Hilda. Millie, make sure Olive is still with us,' she chuckled. 'You know what happens to the fatty at the back!'

The five friends pressed on through the door. It opened out into another, larger chamber. Clarissa felt along the wall until her fingers found a dome dolly light switch. Marvelling at the feel of its antiquity, she flicked it on. A muted glow blinked and pulsated from the wall sconces.

'Oops, son of a b…' Hilda's booteed foot caught on an uneven flagstone, tripping her headlong into the room. She grabbed hold of Ethel's arm to steady herself. 'Jeez, that was close,' she gasped.

Taking the time to allow their eyes to adjust to the low lighting, they stood motionless for a few seconds. 'Where to now, or is this it?' Ethel was most disappointed. Apart from a few large crates, a broken chair and an old painting with a fractured frame propped against one wall, it held nothing that would excite them.

Olive, not to be deterred, had started to move around the room, her hands feeling the stone walls as she went. She disappeared into the small nook at the back, her voice becoming an echo as she checked out its purpose. 'It's just a storage room, how boring. No missing women or spooks in here. What happened to this adventure you promised…?'

Click…whir… click.

Totally oblivious to Olive going solo in her investigations, Clarissa made the executive decision to move their snooping back upstairs. 'Never mind, we can have another little recce upstairs to see if we can find the entrance to the tower.' She ushered her friends up the steps ahead of her, taking the time to ensure they had left no evidence of their presence behind. Emerging into the scullery passageway, they checked their hands for anything untoward that they might have picked up during their adventure into the depths of Abbey Towers.

'Where's Olive?' Hilda wiped her hand on the back of Millie's jacket and inspected her palm. Content it was now clean, she chose to happily ignore the smear she had left on the fabric.

A brief moment followed where they counted heads, checked

behind them and began to blame each other for not keeping an eye on their new-found friend.

Panic quickly setting in, Millie frantically looked around. 'She's not here, 'Rissa, she's gone missing, just like Alice,' she wailed. 'Oh my God, it's all my fault. You were right: the fatty at the back always gets it!'

AND THEN THERE WERE FOUR

*O*live, her fingers still adhered to the cold wall, was suddenly thrown forward into the darkness whilst simultaneously being roughly swivelled ninety degrees. Solid brick grating on flagstone was the only sound that accompanied her small 'Eek...' as she disappeared from the room her new friends were still exploring.

A dank mustiness filled her nostrils, making her breath catch in her throat. She tried to get her bearings, but in the pitch black even her own outstretched hands were invisible. She quickly came to the conclusion that somehow, without making any effort whatsoever, she had found another room but not one that had a regular door. 'Ladies, I've found a secret room...' she shouted, unsure if her voice would be heard through the thick wall. 'I must have pressed something and a section of the wall rotated.'

She waited, listening intently for any response.

'Millie, can you hear me? Ethel, Hilda... anyone?'

Pressing her hands across the wall, she tapped, banged and knocked, desperately trying to find whatever lever or pressure point had thrown her from one room to another as a sudden chill began to creep into her bones. With the darkness becoming more and more oppressive, her imagination began to run riot. Fearing something, or someone might be in the room with her she couldn't see, she slowly turned her head to look behind her, squinting into the blackness. 'Helloo, is there anybody there?' She didn't expect anyone to reply; she was just being a scaredy cat. 'Get a grip, Olive, don't be such a wuss...' she chided, desperate to give herself some reassurance.

But instead of solace, the soft tread of footsteps on the flag-stones confirmed her worst fears. They grew closer and closer with each passing second.

She was not alone.

Olive couldn't see them, but she could sense them. She slowly brought her hand out in front of her, her fingertips probing the void. 'Please, I didn't mean any harm, I was just being nosey.' Her voice quivered with the sheer terror of the unknown. 'I'll just find my way out and I won't trouble you again.' She had no idea whose ears her plea for clemency would fall upon, she just knew that to beg for her safety and freedom was her only choice. Whoever was in here with her was, without doubt in her mind, more foe than friend.

She felt the breath of her unwanted companion, hot against the side of her face followed by a breeze that ruffled her hair. Something slammed against the wall behind her and the sequence that had initially thrown her into this hellhole, began again. Her body, pressed against the wall in fear, swung ninety degrees, throwing her back into the room she had only moments before shared with her friends. She stumbled and fell onto her knees, the flagstones digging hard into her skin, ripping her tights.

'Feck me...' she spluttered in shock, and then just as quickly corrected herself. Even though she was unsure if she had an audi-ence to hear her cuss, she felt the need to redeem herself. 'I mean sweet Felicity Arkwright...'

She remained there, not daring to look back, her breath

coming hard and fast in staccato. The silence continued, giving Olive hope that she was safe. She tentatively took a peek behind her; the wall having returned to its original state gave no indication that anything untoward or mysterious was contained behind it. Taking the opportunity that she had been given, she clambered to her feet and ran as fast as her legs would carry her back into the entrance chamber and up the stone steps.

~

'There's nothing for it; we're going to have to tell Bree what we've done.' Clarissa was very matter of fact about their next move.

Millie was still sniffing into her handkerchief, mortified that she had made a new friend and then lost her all in the space of a day. Hilda, on the other hand, was totally oblivious to anything untoward and was happily sitting on a chair sucking a mint imperial from her trusty white paper bag.

Ethel chewed at the skin on her thumb. 'No, no, that's the last thing we need to do. You know what Bree is like. She'll have the police here, they'll make it a crime scene, and then it'll all go tits up. It'll ruin our job as extras and we won't get to meet Flynn Phoenix.'

'Gosh you're all heart, Eth. So, have you got any better ideas then, Sherlock?' sniped Clarissa.

'Actually, yes I have. We say nothing. We leave here, go on our way as though nothing has happened, and we deny everything if asked.' Ethel buttoned up her coat collar and adjusted her scarf. 'They'll think being in showbiz wasn't for her and that she's just packed it in and gone home.'

'Who's gone home?' Olive, having returned from the pit of doom, popped her head through the cellar door, grateful to see friendly faces.

'Who do you think? The one we've "lost", that Olive Wrinkle-face!' Ethel made air quotes with her fingers, as she turned to who she thought was Clarissa. 'Oops! Oh, there you are, Olive!' Embarrassed, she quickly tried to gloss over her faux pas. 'We were beginning to wonder where you'd got to.'

Olive fanned her face with her hand in a show of personal trauma. 'You wouldn't believe what happened, I was thrust into a dreadful dilemma *down there…*' she silently, and with much exaggeration, mouthed the words 'down there' whilst pointing at the floor.

Quick as a flash, Hilda was all ears to comfort Olive in her hour of need. 'It comes to us all, dearie, that's why we try not to giggle too much, it's all down to underused Elvis floor muscles, apparently. Now my doctor said cutting back on coffee helps; it's a diabetic, you know.'

'Diuretic, Hilda, coffee is a diuretic, and it's pelvis, not Elvis. Also, Olive is talking about the cellar, not her lady-bits.' Aware that Olive was actually quite upset, Clarissa put her arm around her. 'What happened, Olive? We were very worried about you?'

'There's a secret entrance down there to another room. It was so dark, I couldn't see anything, but there was definitely someone else in there with me.' She paused to dab at her eyes with the handkerchief that Millie had given her. 'I thought they were going to kill me, but they let me go.' She glanced at the pink cotton square and grimaced. 'Millie, have you already blown your nose on this?'

THE VIGILANT VIGILANTE

*B*arney Lamb opened one eye and clacked his tongue to the roof of his mouth. The six-pack of Stella lager and a ten-quid bag of piff had done the damage he'd needed the night before, but now he was rattling. His anxiety was climbing, and it wouldn't be long before he would need something a bit stronger.

'Will you get your lazy backside off that bloody couch, Mutton...' Jazzy used his nickname in a deliberate attempt to rile him. He hated it with a passion. 'I'm sick to death of you hanging around here like something that's been dug up from the local cemetery.'

Barney stood up, scratched under his armpit and then sniffed his fingers. He recoiled. Maybe Jazzy was right: he had recently died and was now starting to rot. He made a mental note to have a bath during the next week or two, and failing that, he could always have a dip in the local heated indoor swimming pool for free. He was on jobseekers' allowance, and with that came all sorts of gratis perks. But for now, he was happy to walk around stinking as it annoyed the life out of her. 'Wind yer neck in, give us a cuppa, and then I'll be out of your hair.'

Jazzy looked at him in disgust. So far, she had wasted five

years of her life with him, and if there was any way that she could promptly and effectively get shut of him she would, but aside from murder, there were very few options left to her. Mutton was like a ruddy limpet; he clung onto her like a barnacle to a boat. In truth she had never expected too much from him, as apparently he had been the subject of a difficult birth twenty-eight years previously. An awkwardly bent neck had called for a savage forceps delivery, and a rather abrupt start to life. He claimed the trauma of having his head wedged in a set of barbeque tongs had given him lifelong limited intelligence, but she was of the opinion he was just merely uneducated and naturally very stupid. She picked up his shirt and jacket and threw them at him. 'Get out, Mutton, and don't come back until you've got something to contribute.'

Barney shrugged his shirt on, and without bothering to button it up, he breezed past her and made sure he slammed the kitchen door loudly as he left the little terraced house. The glass rattled in the frame with the force. Sauntering down the back jigger he checked the text on his mobile phone from his mate and fellow criminal, Dog Williams.

It's a goer, meet at the Rec. 12.30.

Barney rarely worked in a team, preferring solo jobs, but this one needed a pair of eyes as a lookout. The target was guaranteed to rake in at least a grand in cash and jewellery. He had his fence on standby, so by tonight, he'd have plenty of money to indulge himself and his habit.

'You gotta love the old dears and their mattresses,' he gloated loudly as he skipped over the low-level wall into the park. 'The "Barney-cle" is about to strike!'

Barney really wished the old dear hadn't keeled over when he'd burst through the French doors. So much for the reliable info that told him she was out at her bridge club luncheon and her cottage would be empty.

He leant over her to check for signs of life. He watched the generous smattering of upper lip hair gently undulate in the breeze from her nostrils, and the slight rise and fall of her chest that was clad in a pink crochet bed jacket. 'Feckin' hell...' was all he could mutter with relief. Satisfied that she had only fainted and banged her head on the coffee table on the way down, he was more than grateful that he wouldn't have to perform CPR on her, not that he would have known what to do. He gave her one more glance, shrugged his shoulders, not caring about her condition, and then set about ransacking the place.

There was very little to be had downstairs. Her knick-knacks were made up of easily identifiable ornaments and paintings that would fetch a few bob, but would be quickly traced by the bizzies. The last thing he needed was another stretch inside. What he was after was upstairs. He pushed aside the velvet door curtain and made his way to the foot of the stairs. He didn't usually feel regret or shame, that wasn't in his nature. Ever since he was a child, whatever Barney wanted, he got, by fair means or foul.

This was no different.

He examined the framed family photographs that lined the wall going up the stairs, and very briefly felt a twinge. What of, he had no idea. He didn't think it was guilt; that was something he had never experienced. It felt more like nostalgia for his own recently departed grandmother and the family that no longer wanted anything to do with him.

Distracted, Barney had taken his eye off the ball. His normal high alert to his surroundings would warn him of imminent danger, but having Dog Williams acting as lookout, he had felt confident that he had his back covered, and because of that he had let his guard down. Reaching the top step, he was all set to follow the instructions and turn left to where the treasure was buried. He laughed, amused that his comparison had made him sound more like an adventuring pirate than a low-life burglar.

'Come to me, my hearty…' he cackled, in a poor impression of Captain Jack Sparrow, the anticipation of sparkling jewellery urging him on in his cruel quest.

'Everything's got a price and a consequence, Barney…'

The voice made him almost jump out of his skin and his heart had the chance to miss only one beat before the blow hit him hard in the face. It was unseen, unexpected and agonising. He felt the bone in his nose crack and shatter, followed by an intense pain that ran across his cheekbones and behind his eyes, and then the blood erupted. Warm, wet and metallic. Before he could react, his neck was caught in an elbow hold and he was dragged across the landing to the top of the stairs he had only just conquered. Barney's eyes bulged, turning white with fear as he kicked out with his feet, trying to retain a hold with the tread of his Adidas Hoops on the Axminster Glenavy carpet.

His fight was futile, the strength his attacker possessed was undeniably more powerful than Barney had ever previously experienced. He'd taken some beatings from dealers over his debts more times than he cared to remember, but this was something else. The hands roughly pushed him, twisting him to face his nemesis. His eyes searched theirs, the only part that could be seen, the black wool of the balaclava obscuring all other features. He began to plead for his release, desperate to see leniency in them.

But they were steel grey and held no kindness, no warmth and no compassion.

Barney yelped loudly, his hands scrabbling for the banister rail, his balance lost. His fingers slipped from the wood as his feet danced a jig on the top stair, pausing him momentarily, suspending him in the air like a cartoon character.

He saw the finger point. He felt it jab at the centre of his chest. Just the merest of touches…

And he was gone, bouncing and bowling down every stair like a human Slinky, hitting both the wall and spindles, until he finally came to rest at the bottom. Broken, bruised, and quite dead.

How ironic that Barney 'Mutton' Lamb had departed this world exactly the way he had arrived…

Sprawled in a heap with his neck bent at a most unnatural angle.

A JOB WELL DONE

*D*ottie emerged from the tunnel into the crisp autumn air. Shoving the balaclava into her pocket, she closed the hatch, tamped down vegetation, and then hauled a broken tree branch over it as camouflage. She quickly checked that the coast was clear before striding out from the woods. She cut across the less well-tended section of Abbey Towers gardens, nipped around the folly, and then nonchalantly appeared from behind the lighting generators.

She was greeted like a long-lost relative by David, the director. 'Ah there you are, Dottie, we've got a small tech issue with one of the moves Flynn has to make in this fight scene. Can we do a run through again under your expert eye?'

Dottie was more than happy to have the distraction, and, of course, should anyone ask, her presence here would be duly noted if an alibi was required. She angled herself between the cameras and the folly and watched Flynn run through his routine, quickly picking up what needed to be done. 'Right, if you move Flynn literally twelve inches to the left, the camera won't pick up the lack of contact with his fist; it'll work so much better.

And then, when the Foley artists add in the sound effects, it'll be spot on.'

David gave her a thumbs up and quickly went back to his call sheet. This gave her the chance to move around the set, ensuring she was seen by as many of the crew as possible. 'If there's nothing more, I'll nip over and give Dana's assistant a hand, I think your star is causing a few waves today.'

Describing Dana's behaviour as a 'wave' had been an understatement, but Dottie was careful not to let her feelings for the diva be noted by anyone else, particularly with what she had planned for her. She looked over to Abbey Towers and was pleased to see the four sweet ladies she had met the previous day making their way to the rose garden with Olive. They were chattering ten to the dozen, no doubt reliving Olive's close shave with the 'Death Collector' in the cellars. Dottie gave a little chuckle. Her guiding hand had ensured Olive was returned to her friends in one piece, but she would have to keep a regular eye on them all if she was to ensure their safety over the coming weeks.

'Let's call it Help the Aged...' She laughed.

The flashing blue lights strobed and bounced from the windows of Lilac Cottage as an array of emergency vehicles, parked haphazardly, littered School Lane. The police crime scene tape had already been strung around the hedging and was fluttering in the breeze. White suited officers were busy erecting a scene tent over the front door, completely obscuring the view, much to the bitter disappointment of passing busy bodies who had gathered in anticipation of gory visuals and a touch of gruesome gossip.

'What have we got?' Andy carefully slipped on his forensic overshoes, zipped up his paper suit and made his way to the tent.

Lucy followed behind him. 'It's "Mutton" Lamb, Sarge; looks like he was midway through a burglary, took a tumble down the stairs, and broke his neck. The occupier is on her way to hospital now with a head injury, a Mrs Evelyn Dalby, eighty-seven years of age.'

'Likely to prove…?' He held his breath, hoping it wouldn't be. He couldn't begin to imagine how he would be able to find the words to deliver a death message to her family, telling them what some thieving lowlife had done to their loved one. The only consolation would be he was dead and the world would be a better place for it.

Lucy shook her head. 'They don't think so at this stage. I've got a uniform up at the hospital with her and I'll follow up to speak to the family who are on their way there.'

Andy stood on the clear forensic stepping plate, towering over Lamb's body. His eyes taking in every detail, from the red welt around his neck to the bloodied nose and missing front tooth. 'I want Bob Limpett for a forensic post-mortem on this one, I'll clear it with Murdoch.'

'Something you're not happy with, Andy?' Melvyn Hibbert, their own crime scene investigator, tipped his head at Barney.

'I don't know, there's something off about it, can't put my finger on it, but the obvious one is the mark on his neck and there's some faint petechiae on the eye whites.' Andy scrolled through his phone searching for Bob's number. 'It'll probably come down to death by misadventure, but for the time being best not to lose any potential evidence, just in case.'

Melvyn offered his clipboard to Andy and indicated for him to sign the form. 'Once the photographs are completed, we'll wrap the hands and head, bag him, and wait for the nod for removal.'

Andy thanked him, and after giving Bob the heads up that the job would be coming through to him once Murdoch, as the SIO, had sanctioned it, he turned his attention to the incident log. 'Who called it in, Lucy?'

She flicked through the screen on her Pronto. 'Anonymous.

Call-taker couldn't tell if it was male or female, but whoever it was, they were more concerned for Evelyn than they were for Barney.'

'Can't say I blame them.' All victims were important to Andy, but the very young and the elderly were always the ones that brought a lump to his throat. They were the most vulnerable at the start of life and at its end. He removed his forensic suit and dropped it into the evidence bag, sealed and initialled it, carrying out the same task for his overshoes. He sat down on the sandstone wall outside Lilac Cottage, the autumn chill giving him the fresh air he needed.

Since a child Andy had only viewed life in three stages. The young, the old, and the inbetweeners. Both he and Pru were inbetweeners, waiting to bring the next generation into the world, and what a world it was now going to be with one less Barney Lamb in it. Once their baby was born, they would be a family, a proper family. He felt a little sad at that thought, as though he was being disloyal to his own family by saying it wasn't a 'proper' one, but blood is the bond, and although he had love and care with his adopted mum and dad, he had always felt incomplete, as though he was an unknown.

He might have been chosen by them, but he had also been rejected by someone.

SALAD DAYS

'*G*et out and take your trashy wig with you!' Dana flung the silver mink hairpiece across the trailer. It hit the wall and fell to the floor like a dead rat. 'It's bad enough playing his bloody mother, without you wanting me to look like I'm a hundred years old!' Attempting to clear the enraged spittle from her mouth, she smeared her lipstick with the back of her hand, streaking the red across her cheek. 'I need a drink!'

Tired of trying to placate her, Mark took the empty glass from her, filled it with less than a first-finger joint worth of Scotch, and handed it back to her. 'Dana, you've got a big scene later; you can't afford to be drunk.' He held his breath, waiting for another inanimate object to be thrown at him. When nothing was forthcoming, he felt it safe to stick his head above the parapet again. 'If you hold up filming without a reasonable excuse, there's a clause in your contract that will cost you dearly, and if word gets round, work will dry up.'

Dana slugged back the amber liquid, relishing the burn as it hit her throat. She held out the glass for another one. 'What you're trying to say, darling, is that I'm getting old and saggy, and there's not much on the market for me – apart from playing the goddam mother of an upstart. What will it be next? The grand-mother? Or how about a rotting corpse? I've not done one of those, yet,' she spat sarcastically.

Dottie listened to the commotion through the open trailer door; the tuna on wholemeal sandwich accompanied by a pink lady apple, wobbled on the plate. She took a deep breath, ready for the inevitable onslaught as soon as she placed one foot on the steps and Dana saw her. She smiled to herself. Now that was definitely something she could help Dana with, and there most certainly wouldn't be any complaints afterwards, such was Dottie's attention to detail in her craft. She could turn the miser-able old trout into a rotting corpse in no time at all. That thought gave her the impetus to proceed with her delivery of refresh-ments, just imagining Dana's final moments at her expert hands. It really was quite a delicious thought.

'Have you got a helmet, Dottie? You're going to need it going in there with the mood she's in.' Mark gave her a wry smile as he skipped down the steps. 'I'm off on my break for a bit of peace and quiet. She can sort herself out.'

Dottie returned his smile. 'Don't worry, you leave her to me. I've handled much worse than our Ms Dana Simon.' She knew that was an understatement. The recipients of her services had not lived to tell their tales and were alas unable to confirm or deny her claim, so she was unfortunately a solo reviewer of her own handiwork. It wasn't as though a search on Trustpilot could bring up the genre of *Assassin* to leave a worthy five stars for. On a positive note, the one thing those experiences had given her was the confidence and enjoyment to deal with even the most difficult of people.

'Lunchtime, Dana.' Dottie bustled through the open door, hopped over the discarded wig and kicked a shoe to one side. She made a beeline to where Dana was slouched, whisky glass in hand. 'Here you go: tuna on wholemeal, and an apple.'

Dana looked at the plate and sneered. 'And which body part

have you dangled all over this one, Dottie?' Her nails picked at the corner of the bread, lifting it up so she could see the quality of the tuna. 'There's no mayonnaise; I asked for mayonnaise!' She thrust the plate at Dottie. 'Get me some. Now!'

Dottie smiled as she handed her a catering cup of salad cream. 'No mayonnaise, but they've got this. It's the best they could do.'

Snatching it from her, Dana stuck her finger in it and licked the yellowing cream. 'It's got a funny taste, but it'll have to do, beggars can't be choosers. You can go now – and next time get catering to send somebody else.' She waved her hand dismissively at Dottie.

Dottie quietly closed the trailer door behind her, leaving Dana to her tasty sandwich and her ungratefully received salad cream, confident that the little added 'extra' she had squirted into the cup before handing it over would have the desired effect in…

She checked her watch. 'Ooh, I'd say about an hour or so.'

FANCY THAT!

The weather-worn bench comfortably held the five hunched figures, their silhouettes against the darkening lake read like an ECG printout, their differing heights adding bumps and waves to the vista. The pale sun was beginning to set in the west, dipping just below the roof line of Abbey Towers, making it look even more eerie than it usually did.

'Are you sure there was someone in there with you if it was pitch black, Olive? Could it have been your imagination because you were frightened?' Clarissa rolled the mint imperial over her tongue.

Olive wiped the dewdrop from the end of her nose with a couple of sheets of 2ply loo roll she'd purloined from the crew toilets in the nearby portacabin. 'Absolutely, without a doubt. I felt their hot, raspy breath against my cheek.' She grinned as she inspected the piece of tissue that had dissolved with one small dab. She held it up to show her friends. 'Wouldn't you think they'd splash out and have thicker toilet paper? Your fingers would go right through this on the first nether region wipe!' Olive gave a grimace of distaste to accompany her toiletry observation.

'"Hot, raspy breath'! Bit of wishful thinking there, Olive!' Ethel smirked and gave her a saucy wink. 'I think the luscious Flynn Phoenix in his leather breeches has had us all in a bit of a tither today, he's probably set whatever hormones you've got left on high alert!'

Millie crunched down on her sweet and waited until she had swallowed, not wanting to indulge in poor etiquette by speaking with her mouth full. 'What we're all forgetting here, girls, is there are secret rooms and maybe even passages at Abbey Towers, perfect for more adventures, but more importantly…' She paused, waiting for their full and undivided attention, because for once she was not the shrinking violet of the group; she had found her feet and was intent on leading the way with her Size 3 tootsies.

Four heads swivelled to look at her.

'Come on, Millie, what? You know my memory is dreadful, too long with a dramatic pause and I'll have forgotten what you said in the first place!' Hilda laughed.

'Alice, of course,' Millie gave a sigh of frustration at her friend's slow uptake. 'Poor Alice Moorcroft. Could she be wandering the secret passages of Abbey Towers, lost, alone and unable to find her way out?'

They sat in silence, mulling over that possibility. Hilda handed her bag of imperials around again, confident that the sucking motion would assist with their thought processes. They watched the late afternoon sun glow weakly through the windows of the tower as they discussed the chances of Alice wandering around the bowels of the old house like a lost soul. They came to the disappointing opinion that if she had found Abbey Towers' secret rooms she would probably have curled up her toes by now. Their money was actually on her having done a flit with a secret lover, tired of caring, tired of sweeping and cleaning, and very much tired of the Gregory's rotary floor mop.

'It's been quite a while. She would definitely have starved to death by now.' Grateful for her mint imperials to keep her hunger pangs at bay, Hilda popped a second one in her mouth. 'We need to do another trip down there, find the secret room that Olive fell into, and see where it leads to. It'll be such fun. I'm getting bored with this filming lark already; we could to with a bit of proper excitement.'

The Four Wrinkled Dears, true to form, knew that leaving Hilda's observation as just a suggestion was not going to be an option. They had a reputation to uphold, one of mischief, madness and mayhem. Ethel jiggled her legs in anticipation, and Clarissa quickly ran through the pros and cons in her mind, not wishing to voice them just yet, but very much of the opinion that she didn't want to be the one to discover Alice's body draped over a beer barrel, dehydrated and very much dead if she had found the secret tunnels first.

'Look, it's Halloween soon and the director is holding a big party in the ballroom, a sort of mid-filming treat for everyone. It's fancy dress.' Olive whipped an envelope out of her handbag and hunched her shoulders up to her ears as she opened it. 'See, it says here that anyone on set or in the film can go, so that includes us, the extras or background actors as they call us now. Can you imagine the chaos on the night, loads of people milling around in costumes, plenty of alcohol on offer, and not many places out of bounds inside? It would be a perfect time for us to have another snoop. What do you think?'

A vote was not required this time. The mere suggestion of them donning costumes and running riot around Abbey Towers had elevated their enthusiasm for fun and games, with a tantalising smattering of danger, to new heights.

'All for one, one for all...' Millie giggled. 'You're on!'

YOU'RE FIRED!

*D*ana woke in the early hours of the morning. The sweat soaking through her silk pyjamas had drenched the bedsheet and duvet cover, making it cling to the entire length of her body. Another wave of nausea swept over her, along with a violent stab of stomach pain. She rolled over and checked the clock.

The red 03:47 flashed out into the darkness, illuminating her phone. She picked it up and jabbed in the speed dial number she needed. Turning on the bedside lamp, she surveyed the room. If she had to make a mad dash to the en suite again, she needed to know what obstacles she would meet on the way. Her discarded jeans, sweatshirt and a pair of cowboy boots lay in a crumpled heap next to the armchair. She listened to the ringing tone. 'Come on, come on, pick up…'

'What's the matter, Dana?' Mark didn't sound impressed, his voice carried an edge to it, no doubt irked that he had been woken at such a ridiculous hour.

'I need a doctor; there's something wrong with me…' she rasped.

He sighed loudly, not caring if she heard him. 'You've got a virus or bug, that's all; can't it wait until morning?'

'No, it can't wait! Get me one now! I think I'm dying!' She dropped the phone as her knees jerked upwards in an attempt to smother the pain as another violent spasm hit hard.

She had put her earlier forays into the bathroom, both on set and when she had reached home, down to a mild case of food poisoning; opting for either the tuna or the so-called salad cream being the culprit. But now she wasn't so sure. She'd had food poisoning before, heck, she'd even had alcohol poisoning once or twice, but this was off the scale, both in discomfort, symptoms and the quantity of bodily fluid production. She suddenly began to shiver uncontrollably, the complete opposite to the burning in the fire-of-Hades feeling she had woken with. As she lay waiting for Mark to do her bidding, she wondered how much compensation she could screw out of Colquitt Productions for making her so ill.

Another spasm of agonising pain ripped at her insides. Curling into a ball she held her breath, willing it to pass, but as the intensity grew, her vision became blurred. A misty darkness haloed across her eyes, forcing the light from her bedroom to become smaller and smaller, like a camera shutter closing for exposure. Her body suddenly became rigid, forcing her jaw to clamp shut.

Dana slowly, and very undramatically, slipped into unconsciousness.

Annie flicked through her listings, gave out the daily call sheets, and crossed out the scenes that wouldn't be filmed for the next day or two since Dana's mad dash to hospital. She knew David was already looking at a replacement for her. He'd gone over the schedule, marked the scenes she had already appeared in, and had been confident that they could reshoot with another actor without losing time or money.

Dana Simon was still very much alive, but she was also very much gone from the credits for *The Haunting of Fallow Falls.*

Annie wished she had been a fly on the wall when the news had been broken to the dreadful diva. She had watched Dana's appalling behaviour with increasing embarrassment and disgust, and it was common knowledge on set that Flynn was giving her a wide berth whenever he could. Her undisclosed illness had been the lucky fortune cookie everyone had hoped for, giving Colquitt the perfect get-out to her contract. The clause had initially been to cover absences caused by her drinking, but had been worded in such a way that any long-term away days from set would also come under the same umbrella.

Annie's concentration was broken by her favourite gaggle of ladies approaching her at breakneck speed, only this time there were five of them. 'Hello, girls, how are things?'

Ethel pushed Clarissa to one side and stepped forward, desperate to be the one to ask the question. 'Is it true?' Her nose twitched like a dormouse in anticipation. Millie, Hilda and Olive held up the rear behind her, waiting for a titbit of juicy gossip.

Annie gave them a knowing smile. 'Is *what* true?' She was definitely going to make them work for any tittle-tattle they wanted.

'For fu… I mean dearie me…' Olive tutted in exasperation, almost allowing another rude expletive to leave her lips. 'Is it true about Dastardly Dana, the geriatric actress that's playing Flynn's mum? The talk is she's been kicked off the film.' Olive wasn't used to beating about the bush: if she wanted answers, the only way to get them was to ask outright.

'Right, ladies, and you didn't hear this from me: yes, she's no longer in the production. But, and I mean this, don't go spreading it around. As far as I know, it could be by mutual agreement.' Annie knew damn well it wasn't, but felt for the morale of the cast and crew, it was best to play down the dreadful scenes that had followed Dana's sacking.

'There you go, told you, nothing gets past me....' Hilda tapped her nose, knowingly. 'I'm that good I could work for MFI!'

'I think we've had this little mix up before, Hilda love, it's MI-5. MFI was the cheap furniture place, remember?' Clarissa tried not to laugh. 'Right, let's get a nice cup of tea. We've got things to discuss.'

Annie was all ears. 'I hope it's something fun.'

Olive nodded furiously to Annie whilst simultaneously executing a perfect stage whisper to her friends from behind her hand. 'Not 'arf...' she laughed, 'you'd be amazed at what the Quirky Quintet can get up to!'

THE FIGURE

*F*iona slammed the casserole dish onto the wooden chopping board with more force than was needed to show her annoyance. She stood with hands on her hips, studying Clement's facial expression. As usual it was the bloody ridiculous serene and pious look that he had perfected over the years when meeting the bishop. 'Why, Clement?'

He shrugged his shoulders and carried on eating his sandwich, making her wait whilst he swallowed and cleared his mouth. 'Why not? They're here anyway, and it'll be nice to have Abbey Towers filled with laughter and fun for a change.'

'But on All Hallows Eve…' She yanked the lid from the casserole and gave the contents a hefty stir with the spoon. 'This will end in tears, you mark my words. Because of what has happened in the past we have never spent Halloween in this house… ever!! Why start now?'

Despite Clement's godliness and belief only in holy matters, since her childhood Fiona had fostered an unwavering fear of the unknown. Having a mother who claimed second-sight and 'the gift' of seeing the dead, had only added to her phobia of anything to do with the autumnal celebration of witches, ghosts and ghouls. To appease his wife, every Halloween since their arrival at The Towers, Clement had taken the care to book a two-night stay in a country hotel with spa facilities, a three-course meal, and a fairly decent bottle of Prosecco for their room, leaving Abbey Towers empty and to the mercy of whatever spectre cared to walk its corridors for the preternatural period.

This year, with the excitement of having Colquitt Productions in their midst and the prospect of some joviality and dancing, he had clearly done the unforgivable by first not mentioning his agreement for the event, and secondly by not booking Bolder-wood Hall as promised. He took another bite of his sandwich, taking his time chewing it to give him breathing space to ponder over another appeasement for Fiona. The slamming of kitchen drawers and crashing of cutlery told him that his offering, when he could think of one, would have to be pretty spectacular.

In fairness, he had originally been the one to voice his discomfort at having a film that celebrated all things unholy and supernatural being produced on the grounds of church-owned property, but if St Barnabas Ealing was to have a new roof, then their generous location fee was a welcome gift. He'd actually become quite enamoured with the workings of moviemaking, and, although he would never admit it, a little bit star-struck too, so what had started out as a reluctant inconvenience had become a welcome distraction from ecclesiastical matters. He quickly changed the subject.

'I see the investigation into Alice's disappearance has taken a new turn...' He let that hang in the air, knowing full well Fiona would jump at the chance to absorb some local gossip so his blunder would be temporarily forgotten. He was right.

Fiona tucked the tea towel into the band of her pinny and sat down next to him at the kitchen table. 'Have they found her?'

'No, but apparently someone in the village has reported seeing her on the Winterbottom to Kings Cross express, so they're now looking at the possibility she just upped and left of her own accord.' Eyeing up the delicately iced cupcakes on the cake stand, his fingers swiftly plucked one from the top.

Fiona tapped the back of his hand. 'They're for the Knitting Circle coffee break, you naughty man,' she chided. 'I'm not buying that. No woman would up and leave without making sure her mother was cared for, and without taking any clothes or toiletries with her. It just doesn't make sense.'

They sat in mutual silence for a while, Clement enjoying the last sticky bits of the cake from the frilly case it had sat in, and Fiona wondering how she could make him pay for his crass decision to open Abbey Towers to all and sundry on Halloween.

'By the way, dear, I meant to ask you. Where did you get this from? I'm pretty sure it wasn't from the collection in the box.' He took the small figure from his jacket pocket and stood it on the table. It was dressed in delicately stitched tweed jacket and faded jeans, with its face obscured by a flat cap. A tiny clipboard was tucked under one arm.

She picked it up and turned it, admiring the detail that had been put into it before placing it back on the table. 'I didn't, I've not seen it before. Why?'

'Strange. It just suddenly appeared in the library of the diorama. I think someone is playing games with us.' He chuckled. 'I'll just pop it in the box; it'll add to the collection.'

Fiona involuntarily shivered. She snatched it from him, kicked down hard on the pedal bin and dropped the figure into the depths of the bucket to join the eggshells, tea leaves and potato peel. 'This doesn't belong, it's not part of Abbey Towers…' she snapped. 'Don't say I didn't warn you!'

COMING OUT

*E*thel lay in bed, the old-fashioned counterpane tucked up under her chin to ward off the chill in their room at The Bell, Book and Candle Inn. The orange glow from the lamp, set on an equally old-fashioned bedside cabinet between the two single beds, barely reached the corners of the rickety walls. She hated this time of night when left alone to her thoughts. No one to distract her, make her laugh or just rankle her. No sharp retorts, no quick-fire jokes, no sarcasm. It was a time when simply being Mrs Ethel Frances Tytherington, wife of Mr Albert Barnard Tytherington, would become just a distant memory.

She was now just plain old Ethel, the widow of the late Albie, bumbling along solo through what was left of her life without him.

Well-meaning friends had told her it would get easier with time, but it hadn't. If anything, it had become harder for her with the dreadful feeling of loss, the emptiness and the actual physical pain that her heart felt being without him. The only things which had remained in her cottage that said he had once been there was the thermostat on his 'infernal piece of tin', set at a constant eighteen degrees in his honour, along with his spectacles, a grey macintosh with the faded smell of Old Spice aftershave on the collar, and his unfinished copy of *The Magic Shop*. She missed his teasing and his nightly kiss on the top of her head, but most of all she just simply missed his presence. 'Oh, Albie…' she whispered as she wiped away the tear that had trickled backwards onto her pillow. She lay staring at the ceiling, hating the silence and the solitude of the hour, wishing for just one last dance with the love of her life, either in her dreams or when it was her time to join him.

'Pst, 'Rissa. Are you still awake?' She looked over at her friend, amused that the pink sponge hair rollers that Clarissa had so carefully applied as part of her bedtime routine had now haloed her head and sunk into the pillow. Her form gave an eerie shadow on the wall next to her. Ethel traced the outline and came to the conclusion that if Clarissa had been wearing her Gossard Lift and Separate Wonderbra, then the silhouette she had cast by lying on her back would at least have a mountain or two as an added interest to the horizon. As it was, she'd removed it in favour of a vest under her nightie, so now her projected contour on the wattle and daub wall was just like the Holstein mudflats. She tried again. 'I know you're still awake, 'Rissa, I can see your eyelids twitching!'

Clarissa sat up. 'Well, why are you ruddy asking, then?' Immediately feeling a bit mean having snapped at Ethel, she quickly caught herself. 'What's the matter? Can't you sleep?'

'Not really.' Ethel threw back the counterpane and swung her legs over the edge of the bed. 'D'you fancy a little tipple?' Before Clarissa could reply, she was up and rummaging around in the wardrobe. Pulling out a bottle of Harvey's Bristol Cream and two plastic cups, she set them down on the dressing table. 'Three fingers or four?' She didn't wait for a response, happily filling both cups to the brim. 'Here you go…' Handing Clarissa hers,

Ethel carefully tucked herself back into bed without spilling a drop.

'Come on, out with it. I've known you long enough to know when there's something amiss.' Taking a sip of her sherry, Clarissa propped her pillows up behind her.

Ethel took a large slurp of her drink, the feeling of it hitting the spot and bringing the Dutch courage she needed to admit to her friend she was not coping as well as they thought she was. Her head bowed, she stared a little longer than necessary at the intricate needlework on the quilt. She picked at a loose thread. 'I miss him, 'Rissa... I miss my Albie so much.'

Clarissa threw back her covers, paying no heed to her rollers or her thermal vest, she sat herself down on Ethel's bed and held her tightly. Bewildered that her friend could be so upset, but also taking herself to task because she had not noticed her deep distress before now. 'Oh, Eth, I thought you were doing so well. I'm so sorry, dear. I wish I could offer comfort by saying that I know what you are going through, but the love of my life was many, many moons ago, and for the briefest of times before their passing. Not like you and Albert, but I do know a little about love and loss.'

Surprised, Ethel shook her head. 'The love of *your* life, 'Rissa? You've never ever mentioned being in love, of having anyone in your life, or losing them. I don't understand, I thought that from choice you were the eternal spinster.'

Clarissa gave a sad smile. She inhaled deeply, giving herself time to consider if this was the right time for her to divulge her own long-held secret. 'It seems like forever ago now, in an age where our type of love was not readily accepted.' She gave Ethel a tissue to wipe her eyes. 'And I never told you, or the girls, just in case.'

'In case what?'

'In case it would change our friendship, I just didn't know

how you would feel about it. It's so different these days. People can now love whoever they want to, and nobody bats an eyelid, which is wonderful.' Clarissa became wistful, the conversation having evoked memories she had always kept close. 'My Freda was absolutely everything to me...'

Ethel dabbed at her eyes. 'Freda? But wasn't that your sister? I've seen the photographs on your sideboard – you and Freda lived together for years until she passed away.'

'She wasn't my sister, Ethel,' Clarissa said very quietly. 'It was a subterfuge, a game we had to play to hide who we were. We could never show our love like you and Albie did; our love was for behind closed doors; we couldn't even hold hands.' Clarissa took a deep breath, waiting to sense any change in body language from her friend, a shift in their fondness for each other, or even, dare she think it, abhorrence. As the seconds ticked by, she began to regret her honesty in the guise of being sympathetic and supportive. She had kept her counsel for more years than she cared to remember, but in a brief moment of vulnerability, she had let go of it.

Ethel finally spoke, trying to choose not the right words, but the true ones. She held her best friend's hand tightly in her own, hoping the warmth of her love and care for her would radiate through touch. 'Oh Clarissa Ruby Montgomery, you utterly daft bat! I knew, in fact we all knew, and we have for bloody years! Not about Freda, of course, but we've always suspected you had lesbionical leanings, that you 'batted for the other side.' Ethel's lumpy fingers formed air quotes as she chuckled, her tears temporarily forgotten, as was her grief.

Clarissa looked crestfallen, amazed that her secret had not been a secret at all. 'Jeez, Eth, what gave it away?'

Ethel winked. 'Your sensible shoes, of course...'

Clarissa sniggered like a teenager before giving a sigh of relief. 'I thought you'd guessed when we stayed at Montgomery

Hall and shared a double bed. You made that joke about being safe, but you never mentioned it again.'

Remembering her quip, Ethel laughed out loud. 'Aye I did, didn't I?' she paused for thought, a wry smile touching her lips and a twinkle in her eye. 'I'm still safe, aren't I, 'Rissa?'

'Oh absolutely, Eth, you're not my type…'

THE CONFRONTATION

*T*he day had begun with a mist that rolled across the ground of Abbey Towers. It swept across the lake and spun eerie tendrils that crept their way over low-lying shrubs and hedges.

David Preece, director and major shareholder in Colquitt Productions, stood facing Abbey Towers, marvelling at its structure, its presence and its history. It was allowing his imagination to run wild, along with his camera and a few select members of his crew. He'd lost track of how many stills he had taken for reference. 'Gwilym, can you pan out over there, pick up on the mist, but try and leave out the sunrise as we can use this to cut in for a night shoot. I'll get them to tighten it up in post-production.'

Gwilym Benedict-Hughes adjusted the lens on his Arri Alexa LF and zoomed in on the areas that his director had indicated. He finished with a steady shot of the tower itself. The tower fascinated and terrified him in equal measure, but every day, once he'd clocked on and before set, he would be drawn to it, mesmerised.

Like now.

'Gwil?' David snapped his fingers.

'Sorry, boss…' Rubbing his temples, Gwilym hoped the gentle action would ease the headache that had begun to tighten like a band around his head. He watched David stride across the grounds like a man on a mission, barking orders as and when crew members came into his line of sight. He followed behind, cursing the weight of his equipment as his quickened pace caused him to stumble over the uneven ground. It annoyed him to think that no matter how hard he had worked to get where he was, he still looked like the little boy that had always been left out. The one that had to constantly run to play catch up with the other boys in the school playground. The tailgater.

He watched David weave in and out of the trailers, stepping over cables as he made his way to see Flynn at the crafty table. As usual, Flynn was holding court whilst munching his way through a plate of waffles. Gwilym was just about to peruse the other refreshments that were on offer himself, when what he could only describe as a screaming banshee ran full pelt across the lot, hurdling the dolly tracks and barging into bemused actors as she focused on her target. Gwilym stood frozen to the spot as Dana Simons, tatted hair blowing behind her, talons at the ready, launched herself at David.

'You bastard! How could you?! You can't sack me…' she screamed. 'It was that goddam bitch that did it. She poisoned me, she put something in my sandwich!' A gnarled finger with a split nail and chipped red varnish jabbed accusingly at Dottie.

Dottie, coffee mug poised, offered her a serene smile whilst shrugging her shoulders to the gathered audience, feigning her innocence. 'Dana, I don't know what you're talking about, there was nothing wrong with the food. It's all been checked out. Whatever made you sick didn't come from here.'

Dana slumped down into a nearby chair. She looked around, taking in the surprised and judgemental faces of cast and crew. Flynn had taken the opportunity to be whisked away by his security, but she knew that those who remained to watch her shame and downfall were all whispering the same.

'It's the drink…'

'She's an alcoholic…'

'Didn't someone say drugs…'

'Oh my God, it's like Sunset Boulevard; she's channelling her inner Norma Desmond!' A chorus of embarrassed laughter followed that quick but hurtful jibe from within the crowd.

Dana's head snapped round to face them. 'Who said that? Come on, don't spout it if you can't flout it!' Her lips curled back as she snarled her rage to anyone within range, spittle flying in all directions.

'Dana…' Mark tentatively approached her. 'I think we should go home, you're still not a hundred per cent, and this isn't going to solve anything.' He gently took her arm. 'I'm sorry, David, it's probably the medication she's taking.' Making excuses for her and feeling somewhat embarrassed, he nodded his apologies to the rest of the crew as he led Dana away to the waiting car.

Dana was not finished. She paused, hanging on to the car door, one foot inside, the other gripping for dear life to the tarmac with her flip-flops. 'That evil cow is the one that did it! Ask her – go on, ask her…' she screamed. 'She tried to kill me – she wants me dead!' The rest of her histrionics became muffled as Mark shoved her onto the back seat, slammed the door shut and quickly got behind the wheel.

Dottie watched Dana with interest, her pallid, mascara-streaked face up against the window of the black Range Rover as it slowly drove away from Abbey Towers, her mouth wide open and screaming unheard obscenities through the toughened glass. She had only wanted to chastise the rancid old boot, not kill her, but now she was deeply regretting that choice of reprimand, particularly if Dana was in a position to point that arthritic finger at her again. Maybe she needed a rethink.

Then again, after that last and final public performance of Ms

Dana Simon, aka 'The Bitch with a Twitch', she really had shown herself to be a sandwich short of a picnic, albeit not one that was dressed with salad cream laced with one of Dottie's very special concoctions.

THE MEANING OF THE WORD

*M*illie carefully dipped her toast soldier into her boiled egg and jutted out her chin to avoid any yolk loss down the front of her blouse. 'You can't beat starting the day with a nice chucky egg.' Her fingers snaked out to grab another triangle of toast from the little silver rack on the table.

'There's five of us having breakfast, Millie, don't be too greedy!' Ethel slapped Millie's hand away and grabbed the piece of wholemeal that had been grilled to within an inch of its life in the toaster. 'So, we've got a day off today. Who fancies doing something a little different?' She scraped the knife across her acquisition, spreading a large dollop of marmalade from corner to corner.

'How about we see if we can find out a bit more on Alice's disappearance, sort of nonchalantly make enquiries around the village? Someone might know something that would give us a lead.' Millie plunged another toast soldier into her egg and inspected the result.

Clarissa shook her head. 'Too close to home. If there is anything suspicious, we could lift the lid on something that might put us in danger. Remember what we promised Pru and Bree.'

'Oh come on, one's in the pudding club, it would take a JCB to lift her off the sofa, and the other one's too busy making eyes at that assistant guy on set. They'll never know,' offered Ethel. 'A little wander around, ask a few discreet questions, and Bob's your uncle.'

'Bob wasn't my uncle, his name was Ernest, god rest his soul, so that doesn't count...' Millie turned the shell of her egg upside down, a family tradition to show she had concluded her breakfast.

Hilda harrumphed loudly. She leant into the table, encouraging her friends to do the same by beckoning with her hand. She furtively looked around. 'I don't think we should wander around anywhere by ourselves, girls, it's not safe.' She nodded sagely, happy her pearl of wisdom would be received by four pairs of attentive ears.

'Not safe? Here in Fallow Falls? Whatever makes you say that?' Clarissa took a sip of her tea. 'Granted there's a lot of spooky history, but other than that it's just a sleepy little hamlet.'

'It can't be a hamlet, it's got a church,' Olive was keen to point out. 'But still, why shouldn't it be safe, Hilda?'

'Because it's got loads of psychopaths...' Hilda chuffed whilst folding her arms, inadvertently hoisting her boobs to new heights at the same time. '*She* told me whilst I was waiting for you lot to come down for breakfast.' She jerked her head towards Hazel who was serving up a full English breakfast to the next table. 'When I said we might have a little ramble today, she said to watch out as there are loads of psychopaths.'

The collective 'oohs' from her friends gave Hilda hope that they had taken the information seriously and would reconsider their plans. Alarmed that potentially there was a madman or two roaming the quaint village, Clarissa sought clarification from Hazel. She beckoned her over.

'Morning, ladies.' Hazel tucked her serving towel into her waistband. 'Is there anything else I can get you?'

She was actually starting to look less like someone that once graced the witches' stocks by the village pond and more like a kindly tavern host. She had brushed her hair and Clarissa was almost sure she could detect a smattering of rouge on her cheeks. Just that small smidge of colour made her appear less menacing. 'Hilda here has just been telling us that you have a small problem with psychopaths around here at Fallow Falls, and that it's not safe for us to be wandering out alone. Is that true?'

Hazel looked confused. She scratched her head vigorously, which only served to facilitate the return of her bedraggled harpy hairdo as tendrils escaped from the plastic clip. 'Psychopaths? When did I say that?'

Hilda allowed her nellies to drop suddenly onto the table with a gentle thud as she unfolded her arms, her aged brassiere not giving them the support it used to. 'Just before, when I said we were going to go out and have a bit of a ramble, you said there are loads of psychopaths in Fallow Falls and to be careful...'

'Oh, Hilda...' Hazel burst out laughing, the tremors and jiggling from her amusement causing more hair to lose its grip and fall foul of gravity. 'I said *cycle paths* not *psychopaths*!' she chortled. 'We have lots of cycle paths around here. I was just saying to be careful, as sometimes riders take no prisoners when they hurtle around the village on two wheels with no bells.'

Relieved to know that they would not be fodder for even one Fallow Falls fruitcake, the Four Wrinkled Dears plus one, giggled and chattered to their hearts content, savouring an extra rack of toast and a pot of honey whilst planning the next part of their great adventure.

OLD FRIENDS

The gentle hum from the Winterbridge CID office confirmed to DI Murdoch Holmes that his troops were working hard towards him having a better clear-up rate this year than the last. His appraisal from the superintendent had been at the very least embarrassing, at best, appalling. He subconsciously willed the heat that had risen from under his collar to abate. He pulled the file towards him and scanned the first page, nodding each time he came to an entry that gave him satisfaction. The death of Barney 'Mutton' Lamb had been an excellent result. Several burglaries had been written off once forensics had linked him to the scenes, and since he'd shuffled off into another realm, their burglary figures had dropped dramatically. Unfortunately, there was a cloud hanging over his 'accidental' death, with Bob Limpett casting some doubt on the veracity of his tumble down a steep flight of stairs, the subsequent carpet burns on his nether regions from a well-worn Axminster carpet and the still missing front tooth adding to that doubt. A full search had failed to recover it from the scene. That was something Andy would have to deal with, as and when confirmation on cause of death and any suspicious circs were reported.

The cashpoint robberies had dwindled to nothing since Jackson Rutter had been smacked in the mouth with a fake Gucci handbag. Having him sent straight on remand from hospital meant the good people of Fallow Falls and beyond could once again draw their pensions without fear. His jaw rewiring hadn't been totally successful, so he was currently sporting a very dodgy facelift and was still sucking cold tea through a paper straw.

His finger traced the next page, the notes making him groan. Two robberies on the canal towpath at Chapperton Bliss, a domestic-related assault with the suspect still on his toes, teen gangs causing havoc by Winterbridge library most evenings, a spate of conmen targeting the elderly, and the missing woman case from Fallow Falls was still active, although currently stagnant with no further sightings. The second page contained known offenders and suspects for each of the outstanding crimes with updates on their status.

His train of thought was suddenly disrupted by a knock on his office door. 'Enter...'

'Hello, Murdoch, I hope the time's not inconvenient?'

Murdoch was delighted to see a friendly face. 'Dottie! Well, how lovely to see you! Come in, come in...' He stood and offered her a chair. 'Tea or coffee?'

Dottie smiled. 'A nice cup of tea would be lovely. It's been too long, hasn't it, but you're such a hard man to get hold of these days.' She looked around his office, impressed with the wall charts and framed photograph on his desk. 'Oh my, the boys sure have grown. Darren and Dirk, isn't it?'

Murdoch nodded. 'They tower over me now, Dottie. Just a thought, you do still have clearance, don't you?' He cocked a secret hand signal to her and laughed.

Dottie leant back in the chair. 'Of course I do. I don't do as much on the intelligence side as I used to for your lot, but I have kept my Counter Terrorist Check up to date.' She gave him a complicit smile.

Dottie and Murdoch had history. She had mentored him when he had been young in service and seconded to her under-cover team in the National Crime Agency many years ago, before she herself had taken a different path. He had remained on the right side of the law, whereas Dottie had forged her own judge, jury and punishment business. Not that Murdoch had an inkling of her extracurricular activities that had been over and above what had been expected of her at the NCA. She had a soft spot for him: cantankerous he could be at the best of times, but he was also an old-style copper that would always have your back.

'Back in a minute, I'll raid the biscuit tin whilst I'm getting your cuppa. I think we've got half a packet of your favourites.' He patted her on the back. 'Custard Creams, if I remember rightly.'

Dottie took the opportunity as soon as he left the room to whip out her mobile phone. She hovered over his desk, quickly turning the pages of the report he had been so invested in when she had first arrived. Fortunately, no flash was needed on her camera to give the game away, as she photographed each page in quick succession. She was back and casually slouched in the chair by the time Murdoch returned with a tray that contained a plate full of broken biscuits and two mugs of tea.

'So, what brings you here, Dottie, and what have you been up to since you retired?' He took a tentative sip of his tea, screwed up his nose, blew forcefully on the hot liquid and tried again.

'Oh, just a social visit, I moved back to Fallow Falls a few months ago, so I thought I'd take the opportunity to pop in and see you. It's nice to be back home.' She split the custard cream and, like a child, scraped the yellow cream with her teeth to relish the sweet mixture minus the biscuit base. 'I'm working on the film that's being shot at Black Abbey Towers. Mainly assisting on the stunt choreography, but also doing my bit on the crafty, dishing out butties and bottles of water to the rich, the famous and the minions.' She laughed, amused that her life had taken such a diversion from the excitement, tension and danger of her previous career. Although with her latest sideline, she occasionally had moments where her bum twitched with the fear of being discovered, if it was a job well done it was always worth the momentary angst.

But not all jobs were well done. Dana's hadn't been; there had been a lapse in her professionalism. Dottie had fallen foul of the slightly softer side of her own nature and had chosen to destroy just her career. Maybe she should have taken the hit and done away with her altogether. That was something she still might rectify at a later date.

Murdoch sighed loudly and pushed the crime file to one side so he could accommodate his mug on the desk. 'Sounds good. I must say I haven't heard Abbey Towers being given its full title for many a year. I went there once as a young constable – to investigate a report of a phantom or some sort of spectre roaming the hallways there. It was more like an attempted burglary, but there was no sign of a forced entry; the place was secure and nothing was stolen. It gave me a headache trying to write that one up without offending the occupier.' He shoved the custard cream into his mouth, hardly waiting to clear the crumbs before he spoke. 'It was as spooky as hell, though, particularly with its history. I definitely wouldn't want to wander around there after dark again.'

Dottie nodded her agreement whilst keeping her counsel on the fabric and truth of Black Abbey Towers. The building's dark stories were a welcome backdrop to mask her own agenda; it kept people on their toes and looking in the wrong direction. She also held a secret; one she hoped would never be revealed. Her return to Fallow Falls had not been solely for comfort in her dotage and the occasional thrill of her old ways.

Dottie had work to do. A helping hand for those that deserved it and, more importantly, wrongs to be righted and dark deeds to be carried out to ensure that secret would be kept.

. . .

'Three may keep a secret, if two of them are dead.'
  Benjamin Franklin

A LOOSE CANON

$\mathcal{M}$ ark stood by the door to Dana's bedroom and watched over his charge. She had been a complete and utter nightmare since her meltdown on set, and as sure as eggs were eggs, he knew with absolute certainty, she would never work in the industry again. Talk travelled fast, and if she hadn't been almost washed up before the Abbey Towers fiasco, she sure as hell was now. He felt some sympathy for her, but endearing herself to others had never been on her list of personable attributes and priorities, neither had consideration for others.

Dana just did Dana.

He braved the atmosphere and approached her bed, offering up the tray. 'Hot chocolate and a croissant, it'll help you feel a little better. Betty will bring up a couple of paracetamol for you, too.' He waited, but there was no acknowledgement from her, just a strangled grunt from under the bed covers and a finger that jabbed the air, directing him to leave the tray on the bedside cabinet. Annoyed, he dropped the tray down a little harder than needed to show his displeasure.

'I'll leave you to it, then.' The tone of his voice was another indication that no matter how much he was paid, it wasn't enough to have to deal with Dana and her vile moods. 'Betty was going to check in on you, but I'll tell her to leave it. Just ring down when you want her. I've got to be at the shoot for a few hours to sort out your trailer.' Taking a risk, he suddenly decided to voice his thoughts. 'Dana you're bringing all this on yourself. I did warn you. You need to sort yourself out.' He waited. After a few seconds it became evident that she was not going to grace him with a reply or tear a strip off him for being so forward. Either way, he was past caring.

Dana waited for the soft click of the bedroom door to indicate that he had left her in peace. She sat up and almost baulked at the smell of the sickly-sweet chocolate. She carefully opened the top drawer of her cabinet and pulled out a bottle of vodka. She grabbed the glass of water and threw its contents into the wastepaper bin, not caring that it was woven wicker and barely contained her cigarette butts, let alone half a pint of fluid.

Slugging back her 'lifesaver tonic', she waited for it to have the desired effect. She refilled the glass. 'Bastards, all of them...' she sobbed. She grabbed her phone and checked the time, which only served to heighten her despair. The cast and crew would be on the late evening shoot, and it was her scene with Flynn. Only it wasn't now. She threw her phone across the bedroom. It hit the wall, leaving a small dent in the plaster. 'But now I'm persona non grata all because of that rancid bitch...'

Dana heaved herself out of the bed and stumbled to the wardrobe. 'You're gonna regret messing with me – each and every one of you,' she half-sobbed, half-spat. Dressing herself in a pair of jeans, T-shirt and a heavy jacket, she tucked her trainers under her arm and staggered to the door. Checking the coast was clear, she tiptoed along the landing, down the stairs and slipped silently out of the front door, pausing only long enough to clad her feet in her Nike Air Force 1s before jumping into her car. She revved the engine of the little Fiat 500 and jammed it into first gear. The driveway gravel crunched under the tyres as she sped off, veering out onto the country lane, following the signs for Fallow Falls.

'How come you're not with them?' Pru heaved her ever-expanding bulk onto the sofa and flopped down. 'I thought you were taking care of them, making sure they didn't get up to mischief.'

Grinning, Bree tipped her glass at her friend. 'It's a night shoot and they didn't need any of the extras for it. As far as I know, Clarissa and pals are dining at the Bell, Book and Candle and having an early night.' She checked the bottle of merlot, closing one eye to see the level line against the glow of the fire. 'There's nothing they can get up to by indulging in a sherry or two and a game of gin rummy.'

'You can't be serious! You know as well as I do those four can get up to anything, and I mean absolutely anything when they're merely together just in the same room, let alone with any outside influences such as copious amounts of alcohol!' Pru shifted position and shoved a cushion behind her back.

'Five.'

Baffled, Pru tipped her head inquisitively. 'Five what?'

'Five of them.' Bree carefully topped up her glass, a touch of guilt washing over her as she watched her temporarily teetotal friend eyeing up the rich red liquid. 'They've made a friend; her name is Olive and she's just as bad as the four of them put together. They actually fit in well with each other.'

Pru groaned. 'So now they're *five* times as likely to get into trouble than they were before. I know you're not their keeper, but nothing will convince me that they won't stick their noses into something whilst they're there.'

'They already have. I'm pretty sure they've been snooping

around looking for Alice. There's been a lot of group huddles and whispering, and I know for a fact Hilda has inadvertently let slip that they had been mooching around Abbey Towers.'

Pru wasn't the least bit surprised that Alice's disappearance had piqued their interest, but the saving grace so far was a distinct lack of grisly murders and dead bodies at Abbey Towers, which usually had all the hallmarks of their involvement at some point. She was more worried that if they failed to respect people's boundaries and privacy, particularly at Abbey Towers, apart from getting into mischief, they could also be the subject of complaints. 'It might be worth having a word with them again, Bree, but...' She was suddenly interrupted.

'Are you tempting her with your wicked ways and a bottle of red, Bree Richards?' Andy laughed as he threw his car keys onto the coffee table. He kissed Pru on the cheek and tenderly stroked her tummy. 'How's my boy?'

She exaggeratedly pointed to her bump as the skin undulated under her T-shirt. 'Kicking like *he* or *she* plays for Winterbottom United. Have you had a good day?'

Andy grabbed himself a beer from the fridge, and flipped the cap. 'Same as usual. I've got the Met police checking the reported sighting of Alice, and a new press appeal has gone out, but other than that, and one of our most prolific burglars getting slinkied down a flight of stairs, it's pretty much business as usual.'

Bree emptied her glass in two gulps. Well, I'll leave you two lovebirds in peace. I've got socks to darn and teabags to count, and I might even wash my hair. You can't beat the joys of being a single, loveless old trout...' She slung her bag over her shoulder and paused by the door. 'And don't forget, any movement in the alien harbouring department, ring me!' Her hand made the universal telephone gesture before she disappeared into the hallway.

'Oh, and a good curry can help get things shifting – as well as you two having a bit of a firkle and a...' her disembodied voice tapered off, leaving Andy and Pru simultaneously voicing their preference for the curry rather than the effort and energy of her saucy second suggestion.

WIN SOME, LOSE SOME

*T*he drive to Abbey Towers had been a blur for Dana. Twice she had oversteered on a bend and almost totalled her Fiat roller-skate into a ditch, but she had compensated and finally, after several missed turns and the acquisition of a dented bumper from a tree stump, she made it to her destination.

Parking at the back of the estate out of sight, she grabbed the jerrycan from the boot and made her way through the trees. Scrambling over the perimeter sandstone wall, she lost her footing and fell hard onto the ground below. Winded, she lay on her back, staring at the darkening skies above her. If she had been sober, that fall would have probably hurt, but as it was, vodka in the quantities she'd quaffed since her humiliation on set had turned out to be a great all-round anaesthetic. After her meltdown and threats, David had upped the security on the front gates, so although this had been the best way to avoid detection, it most certainly wasn't the finest way for Dana to arrive safely and with dignity for her final performance. 'It's like using the bloody servants' entrance,' she snarled under her breath as she scrabbled around in the grass to retrieve the red can that had been thrown during her fall. Heaving herself up, she stood, swaying slightly as she attempted to generate the impetus she needed to slip unseen into the building. She stood watching her target, the moon forming an eerie backdrop for its silhouette.

Abbey Towers was floodlit, the glow from the key lighting on set at the front had formed a halo around the building, making it appear even more menacing than usual. For Dana this was like a moth to a flame. She staggered forwards, her Nikes dragging in the uncut grass and making her stumble as she broke into a haphazard jog towards the stone steps that led down to the boiler room.

Clinging onto the metal railings to guide her down into the depths, she counted each step as she went.

'One, two, three, four, five and we're here...' Her free hand pushed down on the handle. It wasn't locked. Her fingers pressed on the wood, forcing the hinges to groan as the door swung inwards. She felt around the wall, and finding a metal light lever, she pulled down on it. A quiet buzzing from the caged fisherman's lamp hanging from the ceiling filled the room as it flickered on, casting a yellow glow into the middle of the room. It was so weak it barely reached the corners.

In the half-light she could make out the massive copper system in one corner. Pipes like umbilical cords trailed from it, hooked and pinned to the brick wall before disappearing into custom-made holes in the ceiling. A higgledy-piggledy pile of wooden wine crates was stacked in one corner, with several hessian sacks randomly heaped on top of each other. One had spilled open, allowing earth-covered potatoes to roll across the floor.

'Let's see how much of a film you have left without a location, David...!' she muttered, furiously wiping her sleeve across her mouth, conscious that in her haste to exact her revenge for her public humiliation, she was beginning to drool with anticipation. 'Nobody puts Dana in a corner,' she cackled as she began to slosh the strong-smelling liquid around the room, paying particular attention to the stacked crates. She kicked the potatoes out of her way, amused that once her creation would rise and peak, baked spuds would be available to all.

'Bye bye, Abbey Towers, farewell *The Haunting of Fallow Falls* and up yours, Preecy...' She giggled as she flicked her thumb down on the spark wheel of the red plastic disposable lighter. She momentarily stood, the single flame reflected in her eyes, all sense and reasoning gone, replaced by an uncontrollable rage. Dana was so mesmerised by the power she held in her hand, she failed to notice she was not alone.

The blow to the back of her head was swift, harsh and debilitating. The vodka wasn't assisting her this time; she actually felt the pain, like a thousand nerve-endings exploding into a finale behind her eyes. Her hand twitched, dropping the lighter. It bounced and scuttered across the floor, the pressure of her thumb no longer sustaining the flame that was needed to exact her revenge. She slumped down hard onto the stone tiles. Stunned and confused, her limbs resisted her mental instructions to escape from the danger she was in. Dana mumbled incoherently. Aware that her attacker was still present, she wanted to shout at them but the words that formed in her head refused to grace her lips.

She saw the second blow before she felt it. Her attacker, framed by moonlight that shone through the barred window, held their arm high and quickly brought it down on her, not once, not twice, but three times. The force was savage; it held hate and anger in equal measure. The fisherman's light caught by one of the blows, swung from side to side, casting a ghostly strobed glow over the face of her soon-to-be killer.

Dana, her eyes heavy as she fought the darkness that was taking hold of her, forced herself to take one last look. Although the face was blurred, she still gasped in recognition. 'Why?' she spluttered.

She was not to be granted a reason, just another skull-crushing blow that savagely hit its mark.

Dana had died many times over the years. Always dramatically, always with clever scripts and beautiful costumes, and always with applause. Her last thoughts this time, if she had died peacefully in her sleep of old age, should have been of encores and Oscars, accolades and awards – instead they were filled with horror, pity and agony, and the bizarre hook from 'The Real Slim Shady' song.

Will the real Donna Smith please stand up... her brain bizarrely hummed in accompaniment to her final moments.

She tried to laugh, coughing out her life blood in the process. She knew that the real person behind the persona had long since died within her, leaving only the sinister shadow of the self-serving, egotistical bitch she had become.

'Ah well, in this life you win some, you lose some...' her brain offered.

Only this time, without a shadow of a doubt, she had lost.

TRAILER TRASH

The secret passages and tunnels of Black Abbey Towers had always been appreciated by many that had lived there, albeit only by those who had chanced to stumble upon them or those who had been educated in their existence.

The original plans, the amended documents, and secondary building surveys held no trace of the other world within its walls and grounds. It was a realm that was never used for good; rather, it was an underbelly of murder, mystery, witchcraft, smuggling and imprisonment. The only ghosts to walk the rooms, vaults, corridors and passageways of Abbey Towers were those who sought to do ill without being seen, using the darkness of night to cloak them on their travels.

The Collector hauled his latest acquisition along the dark tunnel. Dana's roped ankles had given a perfect hook for her body to be dragged to its final resting place. Considering she drank more than she ate, she was still a pretty hefty heifer, and every few feet he stopped to gather breath before setting off again. The fabric of Dana's jacket gave a pleasant swish, swish sound as it brushed along the stone floor, and every turn of a corner gave a delicious sounding thud as her head hit a bend in the wall. Not that Dana would be bothered, but he was aware that the less additional damage to her bonce, the better.

This had been quite a satisfying kill. It had been on the cards, but came about a lot sooner than planned once he had spotted her creeping down into the boiler room with her little red can. It was pretty much a given that she wasn't going down there to fire up the old petrol lawn mower or add a bit of juice to the long abandoned BSA M20 motorcycle left behind by the military after the war.

Abbey Towers was in danger and he couldn't have that. Dana had to be stopped. It was a frenetic kill, a disorganised one that still held the power needed, but it lacked finesse. Disappointing in one way, but quite enjoyable in another.

Continuing on for several more twists and turns, he finally reached his destination. Abbey Towers was still. The film crews had turned in for the night, the Gregorys were in the land of slumber and the cocky watchman, who had the simple task of keeping an eye on the production equipment overnight, had been easily bought with a carefully positioned bottle of whisky left in his cabin.

It was time to commence the set dressing, to perfect the scenery and to stage the final scene for Ms Dana Simon, the Bitch with the Twitch, the washed-up thespian and all-round pain in the ass.

At 7am sharp, the Four Wrinkled Dears plus one made their way to make-up and costume, chattering ten to the dozen. They had achieved a little success the previous day in their endeavours to assist the police and locate Alice. Their snooping had revealed that Alice had indeed been secretly wooed by a widower in the next village, courtesy of some pretty top-notch gossip from Mrs Ida Barraclough from the Fallow Falls newsagents on the high street. She had apparently seen them smooching in the Waddling Duck Inn at Chapperton Bliss a few weeks before her disappearance.

'Did you tell Bree, so that she can tell Pru, so that she can tell Andy?' Millie was very excited that this snippet of information could possibly break the case.

Ethel rolled her eyes. 'How about we just phone the police directly and cut out the middlemen?' she snapped. It was clear that getting up at the crack of dawn didn't suit Ethel at all. She had been cantankerous throughout breakfast and had continued with her grumbling during their stroll to Abbey Towers to clock in.

'Did I hear my name being taken in vain, ladies?' Bree edged into their group, taking the opportunity to join them after having overheard their chatter. 'Come on, now, we can't keep the director waiting; the call sheets are out and you rabble are due at the lake for the dunking of the Fallows Falls witch trials scene.' She ushered them forward. 'How many times do I have to tell you, girls: don't get involved in things that don't concern you. And that advice is from Pru, your president, too!'

Clarissa gave a wide grin and pointed to her mouth to prove that she had already been 'haggard' by the make-up department. Her two front teeth were blacked out and she was sporting a pretty good fake silicon wart complete with bristly hairs on her top lip. 'I don't normally look like this!' she chuckled, being careful not to lose the clip-on denture in the process.

'Very impressive, 'Rissa. You'd definitely scare the kids!' Bree laughed. 'I've just been thinking, how about...'

A loud, bloodcurdling scream suddenly cut through the air, forcing everyone to stop in their tracks. Heads jerked in synchronisation as people looked for the source, a soft murmur rippling through the crowd of actors and crew. A second scream broke through the melee as knots formed in stomachs and anxieties were raised.

'Oh my God! Oh my God! She's dead...!' A heart-stopping silence followed the unidentified voice.

Bree ran towards the back lot of trailers to where the shouting had originated, closely followed by Clarissa, Ethel and Hilda. Millie chose to remain with Olive who was visibly distressed by the commotion and was busy fanning herself with her hands whilst dramatically hyperventilating.

'I only came for her things; I don't understand; she's supposed to be at home in bed!' Betty, Dana Simon's housekeeper, tears rolling down her pale cheeks, was hysterical. Her hands shaking uncontrollably, she pointed to where a lighting rig had been parked dangerously close to the rear end of what had been Dana's trailer. 'It's horrible, she's been crushed between them, her head is all... all...' Betty's knees began to give way as the shock drained her. She was swiftly caught by Mark who, having heard the high-pitched screaming, had sprinted over from the waiting car.

Dana's body lay crumpled between the two pieces of equipment, one arm draped over the towing bar of the trailer, and her head at an unnatural angle against the thick metal bar of the lighting rig. Her glassy eyes stared out unfocused and unseeing, the dried, congealed blood dark against her pale, mottled skin.

Mark stared at the scene longer than he really wanted to. The horror of seeing the current condition of Dana, who only hours earlier had been lying in bed drunk but very much alive, was just starting to sink in. He finally drew his attention away, the need to take control suddenly forcing him into action. He turned to Bree. 'Can you take care of Betty for me, please?' He strode with purpose to where the screen dividers were stacked. 'There's nothing we can do here; she's gone. Come on, everyone, let's move back...' he began to pull the screens out to block the macabre view. 'Can someone let David know we have an incident?'

Taking out his phone he jabbed in the numbers, trying to retain as much composure as possible. 'Hello, yes, can I have the police...'

FAIR WARNING

*A*bbey Towers had suddenly become the focus of something more than its history and the appearance of Flynn Phoenix, superstar and heartthrob.

The death of Dana Simon was worthy news, and now Andy had to contend with camera crews and reporters from all aspects of the media shoving their faces through the bars of the wrought-iron gates hoping for a grisly scoop. Annoyed that word of a suspicious death had leaked out so quickly, he had immediately locked down the house and grounds pending the forensic investigation and the removal of the body, but that hadn't stopped them turning up in the hope of catching a glimpse of the coroner's van or, dare he think it, a body part or two. There was no common decency when it came to the reporting of a semi-famous death and being the first news media outlet to break the news publicly.

'Have we got a list of everyone on site, Lucy?' He signalled to Melvyn to allow the HSE officer through the cordon. It would be up to the results of the post-mortem to determine if this was a terrible accident or a murder, but judging by what he had seen so far, his money was on the latter. Nevertheless, HSE had to be notified.

Lucy handed the scene log for him to initial. 'Fortunately, the production team are pretty hot on their paperwork, even down to the background actors. They're ready to move her now, shall I give them the okay?'

Andy nodded. He watched as Dana was extricated and transferred to the black bag. The sound of the zip being fastened and tagged before being slotted into the coroner's van was so final. Regardless of the victim, whether it be a no mark like Barney Lamb or a waning film star like Dana Simon, it never failed to touch him. 'I'm just going to have a quick chat with Archdeacon Gregory. Can you carry on supervising here?'

Lucy nodded, and squinting her eyes, she groaned. 'Heads up and fair warning...' she gave Andy a wan smile as she pointed to the posse that was fast approaching.

'Cooee, detective...' Hilda's voice loudly trilled. 'Wait a minute.' She sped up and tottered towards him. 'Good grief! Anyone would think you were trying to get away from us!'

Andy stopped in his tracks, disappointed that his quick getaway from the Four Wrinkled Dears plus one hadn't been fast enough. 'Whatever gave you that idea?' he wryly responded. 'Actually, it's good that you're all here, I need to have a word with you.'

All ears, they gathered in a semi-circle around him. 'This is my friend Olive...' Millie offered. 'We're now known as the Quirky Quintet because there's six of us.'

'Five,' he corrected.

Millie waved her hand dismissively. 'Five, six – what's the difference?'

'Probably one...' laughed Clarissa. 'Anyway, go on, what do you want to tell us? Is it about Alice? We've got information on Alice, haven't we, girls?'

The little alarm bells that usually gave him a heightened sense of foreboding when the Winterbottom ladies mentioned anything to do with one of his investigations, suddenly began to clang loudly in his head. 'No, it's got nothing to do with Alice, and nor should it have anything to do with you. Please, ladies, keep your heads down and your very inquisitive noses out of anything that is police business. I know you think you're helping, but you're not, and that also goes for what's happened here today.'

Millie was crestfallen. 'But we have information; we've been investigating too,' she mithered.

Clarissa was quick to interrupt her. 'It's okay, Millie. Detective Barnes is very busy. We can always have a chat with him later.' She placed a kindly arm around Millie and ushered her away, beckoning the others to follow her, which they did with some reluctance. She waited until they were far enough out of earshot before she started to speak again. 'Right, it's pretty obvious Andy has other things on his mind, and falling short of smacking us over the back of the head to drive home his point, he clearly doesn't want us involved, nor does he want to listen to what we have to say.'

'But that's silly; it could help him if only he would listen to us. It's always the same, everyone thinks that because we're getting on a bit, we're either senile or stupid!' Millie was not impressed, but her thoughts on Alice had suddenly been usurped by another more important investigation. 'Mind you, this could easily turn out to be a murder, couldn't it, girls?'

'Murder...' whispered Olive in awe. 'Do you really think so? I mean, couldn't it just be an awful accident?'

Clarissa shook her head. 'Who moves a trailer and a lighting rig in the middle of the night by themselves. I'll stake my Tuesday night bingo winnings that this will turn out to be a gruesome homicide, you mark my words.'

'Crikey...' Olive's eyes shone with excitement.

Being an old hand at the murder game, Ethel gave a cheeky wink to her friends. 'Yes, a good, old-fashioned murder, Olive. We're good at solving those, aren't we, girls?' She hustled them all together in a line. 'You know what they say, you can't keep a good woman down. Well, there are five of us now, so five times the brain power, wit and guile. What do you say, ladies? All for one and one for all?'

The Four Wrinkled Dears plus one linked arms, danced a little jig, and kicked their heels in a show of camaraderie. This was turning out to be more exciting than they could have envisaged.

Andy watched them disappear behind the folly, a sinking feeling hitting the pit of his stomach. He had seen that display of impish disobedience before and it hadn't turned out well that time, either.

Clement Gregory sat back in his chair, elbows on his desk, and tapped his fingertips together steeple-style whilst deep in thought. After a few minutes he spoke. 'How certain are you that this woman's death wasn't accidental, detective?' His genuine concern for the dead woman was now beginning to be overshadowed by the media hype and the impact it would have on his diocese.

Andy shifted uncomfortably in his chair. 'We'll await the post-mortem results, but forensics seem to think that where her body was found wasn't the actual place of assault, or where she died. There are too many things that aren't adding up.'

Clement stood up and awkwardly adjusted his clerical collar. 'My wife is most distressed.' He failed to add that, although upset, Fiona hadn't actually been a fan of Dana Simon; she had found her incredibly rude and condescending, so her trauma was more to do with the added inconvenience of having even more people trampling through and around her home. 'But we of course send our condolences to the poor lady's family and friends.'

Standing up to leave and believing his audience with Clement was over, Andy offered a handshake. 'Thank you, and as soon as I have any further updates, I'll keep you apprised.'

'Detective, I have something to show you before you leave.' The archdeacon moved with precision towards the diorama. 'This may or may not have any bearing on your investigation, but when I came to my study this morning, I found this.' He opened the front of the Abbey Towers scale model and pointed to a basement room. 'That wasn't there yesterday, and it isn't one from our collection.'

Andy bent down and visually inspected the small figure that was lying, face down, in the middle of the room, a brass enamel painted boiler system acting as a backdrop. A tiny replica candlestick lay on the floor next to it. Using his pen, he tipped the figure onto its back. 'It's female...' Red paint had been meticulously brushed around the face and head to mimic the same type of injuries that Dana Simon had suffered.

The look that Clement and Andy exchanged gave no room for half-truths or prevarications. With this discovery their mutual suspicions had been immediately heightened. They now feared, with very little doubt remaining, that Dana's death was much more than an unfortunate accident.

Andy inspected the model, taking in Clement's represented figure still standing where he had last viewed it, propping up the fireplace in the library. Fiona's figure had moved from the kitchen to the lounge. It had been arranged on the miniature sofa where it appeared to be indulging in a spot of knitting. 'Who is this one, Clement?' He pointed to the figure standing inside the tower itself, dressed in a tweed jacket and jeans, sporting a flat cap and a tiny clipboard tucked under one arm.

Clement peered over his shoulder, his face immediately draining of all colour. 'That can't be there, it doesn't belong. Fiona threw it away...' He snatched it from the diorama and stuffed it into the pocket of his jacket. 'Somebody must be playing games with me, Detective Barnes. No need to worry, I'll soon put a stop to it, it'll just be a bit of harmless fun.'

Andy watched Clement's demeanour and the change in his breathing, unconvinced that it was just a spot of harmless fun. Someone had gone to great lengths to create the scene in the boiler basement and the appearance of a new figure could be part of it. 'Does this figure with the clipboard look like anyone you know?'

Clement shook his head. 'No, not at all. It's not from our collection. I have no idea where it has come from. Fiona threw it away, so whoever has done this...' he pointed to the scene, '... must have found it and put it there.'

Andy indicated to the model of Abbey Towers. 'I'd like you to put it back where you found it, Clement. I'll have forensics take a look at the diorama and the figure too. Now, can you show me where this basement is...'

THE STORY

*T*he atmosphere in the bar of the Bell, Book and Candle was surprisingly warm and inviting, helped along by the huge open fire in the stone grate. The logs cracked and spat sparks that were quickly swept upwards to join the smoke in its rise to the sky through the inglenook chimney. As an added bonus, Hazel had dropped her wizened witch persona for the evening, opting for a more suitable woolly turtle-neck sweater and a pair of thinning leggings tucked into her UGG boots, providing comfort whilst she served her regulars.

Hilda was happily toasting her bootee-clad toes in the nearest chair to the fire whilst Ethel, Millie, Clarissa and Olive occupied the cushioned bench sofas. Four sweet sherries and a bottle of Guinness sat on the table.

'Well, that was a day, wasn't it?' Olive took a sip of her Guinness. 'I can't get over how calm you lot were. Didn't it bother you in the slightest?' She was still very much in awe of her new-found friends and their ability to shrug off blood, gore and intrigue as though it was a trip to the corner shop for half a pound of butter and a pork pie, whilst Ethel was very much in awe that a woman of Olive's years had forsaken a glass and was cheerfully swigging stout directly from the bottle.

Clarissa waved her hand, not dismissively, more as an act of modesty and coyness. 'We're seasoned hands when it comes to murders, Olive; there's nothing that fazes us any more. If anything, it makes us all the more determined to get involved. We love a bit of madness, murder and mayhem.'

'It's what keeps us young at heart,' Hilda offered. 'Did you know they'd cordoned off the old boiler room at Abbey Towers just before we left? Apparently they think that's where it happened.' She offered up her glass for a refill. 'I would like to know more about that place, not what our Olive here found in its depths, but about its history. Surely we can't be the first to stumble upon some of its secrets?'

'Talking about Black Abbey again, are we, ladies?' Hazel pushed a bowl of peanuts into the middle of the table, quickly followed up with four more sherries and another bottle of Guinness. 'I could tell you a few things about that place.' She gave an exaggerated shudder. 'Lived here all my life I have, nothing gets past me.'

The ladies were all ears, desperate for any snippet of information that would assist them in their planned adventure during the Halloween party. 'Here you go, Hazel – sit here.' Ethel patted the cushion of the spare chair next to Hilda.

Hazel made herself comfortable. 'Well, it all started in the 1890s, the Wraithe family had Abbey Towers, then known as Black Abbey Towers.' Her eyes narrowed as she looked at each of them in turn. 'Calduggan Wraithe was a relatively young man who had a penchant for witchcraft, black magic and...' she paused for effect.

An audible gasp came from Millie which was accompanied by the leather of the sofa squeaking its displeasure as Olive's well-rounded bottom squirmed with excitement. 'Go on...'

'… a penchant for young, nubile girls.' Hazel sat back in triumph, content that her audience had been hooked.

'I was nubile once, you know, before I got arthritis in me hip.' Hilda slugged back her sherry. 'Can't go as far as I used to these days without a stick.'

They all looked at her, puzzled, each trying to work out what her arthritic hip had to do with the conversation. It was Clarissa who cottoned on first. 'Not that, Hilda, that's a totally different word!' Not wanting to be the one that would have to explain the difference in detail between mobile and nubile, Clarissa plumped for a simpler explanation. 'They were ladies that enjoyed a bit of how's yer father…' She let that nugget of information float in the air for a few seconds before prompting Hazel to continue.

Hazel was only too happy to oblige. 'Over the years, so many young girls went missing from the village, never to be seen again. Everyone knew it was Calduggan that had taken them for his rituals. They were slaughtered like animals, but he was beyond reproach or punishment. For those that walked Black Abbey Towers dressed in hooded robes as his necromancers, all held important positions within the county. Judges, officers of the law, magistrates – you can see where I'm going with this, can't you?'

Four heads nodded eagerly. The fifth belonging to Hilda remained static, her face deadpan and her eyes glazed. 'Oh blimey, our Hilda is *buffering*…' laughed Ethel, as she touched Hilda's hand to encourage her participation.

The gentle gesture was not lost on Hazel as she continued. 'Calduggan answered to no one, he held the power. That was until All Hallows Eve in 1899 when he called upon a village girl he had been coveting for some time. Florence was young, innocent and very beautiful. In her naivety she chose to ignore the warnings from others and she accepted his invitation to a party.' Hazel beckoned to her husband at the bar to bring her a drink. 'Only there were no guests, no banquet, no games; it had all been a ruse.'

'Oh gosh, how terrible! I bet the poor girl was terrified, all alone with him. He doesn't sound very nice at all. What happened to her? Did she end up like all the other girls, or did she escape?' Ethel was keen to know how Florence had fared.

'Unfortunately not, Florence apparently fought back, a candelabra was knocked over in the struggle, and the place went up in flames. The damage to the ballroom was extensive, Florence's body, or what was left of it, was recovered, but nothing was found of Calduggan. There were rumours that he had escaped through a maze of tunnels underneath Black Abbey Towers, but over the years extensive searches, along with renovations, have never uncovered anything, no tunnels, no secret rooms, nothing.'

They all sat in silence, taking in the story that was both sad and terrifying in equal measure. Clarissa caught Millie's eye and, knowing her friend of old, was quickly aware that she was just about to divulge their own findings at Abbey Towers. She popped her eyes and shook her head at her, giving off very obvious 'don't say it' vibes. Fortunately, Millie was quick to recognise her signal. She shrank back into herself, keeping her counsel. Their secret code message was interrupted by Hazel continuing her story.

'Over the years, Abbey Towers has played host to many owners and residents alike. During the Second World War when it was seconded as a hospital, soldiers reported sightings of spectres walking the corridors, disappearing through walls, and floating down staircases. Most of that was put down to trauma or medication, but some were convinced that Florence's spirit, having been trapped in Abbey Towers, was fated to walk its passages for all eternity, her emerald-green cloak undulating behind her as she wept for her lost life.' Hazel shivered. Standing up she threw two logs from the basket onto the dwindling fire and agitated the poker into the glowing bed, forcing a small flame to rear up and catch the new wood. 'There have been many other tragedies and deaths there. A murder suicide in the 1970s involving a vicar, his wife and their little boy.'

'That is so sad.' Olive swallowed the huge emotional lump that had formed in her throat. 'How old was the little boy?'

'William was just eight when it happened. His father went completely mad, suffocated his son, and then stabbed his wife with a knitting needle. As you would expect, the rumours were rife around here that the darkness had returned and Abbey Towers was to blame.' Hazel took a sip of her drink, her story having parched her throat. 'I'd steer clear, ladies, no good will come of courting evil.'

Ethel, mesmerised by the flickering flames that were now reflected in her tearful eyes, sighed heavily. 'They say every house has a heart. If there is evil within the walls, the heart will absorb the darkness and will become tainted. I think that is what has happened to Abbey Towers.'

THE HELPER

*L*ucy side-eyed Andy and pulled a face. Having her DI's buttocks unexpectedly placed on her desk first thing in the morning wasn't something she had included on her daily wish-list of things that she would like to happen.

Win the lottery, loose 10lbs, eat chocolate without getting acne, drink wine with no hangover, have Murdoch's arse on my desk...

Even thinking it made it seem so wrong. She could see Andy was following her own train of thought as he brought his mug to his mouth to cover up the smirk he was generating.

'We've definitely got a murder on our hands. What did forensics say about the basement?' Murdoch shifted slightly, pushing Lucy's pen pot to one side to accommodate more of his posterior.

'It was definitely the murder scene. The trailer was just the dump site, although for whatever reason, it was made to look like an accident. That's the niggle. Why go to all the trouble to set a scene to steer away from a kill, only to leave clues to prove it was a murder? It just doesn't make sense.' Andy scribbled a doodle with his pen on the corner of the notepad. 'Forensically so far, we've got nothing. The candlestick was the murder weapon, but apart from the victim's blood and Archdeacon Gregory's fingerprints, which was expected, it was clean.' He kept to himself the discovery of the red canister and the petrol fumes that had assailed his nostrils until such time forensics gave him something to work with.

'The whole thing was staged like a performance, wasn't it? It would be obvious that we would have known straight away. For a start, the lack of blood splatter and deposit where she was found. She'd clearly done most of her bleed out a good while before being placed between the trailer and the lighting rig, so it's pretty obvious her injuries weren't sustained there.' Lucy ran her fingers over the smooth curve of the wooden-topped bradawl in her hand; its ultra-sharp point for jabbing holes in files was beginning to look more and more appealing if it was allowed to puncture one of the DI's butt cheeks and make him move.

'Right, I'll leave it all in your capable hands, Andy. Keep me updated.' Murdoch finally slipped off the desk, much to Lucy's relief. 'By the way, how is that wife of yours? Any news?'

Andy laughed. 'No, just as rotund, and just as snappy. Pru has had enough now. It's exciting to be on the final countdown, but she's really starting to feel nervous about it all.'

Murdoch Holmes was inclined to agree with him. He could still remember Mrs Murdoch when she was pregnant, the short fuse, the cravings for sardines and bean sprouts that still made his stomach heave. 'Well, give her my regards when you see her.'

Andy watched him amble back to his office. 'Chance would be a fine thing, hey, Luce?' He was very much aware that the last thing he needed right now was a fresh murder enquiry when he still hadn't been able to finalise Barney Lamb's unfortunate demise, or find the missing Alice Moorcroft, and all when he really wanted to be spending more time with Pru, not less. The only shining light for the misper case was the unconfirmed sighting of Alice on the train out of Winterbottom, and talk of her having a bit more to her life than just cleaning Abbey Towers and looking after her mother, although they yet had to identify and trace her elusive beau. He just had to hope that Alice was somewhere nice, enjoying her new, uncomplicated life.

'Right, I'm off to speak to…' Lucy shuffled her paperwork and found what she was looking for. 'Yep, here they are: Mark Joynson, the general aide to Dana through Colquitt Productions, and Betty her housekeeper. I'll let you know how I get on.'

Andy was grateful for the respite in conversation. He cracked back his chair and turned to face the window. Closing his eyes he began to mentally slot everything he knew so far into place for every case he had on the go, whilst silently bemoaning the fact that his aspirations had been to become a detective not a ruddy circus juggler.

Dottie flicked the switch down on the kettle, pulled out her favourite mug from the cupboard above, and dropped two teabags into the pot. Wick took the opportunity to swirl around her ankles, desperate for her attention. She bent down and picked him up.

'Are you feeling a bit left out, Wick?' She tickled him under the chin, which elicited a gentle mew. 'I'm sorry, I promise once I've finished my list I'll take some time off. Hell, I might even jack it in all together.' She let him nuzzle under her chin. 'I know, I know. You and me against the world, but I have to help somehow, and this will be my gift.'

Dottie forked out a few flakes of tuna for Wick, before placing her mug on the tray, along with a selection of biscuits. Making herself comfortable in front of the open fire, she picked up the manila envelope from the coffee table. Taking out the papers that had been printed from the photographs she had taken in Murdoch's office, she took the time to devour their contents, along with a chocolate biscuit which disappeared in less than two bites.

'Well, I took good care of Rutter, didn't I, Wick? He won't be perusing cashpoint machines for some time to come, although I don't think he appreciated the workmanship of my Louis Vuitton handbag.' She took a sip of her tea. 'Mind you, it did have a house brick in it at the time!' Dottie laughed loudly, the sound of Rutter's jaw cracking when she hit him and the feral wail that had followed, had been an absolute joy. 'Sometimes I bloody love my job.'

Her finger traced down to the next section. 'Here we go again, a nice big tick for that awful Barney Lamb.' Dottie had revelled in the dramatic squeaks he had expelled, making him sound like the voice box of a broken teddy bear each time his body had hit the wall on his way down the stairs. He had finished with a glorious finale of a low growl from his last breath as his neck snapped. 'So, on to our next one. Here we go, someone else who seems to think it appropriate and acceptable to take what isn't theirs.' She memorised the suspect's custody photograph, his name, date of birth, current address and his stomping ground, the canal towpath in Chapperton Bliss. 'Likes to use a bicycle for his getaway, this one…'

Dottie was already formulating a plan to rid the world of another weasel-faced oxygen thief, and in the process, she would be helping the one person she had failed all those years ago.

WARTS AND ALL

*K*itty swept across the trailer lot, her threadbare hessian costume trailing behind her. She furiously picked at the hairy silicon warts on her chin. Her dreams of a glamorous role had been shattered on her first day at Abbey Towers when casting had informed her who she would be playing.

'Urgh…' She shuddered, pulling her thoughts up short. She could barely say it to herself, let alone out loud. 'The old village hag, the pauper, the gossip,' she spat under her breath. 'Do I look like a bloody hag?' Flouncing to the bank of chairs, she sat down with a thump, the two warts previously removed in one hand, ready to return to make-up.

Ethel sat down next to her. She, too, was dressed in similar attire as they had been filming in the village at Fallow Falls for most of the day. 'You've missed one,' she helpfully offered, her finger pointing out the offending mole by Kitty's nose.

Indignant, Kitty riled. 'That's mine, it's my beauty spot!'

'It's got its own bristle, pull the other one, Kitty, it's a wart!' Ethel tried to stifle a loud snort, amused at her own quick retort.

'Clarissa, will you tell her; she's saying my beauty spot is a wart,' wailed Kitty, sounding more like a five-year-old than a grown woman. 'And you wonder why I've been avoiding you lot since we got here! You're not funny, Ethel.'

'Au contraire, ma chérie, I think I'm hilarious!' Ethel was determined to rankle Kitty. The day had been long, her feet were killing her, and she desperately needed a bit of light entertainment. She gratefully accepted the polystyrene cup that held a tepid drink of tea. 'Thanks, 'Rissa, where are the others?'

Still in a huff, Kitty took the opportunity to disappear, leaving her chair free for Clarissa, who sat down and squirmed, trying to extricate the rough fabric of her bloomers from underneath her. 'I know I've got my own knickers on underneath these infernal things, but dear god, they've still been sandpapering my poor foo foo all morning.' She chuckled loudly. 'The girls are sitting with that Dottie woman over there.' Clarissa pointed to the crafty tent. 'Hilda is convinced she's got something to do with the murder of Dana; apparently, they had some sort of falling out a few days ago. Dana was extremely rude to the poor woman, accused her of trying to poison her.'

Ethel tipped her head and narrowed her eyes as she watched her friends engaged in conversation with Dottie. 'Do you think she has something? I know we wrongly dismissed Hilda's ability to pick up on things when we were at Harmony Hollows, but surely she couldn't be right twice in a row?' She pursed her lips in thought. 'And to go from potentially giving someone mild gastro guts to stoving their head in with a candlestick is a bit of a leap of the imagination!'

Clarissa sat quietly, mulling over Ethel's logic, whilst observing Dottie's body language. She had to admit that her interactions with Dottie had been few, but on each occasion, she had found her to be knowledgeable on the film industry and actually quite fun to be with; her quick wit had kept them all entertained during long waits between scenes. There was something, though, something she couldn't put her finger on. It was a bit like an itch that you couldn't reach to scratch. 'Maybe we could do some digging on Dottie, see if we can find out a bit more about her. She does give off an air that says she's capable of very many things, particularly if you take into account her stunt abilities.'

'Maybe so, but to be capable of murder, and a vicious one at that?' Ethel peeled off her own wart and wobbled the silicon between her two fingers. 'Who the devil are these film people that think all villagers have warts?'

Clarissa laughed. 'Probably the same ones who think we enjoy having our lady-bits savaged with strips of hessian-sacking every time we sit down!'

THE PREPARATION

*T*he grandfather clock in the entrance hall chimed three, and when the final reverberation fell silent, the gentle 'tick, tock' once again prevailed over the sleeping edifice. The moon cast its light through the window, turning the vast expanse of marble flooring into a stage.

The Collector stood for a while in the spotlight, admiring the surroundings. The bewitching hour that symbolised all that Black Abbey Towers stood for, gave momentary peace to the dark heart that was carried beneath the robes. It soothed the soul, quietened the voices and gave impetus to walk unseen through the corridors. His feet made no sound as they crossed to the archdeacon's study and the door clicked softly open at the merest touch.

'Ah, there you are...' The architectural beauty of Black Abbey Towers never ceased to amaze and humble him; even though the diorama was small, every detail was perfect. The omissions to its secrets were a source of annoyance, but they had eventually been acknowledged and accepted so that they could remain known only to those who were entitled.

The figure that represented Archdeacon Gregory was quickly

removed from its usual spot and set down in the kitchen, leaving a place in the library for the new figure that had been crafted by The Collector's own hands. Those same hands now deftly worked with silent precision, bringing the diorama to life for a short time. Like a child playing with a doll's house, his hands toiled with care and imagination whilst his melodic voice hummed a strange, hypnotic song.

Oh how they sleep in the strangest of ways
That their cries are not heard at the end of their days
The Collector will go where the innocent tread
Singing bring me their souls and I will give life to the dead

The scene had been set, the script had been written and the star of the next show had been chosen.

The Death Collector was ready.

GWILYM

*G*wilym Benedict-Hughes was not your average kind of guy.

In fact, Gwilym Benedict-Hughes was anything but average. At school he had excelled in all aspects of academia, had led the Tollthorpe Titans under 21s to rugby victory as their captain and flanker, and when he had sat alone in Tollthorpe picture house watching a matinee performance of *The Last Emperor* whilst devouring a bag of stale popcorn, he had made a decision that was to shape the rest of his life.

The film industry was calling him, and once again he excelled in his training, in his work ethic, and in his ability to ingratiate himself with the type of people who would advance his career.

The only thing that Gwilym wasn't good at, or successful in, was love.

If the word 'unwanted' had an image, that image would most certainly be Gwilym. He had suffered the agonies of unrequited admiration from Susan Golding at the age of ten, and relentless teasing from the acne-faced Barbara Butterton at the Young Adventurers Methodist club when he was fourteen. He had endured heartache at eighteen when his life had been turned upside down by a truly magnificent young lady whom he had ravished with much gusto before she had mysteriously disappeared from his life, and just when he thought he had been gifted his future, he had finally been rebuffed by the fabulous Camila Martinez at the age of twenty-five.

Camila had been the love and lust of his life; if only it had been reciprocated. She had smoked Sobranie Cocktail pastel cigarettes, pouted with full lips, seduced him with her thick, throaty accent, and had drawn him in with her smouldering eyes, all adding to her mystique. He had watched her from afar; his heart filled with a deep desire to love and protect her with just a touch of lust to add to his yearning.

Sadly for him, Camila had decided to share her 'smouldering' with someone else: the flamboyant Johnny 'Splodge' Jenkins. Five years and three kids later, Camila was smoking Cuban cigars and coughing like a sea lion whilst constantly rebuking Splodge with those same full lips. And the only smouldering he got to see was the smoke from the local factory furnace chimney, where he turned in sixteen-hour shifts to pay for the pleasure and torment of having his head turned by a once-beautiful woman.

Many times over the years Gwilym had likened himself to the one remaining runt that nobody picked from a litter of cute puppies. But Splodge's experience and Gwilym's own lack of romantic success had finally taught him that a solitary life was preferable to suffering the agonies of the heart. Gwilym had settled down to a life of bachelorhood, sharing his cottage on the outskirts of Tollthorpe with his overweight ginger cat, Mingus the Terrible.

He dropped his pen onto the cabinet and sat his journal beside it. He would finish his latest entry tonight whilst enjoying a nice glass of crisp white Portuguese Douro Branco. What he had discovered had turned his world upside down and needed quality time to document that knowledge and what he would do with it, but right now, it was time for work.

He stood in front of the full-length mirror and hitched up his boxer shorts – and then, just as quickly, pulled them down to sit on his hips. Nothing gave a man's age away more than having his underwear or trousers pulled up so high they would crush his wedding tackle whilst simultaneously reaching his armpits. He sucked his stomach in, held his breath, and turned to give himself a side-angle reflection. Seeing stars, he felt obliged to exhale again rather than take a tumble on the bedroom floor from self-induced vertigo. His stomach took the opportunity to flop and return to its usual resting position. He patted it, wobbled it, and then savagely tucked it into the waistband of his shorts, bemoaning the loss of his youthful six pack.

'Okay, Mingus, what's on the agenda today?' He wasn't expecting the cat to reply, but it always felt better to be talking to something rather than just himself. He slumped down on the bed and flicked through the call sheets for the day. The death of Dana Simon hadn't impacted too much on the filming schedule, but it had caused the Gregorys to temporarily lock down the interior of the house, so the production team had switched schedules to do the outside scenes first. Being stuck outdoors didn't bother him too much; he had always been a lover of nature and fresh air, and if he really needed access to Abbey Towers there were plenty of other ways in besides the front door.

That thought amused him. On his pre-filming recce he had found out so much more about the old building, things that only an adult eye could see, including a few hidden extras that had surprised him. Gwilym had spent his formative years in Fallow Falls before being shipped off to a faith-affiliated boarding school, so he had prior knowledge of the Towers. Knowledge he would have preferred not to have had. He screwed up his eyes and tried to block out the dark thoughts that had suddenly invaded his head space.

Breathe Gwilym, breathe.

In...

Out...

Back in control, he pressed his forehead against the cool glass of the window, taking in the darkening skies. The clouds weren't yet threatening rain, but the dull, overcast atmosphere would challenge the lighting crew. He shoved his journal into the top drawer of the cabinet, quickly dressed and grabbed his jacket and rucksack, ready for the day ahead, pausing briefly in the kitchen to fork out some leftover tuna for Mingus.

'Don't eat it all at once.' He laughed, giving Mingus a scratch under the chin. 'And don't be jumping all over my workbench, either; there's delicate work in progress over there It's going to be my masterpiece!' Turning the knob on the reproduction 1960s style cream-coloured Bush radio, he set the volume to a level that would keep Mingus company.

Outside, a chill wind fluttered orange-yellow maple leaves across the cobbled path of Riverbank Cottage, pushing them over the hedge that was now devoid of its own finery. A solitary figure stood huddled behind a nearby tree.

Watching and waiting.

IN THE CLEAR

'*J*'m telling you, that's *exactly* how she told it to me; it's the truth, honestly.' Olive sat back in her chair, triumphant that her knowledge of Dottie Barker's past history was rock solid after her little chat with Ida Barraclough at the corner shop.

'Pah, you wouldn't know the truth if it bit you on the arse, Olive Periwinkle,' Hilda spat, clearly annoyed that her position as chief gossip teller and mystery investigator was being usurped by the newcomer in their group.

'Feck me! It's Auldwrinkle, dear. Olive Auldwrinkle.' Not even trying to disguise her cuss since her familiarity with her friends had gone on to the next level, Olive sighed her frustration. 'Look, I'm not trying to step on anyone's toes, I just want to help. And now we know what Dottie's penchant is for, we can keep a closer eye on her.' Olive bit into her sandwich, chewed slowly, and then peeled back the top slice of bread to check its contents.

Ethel stirred her tea and let the spoon rattle back into the saucer. 'Well, Olive, considering your weird ten-to-two feet, I don't think you'd have much luck stepping on anyone's toes!' She smirked. 'I know Dottie's pretty nifty on the old stunt stuff. I've seen her in action, and maybe in her youth when she was as fit as a fiddle she could fight like a ninja, but I'm not having that she was some sort of secret agent. I mean how far-fetched is that?'

The ladies continued to debate the career history of Dottie over scones with clotted cream and strawberry jam. They eventually begged to differ over her capabilities as a potential MI6 agent, settling on Dottie being a more sedate member of the British police force because of Millie's input.

'I heard her telling Andy when he came to Abbey Towers. Apparently, she used to work with his boss, Detective Inspector Holmes, on some sort of crime squad thing.' Millie felt she had trumped all four of her friends with that snippet of information. 'So you see, she isn't some high-flying secret agent, she was just in the police. Simples. And anyway, even if she had been in the secret service, nobody would ever know, that's why it has s-e-c-r-e-t in the title!' She spelt the word out for dramatic effect.

'So why would Ida say she was some sort of female James Bond?' Olive was beginning to feel unappreciated for the effort she had put in grilling Ida over a pack of four bath buns and a copy of the *Winterbottom News*.

Clarissa laughed. 'Because she's the village gossip, Olive. What she doesn't know she'll make up, and what she does know she'll embellish. Years ago, a woman like Ida would have been sitting with her head jammed in those stocks by the pond every other Friday whilst the locals, feasting on bread and cheese, were merrily entertained.' She gave Olive a friendly pat on the back of her hand to show no hard feelings. 'But what we can do now is confirm what we've discovered, and then we can dismiss Dottie from our investigation. If she's a retired police officer, then she's definitely not our murderer, is she, girls?'

'Right troops, listen up...' Andy sat on the edge of his desk and waited for his incident team to pick their seats and finish their telephone calls. The usual office murmur that filled the room dropped in volume and then quietened completely.

'Donna Smith aka Dana Simon, our victim. Cause of death, blunt force trauma to the head and face. All the details are in your handouts: we had two scenes for this one, the kill and the dump. So far, forensics have nothing to go on.' He shuffled through the papers on his desk. 'According to investigation and interviews, Dana was very much a fading star; she had an alcohol problem and was on antidepressants. Unfortunately, there is no one person to point a finger at for having a grudge against her, as virtually everyone who met her had a run-in with her at some point. She wasn't a particularly nice lady.'

'What about the stunt advisor? The victim accused her of poisoning her food, surely that's got to be top of the list?' DS Jack Finnigan, Andy's oppo on C team, chewed the end of his pen, waiting for a response.

Andy checked his list. 'Good shout, Jack. Regrettably, whatever Dana ate that she claimed poisoned her didn't come from catering on the film set. As a matter of course they cleared their stock and sent samples for testing. They were all negative. I've asked the hospital for a copy of her medical records for that admission, and from what they've told me, her liver wasn't up to much. Even the mildest bout of Montezuma's revenge can reach crisis point as alcohol irritates the stomach lining, weakens the immune system, and sets up a good breeding ground for bacteria. According to Betty the housekeeper, Dana had a habit of over-dramatising everything, anyway.'

'The stunt advisor is actually one of us, or was many years ago.' Lucy held up the statement she had taken from Dorothy May Barker. 'She worked with our very own DI for a while when she was in the NCA. There are some blanks in her CV, mainly because of the nature of the work she undertook, but I think we can safely rule her out.'

'Thank goodness for that!' Murdoch Holmes grinned. He had slipped unnoticed into the incident room. 'I'm having lunch with her today and it wouldn't do for me to be slurping minestrone soup with a murder suspect, would it?'

Laughter quickly filled the room.

'Okay, enough of the jovialities, I need some progress on this case, something I can give to the press office, and an update on Alice the Misper wouldn't go amiss, either.' Murdoch shrugged his arm into his jacket. 'I know there's been reported sightings of her, and I want those firmed up.'

Andy closed the briefing and sat down at his desk. 'Luce, I've got to grab an early dart from here later; Pru's got a hospital appointment. Can I leave this with you to allocate? It's another robbery on the canal towpath; it came in yesterday, making it number five so far. It's an eighty-two-year-old male victim named Arthur Woods. He's been fairly lucky, a couple of stitches in his head and his pension gone along with his wallet. It could have been worse as he was lying unconscious by the canal for quite some time before he was found.' He handed the red folder to Lucy. 'I think he was more upset about the wallet, as it was a birthday present from his grandchildren.'

Lucy took the file from him and read the first page. 'Not a bad description from the victim; could be promising. Male, white, six-foot, late twenties early thirties, tattoo of a black bird on his neck. I'll get Tim to go over the database now on the tattoo, fingers crossed we might have a name before the day is out if he's offended before.'

TAKING THE ROOK

*D*anny Rook crouched down in the undergrowth and swatted away a rogue twig that had inconsiderately poked up his nose. He could feel the familiar tickle of a sneeze that was brewing deep in his nasal cavity. Not wanting his concealment to be revealed, he squeezed hard on either side of his nostrils with thumb and forefinger. His eyes watered waiting for the reflex to abate.

He had spent time on this one, knowing the reward would be well worth the effort. The old dear from the corner newsagents had boasted to anyone who would care to listen that her takings had tripled since the arrival of the film crews in Fallow Falls. He checked his watch. Today was her regular trip into town to visit the bank, pay in her pennies, and enjoy a spot of lunch with a friend. Only this time it wasn't pennies; it was pounds and lots of them. He had strategically placed a two-pound coin on the ground at the exact spot he needed her to stop. Old she might be, but he knew from experience she had eyes like a warehouse rat. His one and only foray into shoplifting had earned him three months' community service when she'd spotted him in her crummy little shop filling his Calvin Klein's with several Curly

Wurlies, half a dozen packets of Embassy fags, and two tins of Foster's lager.

Danny rocked on his heels, checking that the tension and spring in his legs would be enough to jump out on Ida, give her a dig in the face if she decided to resist him, and then snatch her bag. He peered out from behind the sandstone wall and checked the direction he knew she would take. Seeing a small figure ahead, he relaxed back into the shrubbery, waiting.

'Here she comes...' he half-sang, half-whispered to himself the closer she came to him. He was getting to be a bit of an expert at these types of job; he'd even earned himself a nickname with the bizzies who were investigating his crimes. He'd been given the monicker of 'Canal No. 5', although this job would be number six on this stretch of river so exchanging the 5 for a 6 somehow didn't have the same ring to it. He watched her approaching the spot.

Ida Barraclough, muffled up in a grey mohair coat, red scarf and a matching crochet beret with a black leather bag tucked under her arm, was oblivious to the imminent danger she was in. She bounced along the canal towpath, singing to herself. Drawing level with the sandstone wall that held a lifebuoy hooked in place by a sign giving instructions on its use, she paused to get her breath.

'Dearie me, I'm sure this path is getting longer every time I come this way,' she chunnered to herself. 'Ooh look, two quid...'

She bent down and tried to pick it up, but her gloved fingers were stubborn. She bit down on the wool weave of her middle finger and pulled off one glove with her teeth. Her gnarled fingers poked at the edges of the coin.

Danny took his opportunity. His brain screamed his cue.

Now...

He relished the almost painful burn in his thigh muscles as the adrenaline surged through them. He sprang into action at exactly the same time as the wire was slipped over his head. It caught around his throat, just as his outstretched arm, fingers reaching for the still oblivious Ida, clawed at thin air rather than at the bag he had so desperately coveted. He was savagely yanked backwards, the wire twisting and tightening around his neck, pulling him into his attacker.

'Well, if it isn't Danny Rook! I've been looking everywhere for you. Are you being a naughty boy again, Danny?' The voice was hard and firm against his ear, the heat from his assailant's breath burning his skin. 'We can't have that, can we?' The wire tightened another two turns on the wooden ends.

Danny's body writhed and jerked involuntarily, his feet kicked down hard onto the embankment, causing small stones to dislodged and trickle down towards the towpath. Spittle formed on his lips as the wire cut through his skin, warm blood soaking his layers of clothing. The garrotte wire tightened again with a further turn that was done slowly and with the utmost precision and enjoyment.

Little by little, Danny Rook, thief, addict, and all-round bad boy, was preparing to meet his maker.

In his final moments, he thought not of redemption or reflection on his sins, nor of the steak and kidney pie his missus had promised him for tea when he got home, but of the two hundred and fifty quid he had forked out for the family crest of a large black rook in flight across his neck, which by now had probably been separated from its wings by the maniac behind him with the Amazon Prime cheese cutter.

Contrary to the horror of Danny's demise, and with credit to his murderer, Ida was now gleefully popping a two-pound coin into her purse, still completely oblivious of her narrow escape. She turned in a circle and gave a little jig, an extra slice of Battenburg cake was now on the agenda due to the carelessness of another. 'See two pounds and pick it up and all day long you'll have good luck...' she sang as she went on her merry way.

Dottie watched Ida happily ambling along the towpath,

grateful that she had arrived in time to save her. 'If only you knew how true that was, Ida,' she whispered under her breath as she rifled through Danny's pockets until she found what she was looking for. Quickly stuffing the mobile phone into her own pocket, she checked the coast was clear before pushing his body down the embankment.

A nonchalant kick was all it took to roll him over the edge. She relished the splash his tubby form made as it hit the water. 'Bye bye "Canal No. 5"…' She laughed. 'Although give or take a few days, you definitely won't be smelling anything like that by the time they find you!'

Satisfied it was another job well done, Dottie checked the time and quickened her pace. If she took a shortcut, she'd make her lunch date with Murdoch Holmes in plenty of time. He would be the perfect alibi, not that she would ever need it.

Precision, attention to detail, and being forensically aware were just a few of her many attributes.

CAUGHT IN THE ACT

*A*bbey Towers was a veritable hive of activity. It was as though every star, actor, extra and member of the crew had been called to set to make up for lost time.

Clement had been cajoled into reopening his home to David Preece and his entourage, much to the chagrin of Fiona who was still firmly of the belief that their presence was bringing a host of bad luck to the house. He had spent time locked away in his study over the last few days rather than have to sit in the same room as her and listen to her constant whining. He tentatively opened the door and peeped out to see if the coast was clear.

'Clement Carlisle Gregory!'

Her voice had reached a pitch he had not experienced before; it screeched down the corridor, whistled around the entrance hall and finally settled on his delicate ears.

'Yes, dear…'

Fiona stood firm, hands on hips in what he knew was her fighting stance. 'I take it you're continuing with this nonsense?'

Clement nodded meekly. Anything for a quiet life was his motto. 'Yes, dear.'

'And the Halloween party? Are you still allowing them to use our home?' Her steely eyes bore into him.

'Yes, dear.'

'Even after what has happened with that actress woman? Have you no shame, no sense of respect for the dead?' She stopped abruptly, suddenly realising how stupid her barbed comment had been. Of course her husband had respect for the dead, after all, he was a man of the cloth. She changed tack. 'Look, darling, I'm all for doing whatever we can for St Barnabas Ealing, but carrying out all this for a new roof is just asking for trouble. You know I have the family sixth sense; I just know something is going to happen again.' She waited for his response, hoping her gentle plea would be heard.

She was to be disappointed.

'Fiona dear, I think you are taking this all out of proportion. It was very sad what happened to Miss Simon, but that is something the police are investigating. We can't pull out now, it's in the contract, and we could end up owing them thousands of pounds if we do.' He placed his hand on her arm. 'Let's just get this out of the way. I'm sure you'll enjoy the Halloween party if you put your mind to it, and then in a matter of days after that, they'll be gone.'

Fiona was not convinced, but she knew it was futile to argue with him. The one thing she was certain of was that she would not be attending the party under any circumstances. She had already booked a room at The Bell, Book and Candle in the village for the night.

Whatever was going to happen in Abbey Towers on All Hallows Eve would not include her.

∼

Millie sidled up to her new friend until they were touching

shoulders in order to keep their conversation just between themselves. 'Have you managed to have another snoop around?'

Olive nodded before making a dramatic stage whisper in return. 'Don't look now, but eyes to three o'clock…'

Millie furtively glanced towards the Abbey Towers staircase.

'That's nine o'clock, the other way, silly.' Olive rolled her eyes and sighed.

Millie changed direction, squinting into the distance along the corridor. She scratched an itch that her hessian costume had generated at the back of her neck. 'What am I looking at?'

'The door to the study; it's open. Look at the doll's house thingy in the bay window. It's the exact replica of this place.' Olive was beside herself with excitement. 'If we can get in there, we could have a nosey at it and see if it's got any of the secret passages. That would save us so much time if we knew where they all were and where they lead to.'

Millie was inclined to agree, but she had been thinking long and hard about this passage malarky. 'Remind me again why we want to find these passages and what we're looking for, or are we just being inquisitive with no end game?' She felt quite proud of that turn of phrase, as though she was starting to sound like a real detective. 'I mean we haven't seen anything that would indicate the tunnels, passages, or whatever you want to call them, have any link to anything that needs investigating.'

Ethel, overhearing their rather loud stage whispers, joined them. 'Fair point, Millie, but what about Alice? Didn't we say that secret room and possible passages might have something to do with her going missing? Maybe Dana's killer escaped that way, gosh, maybe they're even living in the secret rooms. And what about whoever was down there when Olive found the room?'

Millie had forgotten about Olive's near brush with death, or at least a brush with something other than a cobweb in the dark, and she still wasn't quite convinced that another entity had been down there with her. Imagination could do wonderful things in the throes of terror.

'I think Olive is right; we need to get in there and have a look at the doll's house. If you two block the doorway and cause a bit of a diversion, I can slip in and take some photographs of it. I can be in and out before you know it.' Ethel was excited at the prospect of having something concrete to help them in their endeavours.

'Ooh, brilliant idea.' Millie rummaged around in her pocket and pulled out her mobile phone. 'Here you go, I don't want to go in there in case I get caught, but you can use mine.' Her finger animatedly jabbed at the device. 'It's turned off at the moment because we were on set, but it still works fine.'

Ethel took it off her. 'Jeez, Millie, where d'you get this? It's off the bloody ark! It doesn't even have a camera!'

'It's a Nookie 3310, and I'll have you know it's the must-have model, too.' Indignant, Millie snatched back her mobile.

'*Nokia*, it's a Nokia, dear, and the only must-have model I'd be bothered with is Fabio Lanzoni. Oh my, did you ever see him on the book cover for *Rogue*? Actually, thinking of Fabio, perhaps nookie was the right word!' Ethel gave a naughty chuckle. 'It's okay, I've got my own phone, I'll use that.'

Keeping watch on the comings and goings of the film crew and other extras, Olive and Millie nonchalantly gossiped together, providing perfect cover for Ethel to slip through the open door. She quietly shut it behind her and tiptoed over to the diorama, camera at the ready. She carefully opened the front sections to reveal the inner workings and began squeezing off several shots.

'Excuse me, can I help you?'

Ethel froze, heart pounding she turned around. 'Oh dear, I… I…' she stammered, trying to find the right words that would both simultaneously explain and excuse her presence. 'I was just looking, it's so unusual and must have a lot of history to go with it.' She peered into one of the rooms, giving herself time to think. 'I love these little figures.'

Clement rose from his desk. 'You only had to ask, my dear. It is such a fascinating piece. It's actually nice to know someone else appreciates it too.'

Ethel stood like a deer caught in the headlights of a fast-approaching vehicle, her mind working ten to the dozen, trying to think of a suitable come back, when an idea suddenly formed. 'That is so kind of you. Actually, what I was wondering…'

Whilst Olive and Millie remained on guard, unaware that their friend had been caught in the act, Ethel was busy putting an exciting proposal to Archdeacon Clement Carlisle Gregory to help solve the disappearance of Alice.

One that she hoped he couldn't refuse.

HOCUS POCUS

'*I* don't think I like him very much.' Hilda sat watching the camera crew setting up for the next scene. She blew on the hot liquid in the polystyrene cup before taking a sip. 'Him, there.' All eyes followed her finger until they settled upon Gwilym. Oblivious to their interest, he continued to fiddle and fuss with the equipment, checking the dolly tracks and car and the angles his camera would take.

Clarissa shifted uncomfortably in her chair, trying and failing to find a way to sit down for more than ten seconds without destroying her already fragile nether regions with the coarseness of her costume. 'He's actually really nice, Hilda; he's very helpful, just a little bit of a loner, I think.'

'I'm with Hilda on this one,' Olive mumbled through a mouthful of custard creams. 'He's a bit of an odd ball; his attic is definitely a little bit dusty, don't you think?' She animatedly tapped the side of her own head to evidence Gwilym's perceived lack of mental agility.

Their conversation continued, with an observation of Gwilym's odd ways coming from Hilda. 'When they found Dana's body, I saw him at the side of the crowd, like he didn't want to be seen by anyone else but couldn't resist being there to watch. I swear he was smiling. When everyone else was in shock, he was grinning like a Cheshire Cat as though he was enjoying her grim death. Now that's not normal.'

Clarissa gave Gwilym another discreet once over. The last thing she wanted to do was make the poor man feel uncomfortable by having a tribe of gossiping old trouts giving him the eye. 'People react in different ways when they're in shock, Hilda, so give the guy a break – in fact you can't talk. Who was it who got a fit of the giggles when Kitty was kidnapped at Harmony Hollows?'

Hilda popped a mint imperial into her mouth and rolled it around with her tongue. 'That was different, how was I to know it was *actually* a serious kidnapping? I thought it was a joke.'

'That was a bit of a hairy time, wasn't it, girls!' Ethel, far from being horrified at the memory, scrunched up her nose and grinned, which in turn brought a twinkle to her eyes. 'Being so close to kicking the bucket actually made us feel so alive!'

Their animated reminiscing of their holiday at Harmony Hollows and their near-death experiences had Olive stunned. She sat open-mouthed, listening to them relate the tale of dastardly doings, murder and mayhem during an apparently innocent holiday stay at a budget Butlins style holiday camp. She was just about to interrogate them for more information when they were interrupted.

'Hello, ladies, how are we doing?' Annie Baines, clipboard in hand, warmly greeted them. 'I'm just doing the numbers for our Halloween party. It's going to be such a good night, we're even having a prize for the best costume, a voucher for Bolderwood Hall Hotel, so is it a tick or a cross for you, girls?'

The ladies, fully up for an evening of fun and a bit of their planned secretive snooping inside Abbey Towers, gleefully gave Annie five ticks, whilst throwing around ideas for their costumes. Annie listened on, amused at the bickering between them when one suggested a character that the other really wanted, and vice versa.

'Without causing offence, girls, when I first saw your head-shot photographs back at the office, I did think of the Sanderson Sisters from the film *Hocus Pocus*: you'd be perfect for that, but as there's five of you, I think that might cause a few problems.' Annie waited to see what their reaction would be.

'Ooh that sounds brilliant. Clarissa could be Winnifred, I'd be Sarah, and Millie could be Mary.' Ethel was already planning their costumes in her head.

'What about me and Olive?' Suitably miffed, Hilda pursed her lips and jutted out her chin. 'And why should you be the pretty one, Eth?'

Ethel chose to completely ignore that remark. 'Binx! You could be Binx the black cat, and Olive could be Billy Butcherson!' She was on a roll, her mind working ten to the dozen on how the five of them would look for the night. 'Oh come on, it'll be such fun.'

Clarissa had to agree: it beat the bog-standard witch costume. They would be themed in their costumes and hopefully stand a good chance of winning first prize. 'Great idea, Annie, thank you.'

Pleased that her suggestion had been taken in the manner she had intended it to be, rather than an insult, Annie gave them one of her winning smiles before she tucked her clipboard under her arm and made her way to the next group.

'Why am I always the bloke?' Olive sighed. 'Even as a kid I had to wear a beard and play Joseph in the nativity play because it was an all-girls school. It's me big feet, isn't it?' She attempted a half-hearted laugh.

'At least you're not someone's pussy...' Hilda giggled.

The ladies huddled closer together, desperate to keep their choice of Halloween costume from anyone who might eavesdrop and steal their fabulous idea. A freebie voucher for a fancy hotel like Bolderwood was to die for. Olive had already steered them in the right direction with a potential visit to 'Fancy Nancy's', a large fancy dress shop in Frampton Falls. They had planned the night in minute detail, with every 'i' dotted and every 't' crossed. They were leaving nothing to chance.

'That reminds me, getting away from playing dress-up for a minute, how did it go with the archdeacon?' Olive tipped her head in anticipation.

Ethel gave Clarissa a conspiratorial smile before she spoke.

'He's up for it, count him in…'

A DROP IN FAITH

*C*lement sat back in his comfy armchair, book in hand and propped his feet up on the old rectory pouffe. The brown leather had seen better days, scuffed and worn, but still serviceable, and the stuffing had left it more saggy than firm, a little like Fiona, but it went everywhere with him. Each time the bishop deigned to move him, his faithful pouffe was the first to be put on the removals van. It was the one thing he had that belonged to him and not the church.

Mesmerised by the flickering flames of the fire, he quickly abandoned any thought of indulging himself with his latest page-turner; his mind was far too active to focus on the pages. Carefully placing the bookmark at the last page he could remember reading, he closed the cover and exchanged the book for his glass of whisky. He glanced over at Fiona, wine glass in hand and nose in her own book. She had spoken very little to him since their exchange of words the previous day. He watched the shallow rise and fall of her chest, the slight tic she had at the corner of her mouth when she was concentrating and the tap, tap, tap of her nails drumming against the wine glass. 'Does this house really make you feel that uneasy, dear?'

She looked at him, a sneer touching her lips. 'Whatever gave the game away?' she sarcastically spat. 'From day one, Clement, from day one. I have hated living in this place from the first time I walked through that door.' She jabbed her finger animatedly in the direction of the main doors to Abbey Towers. 'It's rotten to the core, every square foot of it, but you can't see that.'

Clement wished he could agree with her; it would be so much easier to do so, and in the process pacify her, but in all good faith, he knew he didn't quite share the beliefs that his wife had. Granted, the creaks, groans and odd happenings at Abbey Towers occasionally spooked him, but as a man of God, he had to hold on to the teachings of the church. 'It's an old house, dear, and although I don't believe in ghosts and spectres, I do believe that energy, good or bad, has an impact not just on people, but on the fabric of buildings too, the bricks and mortar…' he paused to check that he still had her attention. Content that she was listening to him, he continued. 'I think they absorb energy, and because negative energy can be a strong emotion, if people don't hold the faith, it sometimes trumps good. Let's face it, Abbey Towers has had its fair share of dreadful happenings over the years.'

Fiona rose from her chair and refilled her glass from the open bottle of merlot in the drinks cabinet. She took a good slug, allowing the alcohol to warm her. 'Fair share! I think this mausoleum has had more than its fair share! How about a bit of devil worship here and there, several murders, and a missing bloody domestic to start with?'

Clement sighed loudly. There would be no reasoning with her, he had to admit defeat. 'It's not *Ninth Gate* with Johnny Depp running riot in our home, trying to summon the devil, dear. Often mental health issues, drugs, alcohol use, that sort of thing, can play a large part in those stories. Shall we just beg to differ? It's not worth us constantly bickering over.'

Fiona grunted and returned to her book. Feeling uncomfortable with the ensuing silence, Clement made a show of indifference by adding a few more logs to the fire and checking the time on the mantel clock before returning to his chair. He resumed his earlier position and closed his eyes, listening to the gentle 'tick, tock' from the antique Hermle piece.

He had, in a moment of weakness, agreed to join Ethel Tytherington and her lady friends on their 'adventure' around Abbey Towers on All Hallows Eve to look for clues into the disappearance of Alice. It was an agreement that had at first hearing seemed fun and informative, but once common sense had returned, he had very quickly begun to regret. He had to admit that the idea of secret rooms and tunnels would send any *Boy's Own* fan – which he had been since his dad had bought him a copy in the summer of 1965 – into raptures. The fact that he had discovered Fiona's intent to spend Halloween away from home had been the icing on the cake and had peaked his excitement to new heights. What better time to investigate the home he now realised he had never really known, whilst she was conveniently absent? But now, mulling over Ethel's proposition, he wondered, in view of his wife's concerns and if his own Christian beliefs were put into question, whether the investigation might risk awakening something that would be beyond his control.

POETIC JUSTICE

*A*ndy edged his way down the embankment to the canal and then cursed under his breath when he lost his footing and slid down the last few feet. He picked himself up and briskly rubbed his hands together.

'Six out of ten for that landing, Sarge.' Lucy grinned as she watched him saunter along the towpath, clearly hoping that she had been the only person to witness him landing on his arse at a murder scene.

Andy stood over the bloated body of Danny Rook. 'I take it the cause of death wasn't drowning, then?' He pointed to the deep cut across Rook's throat that now played host to duckweed and algae collected during his time submerged in the canal. He waited patiently for a response from the forensic pathologist who was still examining the body.

Bob Limpett, his face just visible from the hood of his white suit, stood up. He nodded his acknowledgement. 'There's been some type of garrote used on him, I'll know more when we get him back for the PM, but it won't have been quick. We need to establish the primary scene as soon as possible so we don't lose anything.' He handed an evidence bag to Andy. 'They found this on him. And just so you know, canal water does move. It's slow, but the opening and closing of locks, barges, boats, etc., all have an impact on the flow and where his body went in and where it was found.'

For some unknown reason, Andy wasn't inclined to feel any sort of sorrow or sadness for the victim this time. He stared longer than he should at the milky eyes and wrinkled fingertips, trying to feel something other than the apathy of life being so cheap that it was snuffed out so easily and so often. Rook had been given an interim identification from his driver's licence, but Andy already knew that he had a record longer than the arm of an inflatable Skydancer. 'Who found him?'

'A local woman on her way back from town; uniform over there has got all the details. Ida something or other. She has the newsagent shop in Fallow Falls and takes this route on a regular basis.'

'Sarge, look!' Lucy nudged Andy with her elbow. 'It's a bit mangled where the trauma is, but that's a bird tattoo on his neck. I think this is our suspect for the towpath robberies.'

Andy took a closer look, tracing the wings and beak of a blackbird in flight whilst estimating the height and age of the body. 'Yep, this is him alright.' He checked the contents of the sealed evidence bag and sighed. The initials **A.W.** embossed in gold print stood out on the dark brown leather of the wallet. 'And this is the evidence we need.'

Andy dropped his mobile phone on the desk and ran his hand through his hair, making it stand on end. 'They've found the primary murder site for Rook; there's a lot of blood evidence; forensics are at the scene now. A bicycle has been recovered too, hidden in nearby bushes.' A low murmur from his team ran around the room, each preparing themselves for tasks that would arise from forensic results.

Jack Finnigan handed Andy the search report for Rook's home. 'Everything we need to finalise the outstanding towpath robberies have been located, recovered and booked into crime exhibits. Still no sign of his mobile phone, though. His missus confirms he did have one, a silver iPhone 8. The number is in the report, but we're not getting anything back from it.'

Andy looked at the list. 'Our Danny was more of a magpie than a rook, he just couldn't part with the wallets and purses, could he?'

Lucy closed down the crime report on her screen. 'Trophies, I suppose, but at least we can link every job to him, so that's another serious crime wave solved. Murdoch is bound to be impressed; he'll give us time to breathe now and we can concentrate on the Dana Simon's case.'

Andy angled his mug at Lucy in an unspoken action for a fresh cup of coffee. She nodded, and handed her own empty mug to him. He savoured the current healthy status of the crime investigation board on the wall next to him. 'I definitely wouldn't want to be a prolific offender around here at the moment, that's for sure. Barney Lamb, Rutter and now Rook. Two pushing up daisies and one still drooling soup down his chin.' Andy had a way with words, but ones that would only be used in the sanctuary of their office. The last thing he needed was to be vocal with a throwaway comment and upset a grieving relative. Having said that, he was still amazed at the nonchalant way in which Rook's wife had taken his death. He could almost hear the fizz of the Lambrini bottle being opened in celebration once the fake tears had dried on her bronzed cheeks.

The clear-up rate for their office had been, in the words of Murdoch, 'phenomenal' in such a short space of time. Cashpoint thefts, house burglaries and now the towpath robberies all wiped from the board with just the crime reports to write off. The downside was they now had, in the same space of time, three murders and a serious assault on their hands, with no suspects.

'Whilst I'm on tea duty, Luce, can you send out an email to the whole team, give them a heads-up to a briefing tomorrow, 2pm in this office...?'

Andy was not one for conspiracy theories and he didn't believe in plain old-fashioned coincidences, particularly when it involved three stiffs occupying trays 13, 19 and 6 at the mortuary. If he didn't know better, he would think someone, somewhere, was assisting Winterbridge CID with their clear-up rates whilst dishing out some rather ultimate poetic justice.

FIVE THINGS

*E*thel tottered down the road as fast as her little booteed feet would carry her, the carrier bag containing tasty snacks and the latest edition of the *Winterbottom News*, slapping wildly against her thigh with the momentum of her haste. 'Make way, make way, I have important news…' she burst breathlessly through the doors of the Bell, Book and Candle, almost knocking poor Hazel over in the process. Belying her age, she jumped the two steps to the bar area in one leap to reach her friends who were happily enjoying a cream tea.

'Good gracious, Ethel,' Clarissa dropped her fork. It rattled loudly on the plate, skittering a blob of jam and a sultana across the table. 'What on earth is the matter?'

'There's been another murder!' Ethel bent forward, hands on hips, short gasps of breath showing her physical exertion. 'And Ida Barraclough found the body!'

Scones and jam forgotten, exclamations of surprise, delight and sheer nosiness filled the snug as they chattered animatedly between themselves.

'Girls, girls, we can't all talk at once…!' Clarissa was keen to bring everyone into line. 'Let's hear what Ethel has to say first, and then we'll take it from there.' She brushed several crumbs from her jumper and waited, all ears.

Ethel preened with delight before launching into the story as related to her by none other than Ida Barraclough herself. She remembered to give dramatic pause between sentences and to emphasise certain words to heighten the chills she knew her friends must be feeling, as she narrated the story that was now one according to Ethel Tytherington, with lots of added artistic licence and gory details thrown in, rather than Ida's original offering. 'So the police arrived, it was Andy by all accounts; it's absolute chaos down there. Ida heard them say it was the second man known to the police to kick the bucket in as many days. It looks like we've got a serial killer in our midst, girls, as well as a missing cleaner!'

Clarissa pursed her lips in delight. 'That settles it! We'll put Alice to one side for now, after all, there have been apparent sightings of her, and I put it to the vote that we do some snooping into Dana's murder and see if it's connected to these other two.' She grabbed her notebook from her handbag and, pencil poised, began to delegate. 'Ethel, I'll leave it to you to see what you can find out about the two ne'er-do-well's that have croaked it, and if they have any links with Dana or the film lot. Take Millie with you for backup.'

Millie jiggled with excitement, her eyes twinkling in anticipation.

'Hilda, you can stay with me and we'll write down everything we know so far, just so we don't get muddled up.' Clarissa carefully headed four columns in capital letters, her pen nib pressing firmly on the lined paper.

VICTIM – MODUS OPERANDI – SUSPECTS – SCENE

On the first line she carefully penned Dana Simon's name. The second line went to 'Unknown naughty man 1' and the third line to 'Unknown naughty man 2'. The suspects column remained blank.

Hilda peered over her shoulder. 'Well, that's not a very good start, is it?' she huffed. 'How can we be great amateur sleuths if we haven't even got one suspect? You need to put that Dottie down, she's definitely a bit suspicious, and you can add that awful man Gwendoline too.'

Millie giggled. 'It's Gwilym, his name is Gwilym, it's Welsh, and we can't just put people down as suspects for something as serious as murder just because you don't like them or have a funny feeling.'

'Oh my goodness, that's just brought back a memory! I had a funny feeling once, on my wedding night...' Ethel slapped her thigh like a pantomime prince and gave a throaty laugh.

'Ethel!!' Clarissa was mortified, but also slightly relieved that her friend was beginning to act like her old saucy self again.

Olive sat in silence, her gaze navigating between Clarissa and Ethel, from Ethel to Millie and then to Hilda. Teaming up with this crew of fun-loving women had seemed like such a good idea to begin with, but now she was seriously starting to doubt her decision. Being used to murder and mayhem might be their kettle of fish, but the more she thought about it, the more she was convinced that anything they got up to wouldn't end well, particularly if she had anything to do with it as the newcomer. 'I know I'm new to our little group, so forgive me if I'm being too forward, but in all honesty, we don't have anything at all, do we? We're just playing games with gossip.'

Ethel riled slightly. 'We've got three dead bodies.' She counted that as number one on her finger. 'We've got a missing woman.' That went down as finger number two. 'We know there's dark history to Abbey Towers and the village.' She counted her third finger. 'And lastly we know there's secret rooms and possible passages at the Towers.' Her little finger was subjected to the count whilst she paused thinking. 'Oh, and we've got photographs of that miniature house which could give us leads.' Ethel stared at her hand, aware that only her thumb was remaining for the count. 'So you see, we've got five things.' She jiggled her hand at Olive, fingers spread in a challenging fashion.

Olive wasn't convinced. 'We've got absolutely sweet Felicity Arkwright girls! What we've got is five nothings, five zeros, zilch – none of them link. We don't even know who the last two victims are, or if they have anything to do with the Towers or Dana.' She wiped her chin with a paper napkin. 'I think we should just concentrate on having a bit of fun with the secret passages, look for Alice, and leave the murder stuff to the professionals.' She sat back, pleased that she hadn't let another F-bomb slip from her lips. Being a barmaid in some of the roughest beer houses known to dockers and steelworkers alike for more years than she cared to remember, had gifted her with a choice 'blue tinged' vocabulary that frequently slipped through her acceptable social filter.

'And that's where we're going to start our investigation, as I've just said,' Ethel continued. 'We'll see if they're linked and take it from there. In the meantime, Hilda, take Olive with you and see if you can find anything on this Gwilym. if you're so intent on him being suspicious.' She gave Olive a side-eyed glance and grinned. 'And if your much-mentioned mate *Felicity* hasn't got anything better to do, perhaps she'd like to come along for the ride too!'

Olive at least has had the decency to blush slightly whilst making a mental note to consider other options to replace the original F-bomb cuss and her much used alternative of 'sweet FA'.

Clarissa was a little unsure on their new friend's motive for putting a spanner in the works. She stared longer than necessary at Olive. Their previous adventures had taught them that nobody should ever be discounted for being capable of doing dark deeds.

Her pen hovered over the 'Suspects' column as she wondered if Olive Auldwrinkle was just a bit of a scaredy cat, or whether she could indeed be someone they should add to their list.

TWO GO HUNTING

*A*bbey Towers had at last fallen silent.

An ethereal mist undulated across the vast grounds, snaking towards the folly, which was bathed in a pale light from the waning moon. Here and there, its eerie glow picked out the metal of the studio dolly tracks that were settled on the grass, making them glisten as though wet, although no rain had fallen.

Gwilym, shrouded by the boundary hedges, stood watch. The building, in all its glory, still fascinated and terrified him. He shivered and pulled up the zip on his jacket so that it met his scarf. It had been a long day: filming had been fraught with star temperaments causing drama and unavoidable technical hitches. After the last key grip had departed through the main gates, he had been on target to follow him, yearning for a hot shower and something to eat, but Abbey Towers had other ideas for him.

Gwilym watched, mesmerised by the mist as it took on a life of its own, swirling and dancing in the dusk, its tendrils snaking out to brush against shrubs, fountains and statues that now with its touch, almost glowed through the darkness.

'Master of my nightmares...' he whispered to himself as he broke cover and made his way across the grounds, keeping as much as he could to the parts that would afford him cover. Abbey Towers had many windows from which he could be seen if he wasn't careful. He lumbered across the final expanse of ground and disappeared down the stone steps and into the boiler room.

Clumsily feeling his way around, he finally found what he was looking for. The sound from under his feet from the loose floorboard told him he was in the right place, just as he remembered. He knelt down and, with his fingers splayed, he took a deep breath and pushed on the panel of the store cupboard. A soft click broke the heavy silence as the section above swung open revealing a second, hidden room.

Gwilym took one last look around before quickly disappearing inside.

Dexter 'Dexy' Clapton squeezed his nimble frame through the open door and gave himself a few seconds for his eyes to adjust to the darkness. He had been astounded as to how easy it had been to get in. When he was sure he'd made it into the basement of Abbey Towers without being seen, he clicked the button on his torch. A weak beam of light spanned the room.

Cursing, he hit the rubber body of the device twice in the palm of his hand, hoping to elicit a little more power from the fading batteries. 'Bloody hell, Marge!' he berated his wife under his breath. The old bat had clearly been using it when insomnia struck to entertain herself with shadow rabbits on the ceiling of their two-up, two-down council house in the wee small hours. He'd be having words with her when he got home; he'd lost track of how many times he'd told her not to touch the tools of his trade, but did she listen? Hell no! He might as well talk to the wall he was standing in front of.

The tragic passing of his old mucker, Barney Lamb, had left a gap in the market which Dexy was only too happy to step into, and Abbey Towers had been one of the rare jobs they had earmarked to do together. He was pretty confident he could carry it off on his own, but he was working blind as Mutton had taken all the inside info on the place with him to his grave. That was the trouble with honour amongst thieves: it rarely got shared until the last minute, and Mutton's last minute had been very final.

The torch light scanned the walls, forcing Dexy to chunner under his breath. A dead end, a room going nowhere, he couldn't even steal the copper from the boiler in the corner to make a fast buck. He should have known it would be too simple to just walk in through an open door; he should have stuck to his speciality of scamming old dears out of their jewellery and life-savings. He slumped against the cupboard in the corner, pausing to give himself time to think.

The movement was sudden and unexpected. One minute he was propped up against an old cabinet, the next he was on his arse in another room.

'Hey, Dexy lad, you're in…' He laughed to himself.

Picking himself up from the stone flooring and not caring how he had arrived in the room or how he would get out, he gingerly made his way further inside, searching for a means into the house itself. His torch picked out an old door set in the far wall, its large, rusted hinges and fractured wood providing an air of mystery. A second door was barely noticeable in the corner of the wall closest to him. He played *eeny meeny miny moe* in his head before plumping for the first door. It had a grandeur about it, as though it would lead to the treasures he was seeking. He adjusted his balaclava and waited, listening for anything that could be on the other side.

A high-pitched whine suddenly filled his left ear, accompanied by a piercing whistle in his right ear. 'You're havin' a laugh…' he spat, as he poked his fingers under his balaclava and tried to adjust his hearing aids. Not content with Marge running his torch battery flat chasing rabbits, he now realised that he had forgotten to charge his NHS-supplied Danalogic DNs.

Ripping them out of his ears to alleviate the painful sound, he stuffed them in his trouser pocket. Now he was not only working half blind, but also completely deaf. If the door opened and failed to yield anything immediately worthwhile, he had made the executive decision to jack it in for the night and return when he had at least one ear that was useful to him, and four AA batteries to fuel his trusty torch.

He tentatively pushed open the door.

SACRIFICIAL LAMB

The Collector, eyes closed, inhaled deeply. The dampness of stone, the odour of earth and the mustiness of relics and antiquities never failed to awaken the spirit. The sacrificial room vault of Black Abbey Towers, set in the deepest part of the building, was a sensory overload of ungodliness.

The heavy robes that hung from his shoulders swept along the tiled floor, throwing up decades of dust and debris across the ornate pentagram, as each wall lantern was lit, one by one, with a flaming torch.

'*In nomine Dei, Nostri Satanas Luciferi excelsi…*' he rasped as the glow flickered in a rhythmic pattern across the domed ceiling, bringing life to each quarter of his sanctuary.

His haunting chant echoed around the vast, empty room as light began to bathe the darkest corners. He stood proud in the centre of the pentagram, breath almost stilled, heartbeat barely perceptible. His mentor looked on, a mummified version of Calduggan Wraithe, reclined and regal on the Devil's Chair, his life having been lost more than a century ago.

The Collector held out his arms, beseeching an unseen benefactor. 'Grant me the indulgences of which I speak, bring to me the sacrifice so that I may serve you.' The lust for death had returned to him, and he was slowly being driven mad by a desire that required immediate fulfilment.

Creek...

The sudden sound of the entrance door being opened, which under other circumstances might have gone unheard, amplified itself within the confines of the room, bouncing from each curved wall. He waited with bated breath, reassured that there would be no hunt required on this eventide.

This time the prey had delivered itself.

A chilling, low hiss preceded his welcome. 'Will you walk into my parlour said the spider to the fly...' he growled.

And as if accepting the invitation, the prey willingly entered the room.

The figure standing in front of Dexy was lightning fast. He felt the blow before he saw it. It spun his head sharply to one side; his jaw cracked under the pressure, radiating an agonising pain across his face. He slumped to the ground, moaning softly, tasting the first gush of warm, metallic blood in his mouth that soaked into his balaclava. Stunned and slipping in and out of consciousness, hands were wrapped around Dexy's ankles as he was dragged across the tiled floor. His body slithered from side to side with the momentum until he was dropped in perfect alignment with the pentagon. His assailant was speaking, but he could hear no words, the flickering flames of the wall sconces adding to the horror that was being played out before him.

'Please, I'm sorry, don't ...' he wailed as best as his broken jaw would allow him. Blood frothed from his mouth making his terrified words garbled.

He watched as the hooded figure stood over him, a ceremonial dagger in hand that was swiftly and with perfect precision brought down with brutal force to pierce Dexy's heart.

Dexy didn't feel any pain at first, apart from a jarring thud to his ribcage, which gave him false hope that the knife had missed. A seeping coldness then swept over him as he gurgled and moaned, his staccato breath wracking his body. He reached out with his hand, trying with his last ounce of fading strength to grip the handle of the dagger, only to touch the gloved hand of his killer. The blade was savagely forced down to the hilt and held there, the eyes of The Collector holding his own, as though searching for the final image on a dying man's reflection.

'Up jumped the cunning spider and fiercely held him fast,' his assailant hissed. 'And dragged him up the winding stair into his dismal den…'

In the quiet that followed Dexter Clapton's last breath, and once content all life had expired, The Collector began the next part of the ritual.

MEMORIES

*D*ottie's hand ran the full length of Wick's back, which in turn encouraged him to stretch out and elongate himself. He slid down the back of the sofa and wedged himself into the boucle cushion, purring loudly. She continued to stroke him, distracted by her thoughts.

'What a ridiculous time of the morning to be awake, hey, Wick?' Dottie frequently had bouts of insomnia where her secrets would invade her dreams, but this time it had been quite exceptional. This time, instead of her psychological safety net waking her just before she reached the locked door, her hand had touched the cool metal of the handle and she had opened it. She had then been forced to relive each painful second in vivid detail, a cinematographic masterpiece that should never have reached the big screen, finally forcing her to wake.

Dottie shuddered, an emotional sob catching in her throat. She savagely wiped away the tear that had trickled down her cheek with the heel of her hand. Dottie didn't do emotion, Dottie didn't do weeping and wailing, and Dottie most certainly didn't do guilt. But she did do regret.

That was her Achilles heel.

The small box that she had gently and reverently laid on her knee was a constant reminder of that. She closed the lid, not wanting to block the memory, but to alleviate some of the pain she still felt after all these years. Having had the misfortune that very morning at Abbey Towers to recognise the instigator of that pain and remember the choices she had subsequently been forced to make, had brought fresh torment to her heart.

'Right, this will never do, time to get back on track if I'm to make amends and atone myself.' She placed her treasured box back into the cupboard, kissed her fingers, and softly placed them on the lid before closing the door.

Wick followed her as she made her way into the kitchen, weaving in and out of her legs in the hope that food would follow. 'Yes, yes I get the hint, buddy...' She placed the small metal dish on the mat for him. 'Right, tea and toast for me, see you back in there when you've finished.'

Her slippers tapped across the tiled floor as she transported her breakfast on a small tray back to her cosy morning room. Making herself comfortable in front of the fire, she pulled out her special file and, with pen poised, began making notes between small nibbles of toast.

'I'm looking forward to this one, he's been quite the career criminal...' She picked up her highlighter pen and struck a line through a name on the suspects' file she had photographed in Murdoch's office. 'Eliminate him, and the life savings and family heirlooms of the elderly in Fallow Falls and beyond will remain safe.' She chuckled. Her keen observations on her target had not been wasted, she had devised and planned quite a special death for him, based on his predicted movements.

The florescent yellow stripe that ran over the name was stark against the white paper and gave Dottie a feeling of order. She liked things to be orderly, to be neat, and to be in place.

It was just a pity that Dexter Clapton was going to disappoint her.

Gwilym slammed the front door shut and jacked his rucksack onto his back. He rubbed his eyes with his bunched-up fists, cursing the late hour he had returned home from his jaunt at Abbey Towers. The morning was bright and crisp, which only served to make his eyes sting as he sauntered down the path on his way to work. As he blinked rapidly, trying to clear them, in his peripheral vision he caught a fleeting glimpse of movement in the trees.

'Hello, can I help you?' He felt quite stupid to be shouting out to what could just be a breeze ruffling branches and autumn leaves, but over the last few days in his comings and goings from his cottage, he had experienced a feeling of being watched. He licked his finger and stuck it in the air. The morning was still; not a breath of wind to be had. He edged closer to the fence line and peered into the trees. Everything had fallen still once again. He rubbed his eyes for a second time and gave a cursory look. There was nothing untoward.

'I must be losing the plot...' he murmured to himself as he set off at a brisk pace on the route for Abbey Towers for the second time in less than eight hours. His little foray into the depths of the building through old haunts the previous night had yielded some surprises, but not enough to satisfy his curiosity. He was sure there was still so much to Abbey Towers that he had yet to discover.

He just needed more time.

FANCY NANCY'S

The Four Wrinkled Dears plus one sat patiently together in the little shelter that resembled a hobbit house. The peaked roof, grey shingles and wooden walls played host to two small benches either side that were now currently cosseting their respective bottoms. A slightly skewed glass-fronted cabinet had been hung on the wall, it's sage-green paint, chipped and peeling, had seen better days, but it complimented the rustic feel of the little bus shelter. It was stuffed full of paperback books, some old, some new, some curled and bent, and some with missing pages. The hand-painted sign above announced, 'Book Swap'.

Hilda stamped her feet. The cold was beginning to seep through the soles of her boots to grip her toes. 'How much longer before the bus comes?'

Four faces turned simultaneously and stared at her.

'What? I'm just asking when it's coming. I'm cold,' she huffed.

'Hilda, love, it's the fourteenth time you've asked. If you carry on like this, can we expect twenty-two "are we there yets?" from you when we get on the damned thing?' Clarissa, her patience wearing thin, tried her hardest not to sound too mean and snappy. She hadn't slept well the night before, partly due to Ethel's warthog snoring from the adjoining single bed, and was now beginning to feel the effects the lack of slumber could have on a woman of her advancing years. Her head felt like cotton wool and her eyes wouldn't stop watering.

'Wait no longer, Ms Jones, our chariot has arrived!' Ethel jumped to her feet, popped her head out of the shelter and stuck out her umbrella. The bus, obeying her command, pulled into the kerb. The gentle hiss of the pneumatic doors opening signalled that they were allowing the ladies entry. Clambering on, they ambled their way along the aisle to take their seats, bumping from side to side as the bus started its journey before they had a chance to sit down. Reorganising themselves, they finally sat in silence to allow Clarissa to rest her eyes whilst the bus bounced along country lanes that proudly displayed the orange, reds and browns of autumn colours on the trees.

Twenty minutes later, they had reached their destination.

'Wakey, wakey, 'Rissa.' Ethel gently nudged her friend to bring her back to the land of the living. 'Here we are, ladies, Frampton Falls. Don't forget your bits and bobs. Millie, can you grab my umbrella...' She waved them off the bus.

'Jeez, Eth, who died and made you the boss?' Hilda harrumphed in annoyance. 'I'm not a ruddy cow that needs herding.'

Ethel chose to ignore Hilda's barbed comment. She continued to gather her friends together and chivvy them across the road and through the little ginnel that led to the town centre, following Olive's tour-guide instructions as they went.

'Here we go...' Olive stood to one side and eagerly presented another cobbled entry that was tightly enclosed by the walls of shops either side.

Being careful not to trip, slip or slide on the shiny stones, the ladies made their way to a lopsided, weatherbeaten door ahead of them. The bull's-eye window glass was lit by twinkling fairy lights and bright coloured fabrics hung on rustic ladders. A selection of false noses, elf ears and plastic teeth were artistically scattered on a shelf. The sign above the window, decorated with red toadstools, witches brooms, black cats and bats, welcomed them to Fancy Nancy's.

Millie pressed her face and hands against the window, in awe of the magical little shop. 'Ooh, this is so exciting.' She wrinkled up her nose and hunched her shoulders in delight.

Olive pushed open the door, allowing the bell to loudly herald their arrival. One by one they fell inside the quaint shop, pushing each other to claim space to move more freely.

'Morning, ladies, and welcome to Fancy Nancy's! I'm Nancy, so anything I can do to assist you, just holler.' The young woman with mesmerising green eyes and a shock of jet-black hair gave them a warm smile from behind the counter. The numerous beaded bangles on her wrist jangled and clattered together, a strange symphony of sound.

Hilda pushed herself to the front, eager to place her order. 'We're going to a fancy dress party and would like to be the Anderson Shelters, please.' She thought for a moment. 'Well, not me personally. I've got to be a cat.' She curled up her top lip and gave Ethel a sneer.

Clarissa quickly intervened. 'It's the Sanderson Sisters, please. We definitely don't want to be air raid shelters!' She stood behind Hilda, silently mouthing the word 'sorry', whilst indicating with a twirling finger that not all the bats had made it home to Hilda's belfry. 'We're hoping you might have the costumes for them, a black cat costume for Hilda here, and Olive is going to be Billy Butcherson.'

Nancy thought for a moment, biting down on her bottom lip as she mentally ran through her stock list. 'Mmm... now that's quite a tall order so close to Halloween, but let me see what I can cobble together for you.' Her voice tapered off as she made her way into the back of the shop. 'Just take a seat, ladies, I'll be with you in a minute.'

They could hear coat hangers being swept along metal rails and drawers being opened and closed. Nancy eventually bowled through the curtains, her arms full of cellophane-draped costumes. 'Here we go...'

Twenty minutes later after much fussing, huffing and puffing, the ladies were party ready. Nancy stood back to admire her customers. 'Even if I say so myself, you're all marvellous and truly look the part.'

Clarissa, Ethel, Millie and Olive were beside themselves with excitement as they admired their reflections in the floor-to-ceiling mirrors.

'You'll have to droop your face to one side, Millie, just like Mary does in the film.' Ethel ran her fingers down the long blonde wig she was wearing. 'Although 'Rissa won't have to bother with Winnifred's false teeth, will you, dear? You've got a perfect set of your own!' She chortled loudly, making rabbit-teeth noises as she swished her burgundy skirt in a circle.

'Hold on, where's Hilda?' Clarissa began to check behind the racks of clothes dotted around the shop.

'I'm here...' the muffled voice came from the corner near the changing cubicles. Two sad eyes peeped out from an explosion of black fur, making her almost impossible to see against the black-curtained backdrop. 'I'm hot, it smells in here, and I keep falling over its appendage. Nobody told me I was going to be a boy cat. I can't be dragging a percy pecker across the dance floor,' Hilda wailed as she stepped forward. 'Look...' She grabbed the offending piece in her hand and twirled it around like a rotor blade on a helicopter. 'It's bloody huge!'

'Oh dear...' Ethel howled with laughter. 'It's on back to front. You've got the costume on the wrong way round. That's the *tail*, Hilda!'

AFTERMATH

'Who found him?' David Preece closed his eyes and mentally prayed to anyone, God or otherwise, to save him from yet another disaster.

Annie, the colour having barely returned to her cheeks, swallowed hard before she replied. 'On site security. They were doing a perimeter check. It looks like he slipped from the window above and impaled himself on those spiked bits on top of the railings.' She pulled a face and impulsively shrugged her shoulders up to her ears at the thought of one of the large decorative spears piercing her own chest. 'He was just lying face down on it, sort of dangling.' She inhaled deeply again, trying to push down the nausea she was feeling, and wishing she hadn't gone to see what the commotion had been. It was a sight she would never forget.

'Do we know who he is?' He was keeping his fingers crossed that it wasn't another member of the cast or his production team.

As if reading his mind, Annie was ready to reassure him. 'No, definitely not one of ours. The police are here now, but talk is he's known to them, so whatever his reason for being here, it definitely wouldn't have been legal.' She gave David the call sheets for the day, her hand shaking so much the paperwork trembled in unison. 'The back section of Abbey Towers is cordoned off, but they've allowed us to keep our bit open. I've spoken to Gibson, and they've rescheduled some of the scenes, so this is what we'll be doing today.' She paused, waiting for his response. 'Oh no, shoot me now! It's them again...'

David looked to where Annie's focus had been diverted to, taking in the five ladies, in scene costumes, marching with purpose towards them. Annie let out a loud groan.

'It's okay, I'll deal with them.' She angled herself towards Clarissa and friends to give David the opportunity to slip away quietly. 'Ladies, how lovely to see you. You should be in the waiting area. Is anything wrong?'

Ethel pushed through so that she led from the front, eager to be the first to speak, leaving Clarissa in her wake and still showing the strain of having a costume that sandpapered her nether regions with every uncomfortable step she took. 'We heard there's been another murder!' Ethel had decided to get straight down to business, there being no point in prevaricating and wasting time.

Annie was aghast. 'Who told you that? There is nothing to indicate that what has happened is anything but an accident, Ethel.' She clapped her hands together like a school teacher. 'Come on quickly; let's get you back. You'll be due on set shortly.'

A clamour of voices from the five ladies posing question after question followed her as she set off across the undulating lawn with them in tow, very much the Pied Piper as she led them back to the background actors' tent. 'Right, get yourselves a cuppa and no more snooping, please. If there's anything for you to know, I'll be the first to break the news, okay?'

Five disappointed faces reluctantly nodded their agreement. Annie was under no illusion that as soon as her back was turned, they'd be up to something. Just what, she didn't know, but they hadn't nicknamed them the Meddlesome Maidens for nothing.

~

Dottie stood watching for longer than was really necessary, making her aware that any actions that appeared to be out of the ordinary would highlight her as being a bit dodgy. The last thing she needed would be people, and by 'people' she really meant the quirky quintet headed up by Clarissa Montgomery, pointing their fingers at her. As charming and funny as they were, she was in no doubt that their talent for sniffing out suspicious activity could be her downfall if they got too close to the truth.

She seamlessly blended in with the rest of the crew who were still finding difficulty in drawing themselves away from the scene that was playing out in front of them. The body was in the process of being photographed and their presence and curiosity showed that there was no dignity in death.

Dexter Clapton had become a macabre sideshow for his uninvited audience.

Dottie bit down hard on her bottom lip, a range of emotions sweeping over her: anger that Clapton had slipped through her fingers, annoyance that his death at the hands of someone else could throw her plans into disarray, and a sense of unease because, after all, if she hadn't exterminated him, who the hell had?

She knew with certainty that his death hadn't been the accident it had been staged to look like, and she had a pretty good idea who was responsible, but proving it was going to be another matter. She would have to call upon all her years of surveillance training for this one, but if she played her cards right, Fallow Falls and the surrounding villages would reap the benefits. Her target would not only be brought to justice, but every little service to the community that Dottie herself had so selflessly carried out, would be attributed to them.

She gave herself a little mental curtsy for her endless empathy and sense of duty, which in turn made her snort with laughter.

She felt her lip curl into a sneer as she watched Dexter being lifted from the railings, the spikes still in situ through his chest having been cut to preserve evidence, with the unzipped body bag waiting for him. Whoever had been the perpetrator of his demise had also robbed her of quite a delicious moment and they would have to pay heavily for that.

'Dottie, they're ready for you on set…'

Startled out of her reverie, Dottie caught herself, quickly masking any facial expression that was not the norm for her. Her face softened into a smile, the harshness of darker thoughts being pushed away. 'Mark! I'm so sorry I was miles away.' She jerked her head towards the boiler room railings and Dexter. 'Now he's finished "hanging" around, we can get back to work, hey?'

Mark's eyes widened in astonishment. 'That's not like you, Dottie, you're all heart there.' He laughed. 'First Dana and now this. I'm beginning to wonder if any of us are safe; there's rumour that it wasn't an accident.'

Dottie smiled, taking in the gentle giant standing beside her. She patted him on the arm like a doting grandmother. 'Oh don't you worry, dear, no harm will come to you, old Dottie here will make sure of that!'

Mark, overcome by her sweet warmth looked down on the diminutive lady with the remarkable rugby-player-size calves and thighs. He was in no doubt that with her stunt skills, fitness and agility she could more than handle herself, but to be *his* protector was a bit of a stretch of the imagination. 'I think it'll be me looking after you, Dottie, and I promise I'll do a better job than I did with Dana!'

She gave a knowing smile and tapped the side of her nose. 'I'm sure you will, Mark, I'm sure you will…'

UP IN FLAMES

*I*f the doors to the incident room hadn't been fitted with a pneumatic silent close system, Andy would have relished the idea of slamming them to evidence his current mood. As it was, he had to make do with their soft hiss and his own voice to announce his arrival.

'Right, troops, settle down...' he snapped as he slapped the file onto his desk. He waited until all conversation had abated. 'Dexter "Dexy" Clapton.' He pinned a custody photo of Dexy on the board, alongside the ones for Rook and Lamb. 'If I didn't know better, I'd say we've got some sort of vigilante running riot in the county.'

'Well, if there is, and we find them, can I be the first to buy them a pint?' Jack mumbled through a mouthful of biscuit, spluttering crumbs across his desk before regaling them with a loud guffaw of laughter which also amused the rest of the team.

'Okay, folks, enough of the jokes. We've got a "did he fall or was he pushed" scene at the moment; we're treating it as a suspicious death until the evidence tells us otherwise. Forensics are pretty sure the chest wound doesn't match the railing spikes he was found on, so that's our first piece of evidence to rule in or out. Where are we up to on that, Lucy?'

'Clapton is currently en route to the mortuary with his special body piercings still intact. I believe Winterbridge fire service had a field day cutting through those railings; they didn't give up their hold easily.' Lucy began to hand out the intelligence sheets to the team.

Andy nodded his appreciation. 'Right, Clapton had his usual "working" kit on him,' he gave air quotes with his fingers. 'So we can take it that he was at Abbey Towers for nefarious reasons and not working for Just Eat delivering a late-night pepperoni pizza and a bottle of Diet Coke.'

Lucy ticked off the list of actions the Clapton case would now need to be allocated out. She was pretty used to their team being involved in several murders at the same time, but never one where all the victims, bar Dana Simon, had been known to them as prolific offenders. Maybe Andy was right and someone *was* giving them a helping hand with their crime stats.

'The scene is still being processed, particularly upstairs. The open window is on the first-floor landing, so I want to know asap if any fingerprints are lifted from that area.' Andy took a sip of water. 'Jack, can you start the team interviews? I want the night security pinned down on this one. What time did he do his regular perimeter checks, and where are they logged? They need to fit in with the time of death once Bob has completed the post-mortem. If they don't, I want to know why.' He looked around the room to satisfy himself that he had covered every base and everyone had a task. He tensed his shoulders and exhaled loudly; the constant ringing of his desk phone was beginning to annoy him. 'Lucy, will you answer that for me, please.'

Lucy obliged, turning her back on him whilst she listened. 'Ah yes, of course. I'll just put him on.' She held out the receiver. 'Sarge, it's for you. It's Clement Gregory from Abbey Towers, there's been another interference with the miniature house.'

~

Clement sat deep in thought at his study desk. His comforting go-to habit of his fingers shaped like a steeple, tapped a rhythm on his bottom lip. Eventually he spoke. 'I don't know what's happening here, detective. Perhaps my wife was right all along and bringing in these people has set off a chain of events.'

Andy shifted uncomfortably in his chair. 'Well, what we do know is that someone is replicating murder scenes utilising your diorama, sir.' He was loathe to confirm Clapton's death as a murder before the PM results were in, but he had no doubt in his mind that this was exactly what they were dealing with. 'They're playing a very dangerous game.' He gave Lucy a nod for her to continue the conversation.

The diorama, backlit by sunshine from the large window, had the front open where Clement had revealed to them the return of the man in the tweed jacket and clipboard. The figure had been placed by the window that overlooked the metal railings leading down to the boiler room. Perfect in every small detail. Lucy had marvelled at how accurate the ornamental railings had been replicated, even down to the miniature body that was draped across it. 'Did you hear anything at all last night, Mr Gregory, or did you notice anything had been disturbed?'

Clement shook his head. 'No, we slept the sleep of the dead last night – both of us, which is very unusual. I didn't even notice the window was open, but that's a section of the bedrooms that we rarely venture to.' He rubbed at his temples as he cast his mind back to that morning's routine. 'I came downstairs, Fiona went to make breakfast, and I came in here to do a little ecclesiastical work before eating – and that's when I saw it: it was back. The awful little man with the clipboard.'

Lucy stood up and using her pen, angled the figure to get a better look. 'Where did you leave it last time in the diorama after our forensics had looked at it?'

Clement's eyes widened and a flush of colour rushed to his cheeks. 'That's the point – I didn't. I got rid of it; I threw it on the fire in the library.' He paused for dramatic effect. 'I stood and watched it burn!'

HEDGING IT

'Oh my! Did you hear that?' Ethel could hardly contain her excitement. Her head bobbed up over the windowsill that led to Clement Gregory's study.

'For goodness' sake, woman, keep your head down!' grunted Clarissa as she bopped Ethel on the head with her hand and pushed her back down into the shrubbery. 'The window might be open only an inch or two, but they can still hear you!'

A loud rustling behind her gave way to a whispered squeal. 'Ouch! Mind my fingers,' Hilda indignantly spat at Millie. 'You've just trodden on them with your huge trotters!'

Olive sat with her knees up to her chin in the undergrowth, very quickly regretting Ethel's idea to listen in on the archdeacon's conversation with the police. Her bottom was damp from the fallen leaves and moist earth, and a serious twinge of cramp was just beginning to creep up her calf.

'Excuse me, may I ask what you ladies are doing crouched on a large euonymus?' Bree was trying her hardest not to laugh.

'Ooh, chance would be a fine thing.' Ethel chuckled, totally nonplussed that their snooping had been discovered by the one person they had tried to avoid knowing. 'We're actually just enjoying Abbey Towers beautiful gardens.' She picked a leaf and pretended to inspect it. 'Look, it's green!' She proffered it to Bree with a smirk.

Clarissa took the opportunity to stand up, stamping her feet to return some feeling to her toes. 'It's not what it looks like, Bree, we were just… er… just…'

Bree folded her arms. 'Yes?' She tipped her head, waiting for whatever excuse Clarissa could come up with for the five of them to be away from the film set and squatting like an arrangement of garden gnomes under an open window.

'Cleaning, we were helping to clean the windows,' Millie offered. She quickly whipped a duster out of her costume apron, waved it in the air and tried her level best to look innocent of any wrongdoings.

'And you think I'm going to believe *that?*' Bree didn't wait for a response. 'Pru's going to be so disappointed in you; you promised you wouldn't get up to mischief whilst we're here. Come on, back to set – all of you!' She glared at Ethel who was rather stubbornly still clinging to the windowsill.

'But, Bree, listen, we've just heard something. The archdeacon has just told Andy and Lucy that someone's been fiddling with his diorama!' Ethel almost ran out of breath, trying to explain very quickly what she had overheard before Bree shut her down.

'You can go to prison for a long time for doing that, you know…' tutted Hilda in embarrassed disgust. 'There's no accounting for some people's preferences, is there?' She didn't so much as pose a question to the others but to herself, which was just as well as her friends were too busy trying to persuade Bree that all was not well in Abbey Towers.

Ethel clambered over the low feature edging of the flower bed to join the others and stamped her feet on the grass to dislodge the clay soil caught in her boots. 'Don't you see? Whenever there's a death around here, that little house seems to feature in it somehow. Well, that's what they're saying in there. It's as though the story is being played out through the miniature.' She trailed behind Bree, desperately trying to keep her attention. 'I just heard Clement say he burnt one of the figures, but now the exact same one has turned up again in the diorama. Unless it's a ghost doll thingy that reincarnates itself, my guess is there's someone around here that's made a new one.'

Bree had to admit that under any other circumstances, and if her best friend and fellow mystery-meddler Pru had been with her, she would have been as excited as Ethel and her friends currently were to get involved and investigate further. She watched them chattering amongst themselves as they made their way back to the set, animated, excited, and full of mischief. A frown knitted her forehead as she weighed up the possible consequences of allowing them a free rein.

Who was she to stop them from living their lives to the fullest? Apart from them being her responsibility for health and welfare as the WI vice president, she couldn't be their conscience or their decision-maker twenty-four seven. Sometimes they just had to make their own chaos and deal with the implications...

Just as they had done on other numerous occasions!

BEST BEFORE

*T*he odour was starting to become a little unbearable for The Collector. He stood admiring the rapidly deteriorating form of poor Alice Moorcroft, still slumped in the chair. With each passing day she was shrivelling and becoming smaller, and smaller, like a slowly deflating balloon.

He wrinkled his nose as he approached her, viewing her from every angle. He was a little disappointed at her inconsiderate decomposition. The bloat phase had passed, and now she was creeping into decay. He had hoped for more time with his first kill, but it was now quite apparent that dead bodies really should have a 'use by' date - just like the nice piece of rump steak he currently had stashed in his fridge.

'They've stopped looking for you, you know…' He rearranged her hair, carefully brushing a tendril behind her ear whilst praying that his actions wouldn't cause the auditory appendage to fall off. That was the last thing he needed; a carelessly dropped ear could really give the game away. He began to laugh. imagining various body parts littering the floor like a dismantled Mrs Potato Head figure. 'They think you've run off with a lover,' he tormented the corpse. 'And who am I to correct them?'

The Collector had been wily in his trail-laying, with a quiet word in the right ear. For him it had been the renowned village gossip who owned the newsagents, and suddenly Alice had a story to explain away her absence along with a sighting on a train, thus scaling down the search for her. He had still been put on his toes a few times, though, when the local plod had been rummaging around Abbey Towers and the grounds for clues to her whereabouts.

Alice had been a simple pleasure; she had not been part of the plan and now it was too late to use her for any form of ritual. The same had to be said for the actress. That was a thrill kill with a little revenge thrown in, but most importantly it had saved Abbey Towers from destruction. The first two had been practice runs, honing his skills ready for what was to come.

Raising the dead on All Hallows Eve.

Abbey Towers had held him in its grip once before, a grip that had changed his life. Now it was time for him to be the one in control. He busied himself trying to make Alice appear as a silk purse rather than the festering sow's ear that she actually was, just so that he could extend the pleasure of her company. His carefully positioned room fresheners had gone some way to masking the stench, but it wouldn't be long before the latter would reach new heights of putrefaction before finally petering out, leaving only an undercurrent of foul air.

He had read extensively on the various stages of decomposition and was finding the whole process that was playing out in front of him rather fascinating. He peered closely at her eyes, searching for any sign of the much talked about and often debunked, retinal optography, the last moments before death. He certainly didn't want his image being left behind for all to see. Satisfied all was well, he gave once last stroke of her hair. 'See you tomorrow, Alice…' he cooed.

And with a jaunty step, he disappeared through the wall.

POINTING THE FINGER

'Why on earth would she do *that*, though? She's an intelligent, educated woman.' Lucy doodled a five-petal flower on her jotter, adding a couple of feathery leaves for effect. She was astonished that Archdeacon Gregory had so easily pointed the finger at his wife.

Andy sighed heavily, pulling his eyes away from the board that contained the pictures of Rook, Lamb and Clapton. 'She's also very superstitious. Apparently, her mother had second sight or something, so Fiona believes she's attuned to ghostly goings on. She's hated living at Abbey Towers from day one, and two deaths and a disappearance has now given her the leverage she needs to get Clement to beseech the bishop for a move to another diocese with less haunted living accommodation.'

'So, potentially she could be the one behind things that go bump in the night and the spooky moving figures in the diorama. But how did she replace the one that was burnt? That can't have been easy.' Lucy tipped her head, waiting for pearls of wisdom from Andy.

'Easy when you know.' His thumbs clicked over the keys on

his mobile phone. 'There you go, you can pick them up at model-making shops, Ebay, Etsy, even Amazon. You can actually buy them stark naked and make your own clothes and accessories. Not terribly difficult if you run the Church Needlework group! But I'm not convinced, I've just gone over the scene notes for Dana. Now, unless Fiona is actually our murderer, how did she know how to paint the blood, arrange the figure of her, and pinpoint the kill site? Until something proves otherwise, we still go with it being our suspect playing games with us.' He flicked through the slide on his screen which gave detailed photographs of the boiler room. 'It just doesn't add up. I think Clement is clutching at straws to make the whole situation a little more palatable when he has to explain it to the bishop. It's much easier to say my wife's lost the plot than we have either a haunting or a serial killer running amok in church-owned premises.'

They sat in silence, the shuffling of files and loose sheets of A4 paper being the only sound between them. Lucy checked that all investigative actions had been carried out against the three bodies. Her enthusiasm dipped when she saw the results of the CCTV from the cashpoint assault on Jackson Rutter. The report gave poor quality for the video and the stills were even worse, dark, grainy and virtually impossible to identify anyone from it. She peered closer at the two figures.

'Hard to even tell if it was a woman, Andy, but that handbag must have had a brick in it to do that sort of damage to Rutter's kisser.' She pulled out the desk drawer and grabbed the magnifying glass that she usually kept for small print, homing in on the bag. 'If I didn't know better, I'd say that's not a Gucci; it's a Louis Vuitton, but probably a fake. Not that it will make any difference.'

Jack Finnigan lumbered his way across the room and sat down on the spare chair next to Andy. 'How's the sprog birthing department progressing?'

'Slowly.' Andy rolled his eyes. 'These last few weeks seem to have taken longer than the whole pregnancy itself. Poor Pru is feeling it so much, and I'm here more than I'm at home at the moment, which doesn't help.'

Jack nodded sagely. A father himself, albeit his children had all grown up and left home for universities and work, he had every sympathy with Andy. 'Aye, our Morgan moaned like a devil in the last few weeks: she was too hot, too cold, too tired, couldn't sleep, fat, bloated, you name it, she felt it – and so did I!' He decided to leave out the bit where each time Morgan had endured a pregnancy-related symptom to excess, she'd wacked him across the back of the head with her support cushion. He was still amazed that the loss of one eye when their family pressure cooker had exploded hadn't impacted in the least upon her accuracy. He chuckled at the memory. Morgan hadn't earned the nickname 'Cyclops' for nothing. 'Getting back to the subject of work, I've just been going over the Rook, Clapton and Lamb files. I know it's a long shot, but you know they all ran with opposing organised crime groups up until about eighteen months ago?'

Andy nodded, fully aware that their organised crime groups had given them more than a few problems over the years, not just their offences, but their in-fighting and, without sounding too American, their turf wars. 'Yep, Clapton and Lamb ran together in The Renegade Rogues and Rook was part of The Teflon Cruisers. All low-level OCG, not up there with the big boys, although they wanted to be. Why? What are you thinking?'

'The possibility of between gang hits. Let's face it, pickings are hard to come by, lately, they're all struggling to make their mark and bring home the goods since the NCA did the business, and intelligence supports the talk that lines are getting blurred and being crossed.' Jack paused, waiting to see what Andy's reaction would be.

'Well, we haven't got anything else, Jack: no forensics, no suspects, so let's go with it. We can't lose anything by at least having a go. Speak to your contact in the NCA and see what they come up with.' Andy's mobile phone suddenly buzzed loudly, vibrating across the desk. He checked the caller ID. 'Sorry, Jack, I've got to take this...' he gave him an apologetic smile as he tapped the green button.

'Pru, everything okay?'

STUCK ON YOU

*P*ru sat stark naked on the end of the bed, her wet hair dripping down her back as she contemplated the amount of energy and effort it would take for her to stand up again to grab a bath towel. She checked the three vivid red welts that ran vertically along the skin of her huge tummy, unsure if she should laugh or cry.

She had never, ever phoned Andy at work unless it had been really important, particularly when he was so busy in the midst of several murder investigations, but her frantic phone call to him just now really had been an emergency. Baby Barnes took the opportunity to give her a hefty kick. She gently stroked her tummy. 'It's okay, mummy just misjudged how big she's got...' she soothed, amused at how quickly she had adopted the rather sickly-sweet baby talk tone to her voice, the one that she had sworn she would never use.

Big was actually an understatement. Pru had expanded to the size of a constipated hippopotamus, and there was still no sign of baby making an appearance any time soon. She had visions of being airlifted out of the house through the bedroom window if she couldn't squeeze down the narrow staircase of their cottage when the time came. Her line of sight into the bathroom only served to remind her. The shower door, torn from its slider rail, lay on the tiled floor, its rubber seals holding on for dear life from the frame, dangling like snakes in a jungle as the second panel tilted to one side. It looked for all intents and purposes as though a herd of elephants had barged through it.

She looked down again, the hefty girth obscuring everything below it. 'Not a herd, just one elephant...' she cried. Her eyes began to sting as the first tears plopped over the top of her bottom lashes, just as Andy arrived home. She could hear his footsteps pounding up the stairs.

'I got stuck...' she wailed as soon as he appeared in the bedroom doorway looking concerned and flustered.

Andy grabbed the fluffy bath towel from the back of the chair and wrapped it around her, hugging her tightly. 'As long as you're okay and not hurt, that's all that matters,' he comforted her. 'What on earth happened? Did it just fall out?'

Pru shook her head. 'No, it was me!' She pointed to the red welts either side of her tummy. 'I tried to squeeze out one way but I got stuck, so I turned around the other way and tried to come out backwards.' She pointed to the red welt on her left side. 'But it was just the same, I was traumatised.'

Andy didn't want to state the obvious: that regardless of which side she had led with, it was the overall size of her stomach that mattered. He could feel his mouth twitching at the corners as he visualised her dilemma. He bit down on his bottom lip, holding the urge to laugh tightly in.

'So I thought don't be such a wuss, just edge out sideways. I mean I got in it, so I must be able to get out of it. There's no way I could have got bigger in the ten minutes I was having a shower...' she sniffed loudly as her voice wobbled. 'But I got well and truly wedged in it. I had the side of the door stuck on my tummy and the frame wedged between my bum. I couldn't go backwards or forwards, Andy, I was trapped...' She started to cry again.

Andy got up and surveyed the damage. 'I was thinking the other day that we should get a better door system for it anyway, maybe a pivot one. Even me with my sylph-like masculine figure can struggle with this old one at times.' He gave Pru a sympathetic grin, trying his best to make her feel better. 'So how did it fall off?'

'It didn't, I hit it in temper and it just sort of went...' she made a dropping motion with her hand and arm, '... bang.' She searched his eyes, looking for any sign that he might be annoyed with her for dragging him from work, but all she saw was the twinkle that had attracted her on their very first meeting many years ago. She felt the urge to explain further. 'I think maybe baby moved into a new position whilst I was washing my hair; it must have made me bigger. I had visions of me being starkers and the fire brigade being called, so I panicked and just hit it. I was distraught!'

Andy gave a hearty laugh as his hand rested on a packet that had been hidden underneath *The London Library Magazine* that Pru had been reading. 'Nothing to do with this, then?' He held up a large block of mature cheddar and waved it like a trophy. The wrapping had been peeled back and several bite marks were decorating the edges.

Pru looked sheepish. 'I was hungry...' She pouted as she pulled her maternity leggings up. Andy passed her a warm fleece sweatshirt. 'Anyway, changing the subject, Bree called before. I think you might need to keep an eye on our Four Wrinkled Dears if they step anywhere near your investigations. She's pretty sure they're up to no good again; they're giving off the old mischief vibes that we've experienced before with them.'

Grabbing a small hand towel, Andy gently rubbed Pru's wet hair. 'Don't I know it. Each time I turn round I hear "*Coo-ee, detective...*" from one of them and my stomach churns while my heart misses a beat!'

'I thought it was only me that had that effect on you, my

Delectable Detective?' Pru giggled, all thoughts of being wedged in a shower door already consigned to the back of her mind.

Andy laughed. 'And I thought I was the only one you went out of your way to get close up and personal with, Mrs Barnes, but now I find myself competing with a Mira Shower Slider that has somehow managed to touch parts of you that are just a mere memory for me!'

THANK YOU VERY MUCH!

*H*azel busied herself behind the bar of The Bell Book and Candle. Business had been booming since the film crews had descended upon Fallow Falls, an event that she had been extremely grateful for. The pub and B&B ticked over quite nicely during the late spring and summer months with plenty of tourists and guests, but making ends meet became a bit of a challenge in the winter months when the fair-weather walkers and ramblers kept their toes toasty at home rather than in front of her fire. Her regulars from the village were good stalwart customers, but every year around this time, she had taken on the idea to jazz up the pub by playing on its spooky history of witches and wickedness for the Halloween period.

She looked over at the couple that were enjoying a cosy drink in the booth nearest to the log fire. It reminded her of her younger days with Gareth, before marriage, kids and running this place had taken the shine off the first flushes of love. She balanced the glass of red wine on the tray and set the pint of Old Speckled Hen ale next to it, along with two packets of cheese and onion crisps. She carefully made her way over to the table.

'Here we go, one merlot and a pint of Speckled...' She placed the glasses on the table and handed out the crisps. 'I've not seen you around here before?'

Bree smiled. 'I'm from Winterbottom, but I'm here for the filming at Abbey Towers. A few of our Women's Institute ladies are appearing as extras.'

'And I'm from Nettleton Shrub, not far from…'

Mark was quickly interrupted by Hazel. 'Harmony Hollows! Ooh that was such a to-do last year, wasn't it?' She didn't really mean to beg the question; it was more of a statement.

Mark gave Bree a wry smile before replying to Hazel. 'Yep, that's the one. Such a shame that a beautiful place like Nettleton should get a bad name because of it, though.'

Hazel made a show of wiping a few drips of beer from the table, giving herself more time to linger beside them. 'I suppose Fallow Falls will get that sort of publicity now with all the murders happening around here, not that it was whiter than white beforehand with the stories from Black Abbey Towers and what happened to the young girls from around here.' She tucked the cloth into her pocket. 'I've lived here all my life, and what I don't know about that place ain't worth writing on the back of a stamp.'

Bree was all ears. She knew enough from her own investigating and had garnered a little more from local gossip, but to actually know someone who was claiming to be an expert on the place was too good to miss. She looked at Mark who seemed as keen as she was to hear stories of dark deeds. 'Well, if you've got the time, we'd love to hear about it…'

A sudden clamour of laughter and noise filled the little nook as new arrivals made their way down the two stone steps. They buzzed around each other, vying for the best seat at the table in front of the fire, arguing over who had the coldest feet or the chilliest hands.

'Oh gawd, don't look now!' Bree dipped her head and slunk down on the bench. 'It's Clarissa and friends.' She could have kicked herself, a first 'date' with Mark, if that's what she could call it, and she'd stupidly chosen the one place she had the highest chance of bumping into the WI ladies. 'What was I thinking?' she softly chided to herself. She watched them arranging themselves into a circle, much like the witches of Fallow Falls would have done when gathering their coven. It made her want to laugh at their intensity and focus, actions she knew would be the introduction to them causing chaos somewhere.

'So, let's see where we're up to. Hilda, Olive, what have you got on our boy Gwilym?' Clarissa sat with pencil poised, eagerly waiting to take notes.

Olive looked very sheepish. 'Nothing really, he's a bit of a loner with a nervous disposition, lives out in Tollthorpe with just a fat ginger cat to keep him company. He's worked for Colquitt for about six years and does a weekly shop at Thinsky's Grocery store every Saturday morning.' She shrugged her shoulders in defeat. 'Maybe I was a little hasty pointing the finger at him.'

Hilda quickly took her to task. 'I thought my memory was bad, you've forgotten the important bit. He was the freelance diocese photographer for Abbey Towers in early 2018 when they did an update on the ballroom and library and wanted it documenting. So he's definitely got history with the place.'

Clarissa, impressed with Hilda's small window of clarity and memory that were becoming less frequent of late, pondered the new information before making a decision. 'Okay, we'll take him off the suspects list, but keep him in mind if anyone spots anything that jingles the old spider senses. Agreed?' Four heads enthusiastically nodded back at her.

Bree, still keeping herself out of their visual range, took a sip of her merlot. 'See what I mean,' she whispered. 'They're like a bunch of naughty kids!'

Mark pinched his lips together trying not to laugh. 'Oh come on, they're living their best lives. Probably way off the mark with who they've got as suspects, but they were pretty spot on at

Harmony Hollows. Give them some credit, Bree. They're just having fun.'

They both sat in silence, eavesdropping on the rest of the ladies' conversation whilst quietly admitting it was pretty good in-house entertainment, providing them with a few chuckles along the way.

'So, Ida said she'd seen that actresses' assistant-cum-body-guard guy a couple of times acting a bit shifty, and as we all know he was the last to see her alive.' Ethel rummaged around in her handbag and pulled out her notebook. She flicked through the pages and ran her finger down the lines. 'Here we go, Mark something or other. She couldn't remember his surname, but he's got big feet. I'm almost sure he was at Harmony Hollows when we were there.'

Millie nodded her agreement. 'Yes, he was. He was the guy that sort of did everything there. He was the lifeguard too; he was very nice.'

'Pah, the only nice bit you probably remember about him, Millie, would be his Speedo swimming trunks!' teased Ethel. 'Anyway, I think we should add him to your book, Clarissa – as a suspect. After all, he was at Harmony when all those murders took place, and now he's here and we've got more dead bodies turning up. Too much of a coincidence, methinks!'

Clarissa waved to Hazel to give her the heads up that they were ready to order a drink before returning her attention to Ethel. 'He had nothing to do with the murders at Harmony. Just being there doesn't mean someone is guilty. *We* were there; were *we* guilty?' She pressed out her notebook on the table. 'And if he was guilty of anything, it was how tight those darned Speedo's were,' she stuck out her tongue and smirked.

Bree couldn't contain her laughter. 'Do you still think we should give them "some credit and they're only having fun", my Mr Mark Joynson of the skin-tight Speedo's and big feet?' she teased.

The challenge from Bree kicked Mark's mischievous nature into overdrive. He quickly edged his way out of the snug booth and made his way over to their table. 'Well hello, ladies...' he suavely simpered whilst desperately trying to contain his laughter. 'I couldn't help but overhear that I've made it into your little book.'

Five horrified faces met his.

'It's our thank-you list...' A panic-struck Ethel spluttered, embarrassment written all over her face. She desperately tried to think of what to say next, mortified that they'd been caught being indiscreet with their investigation. 'What a coincidence, we've just this minute put your name down on our thank-you list.' She looked to her friends for reinforcement of her little fib, but none was forthcoming, they just shuffled their feet and suddenly became very invested in the worn and marked oak of the drinks table rather than support for their friend.

'And what would you be thanking me for? The artistic arrangement of Ms Simon's body or the specialist body piercings for the Abbey Towers burglar?' He gave Ethel a playful nudge with his elbow, as though they were sharing an in-joke. 'Honestly, ladies, there's no need to thank me, I mean what's a murder between friends.' Mark gave a cheeky wink, took a princely bow and returned to the booth and his pint of Speckled Hen. He sat down with a jubilant thump. 'There, that'll keep 'em guessing.'

Bree pinched her nose to stop herself from snorting with laughter. 'That's so mean, they're either going to believe you really *are* the murderer, or they'll think you're totally bonkers!' She watched him sup his pint, a beer moustache beginning to grace his top lip in the process. He gave her a mischievous grin, and in that moment, she realised that she couldn't adore this man more. He had everything: humour, kindness and a protective presence.

She hadn't come to Fallow Falls to find romance, but maybe, just maybe, romance had finally found her.

FORBIDDEN RITES

*T*he fast-approaching All Hallow's Eve had blanketed Abbey Towers in a mixture of excitement, anticipation and, for some, a feeling of dread.

Clement was happily going about his daily life, desperately trying to be oblivious to Fiona's festering hatred of her home, which was increasing hour by hour. Her annoyance at the continuing presence of Colquitt Productions and their hordes of actors, crew and 'interfering old biddies' as she had so succinctly put it the previous evening over her fourth goblet of brandy, was also adding to her current mood. Clement had quickly chastised her for her lack of Christian values and kind heart, baffled that his once loving and empathetic wife had turned into someone – or something – he no longer recognised.

Maybe Abbey Towers had more to answer for than he gave it credit. He made a mental note to speak to the bishop once filming was finished. Perhaps Fiona was right and it was time to request a new posting. It would be a pity as he rather liked Fallow Falls and all its superstition, strange practices and odd residents: they made for an eclectic bunch at Sunday service. Granted it had been a challenge at times, their beliefs had been well and truly embedded in the past and their long-standing fear of his current abode did nothing to assist him in their conversion, but he had stuck it out and had seen his congregation grow over the years.

He stood in front of the diorama, desperately wanting to open it up and see if anything was out of place. His fingers touched the clasp and then just as quickly, he withdrew them. Sometimes ignorance was bliss. He had lain awake at night, toying with his idea that Fiona was responsible for the appearing and disappearing little figure with the clipboard, her way of making him fearful of Abbey Towers. Could her mental health really be so poor that she would stoop to that? She had always been such a strong woman, the stalwart of their marriage, the one that was more likely to be in control rather than lose control.

'Clement…'

'Yes dear.' He turned to see her framed in the study doorway, her chin covered in a smattering of self-raising flour.

'Is this what you're looking for?' Fiona held up the little clipboard man pinched between her finger and thumb. 'I found it in the pantry, behind last year's crab-apple jelly pots.' Her bottom lip wobbled slightly.

Clement gingerly took it from her, unsure what he should do with it. 'Thank you, dear, don't you worry, I'll put it back,' he soothed.

Fiona turned to leave, but then abruptly stopped in her tracks.

'I know what you're thinking, but it's not me; it's got nothing to do with me and I'm really hurt that you could even think it.' She gave him a look of anguish before disappearing out into the corridor and back to the kitchen.

Clement sat down at his desk. He placed the figure on the worn and aged leather of his desk and stared at it. 'How can something so small, so insignificant and so unremarkable as you, cause so much distress, I ask myself…?'

He didn't wait to answer his own question. Grabbing the figure, he threw it into the drawer of his desk, locked it, and dropped the key into the breast pocket of his jacket. He patted the material as a form of comfort, safe in the knowledge that the damned thing would not see the light of day again, either in the diorama or behind a pot of crab-apple jelly, unless he himself chose to reveal it.

~

The Collector waited silently in the darkness that had enveloped Black Abbey Towers and its grounds.

All the drapes had been tightly closed shut to keep out the autumn chill, and the last lamp had been dimmed. He stood inside the wall and watched through the eyes of Geneviève Wraithe's portrait as Clement wearily climbed the stairs to his bedroom, his cassock sweeping from side to side with each cautious tread that he took.

He was a man lost to this world, a world that weighed heavy upon him.

At any other time, The Collector might have felt some sympathy for him – after all Clement was not the conductor of his own misfortune. He wasn't leading the great orchestra of shadows that Black Abbey Towers entertained. He was simply in a place that, regardless of godliness, devoured even those with good hearts that were true.

The Collector's own experience gave him that knowledge.

In the minutes that passed, the house sighed and settled, until confident his path would not be hindered nor discovered, he gently pressed the panel with his hand. It gave a muffled click and swung open, allowing him to step out into the great hall. Pushing open the door to the study, he slipped inside.

His hand carefully held the new figure he had crafted, the one he had poured his heart and soul into. He held it aloft, allowing a slim shaft of moonlight that had found a sliver of curtain unmet, to illuminate it. He smiled and touched the worn leather binding of the book he reverently held in his other hand, a transference of energy. The comfort of its presence and its promise through the words he had read, translated and memorised, filled him.

'Forbidden Rites…' he breathed heavily. He had been a good student over the years. Now he just had to find his sacrifice.

The countdown had begun.

THE HITMAN'S CODE

*D*ottie straightened her back and jiggled in her chair. It was not a full-on obvious jiggle that would draw unwanted attention to herself, just a small wriggle to ensure she was perfectly positioned. She looked around the Waddling Duck Inn at Chapperton Bliss, waiting for the familiar face she was expecting to walk through the weather-worn oak door.

The gentle hum of friendly conversations borne over pints of real ale and the odd glass of wine was strangely comforting to her. She was not the most social of people, preferring the safety and solace of her cottage and the sole company of Wick, but she had made an exception for Murdoch. She had ensured her arrival was before his so that she could choose the table they would dine at. Wherever Dottie went, she always sat near a fire exit for a quick extrication and with her back to a wall for safety to give her a perfect view of everything and anything that played out north, east and west of her.

They were rules number 1 and 2 of the *Dorothy May Barker Hitman's Code Book on Personal Safety.*

She chuckled to herself, the irony of her sitting opposite a detective inspector whilst she had carried out some pretty impressive murders these last few weeks, was not lost on her. She touched the chiffon scarf around her neck, the feel of the soft material comforting her as she checked her reflection in a little hand-held mirror. Pushing up a pretty coral lipstick from its gold compact, she carefully replenished her previous application and smacked her lips together.

The brass latch of the main door suddenly clicked open, allowing a swirl of autumn-coloured leaves to pepper the flagstone tiles of the pub floor. Murdoch tipped over the threshold and stamped his feet to rid himself of the debris his shoes had picked up en route from the car park. He folded down the collar of his coat. 'Ah, Dottie...' He grinned on spotting her. He made the universal sign language for 'drink' by jiggling his hand in front of his mouth, glass style. Dottie nodded enthusiastically and mouthed 'rum' to him. She had a feeling he would still remember her favourite tipple and mix from their days of working together at the NCA.

She watched him standing at the bar, a twinge of melancholy touching her. She had been so fond of Murdoch, a fondness that was a little more than just a colleague friendship all those years ago. At 5'8" he might have been a little on the short side to be her type and a little young too, but he had made her laugh out loud and they had been fun together. That had overridden any difference in inches and years between them. If he had not been so enamoured with Suzy at the time, she might have stood a chance.

Now Suzy was the wife and mother and Dottie was just simply the spinster with a twist. She watched Murdoch balance the two drinks in his hands as he weaved in and out of the small crowd by the bar.

'Here you go, Captain Morgan's spiced with Coke.' He gave an expectant look, hoping he had remembered correctly. 'So, how's it going with the filming?' He shrugged off his coat and sat down opposite her.

Dottie tipped her glass in greeting to him. 'It's good – well, apart from the few slight delays we've had due to "unforeseen circumstances"; she executed air quotes with her fingers. 'Are your team any further on with the investigations?'

Murdoch grinned. 'Have you *still* got the security clearance, Dottie?' he teased. 'Unfortunately, not. We're currently looking at the possibility that it's gang-related for three of them. As for the actress, well, that's a whole different ball game.' He took a gulp of his pint. 'She wasn't particularly popular; there were plenty of suspects who could have planned a dramatic exit for her, a terminal one rather than as per a film script, so...' he hunched his shoulders and held his hands out, palms up in resignation, 'who knows? We certainly don't at the moment.'

'You've got a good team; it won't take them long to join up the dots.' Dottie paused, knowing full well that what she had planned would ensure there would be plenty of clues and evidence to guarantee they did exactly that. 'The one that's heading it up for you, Sergeant Andrew Barnes, he comes across as extremely competent, and has clearly got a lot of respect from his colleagues.'

Grabbing the menu, Murdoch slipped his glasses on and gave it a cursory glance. He really didn't need to read everything listed, The Waddling Duck was famous for its steak and ale pie with chunky pub chips. His stomach grumbled in anticipation at the thought of having something other than the soggy Greggs steak-bake offerings that Suzy usually gave him on a Thursday night. 'He's an asset to me, Dottie, good coppers like him are hard to come by. Great work ethics and honest as the day is long, although don't tell him I told you that, as he'll be wanting special privileges.'

Dottie smiled. 'What "special privileges"? Like going home on time for a change? Is he married – children?' she sipped her drink, not taking her eyes off Murdoch and watching his every facial expression. 'I mean, the job is so demanding it would be difficult for him to be so professional and focused without it causing some ructions at home. Remember what it was like for us?'

Murdoch nodded; he most certainly could remember. It had almost cost him his wedding breakfast at the Winterbottom Wells Social Club when a particularly nasty murder had interfered with his and Suzy's plans, and the seventy-five per cent non-refundable deposit on the place when all leave had been cancelled. 'He manages it well, his wife Pru is a good egg and very understanding of his job. They're actually expecting their first baby.'

Dottie's throat suddenly constricted, making the mouthful of Captain Morgan's difficult to swallow. 'A baby?'

'Yep, their first, due any day now I think,' he passed the menu to Dottie for her perusal. 'Anyway, getting back to you, how on earth did you find yourself doing stunt advisory? That's a whole world away from your last job.'

She gathered her thoughts and quickly brought herself back to the moment. 'Oh, you know, specialist training for the secret squirrel squad I was in at the time. It's amazing what you learn and what you pick up on the way, skills I was able to bring to the film industry.'

Dottie watched Murdoch politely ordering for both of them. The knot in the pit of her stomach had unfortunately taken away whatever appetite she had arrived with. What she had just heard was something that she had not factored into her plans. Maybe it was time to reassess and reconsider where she would go from here.

THE ARRIVAL

*P*ru jiggled the cushion behind her in an attempt to get comfortable on the sofa. She checked the booklet the midwife had given her and marked down the time of the latest mini-contraction. The small ripples were competing with a myriad of additional feelings: anxiety, apprehension, excitement and a stonking great wave of nausea that almost, but not quite, put her off the bacon butty she was tucking into. She was just so grateful that Bree had broken away from her chaperoning duties in Fallow Falls with the WI ladies to come and sit with her.

Bree looked over at her. 'Are you sure you don't want me to phone Andy and let him know?' She was quite concerned that Pru was adamantly refusing to let her notify him.

Pru shook her head. 'Nope, not yet, it's early doors. I don't want him going all Frank Spencer on me, running around and fussing; it's too soon. According to this booklet, I'm in what they called the "latent phase", so odds on I'll have ages yet.' She watched Bree dollop two heaped spoonfuls of chocolate powder into a mug. 'Can I have some marshmallows on the top as well, please?'

Bree tutted loudly. 'Sure you don't want half a can of cream too, just to add to the excess cheese calories you've had today? Honest, Pru, you're going to regret stuffing your face when this is all over. In fact, are you sure you're in early labour and it's not just violent indigestion?'

Pru scrunched up her nose and gave her a mischievous grin. 'I've been to KFC too, and been regretting it ever since I finished the last mouthful...' She let a very unladylike burp escape as she patted her huge tummy. 'I did have a good laugh whilst I was in there, though. This woman came right up to me when I was minding my own business, tucking into a Bargain Bucket. She pointed at me and said, "Aww what are you having..." So just for the hell of it I said "Chicken!" She wasn't amused.' She began to giggle, causing her stomach to jiggle wildly which caused a loud groan and for her to double over. 'Ooh blimey!!'

Bree dropped the teaspoon she was holding with a clatter. 'What's the matter?'

'That was a bloody big one...' Pru huffed, '... and I think my waters have just broken!' Trying to be as elegant as possible under the circumstances, she heaved herself up from the sofa to check the damage. 'Yep, it's that, or I've suddenly become incontinent!'

'Right! That settles it. I'm phoning Andy.' Bree jabbed her finger on the fast dial of her mobile phone and waited. 'Hi, Andy, it's me, don't panic but I think you should come home.'

Pru doubled over, pressing her face into the cushion to muffle the loud groan she had no control over as another wave gripped her stomach. She breathed through it and surfaced quickly, her hair plastered all over her flushed face. 'Wait, wait don't hang up yet. Can you ask him to pick up some Cathedral City cheddar on his way...?'

'It's a beautiful little girl...' Jenny, their midwife, wrapped the tiny bundle in a fluffy white towel and placed her in Pru's arms. 'And she's got a pretty good set of lungs on her, to boot!'

'You owe me a fiver, Mr Barnes!' Pru gave him a 'told you so' look. 'I just knew it was a girl.'

Andy watched in complete awe as Pru's fingers curled around the tiny plump hand of their daughter, the physical contact immediately soothing her. His hand gently swept Pru's forehead, pushing a tendril of hair from her eyes. He tenderly kissed her. 'I love you to the moon and back and all the stars...' his voice broke. He wanted to say more, he had planned in his head for weeks all the clever things he was going to say to show his love and admiration for the woman he adored. He was still in a state of shock as to how incredible women were, that the strength their bodies held could accomplish such a miracle, but those words were now failing him as a myriad of emotions and a hot flush of nausea washed over him.

Tearful, Pru gave him one of the most beautiful smiles he had ever seen as her finger softy traced her baby's cheek. 'Welcome to the world, Phoebe Grace Barnes...' she whispered to their newborn daughter. 'I'm your mummy and this is your da...'

Pru's introduction was suddenly and unceremoniously interrupted by the rapid disappearance of Andy from the side of the bed. An almighty thump followed a 'now-you-see-me, now-you-don't' moment, which left Pru stunned. Staring into the space he had just vacated, she looked at the midwife for an explanation on his vanishing act.

Calm as a cucumber, Jenny peered over the side of the bed at the body sprawled out on the floor tiles. 'He'll be okay, it happens to a lot of them. All the excitement and breath-holding play havoc with their blood pressure – they just don't make 'em like they used to!' She laughed.

THE SWAN SONG

Wick sat on top of the old Aga stove, the lingering warmth from the top plate that had held his mistress's culinary delight earlier in the evening was rather pleasant and comforting. His eyes narrowed and his tail twitched as he watched her bustling around the kitchen. She paused by the drinks cupboard, her fingers tentatively reaching out for the rum bottle. They rested momentarily on the glass housing the amber liquid, before pulling away.

'Absolutely not, Dottie…' she chided herself. 'Wits about you, girl, no point dulling it with alcohol.' The first rule of her chosen profession had always been a total ban on alcohol or any other substance that could impair her perfect and precise reactions whilst on a job. She sat down at the table, snapped on a pair of latex gloves, and pulled the red leather-bound book towards her. In truth she didn't need to read or recap on any of its contents, she had almost burned them into her memory. The fragile ramblings of a frightened child and the savage brutality of a madman combined, was how she had concluded her findings at the last page. It had been a tricky task obtaining the book, but one that had been necessary to put her plan into action.

She had no doubt in her mind that the author of those words had to be stopped. She would have to temporarily step away from her other tasks to deal with this one, but it would be a job well done when completed.

'Whatever did I do with it?' Dottie chunnered under her breath whilst lifting well-thumbed magazines, a tea towel and finally the knitted red-and-green tea cosy she had purchased from the village fete in the summer. 'Ah, here we are.' She cosseted the Stun Master Defence gun, her fingers feeling the curves and contours of the moulded hand section, before clipping it to the belt underneath her costume. 'Well, what do you think, Wick? She gave a twirl, the creamy-white fabric billowing and undulating behind her. 'Say hello to the Bride of Frankenstein.' No sooner had the words left her lips, than a great sadness befell her. Dottie had never been a bride, neither Frankenstein's nor anyone else's for that matter, so it really hit home at times like this.

She was, and always had been, a spinster.

Oh how that word conjured up an archetypal vision of a sad, lonely old woman, one who had never experienced the joys of love, companionship and matrimony. It screamed 'undesired' or 'unfulfilled' – which was absolutely ridiculous. Just because a woman remained single did not make her a thornback. She could certainly show otherwise with her own exciting and exhilarating life, the places she had been, the people she had met. She subconsciously touched the small box on her sideboard.

And the ones she had let go.

'Right, this will never do...' she loudly chastised herself. 'Tonight is going to be the night, Wick, and I'm going to need all my skills, wits and courage for this one.' She adjusted her wig in the hall mirror and checked her reflection. Satisfied that she would pass muster, she checked the belt under the gown and feeling the comforting outline of the Stun Master. Now all she needed was her trusty old faithful.

Her fingers found the hidden button at the side of the large wood-framed mirror, which gave the satisfying click she had not heard for so long. Pulling open the mirror, she deftly keyed in the numbers on the pad, the display flashing with each decisive touch. The door to the hidden safe swung open and she reached inside.

'I've missed you, Gertie...' she cooed to the Glock 17 as she wrapped her fingers around the grip, pulling it from its position in the case. 'One more mission, girl, and I promise, you can continue your well-earned rest.' Her fingers hesitated over the silencer. She tapped it gently with her forefinger whilst considering her options. A silencer would indicate a professional hit, something she would prefer not to have associated with this particular kill, but she grabbed it anyway. 'Best not to go it alone, Gertie.' She laughed. She opened the front of her costume and clipped the Glock into the shoulder-holster before placing the book inside for safe-keeping. She would ensure it fell into the hands of the police once she had completed her mission, but until then, the evil within would remain under lock and key. Closing up the safe and returning the mirror to its proper position, she checked her reflection for a second time to ensure no telltale bulges or outlines would give her away.

She hesitated before opening the front door, her analytical brain running through possible scenarios, just as she had been trained to do. Pressing the Velcro fastening together on her costume, she closed her eyes, took a deep breath, and began her preparation ritual.

All Hallows Eve had finally arrived for Dottie. Her planning had been meticulous, her target had been thoroughly researched, and what she had uncovered had shocked her. If she went to the police, it might spell danger for those she cared deeply for, and that was something she couldn't risk. This was a mission that she would have to carry out alone, and for all her vast experience, it was the one that terrified her the most.

It was her swan song and the most important and difficult hit she had ever undertaken.

∼

Gwilym felt pretty ridiculous in his costume. What on earth had possessed him to choose *Beetlejuice* was a question he'd been asking himself since he'd stepped into the black-and-white striped suit.

He looked around the room packed with Halloween revellers and picked out at least two other *Beetlejuices*. It was like a convention for green-haired idiots of whom he was now one. He hated Halloween with a passion that bordered on the psychotic, but Lucas Sullivan and Colquitt Productions expected everyone on the team to be in attendance for what was being hailed as the party of the year.

He slugged back his drink and cursed under his breath as he watched his fellow revellers spinning and dancing around the vast ballroom that had been opened to accommodate them. Halloween held a lot of anxiety and trauma for Gwilym, his experiences on this day had shaped his life and had created who he now was. He wondered if that was why he had become so paranoid of late, the approach to the season was making him lose touch with reality. The feeling of being watched, of being hunted, but with no evidence to prove his bizarre thoughts.

Suddenly Annie Baines, dressed as a Fallow Falls witch, accosted him. She grabbed his arm making his drink slop over the top of the glass and breaking his train of thought. She pulled him into the centre of the room, swinging him around to the strains of *Monster Mash*. He desperately wanted his feet to obey the beat, to be part of the in-crowd and not be the outsider he knew he was, but they failed him. He stumbled forwards, landing heavily on his hands and knees, his glass skittered across the floor but fortunately did not break as it rolled underneath a console table. The green wig slipped forwards over his eyes, temporarily masking the multitude of feet that had stopped dancing. He slowly pushed it back into place, his breath coming in short, sharp bursts.

Time stood still for him. Annie, her hand covering the large 'O' her lips had just formed in surprise, suddenly began to laugh. Her infectious giggle rippled across the room, catching everyone in its wake, inviting them to join her in the fun. Their collective mirth echoed in his ears, wavering in and out, loud one minute, muffled the next. He remained on all fours, staring at the marble flooring, tracing the veins and life lines of Abbey Towers as they spread out across the very fabric of the building.

Boom, boom, boom...

The heartbeat was steady and strong. He rocked back onto his knees, sitting on his lower legs, one hand on his heart, one hand remaining on the tiles to feel the transfer of energy.

Boom, boom, boom...

Man or mansion? He couldn't be sure where the heartbeat lay, but he had never felt more afraid. Scrambling to his feet, he fled the ballroom.

Abbey Towers had finally awoken and time was running out for him.

ALL HALLOWS EVE

*C*lement hugged the crystal whisky glass close to his chest, relishing the warm glow the large slug of Glenfiddich Grande Couronne had given him. He held the glass to the light and marvelled at its rich, amber colour. It had been a special gift many moons ago, and until now, had remained stored and unopened. At £500 a bottle it had been a pretty expensive largesse, one that he had been reluctant to indulge in for fear of pandering to the sin of greed with a frisson of gluttony thrown in for good measure.

But tonight was different. Helped along by several glasses of the cheaper Scotch he kept in the cupboard for unwelcome visitors, he had fallen to temptation and opened it. He checked his image in the ornate mirror above the fireplace, adjusting the folds of his cloak. He held his glass aloft and toasted himself. 'Well done, Clement, you couldn't have upset Fiona more if you had announced you were the Devil himself…'

His bright idea of dressing up as Count Dracula hadn't been one of his finer moments. Fiona had flounced out of the house, mini suitcase bumping and squeaking behind her on the way to the village pub for her night of sanctuary from demons, devils and whatever else her imagination could conjure up. Her annoyance had been on level three of her usual vexation scale until she had seen him in his costume; it had then quickly racked itself up to level nine, convinced his involvement in the night would bring forth all manner of evil. He had tried to placate her, reassuring her it was just a cheap way of being part of the fun, as being archdeacon, he had an array of cloaks and vestments that he could wear as his costume, and a fun Halloween Party was not tantamount to summonsing Satan, but to no avail. She had slammed the door behind her and was last seen stomping along the driveway towards Fallow Falls. He drained his glass and contemplated a refill, but the gentle facial buzz of the liquor was already starting to make itself known. He despaired of Fiona at times, her attention-seeking behaviour was testing to say the least, in fact he was of the opinion that the diorama mystery probably *was* down to her. This was a thought he had already shared with Detective Barnes, although how she had obtained a replica figure to replace the burnt one was something he had yet to fathom.

Regardless of her opinion, he was actually quite pleased with the way he looked. A little bit of white face paint from the film crew's make-up tent and then the only thing he had to source was a set of teeth, which were currently nestled in his hand for practical reasons. His first two slugs of the cheaper whisky earlier on when he had been wearing them had shown him that vampire teeth didn't hold liquid particularly well, and the last thing he needed was to lose eighty quid's worth of Glenfiddich down his shirt with one dribble through the plastic gnashers.

The clock on the mantel chimed 10pm. He checked his watch to ensure they were both running at the same pace. The invitations had stipulated the opening of *Halloween at Black Abbey Towers* for 7.30pm, with carriages at two hours past midnight. It had been quite enjoyable watching the guests arriving in an array of diverse and imaginative costumes. Some were so clever they had him guessing the wearers' true identity. The party was in full swing with plenty of food and drink. It had to be said that the film lot knew how to enjoy themselves and it was good to see Abbey Towers being brought to life. In all his time here, they had not once held a fun, social gathering. Fiona had been too ashamed of the building's history to foist it upon her well-heeled friends, and her fear of the imaginary ghosts of the past continued to terrify her.

A gentle knock on the library door interrupted his thoughts. 'Come in...' He quickly shoved his plastic fangs into place and draped his arm over the back of the chair, posed and waiting, eager to show his acting abilities. The door opened, allowing the tuneful beat of *Monster Mash* to worm its way into the previously quiet room.

'Ta-da!' Ethel flounced into the room, the purple and burgundy skirt swishing around her as she flicked the tresses of her blonde wig, Sarah Sanderson style. The nylon strands free-floated for all of two seconds before getting caught in the ornate scroll work of the metal wall sconce. 'Oops, shit...' she cussed as her head jerked backwards.

'Ethel!! For goodness' sake, woman, not in front of the vicar,' wailed Clarissa, mortified that her friend had uttered a most unladylike word in the presence of one of God's representatives. Before she had the chance to continue to berate her friend, she was suddenly pushed forward propelling her into the centre of the room, by a tatty black cat and a festering corpse in a three-quarter length jacket and cravat. The impetus dislodged the huge goofy plastic teeth she had been wearing. They shot out of her mouth, landed on the coffee table and skittered across the highly polished wood, coming to rest next to a crystal whisky glass.

Clement took in the vision before him, unsure if he should laugh or be afraid. His gut reaction was to guffaw loudly but then he remembered he had agreed to investigate the bowels of Abbey Towers with this shower of misfits and would probably be spending the best part of the next three hours with them up close and personal whilst entrusting his safe-keeping to them. What on earth had he been thinking?

'Well, ladies, what can I say?' His attempt at a diplomatic opening felt rather weak. The five of them stood before him, one sucking on a set of false teeth that put his own fangs to shame, one desperately trying to reposition a poorly fitting wig, one who, if he didn't know any better, appeared to have fleas with the amount of scratching she was doing in her furry costume, and one that looked as though she had suffered an unfortunate bout of Bell's Palsy. The festering corpse in the three-quarter length jacket and cravat was happily crunching away on the handful of peanuts she had purloined when no one was looking.

Clarissa, having rammed her false teeth back in place, the two front teeth overhanging and digging into her bottom lip, gave Clement a satisfied nod. 'Looking good there. archdeacon, very dark and mysterious.' She did her best Winifred Sanderson pose, index finger on her cheek. 'Anyway, we just wanted to know what time for our little foray, I was thinking we might meet in the scullery in about an hour's time and take it from there.'

Clement could only nod; any prospect of voicing an opinion or contradicting Clarissa's suggestion had disappeared with the onset of a rather flourishing Glenfiddich Glow that had affected his power of lateral thinking and the use of his lips.

Ethel, having extricated herself from the fixtures and fittings, gave a happy jig around the room. 'Excellent, see you later, master…' she chortled as she slammed the door shut behind them.

GENEVIÈVE

*R*oom 6 at the Bell Book and Candle was definitely not up to the standards of Mrs Fiona Gregory. She expected, and usually demanded if they were not automatically present, the highest quality room accompaniments.

She plucked at a loose thread on the thin white bath towel and checked the label. She was used to towels that carried a rating of 900 GSM, not the dishcloth quality of this one that currently hung over the edge of the bath. Her fingers danced over the white porcelain sink, pausing only long enough for her to inspect the tips. She rubbed them together and tutted. The toilet roll was the next to come under her scrutiny. She pulled off a sheet and inspected it.

'Dear God, 2-ply! Whatever next – SuperSaver teabags?' she uttered in disgust.

She slumped down onto the end of the bed, defeated.

Fiona had hoped that her emotional show of annoyance and her threat of a dramatic exit from Abbey Towers would have encouraged Clement to be more understanding of her feelings, not just for Halloween but for their future. She had harboured visions of him conceding to her desires by agreeing to approach the bishop for a new posting and in turn a new home for them. She would have happily repaid him for his sacrifice and would have met him halfway by joining him for the evening. Instead, he had called her bluff and allowed her to go without a backwards glance.

She stared forlornly at the Halloween costume hanging on the wardrobe door. The rich greens and golds of the gothic cloth gave a warmth that belied its significance. She wasn't really sure why she had brought it with her; she had just felt at the time of their argument that ripping it from its hanger and stuffing it into her suitcase had added to the moment. 'You stupid, stupid man...' she griped. 'For one night only, I would have been your Elisabeta to your Dracula, just for the fun you promised.'

Grabbing the colourful plastic glass from the nightstand, she opened the bottle of Antinori Tignanello 2021 that she had sneakily swiped from Clement's special stash in the cellar. She sniffed its bouquet before pouring a large slug, embarrassed that she was being forced to drink a wine that was worth almost a hundred and seventy quid from something that resembled a Tommee Tippee kid's beaker.

She had earlier watched the commotion and excitement from the group of ladies who were also staying at the inn, dressed in their Halloween fineries. Giggling like silly schoolchildren about the arrival of a new baby, they had squeezed past her on the stairs, not giving her any heed whatsoever. The whole day had made her feel so insignificant and virtually invisible, as though she didn't matter, a feeling that was very alien to her.

Fiona had always mattered, she had always been privileged, cosseted and indulged, so this turn of events with Clement had completely floored her. The more she festered on her current lot, the more bitter she became and the more she drank until, in her increasingly intoxicated disposition, she was suddenly gifted with a fabulous eureka moment.

'Well, they're not getting rid of me that easily...' she spat.

Jumping up from the bed she grabbed the bottle of wine and sloshed a lot more than she intended into the beaker. Her anger was now so much stronger than her fear.

Her plan, once she had worked up enough Dutch courage to carry it out, would be sublime. She'd teach Clement a lesson. A few little tweaks here and there with her costume and she would become the ghost of Abbey Towers, the late and very great Geneviève Wraithe, mother of Calduggan. She had endured the fearful woman looking down on her every single day from the huge portrait in the great hall. She knew every crease, line, wrinkle and lash of her.

It was payback time.

A few spectral passes along the corridors of Abbey Towers later that night in her dress with a few 'woos' thrown in the for good measure, would suffice. He would have no idea it was his poor, distraught wife. In his mind she would be back at the inn, tucked up in her bed, sulking. She'd have Clement running scared to the bishop tomorrow morning, cassock billowing wildly behind him, as he begged her for forgiveness. She squeezed her shoulders up to her ears in delight. This was going to be so delicious, particularly after he had tried to lay the blame on her for the weird goings-on with the diorama. As if she would stoop to something so childish.

The irony of that thought and what she was about to do was completely lost on her. In Fiona's world, there were no rights or wrongs. There was just Fiona's way or nothing at all.

She stepped into the dress and pulled at the bodice laces, taking a deep breath as she did to ensure a small waist. Tipping out the contents of her make-up bag she picked a rich brown eyeliner and a deep red lipstick and began her creation.

'Oh, my dear Clement,' she undulated her arms in a ghostly manner and admired her reflection in the ancient silvered mirror. 'This is going to scare the absolute shit out of you!'

Relishing the prospect of a new ecclesiastical residence, minus ghostly goings-on, spectral sightings and murders, within a matter of weeks, she knocked back another large beaker of fine wine and plotted her infiltration into Abbey Towers without being seen.

THE GATHERING

$\mathcal{A}$s the grandfather clock chimed 11pm, the All Hallows Eve party at Abbey Towers was in full swing. Whilst the rest of the house remained dark, silent and devoid of human presence, the ballroom had become the epicentre of light and life. The cast and crew of Colquitt Productions were making merry with copious amounts of cask beer, wine and good food.

Clement watched them whirling, dancing and laughing, pleased to see that for once the only 'spirits' being talked about were the ones that came from a bottle. The costumes added an array of colour, dazzle and frivolity to the event, and he was quite surprised to see that apart from a couple of 'go-to' witches, there had only been one other popular duplication. So far, he had spotted three *Beetlejuices*. One was dancing the light fantastic with Clarissa from the WI ladies, one had clearly had a sherry too many and had disappeared after falling over on the dance floor, and the third one was currently flirting with the WI chaperone. Aware that time was ticking by, he gave a cursory last glance at the room before quietly slipping out to meet his co-conspirators.

'I don't suppose I could be your Michael Keaton to your Winona Ryder by any chance?' Mark gave a wide grin, ensuring he was showing off a fine set of festering gnashers at their best angle.

Bree playfully slapped him on the arm. 'Maybe, as long as there's no funny business.' She peered intently at his make-up, admiring the attention to detail and the obvious care he had taken to become *Beetlejuice*. She poked at a piece of decomposing greenery hanging from the side of his mouth, in awe that he had gone to so much trouble to look like his chosen Halloween character. 'Impressive! How did you manage to get that to stick?'

Puzzled, he scratched the area she had pinpointed and inspected the tip of his finger. 'It's actually a rogue piece of lettuce from the burger batch I've just had.' Laughing, he wiped the back of his hand over his mouth. 'Can I get you another drink?'

Bree nodded and held out her glass for him. 'Yes, please. I think everyone is thoroughly enjoying themselves, don't you? Just look at Ethel and the girls over there. They're giving it everything they've got on the dance floor. I must admit, maybe I was wrong about them, I really did think they had some mischief planned.' She glanced at her watch. 'They won't be doing much more tonight, it'll soon be past their bedtime, so we're safe.'

Mark handed her a glass of red. 'And what time is your bedtime, Miss Richards?' he cheekily propositioned with a wink.

'Why, fine sir, are you thinking of sharing my coffin?' She giggled.

He grabbed her free hand and pulled her towards him. 'Somebody told me that you're into architecture.' His eyes indicated to the doorway, giving her a promise of fun. 'They've got a nice quiet room here full of architectural bits and pieces, and I'm led to believe that its vacant at this exact moment in time, so would you like to feast your eyes on a pretty impressive diorama?'

Bree's eyes widened. 'I hope that's not a euphemism for something else!'

'Very funny…' he gave her a saucy smirk. 'Nope, it's that doll's house thing. Surely you've heard them talking about it on set? Apparently, the police think someone is using it to give clues to the murders; not that it's been any use so far, apart from giving the archdeacon the heebie-jeebies. Each time someone dies, a little replica image of them suddenly appears in one of the rooms. Come on, I'll show you.'

They quickly took the opportunity to slip out together from the ballroom unseen, Bree laughing, whilst trying not to spill any of her wine in the glass that she now held aloft as she skipped after Mark.

Unbeknown to them, Ethel and friends were doing exactly the same. The ladies had skirted the edge of the ballroom, dodging in and out between revellers until they reached the main doors into the great hall seconds after Bree and Mark had vacated the same spot. The very same spot that Clement Gregory had stood only moments before.

'Right, girls, this way. No chattering, no giggling, and definitely no going off on your own.' Clarissa checked to ensure they had understood the rules of their adventure before ushering them across the expanse of marble flooring and through the carved arch into the corridor.

A bottleneck quickly ensued as they attempted to squeeze themselves five abreast down the corridor to the scullery to meet Clement. Not one of them wishing to be the 'fatty at the back' for this particular event, they continued to vie for position, pushing and shoving each other. Eventually seeing sense, they broke themselves down into what they considered to be a safe two-plus-three formation before continuing on.

Clarissa suddenly flung her arm out to stop their progress. 'Hush…' she hissed as the study door ahead closed with a click.

Flattening themselves against the wood panelled walls, they held their breath. The seconds ticked by with no further disruption or surprises.

'Okay, ladies, onwards and downwards we go…'

SEEING DOUBLE

*D*ottie stood watch from the staircase balcony. She, too, felt the marbled veins of the great hall floor pulsating with life, but not in the same way that Gwilym had experienced it. Her perception was more of this world than the next. It had been the patter of human feet – several pairs of them to be exact – that had alerted her to the nocturnal wanderings of not just her target, but of the ones that were supposedly in her care.

Gwilym had been the first to burst through the doors from the ballroom, the raggedly green hair of his Halloween costume wig askew on his head. Clearly upset, he had quickly disappeared through the arch towards the scullery and kitchens. He had been closely followed by Clement, then Mark with his new lady friend, and close on their heels, the gaggle of ladies from the Women's Institute, once they had finished arguing over who would lead and who would be the most vulnerable 'fatty at the back'.

Dottie exhaled loudly. This hadn't been part of her plan, it was supposed to be a quick hit and then blend in with the revellers before the body was discovered. Now she would have to dodge a vampire vicar and five Miss Marples who, without doubt, would be up to no good, and Fallow Falls latest answer to

Romeo and Juliet. Plus she now had the added dilemma of two bloody *Beetlejuices*. She would have to take care with that unfortunate turn of events; a case of mistaken identity would be a disaster.

The one saving grace as she observed them all, was that they appeared to be going the same way – into the depths of Abbey Towers. Apart from Mark and Bree who were more than likely indulging in a little bit of hanky-panky in Clement's study.

Now she had two tasks to deal with. The original hit, and because plans can sometimes be fluid and any one of them could become a victim, she now had close protection duties to fulfil.

'Oh my, it's stunning…' Bree lifted the little latch and opened out the front of the diorama. 'Just look at the detail and how tiny the furniture and figures are.' She carefully picked each figure up and inspected it, ensuring she replaced it exactly how she had found it. 'Did you know in Victorian times households would often have replicas of their homes made for their children as dolls' houses, identical in every detail? Then the children would play out stories from within the home as a means of entertainment.'

Although impressed with her knowledge, Mark was quickly regretting his decision to utilise the study as his charm offensive. He thought Bree might take a cursory glance at the doll's house and then be instantaneously won over by his irresistible animal magnetism. What he certainly hadn't envisaged was her becoming so enamoured with it that she had forgotten why they had entered the study in the first place.

He stood behind her and nuzzled her neck. 'You smell gorgeous,' he whispered.

'Oh my goodness, oh, oh…'

Her breath coming in short sharp bursts of excitement

alarmed him. 'Blimey, Bree, I've barely started, I didn't know I was *that* good!'

Bree swivelled to face him, a flush of pink hitting her cheeks. 'No, no, it's not you, it's this, look…' She held out a small figure she had plucked from the diorama. 'Look who this is!'

Mark took it from her and studied the little figure dressed in a tweed jacket and faded jeans, its face obscured by a flat cap. A tiny clipboard was tucked under one arm. 'If it's got what I think it should have, then I'll have a good guess.' He carefully used his finger to slightly lift the cap, the telltale scar was there on the cheekbone, just under the right eye. 'Bloody hell, it's – it's Gwilym, our cameraman in miniature!'

Panic beginning to rise in her chest, Bree gripped Mark's arm. 'If it's true what they're saying about the diorama, then he's in danger! We've got to find him.' Her eyes darted from side to side, her thought process taking her to somewhere she wished it wouldn't. 'Oh no, he's dressed as *Beetlejuice* too, just like you. I saw him earlier in the ballroom, his costume is exactly like yours. You could be in danger as well, Mark!'

THE RETURN

*G*wilym stumbled across the great hall, a rage building within him. He could hear their laughter, a loud symphony of humiliation throwing itself through the open doors from the ballroom to assault him.

He held his hands tightly over his ears trying to block out their provocation. He wasn't ready and it wasn't time. If he allowed them to push him, everything he had worked towards would be lost. He needed to find his way back to his sanctuary. Forcing himself onwards, he ran through the arched entrance to the corridor and followed the route he knew so well. He held out his arm, allowing his fingers to barely touch the wood panelled walls, feeling his way. They stopped abruptly as they came to the door that led to the tower. Pressing all ten fingers against its warm wood, he listened.

The silence that came from behind the door was as fearsome as the laughter from his colleagues had been soul destroying. He allowed his head to drop, his forehead resting against the wood. How had he got it so wrong? Coming back to Abbey Towers was supposed to give him answers, instead it had thrown him back into the darkness.

Weary, he continued on, passing through the scullery corridor until he found the second door. This time he didn't wait to feel an invitation or hear a welcome. His hand clasped the tarnished brass knob as he waited for his heart to return to a steady beat.

His fingers clicked just one small quarter turn to the right and he stepped down into the depths of Abbey Towers. Clinging to the curved iron handrail he mentally counted the steps until his feet touched the cold flagstones. He stood still in the darkness, allowing his senses to adjust whilst inviting the ghosts to greet him.

His wait was not in vain.

Good evening, sir, so nice to have you back with us. May I show you the way?

Gwilym nodded. 'Yes, yes, please…' he breathlessly whispered to the nothingness.

Well done, sir, a good choice if I may say so.

Gwilym held up his arm, offering the crook of his elbow. He struck a strange solitary figure as he now gently ambled along the secret corridors of Abbey Towers, no haste in his step, no panic in his soul, and no fear in his heart.

'Why are you helping me?' Gwilym asked his chaperone.

Why? Because you belong, sir, you have always belonged. You are just a little late. Can you now see how that delay has upset the balance? We must put it right, sir.

Gwilym meekly nodded to the nothingness, a deep sorrow overwhelming him. 'I would have come but it wasn't my time, that's what they told me.' A single tear ran down his cheek, pausing briefly as it touched the scar beneath his eye.

'… it just wasn't my time.'

BE PREPARED

*H*ilda stood with her hands on her hips in the scullery of Abbey Towers. A small rucksack flopped to one side on the large pine table with its drawstring wide open, waiting for her to finish packing. Several small, white paper bags sat regimented next to it. She carefully counted each one before stuffing them inside.

Clarissa watched her, dumfounded. 'And what may I ask is in those?' She jiggled her index finger at the rucksack. 'Please don't tell me they're a bulk buy of mint imperials!'

Indignant at her tone, Hilda pursed her lips and jutted out her chin. 'Might be, might not. It might also be some Uncle Joe's mothballs too.'

'*Mint* balls, they're Uncle Joe's mint balls…' Ethel chuckled. 'You'll have denture rot by the time we've finished this little adventure with the amount you're chomping through.'

Nonplussed at their amusement, Hilda continued packing her rucksack. 'You'll be thanking me later when we'll need them to find our way back. Remember what happened at Rookery Grange Retreat. I'd never have found your room, Clarissa, without these little beauties.' She popped a mint imperial into her mouth, rolled it around her tongue, spat it out and returned it to the paper bag she held in her hand. 'I'll save that one for later.' She grinned.

Clarissa rolled her eyes in disbelief. 'You would never have found my room because you'd been indulging in the expensive stock in the wine cellar. You were as drunk as a skunk if I remember rightly. Just because you'd dropped a few half-sucked sweets as a trail doesn't make you Bear Grylls!' Clarissa swooshed her cape around her shoulders. 'Anyway, here's Clement. Please don't let him think we're just nosey old trouts with nothing better to do.' She quickly turned to face him as he swept through the door. 'Ah, Clement, are we ready? Yes? Fabulous, let the adventure begin.'

Creeek...

They all froze, listening.

Ethel lifted her hand to stay any conversation. 'Did you hear that?'

They waited, breath held and ears on high alert. As the seconds ticked by, Clarissa made the decision for them. 'Old house, girls, lots of creaks, clicks and bangs to be expected. Now come on, we haven't got all night.'

Clement would have been content to say a few words before they embarked on their exploits, but that opportunity was swiftly taken from him as five sets of hands suddenly turned him around and bundled him out of the scullery and into the corridor.

Ethel took the lead. 'Right, it's this door here...' She clasped the tarnished brass knob that only minutes before Gwilym himself had turned, prior to disappearing into the depths of Abbey Towers.

Puzzled, Clement pushed forward to stand by her. 'This just goes down to the cellars where we store surplus-to-requirement furniture, paintings, that sort of thing, I don't think we're going to find anything exciting down there, ladies.'

Ethel looked to the others for approval. Four heads nodded in unison. She cleared her throat. 'I must apologise for leaving a few things out when I first suggested a fun pokey around Abbey Towers, but we knew if we told you everything, you might not allow us to have our adventure. We had a little nosey around when we first got here and made a discovery.' She paused, watching his face for a reaction. He tipped his head, listening but not prepared to say anything until he had heard their addendum. Ethel took his silence as an indication to continue her confession. 'We know there are secret rooms down there – because we've already found one!'

Far from Clement being annoyed with them, his face lit up. They watched his fingers as they fidgeted with the clasp on his cloak, all a-dither, his eyes twinkling. 'Oh my goodness! Really?' He executed a little jig on the spot. 'This is just like the adventures in my *Boys Own* magazine when I was a child, or Enid Blyton and the *Famous Five* books.' Clement was beside himself with excitement. 'Come on, ladies, what are we waiting for then?' He pushed Ethel to one side and opened the door. 'I'll lead, you follow...' he commanded as he began his descent, his cloak billowing behind him.

The Sanderson Sisters, Binx the cat and Billy Butcherson reluctantly took a back seat to Clement. They rearranged their formation and began to follow him down the winding staircase to begin their adventure.

'I take it I'm the fatty at the back again...!' wailed Millie as she slipped through the threshold behind Hilda. She gripped Hilda's tail and wound it around her wrist. 'If anything happens to me, I'm bloody taking you with me.'

DUTCH COURAGE

*H*aving consumed the whole bottle of Clement's expensive fine wine, Fiona had gone on to order room service with a second bottle of red, although this time it had carried the dubious label of '19 Crimes'. She had gulped more than half the bottle before her finely tuned tastebuds had warned her that it didn't quite match up to the Antinori Tignanello 2021 that was now lying empty and discarded in the plastic wastepaper bin.

With her Dutch courage now almost full, she was ready to embark on her mission. Being too drunk to drive, Fiona had summonsed a taxi to take her back to Abbey Towers and after a bout of hiccups and a loud burp, she had managed to inform the driver that she wished to be deposited at the rear of the estate. This he had done without much pomp, ceremony, or a thank you for her custom.

She now stood alone in the dark watching the red tail lights of the cab disappear into the distance. She looked across at her home, which was alive with glowing lights and the thumping beat of disco music that was just about reaching her ears. It all seemed so surreal; until a few weeks ago a spectacle like this would be unheard of. Forcing herself forward, she made a two-steps-forward, two-steps-back progress towards the scullery door. She didn't intend to announce herself by entering through the front door, even though she was pretty confident that her costume offered her a perfect disguise, and, of course, due to her negative stance on the event, nobody would expect to see her there anyway.

She found her position behind the vegetable store and waited.

When the timing had been right, she had slipped silently into Abbey Towers and secreted herself in the large walk-in pantry, allowing time to get her breath back. The hike across the lawns had been quite gruelling and being slightly tipsy – which she knew was an understatement – plus the weight of her costume, had all added to the feeling of wading through mud. She had been just about to make a move to the back staircase when she had heard voices. Peering through the gap in the door the source was obvious to see.

Clement, still in his Count Dracula outfit, was cavorting with several old dears from the local women's institute, all just as ridiculously dressed and all furtively discussing an adventure.

'I'll give you bloody adventure, Clement Carlisle Gregory...' she had hissed through gritted teeth as she sank back into her hidey-hole. She pushed the door closed, its rusty hinges letting out a creak that was louder than she expected, which in turn alerted one of the Sanderson Sisters.

The seconds ticked by giving Fiona time to rue her decision to be petty and childish with Clement. She could be tucked up in bed now, warm and safe, albeit under a cheap cotton duvet set from Temu. Instead, she was hiding in her own pantry, waiting for her saintly husband and his new friends to bugger off.

Eventually they complied with her mental wishes. She slipped through the door, tiptoed across the scullery and popped her head out into the corridor to check the coast was clear. She was just in time to see them disappear into the cellar, one by one.

Fury built up in her throat threatening to choke her. She wanted to shout out, call him back, find out what they were up to, but something stopped her. Whatever he was doing down there would certainly bring more darkness to the already unholy Abbey Towers, and there was no way she would now walk its corridors alone, prank or no prank. Her desire to move house just wasn't strong enough to battle the ghosts and demons on her own.

She had a split second to make a decision. One that would take her back to safety, or one that would allow her to see her husband for what he really was, a silly boy who refused to heed the signs.

'Fasten your seatbelt, Fiona…' she muttered to herself. 'We're going in!'

She slipped through the cellar door and tentatively began her descent.

FINAL CAST CALL

Mark couldn't believe how quickly his moment of attempted seduction had gone so terribly wrong. Of all the things he could have asked Bree to look at as an opening line, even the naughtiest and most obvious would have been better than 'would you like to ogle a huge diorama?'. Because ogle it she had and in turn it had distracted her from his attempt to woo her. She was more interested in the Colquitt cameraman than him.

'I'm being serious, Mark, I've been in enough situations like this over the years to know something isn't right.' Bree popped her head out of the study door and looked left and right along the corridor. 'There he is...' She quickly pulled back and clicked the door softly shut. 'Gwilym has just gone through a door down there.' She jerked her head to show the direction.

'I think you're overreacting. Granted the police seem to think the little figures are some sort of distraction or clue, but you're jumping from the sublime to the ridiculous!' He hoped he hadn't sounded dismissive of her observations. 'And anyway, that door leads to the cellar, we went down there when we first arrived to collect some stuff for set dressing. What on earth is he doing going in there?'

Bree bit down on her bottom lip, deep in thought. 'People don't go into cellars at this time of night unless there's something amiss. We need to find him, to warn him. It's better to be safe than sorry.' She popped her head through the door for the second time in as many minutes, but quickly pulled back. 'Oh dear lord, I don't believe it! It's bloody Clarissa and friends too, and they've got the vicar with them!' She checked again, watching the entourage of costumed misfits making their way through the same door to the cellar. 'Right, that settles it. They're definitely up to no good.'

She kept watch until Millie, the last in line, had disappeared and the door shut behind her. She was just about to make her move again when a spectral sighting in the form of Fiona Gregory rushed out of the scullery, the fabric of her dress swishing behind her, and much to Bree's surprise, she, too, yanked open the cellar door and disappeared inside.

Bree danced on the spot as pent-up energy fizzed in every limb. 'Fiona's just gone down there, now; it's getting more and more like a comedy farce. Come on, we really do need to find out what's going on...'

Before Mark could stop her, Bree had slipped out into the corridor, leaving him no choice but to go after her. She ran the length of the corridor and gripped the brass handle of the door. 'Hurry up, we've got to stop them.'

Mark reluctantly followed her. 'Stop them from *what?*'

Bree turned, and with a look of exasperation shook her head. 'From doing whatever they've either got themselves into, or whatever they've got planned. Believe me, Mark, anything they get involved in won't be akin to knitting, baking or crafting. Their forte is murder!'

The depths of Abbey Towers were now playing host to all the players in its production.

Not by planning, not by chance, and not by direction had they all come together, but by misfortune and the dark forces that swept the corridors, passages and vaults of a house that had fed on so many lost souls.

It was beckoning them for the final curtain.

EUREKA!

*O*live stood in front of the wall that had previously spat her onto the flagstone floor. She had pressed virtually every brick, pushed, shoved and shoulder barged, to no avail. Not a stone turned nor a crevice widened for her. 'I can't understand it, it was definitely here. I know it was.'

Her entourage, dotted in a semi-circle around the nook, waited patiently for the grand opening of the secret chamber. Clement was the most excited, his boyhood dreams on the brink of becoming a reality.

'What did you do last time?' Ethel helpfully suggested.

'I just pressed my fingers here...' Olive thumped eight finger-tips and two thumb tips on the wall.

Click...whir... click.

And suddenly Olive was gone.

'Oh fluff...' gasped Millie. 'Quick!' Without any warning Millie grabbed Clarissa's witches' broom and darted forward, jamming it into the gap before the wall fully closed. A juddering and grating noise filled the room and then all was quiet and still.

Ethel clapped her hands in delight. 'Well, how clever are you, Millie Moo...'

Millie beamed with pride, overjoyed that for once, rather than being the afterthought and the one that was most likely to mess up, she would now have a different standing within the group. And as an added bonus, Ethel had called her clever!

'Olive, are you okay in there?' Ethel's cheek was pressed against the brick as she tried to see through the gap.

'Well, I'm still in one piece, if that's what you're asking...' Olive's voice quivered from the darkness. 'I must say to fall in here once is a misfortune, to do it twice is just downright carelessness!'

Relieved their friend was safe, Clarissa took charge. 'Right, ladies and gents, let's synchronise our watches, ensure our torches are working, and...' Before she had chance to finish, she was rudely interrupted.

'And ensure I have our mint imperials!' Brandishing her rucksack, Hilda tottered forwards, her wired tail swishing from side to side. 'I've wedged the other door open and I've started a trail.' She jiggled one of her white paper bags at them.

Whilst the ladies discussed the merits of laying a trail, Clement was busying himself looking for something more permanent than Clarissa's broom to hold the entrance in the wall open. If they had to beat a hasty retreat back the way they came, the last thing they needed would be to frantically play a game of upright Twister with a wall trying to find the winning combination. He dragged a battered mahogany mariner's chest across the stone floor. 'The wall's on a pivot, so I'll wedge this on the left side to keep it open and we can all go through this bit.' He curled his fingers around the brickwork edge and pulled. The wall swivelled out and, with the help of Ethel, the chest was pushed in place.

One by one they slipped through the opening to join Olive.

Fiona, fuelled by annoyance at Clement being so darned oblivious to her needs, and a hint of jealousy that five elderly women could command his attention more than she could, clung to the metal railings as she stumbled down the stone steps to the cellar. Faced with two doors, she chose the one that led to the larger of the storage rooms.

She had only been down here once before to retrieve an old dolly mangle when her washing machine had given up the ghost halfway through laundering the choirboy's robes. It had spooked her then and it spooked her now.

Carefully edging her way into the room, her eyes scanned each corner. 'Come on, Clement, I know you're here, I saw you with those geriatric trollops,' she spat into the void. He had been here: she could smell his aftershave as it was still festering in the dank atmosphere.

She peered around the recessed nook. 'Well, well, and what else have you been keeping from me, you old fool?' She marvelled at where the bricks of the wall had parted company affording her a glimpse of an unknown room beyond the cellar. The whole mechanism had been wedged open by her late father's old mahogany chest, further proof that Clement had passed this way. Pushing herself through the gap in the wall, she stumbled over the hem of her costume. It knocked her off balance and she fell into the secret chamber, landing awkwardly on her hands and knees. Relieved that the alcohol she had consumed was acting as an anaesthetic for her bruised skin, she rolled onto her bottom and sat on the cold flagstones, pondering her next move.

Should she shout his name, or wait until she had caught up with him? The latter option was more enticing as it gave her a perfect chance to surprise and humiliate him in equal measure. She chuckled to herself, amazed at how juvenile and full of bravado she had become since downing far too much vino and filling her soul with pettiness. She actually quite liked the new Fiona Margaret Mary Gregory. Instead of being afraid of her own shadow she could actually see herself making shadows afraid of her – particularly if that shadow belonged to her husband.

Scrambling up from the floor, she rearranged the vast folds of her costume and pushed up the pagoda sleeves so the ends returned to their natural position, draped against her body. She allowed her eyes to adjust to the dim lighting of the chamber, searching the corners and walls until she saw the arched opening. The stone flooring stretched beyond it, giving promise of a passageway that would take her to Clement.

'To infinity and beyond…' she snorted as she ambled across the flagstone floor and through the opening, the full fabric of her dress swishing in time with her gait as she pressed on in her mission with renewed gusto.

UNLEASHED

Here we are, sir, everything is ready for you.

Gwilym stood in the colossal arched vault, a damp chill seeping into his bones. He walked the circle in the middle of the stone flags, the five points of the pentagram within it seeming to glow a life blood as he passed each one, giving rise to the glorious pentacle of Calduggan Wraithe. With every rotation he could feel the strength pulsate within him.

Can you feel it, sir, is it reaching you?

He nodded, holding out his arms to the side as the ceremonial robes were placed upon him once again. He discarded the green wig, flinging it to a far corner and pulled up the cowled hood. The vibrations shook his whole being, the deep hum of voices filling his ears. Gwilym could feel himself slipping away. It was gradual at first, a slow burn, followed by a strange cold heat that swept over him. He welcomed it with open arms, a black heart and a mind that had been twisted beyond its ability to rationalise consequences and grasp reality.

In the smallest sane atom that was still left of Gwilym Benedict-Hughes, he knew there would be no going back. There would be no opportunity to change between what he had been and what he would now become. This time the transition would be permanent.

'Is it time?' he asked the nothingness.

Yes, sir, it is time. Find the final sacrifice and bring them here, everyone is waiting. This is, and always has been, your destiny.

Static filled the air merging with the bone-chilling dampness of the vault giving rise to an earthy odour of decay. The Collector, his eyes black and lacking reflection, rose from the pentacle to stand tall, menacing and devoid of reality.

The little boy had been replaced.

The grown man had been defeated.

And a monster had been unleashed…

FOUR CHOICES

*D*ottie stood in the central chamber which fed the smaller cellar rooms of Abbey Towers. Over the weeks she had been here she had walked the corridors and passages from its depths to its heights, committing them to memory.

Her research had been intensive, not just for the building and its secrets, but for her target. She just had to pray that she hadn't left it too late. What was unfolding now hadn't been part of the plan and made her feel that she was getting sloppy in her old age, but she had wanted to give the benefit of the doubt to him. A tragic childhood leading to a lonely life, coupled with their history had opened her up to an emotion that was usually quite alien to her – empathy.

But that empathy was now putting innocent people in danger.

She pressed on, knowing that one of those innocents was perilously close to losing their life.

But which one?

Her money had been on the archdeacon. He would have been the most perfect sacrifice for an unbalanced mind dabbling in the occult. But Olive and her friends had thrown a spanner into the works by giving her another five people to worry about, and if that hadn't been bad enough the appearance of Fiona Gregory tripping the light fantastic down the cellar steps off her tits on red wine dressed as Geneviève Wraithe had been the bloody icing on the cake. The evening was beginning to play out like an episode of *Ghosts*, only her charges were still in the land of the living – for now.

Dottie stood at her crossroads where the passages of Abbey Towers traversed each other. She had to choose which of the four would take her to Gwilym. 'Find Gwilym, find his victim…' she muttered to herself as her brain attempted an analytical option based on her previous sorties along the spidery tentacles of tunnels, rooms and chambers. She had checked two passages previously to their full extent: each had led to a small chamber with evidence on the walls of rusted chains and manacles. Passage number three had only been explored to the halfway point. It had been blocked by large rocks and debris piled on top of each other forcing her to turn back.

'Number four,' she whispered under her breath, before swiftly turning to face the arched opening. The only one she had yet to explore. The choice made, Dottie advanced with renewed purpose. She was now mentally placing bets on Fiona being his next unsuspecting victim. From the moment Fiona had donned her costume to cosplay Calduggan's mother, she had become the catalyst. She was in no doubt that Gwilym was following the script he had set himself in his book, and if that was the case she had no time to lose.

The curse of Abbey Towers, fuelled by Gwilym's need to resurrect part of his past, had begun, and Dottie was the only one that could stop it.

TRUST IN ME

*C*lement tested the top of the dusty wooden chest and, once content it was sound and would accommodate his posterior, slumped down on it, flicking his cloak behind him. He unclipped his vampire teeth and ran his tongue across his gums. 'Well, it's been fun, ladies, but I think we should turn back now.'

'Turn *back*! Turn *back*!?' Ethel was beside herself with annoyance at his suggestion. 'We've only just started, Clement; this is an exciting adventure, not a quick nip into Aldi for a middle aisle bargain.'

Hilda began to jiggle on the spot. 'I went in there once for a tin of beans and came out with a really nice dog bed. Lovely colour, and with a padded cushion too. It was an absolute bargain.'

'How can it be a bargain when you don't have a dog?' Clarissa was genuinely interested.

Ethel bristled. 'Oh for goodness' sake! Forget the ruddy beans...'

'That's the point, I did...' Hilda mischievously interrupted.

Not amused, Ethel snapped back. 'Look, what I'm saying is let's concentrate on what we're doing now. I think we should carry on for a bit, see where this passage takes us, and then if we haven't found anything exciting and you all feel the same, we can go back upstairs and carry on partying. Agreed?' Waiting for a response, Ethel looked to take a show of hands. She scanned the chamber. 'Er... I hate to be the instigator of anxiety, but where's Millie?'

'She's with Clement over there...' Olive pointed to the corner where Clement was resting his legs and waiting for the ladies to make a decision.

Clement looked surprised and shook his head. 'She's not with me. The last I saw of her was when we were all coming down that passage, just before they all met and criss-crossed in different directions. She was at the back behind Hilda.'

Frantic, Hilda grabbed the tail of her costume and checked the end of it for Millie. 'She must have let go...' she wailed. Suddenly becoming hysterical, she railed at Clarissa. 'There you go! She warned you, didn't she, but oh no, nobody listens to poor Millie.' She grabbed her tail again and began to wring it in angst with her hands. 'You made her the fatty at the back, and now she's disappeared!'

Millie had been happily trudging behind her friends, occasionally gripping Hilda's tail to ensure that if anything were to happen to her, Hilda would be forced to accompany her, not through choice but through necessity. This had seemed such a good idea initially, but as the passages took on twists and turns with uneven flag-stones, it was easy for Millie to drop slightly behind everyone else as her pace was not as swift, thus losing her grip on the furry tail.

'Wait for me, girls...' Her voice had been slightly breathless with the effort to catch up with them. She watched the back of Hilda disappear around a curve in the wall, lit by the dim, caged

313

lights along the route. She broke into a little run, eager not to be left behind.

'Oh dear,' she sighed.

The passage opened out into a small central chamber leading to three more passages, but with no sign of her friends. She stood, hands on hips, catching her breath, bemused as to where they had disappeared to in such a short space of time. She checked the ground for mint imperials but there was nothing that would indicate the route they had taken.

'Well, thanks for nothing, Hilda! Even an Uncle Joe's minty ball would have helped.' Millie lifted her finger and pointed ahead of her, ready to make her choice. 'Eeny, meeny, miny, moe…'

The sound of footsteps from behind startled her. Unsure if it was friend or foe, she quickly turned, her witch's broom held aloft ready to strike if needed, but her assailant was fleeter of foot and stronger.

Millie was gripped by the shoulders and pulled backwards, her broom clattering to the stone floor as her cloak was swiftly wrapped around her head, completely covering her face.

'Please don't hurt me…' Her terrified voice muffled by the velvet fabric seeped out from the darkness she was suddenly experiencing. Strong arms wrapped themselves around her, bundling her slight frame upwards, slumping her over and down, almost bent double. Her mind racing, partly fuelled by fear, partly sparked by desperation, tried to fathom out what was happening to her.

A slow, precise gait followed, and with each step, Millie's head wobbled from side to side. She was slung over someone's shoulder, and they were taking her away from her friends. Gathering every ounce of breath she had left, Millie took a deep breath and opened her mouth to scream.

'Don't scream, don't shout, don't make a noise, just do as

you're told,' the gruff voice rasped. 'You have to trust me; I'm all you have right now...'

Several twist and turns in their progress followed, with Millie desperately trying to figure out in her mind's eye where she was being taken. The time she had to consider her options had been brief, but it had been just long enough for her to decide the least trouble she gave her captor, her chances of getting out of Abbey Towers alive would be much improved. Her captor's breathing was becoming laboured, until suddenly they stopped. Millie was roughly dropped to the floor, grateful to feel her two feet on solid ground, but her joy was to be short-lived. She heard a creaking sound ahead of her, followed by the loud metal clang of a door being banged firmly shut.

Millie waited in the darkness, listening for any other sounds. 'Is there anyone there?' Her voice was small and wobbly; she had never been more terrified in her life. 'Hello...'

She lifted the hem of the cloak and peeked out from underneath it. She was alone. Pulling the velvet fabric from her head, she looked around the tiny room lit by a low wall lamp. It was empty, no windows, no furniture, nothing. Just an old door with a grated hatch that had been bolted shut. She pushed at it with her hands, felt around for a handle, tried to prise her fingers between the railings in the hatch, all to no avail. She was trapped.

Millie dropped down onto the floor, a loan moan escaping her lips as she began to cry. 'I was right, it *is* just like the movies, the fatty at the back always gets it...'

THE SEARCH PARTY

The Death Collector recoiled. His fingers had almost touched his prize before it was cruelly snatched away from him. He slid back into the wall recess and held his breath. He was not alone. His mind raced to rationalise his loss and to identify the ghostly creature that had stolen her from him.

Could there be another with a heart as needy and as dark as his? Had the nothingness brought them together for what was to come? He willed the voice to return, to advise him. It didn't disappoint.

Very unfortunate, sir, very unfortunate but these things are sent to prove our worth. May I suggest a little variation from our agreed ritual? A change of offering, someone who will make the power so much stronger.

The Collector gave a barely perceptible nod to the nothingness. His fingers toyed with the miniature hand-made doll in his pocket. Unlike his others, this one was personal. He knew every single curve, line and feature; it had been his special project. It was his masterpiece.

Here we are, sir, she's coming this way. She is just perfect, simply perfect. This is most definitely the one.

The nothingness stepped to one side to allow its master a clear view. The Collector smiled, a slight tic crinkling the scar under his right eye. He adjusted his robes and allowed the force to flow through him. He watched her float along the passageway, her gown trailing behind her. The soft 'swish, swish' of the fabric against the flagstone floor sent shivers along his spine.

'Geneviève!' His breath was snatched away from him as he gazed upon her, his mind confused, the terrors of his childhood returning. Fear gripped his heart.

She is the one, sir, you must take action now before the moment passes...

His movements were precise and his actions were carried out with the utmost impact. His sacrifice fell at his feet, in a pose of macabre genuflection. He bent down and with one finger traced along her cheek. His black eyes, reflecting the dim amber lighting that lit the bowels of Abbey Towers, gave further proof that the man within was now completely lost.

'*Sorem est*, Geneviève, through you she will live again.'

The flowing gown of Fiona Gregory once again made its trademark 'swish, swish' sound – only this time her limp body encased in it was adding to the slow progress along the cold, damp stone.

'Oh gawd, did you hear that?' Flustered, Olive pulled up her breeches and frantically looked around for a means of escape. 'I don't want to stay down here any longer,' she wailed.

Clarissa flapped her hand at her in a shushing motion. She stepped back into the central chamber and listened. 'Could be the wind; there's bound to be some sort of ventilation down here.' She didn't believe her own reasoning, but she could see Hilda beginning to panic, and even in the dim lighting, it was obvious that Clement had lost some colour. Only Ethel was brazening it out.

'We're going nowhere until we find Millie.' It was evident from the look on Ethel's face that she was wholly unimpressed with Olive's lack of camaraderie and support when the going got tough. 'We always stick together, that's the unwritten rule of being part of the Four Wrinkled Dears,' she firmly added.

Olive huffed. 'Well in that case, count me out! I'm not like you, Ethel. I'm scared.'

Ethel felt a little guilty for being so judgemental. Just because they were used to adventures that sometimes got a little hairy and scary, it was unfair to assume that others would have the nerves of steel that their little quartet had developed over the years.

Before there could be a further falling out, Clarissa intervened. 'We need to formulate a plan and stick to it. Our first priority is finding Millie, and as soon as we do, we get our asses out of here...' She picked up Hilda's rucksack and pulled out a bag of mint imperials. Holding them aloft she beckoned everyone over. 'Okay, here's the plan. We need to be methodical in our searching. May I suggest that you, Olive, take charge of the mint imperials.' She threw the bag at Olive hoping that by giving her a task it would quell some of the reticence she was currently experiencing. 'We'll lead the way and you lay the trail as we go, that way we know which passages we've been down and which chambers we've visited. By a process of elimination, we should be able to search parts we haven't been to yet.'

Olive rankled. 'So now I'll be the fatty at the back? Not a bleedin' chance in hell!'

'Oh for goodness' sake, Olive! Go at the front, then, and do it that way...' muttered Ethel.

'Ladies, please!' The 's' at the end of 'please' suddenly played havoc with Clement's plastic Dracula gnashers as they tipped forwards to hang on his bottom lip. He quickly rammed them back into his mouth and clacked his gums together to form a seal. 'There's no point in being mean to each other when we need cooperation for our survival.'

A silence fell over them as they considered the implications and potential dangers in wandering further into the depths of Abbey Towers whilst bitching at each other. The little group, made up of the feisty, the frightened and the faithful, quickly put aside their fears and quibbles to begin their search for their friend, led by Olive randomly chucking mint imperials on the ground as they went.

The race was on to find Millie.

A PERFECT SHOT

*F*iona had been carefully laid out to fill the pentacle like a human star. Each point of the inner pentagon was marked by her head, arms and legs. The flaming torches on the pillars of the vault, bringing light but no warmth, cast eerie shadows around her as the desiccated remains of Calduggan Wraithe looked on.

Her eyes flickered momentarily before fully opening. She frowned, the painful sparks of a headache touching every nerve, made her wince. Her natural reaction to bring her hand to her forehead to soothe was thwarted by heavy chains that dug deep into the skin of her wrists. Disorientated, she snorted with laughter. If she didn't know better, she would think she was in the middle of one of Clement's boudoir games, the type they used to play before he had taken the cloth. Her arms strained against the shackles as she turned her head left and right, trying to bring her vision into focus. The dim lighting was suddenly replaced by a dark shadow that crept over her. Her rapid intake of breath was sharp and painful.

'You?' Her voice seemed small and weak, as though it belonged to someone else. She was unsure if she was challenging him or simply acknowledging his presence. 'What are you doing? Get these things off me now...' she demanded as she yanked her arms, making the chains rattle. The cold tentacles of fear had begun to wrap themselves around every vein in her body, making her shiver uncontrollably.

He stood over her, holding a gilt-edged book, his dark ceremonial robes giving him a façade of importance and menace, a far cry from his usual tweed jacket and clipboard persona. She desperately tried to remember his name, but at the best of times he would probably have been insignificant to her and now her mind, encased in terror, was refusing to play the memory game.

There's no time to waste, sir, your mother is waiting for you.

He tilted his head, listening, a childlike smile gracing his face. 'How soon?'

As soon as you complete the ritual. A life for a life, that is the price of resurrection, sir.

'A life for a life...' he repeated. 'A life for a life. Of course, I understand, I am, after all, the Death Collector.'

Fiona watched on in horror. 'Who are you talking to? Please let me go, you can't do this, this is ridiculous, stop playing games.' In her heart she knew this was no game, no Halloween prank that was getting out of hand. Her screams rose up and filled the vault, bouncing from the walls and ceiling, swirling around her and echoing back. Had those screams reached the corridors to highlight her danger or had they remained here with her? She had no way of knowing.

His feet made no sound on the stone floor as his robes swept along behind him. He reverently placed the book on the lectern, exchanging it for the black-handled Athamé dagger. He turned it in his hands, feeling the cold metal against his fingers. His books had taught him it could not be used for harm, but the nothingness had told him otherwise. He pulled an ornate red stone amulet from underneath his robe and reverently held it up to the light before placing it upon Fiona. Moving stealthily around the curves of the pentacle, the dagger held aloft, he began his incantation for *resurgere*.

'*Ut Vectas, Vitas Phasmatos, Ex Salito…*'

The rapid beating of his heart, the surge of dark blood through his veins, and the breath of a life to be resurrected spurred him on. He stood over Fiona, ignoring her screams and pleas for mercy as he dropped to his knees and straddled her, providing himself with the optimum position to achieve her swift death. Bringing the dagger directly over her heart, his muscles tense, his fingers firm and strong around the hilt, he brought it down with precision…

Crack.

Fiona, her eyes wide in terror watched as he momentarily shuddered and jerked, his head thrown savagely backwards, and then like a movie on pause, he sat rigid, unmoving. The dagger clattered to the stone floor as his fingers lost their grip, a dark hole suddenly burgeoning in the middle of his forehead.

The trickle of blood was slow at first. Mesmerised by the flow of red that glistened in the half-light as it spidered down his face, she searched his eyes, only to see her own reflection and a brief realisation of his surprise within them. His mouth drooped as his jaw slackened, allowing him to emit a slow groan before slumping forwards, his head coming to rest on Fiona's chest.

If nightmares were made of moments like this, then Fiona Margaret Mary Gregory was currently starring in her very own version of purgatory. Not one that was created by her imagination or her irrational fears, nor was it fed and nurtured by her obsessions with the supernatural.

This one had a more earthly origin.

In the form of Gwilym Benedict-Hughes.

THE RESCUE

*M*ark suddenly stopped in the chamber, holding out his arm to halt Bree, keeping her safe behind him. He turned his head, listening. 'Did you hear that?'

'Hear what?' Bree was on the point of exasperation. They had been up and down passages, taken wrong turns, doubled back on themselves and were still no closer to finding anyone. The whole underground of Abbey Towers was like a rabbit warren and she was still convinced that a good proportion of it actually spread out under the grounds of the estate. 'It's probably some spectral spook wailing and hollering and smacking their hands together in angst because we're trespassing in their domain.' She giggled.

'It sounded more like a scream in this realm than a banshee wailing in the next.' Mark peered around the opening to the passage on their left. 'This place is huge, we could still be here at Christmas, never mind Halloween. I bet you that lot have already had a little snoop around, and whilst we're down here scaring the bejeezus out of each other, they're now back upstairs tucking into the finger buffet!'

'The sink hole!' Bree had suddenly put two and two together. 'The sink hole that Alice Moorcroft's dad fell into on the Abbey Towers estate. I think it was part of this underground set-up, maybe a weakness in the structure. No wonder they'd tried to keep it hush-hush. I bet this was used for smuggling and all that black magic stuff the original owner dabbled in.' Squinting, she checked her watch for time. 'How about another five minutes down here and then we can go and see if they actually have returned upstairs?' She waited for him to respond. 'Mark?'

It wasn't that he hadn't heard her, he had just become distracted by something else that was far more interesting than an old sink hole. He bent down and picked up the silver earring set with a ruby stone that had caught his eye. Turning it in his hand, he looked from the earring to the large metal door with a grated hatch set into the wall in front of him. It was almost obscured by the curve of the passage and the lack of lighting in that section, and if it hadn't been for his curiosity with the trinket, he would probably have missed it.

'Quick, over here! Look what I've found...'

A loud bang on the other side of the door startled him. He jumped back, holding out his hand to stop Bree from getting any closer.

'Is there anybody there, please help me I'm locked in...' pleaded a weak but very familiar voice, muffled by the thickness of the door.

'That's Millie,' gasped Bree as they both gripped the metal barricade bar, pushing it up to unlock the door. 'It's okay, Millie, we're here...'

Crack.

Crack.

The sound of high-pitched screaming and a loud bang had thrown Clement and the ladies into sheer panic. Their carefully laid plan was suddenly hurtling into disarray as they ran around like ants from a disturbed nest.

'Oh shizzle, what in darnation was that?' shrieked Clement, his usually calm manner deserting him. 'Correct me if I'm mistaken, ladies, but in my humble opinion as a one-time army chaplain, I think that was a gunshot…' he helpfully offered.

The noise they had heard had ricocheted through the passages, amplifying and duplicating as it hit bricks and stone.

Ethel held her hand up to her ear, an action she mistakenly thought would allow her to identify where it was coming from. 'I think it's this way.' She set off at a blistering pace, closely followed by the others. Under normal circumstances she was sure they would have fled in the opposite direction at the prospect of coming face to face with a gun, but not this time. This time they had Millie to consider. Finding her was their priority.

Twists and turns became endless passages and small chambers, none of which led them any closer to finding Millie or to discovering where the screams and gunshot had emanated from. 'The mint imperials!' Hilda helpfully offered. 'Let's at least check where we've been.'

Scouring the floor, they were dismayed to see not a nice neat line of the white confectionary but a scattering of little balls rolling in different directions.

Exasperated, Ethel shook her head. 'Not our best idea making Olive the fatty at the front, was it? As quick as she's been dropping them, we've been following behind and kicking them all over the ruddy place.'

Before any of them had time to react, frantic footsteps clattered over the flagstones coming towards them. Whilst they considered a flight-or-fight response, Ethel brandished her broomstick out in front of her ready for combat.

'Whoa, drop your weapon…' Mark half-laughed, half-instructed. 'It's only us, we've just found Millie!'

HOLE IN ONE

*G*ertie the Glock had found its mark on the first shot.

Not that Gertie could take all the credit, that kudos belonged to Dottie. Her cool head, eyes as sharp as a tack and the steadiest hand this side of the Atlantic, had all contributed to a rather fabulous 'hole in one'.

From the shadows Dottie had taken aim and fired. Not before time too, she had cut this one far too close. She would have preferred not to have traumatised Fiona Gregory for all eternity, but when it had been a choice between her life and a more private execution for Gwilym, it was a no brainer that it had played out the way it had.

No sooner had Gwilym slumped down dead and the final strains of Fiona's ear-splitting scream had dissipated into the ether in favour of a very dramatic faint, did Dottie reveal herself and jump into action. There was work still to be done. She had quickly checked Gwilym for signs of life. The neat bullet hole in his forehead belied the rather large section of skull that was missing from the back of his head courtesy of a 9mm Luger bullet.

Confident that any risk from him was now terminated, just as he had been, she pulled back his robe and dipped into the pocket of his jacket. Her fingers found his masterpiece. Holding the small figure in her hand, an unexpected sadness swept over her. She swallowed hard, trying to rid herself of the alien lump that had formed in her throat as she battled the onset of tears. At some point Gwilym had been just a little boy, someone's son, a lost soul that had grown into a very damaged man who had been carrying a grief that would never be healed and a hatred that could never be fully avenged.

Sometimes Dottie, for whatever reason, found herself in the right place at the right time. She had come to Fallow Falls for another motive, a personal one, and in the process had stumbled across a more pressing dilemma. She had very quickly realised that when the needs of others had begun to overshadow her own want, it was time to step back and reassess her direction and her reason for being there.

Maybe it was also time for her to reassess what direction her new life could take her. After all, this had been her swan song.

Her temporary reverie was rudely interrupted by a cacophony of high-pitched female voices echoing along the passage, sprinkled with the deeper baritone timbre of Mark and the archdeacon. They were coming her way. Quick as a flash she melted back into the shadows, her presence and her identity once again secure.

Dottie watched them all wittering and dancing around each other, their excitement at their missing friend being found was completely obscuring their awareness of what lay ahead of them on the floor. She had felt a tad guilty at having abducted poor Millie in such a disorganised and frightening way, but time had been of the essence. Knowing what was about to play out, she had been forced to ensure her safety by quickly removing her from imminent danger without being seen. The last thing she had needed was a loose cannon dressed as one of the Sanderson

Sisters wandering around alone with her broomstick. The old holding vault had been her only option.

She held her breath, waiting for the expected reaction to her handiwork. She didn't have to wait long.

'Oops, I think we've stumbled upon your Fiona, vicar. She doesn't look very good, does she? Too much of the old vino perhaps.' Hilda tipped her head to get a better look. 'Mind you, she's faring better than her mate here, look at the state of the poor bugger.'

Bree bent down to check on Fiona's comatose state, her hand accidentally touching the black pool that had already started to seep into the flagstones. She checked her fingertips and sniffed the red liquid, whilst simultaneously catching sight of the damage to Gwilym's head. Her heart raced just that little bit faster as her stomach flipped.

'Mark...' Bree held out her blood-stained hand to show him, forcing down the urge to retch. 'This isn't fake, it's not part of Halloween. Get them all out of here, *now*!'

THE DISCOVERY

*B*lue lights strobed the darkness, bouncing from the trees and walls of Abbey Towers. Numerous police vehicles from standard patrol to forensic vans cluttered the vast driveway in random patterns.

Wrapped in blankets, the Four Wrinkled Dears and Olive accompanied by Bree as their chaperone and Mark as her support, sat on a line of chairs and watched the drama unfolding before them. The white suited forensic officers moved swiftly and with purpose between the hastily erected tents and the route that had been chosen to enter Abbey Towers. The partygoers in their plethora of eerie costumes were being shepherded with professional care to the holding area.

The heavy silence that had settled between the friends was one of relief, disbelief and a strong sense of gratitude that they were all safe and well. Curling their hands around polystyrene cups of tea to warm themselves, each caught in their own thoughts, they huddled against each other for comfort. The chill night air turned every exhalation they made into a misty supernatural dance.

'We did it again, didn't we, girls? The Fearless Foursome have triumphed.' Ethel paused for thought. 'Oh, and you too, Olive. Just goes to show, though, you can't keep good women down.'

Bree spluttered the mouthful of lukewarm tea she had just slugged back. 'Triumphed!? You're joking! You almost got yourself hurt again; in fact you almost got yourselves murdered. I literally can't keep up with you four. And you, Olive, I thought you might have been a good influence on them, but clearly I was wrong.'

The silence returned as they pondered Bree's fairly accurate observation of them.

'I think they've found poor Alice. I overheard them talking when I went to the little girls' room for a wee...' Hilda stuck out her chin, using it as a pointer to the second black van with tinted windows that had been brought to the front of Abbey Towers. 'I don't think it's good news, though.'

Although they hadn't known Alice, they had been invested in her disappearance and Hilda's update on her status had added to their already heavy hearts. They settled back into mutual silence once again, grateful for their individual safety, horrified by the events that had unfolded, and devastated at the tragic loss of life.

'I wonder where the young girl that helped us find our way out has gone, I haven't seen her since we hit fresh air.' Millie's teeth chattered together, still not fully recovered from her ordeal.

Puzzled, Bree gently patted her hand. 'You were the one that turned superhero, Millie, you knew the way, you led us out. There wasn't anyone else there.'

On discovering Gwilym dead as a doornail face down in the ample bosom of Fiona, panic had ensued and not one of them could remember which of the four passages they needed to take to escape and raise the alarm. It had been Millie who had calmly stepped forward and with a confidence they had not seen her exhibit before, she had navigated every single passage with ease, almost gliding ahead, animatedly chattering away to herself.

Millie pulled her hand away, a look of confusion spreading

over her face. 'No, no, I was following her, she was the one that told me which way to go and then you all followed me. She was ever so pretty, she told me her name was Florence.' Millie took another sip of her tea. 'She was wearing a lovely green cloak, it sort of matched her eyes but once we got outside, she disappeared. You must have seen her!'

Breathing deeply, Bree took a moment to think. There had been no woman in a green cloak with them, it had only been Millie leading the way through the twists and turns of the tunnels. The hairs on Bree's arms suddenly stood on end and a shiver ran along her spine as her brain raced to rationalise Millie's account of their escape. Maybe she was just confused and delirious from her forced imprisonment, that would be the most logical reason.

The only other reason would be that Millie had been offered a little bit of supernatural help from the other side from none other than the girl she had read about in *Tales from the Black Abbey Towers*: Florence Rose Clancy. She quickly checked herself for being ridiculous, but the knowing look of certainty on Millie's face told her otherwise.

Perhaps a faint glimmer of goodness and light had shone through the darkness of Abbey Towers after all, and the ghost of Calduggan's victim had risen to lead the way. She looked back at Abbey Towers, her eyes searching the windows, hoping for a glimpse of its spectral inhabitants, a vision that would help her believe.

The heavy darkness of the tower gave nothing away, it offered no hope, no welcome, no peace and no life.

Black Abbey Towers was preparing to sleep once again.

Clement, who was busy saying his goodbyes to Fiona as she was carted off to Winterbottom Royal in the back of an ambulance, was starting to feel his own sense of gratitude and relief. As much as Fiona gave him the proverbial dog's life, he truly couldn't be without her. Granted some changes would have to be made on her return, which would probably mean saying goodbye to Abbey Towers, but it would be worth it to have a little normality back in their lives that didn't include imaginary spooks, spectres, and unnatural whisperings.

He had heard the whispers many times over his years at the Towers, but to him it had been the voice of temptation, a way of testing his faith. Each time he had bellowed into the darkness commanding Satan to get behind him, and he had triumphed. Something others had so clearly failed to do.

He gave one last wave to the red tail lights of the vehicle as it crunched along the gravelled driveway before ambling over to Bree, his cloak billowing out behind him.

'Ladies…' He gave them a cursory nod of greeting. 'Fiona is just fine and dandy, a minor bump to the back of the head. Nothing to endanger her feisty spirit nor impact on her sharp tongue – more's the pity!' Clement grinned, amused at his own quip. He watched their faces looking for a sign that they too had found him witty. 'Too soon, hey?'

Hilda shrugged. 'Whatever floats your boat, vicar…' she tittered as she rummaged around in her backpack. 'Anyway, I've got a little something to cheer us all up.' She continued to plunge the depths of the canvas bag.

'Oh please, Hilda, not more ruddy mint imperials!' Ethel sighed. She didn't think her teeth could take any more of the rock-hard sweets.

'Something much better…' chuckled Hilda as she pulled out a litre bottle of Harvey's Bristol Cream sherry and a stack of plastic cups, which she eagerly handed out before filling each one with the warming liquid, much to the delight of her friends and Clement who also gratefully accepted a cup. It might not be the expensive whisky he had been used to, but it was most definitely welcome.

'Cheers…' They held their cups aloft and toasted each other and their good fortune to be alive and kicking.

Clarissa patted the empty chair next to her, indicating for Clement to sit down. 'Is it true about Alice?'

He pinched his lips together. 'I'm afraid so. They found her body in a secret room in the tower. I didn't know the space existed, and it would probably have gone undiscovered if it hadn't been for the HRD dog they brought in.'

'HRD?' Puzzled, Ethel was keen to understand the acronym.

Clement visibly shuddered. 'Human remains detection dog. Apparently it went ballistic by a wall in the top of the tower and they eventually found it.' He looked up at the tall edifice, the carbuncle of Abbey Towers, mesmerised by the full moon reflecting from the glass of the windows. 'This place has far too many secrets, not just the passages, vaults and chambers, but the terrible secrets of those that have dwelt within its walls. The whole building is adulterated with their horrors, their pain and their suffering.' He swiftly wiped a tear from his cheek. 'In my humble opinion it should be burnt to the ground...'

The bricks and mortar of the house are pure;
it is the evil of man that will taint the fabric and infuse the ground
upon which it stands.
— **The Author**

A JOB WELL DONE

*D*ottie slumped down in the floral-patterned fireside chair and plumped the cushion up behind her, happy to be home and warming her toes in front of the roaring fire. The ice cubes in the large glass of Captain Morgan's spiced rum rattled against the sides as she toasted a job well done. Gertie the Glock had been cleaned and placed back in the safe until the next time it would be required and the red leather-bound journal now sat on her knee. Her quick exit from Abbey Towers had only been delayed long enough for her to place Gwilym's hand-made figure in its rightful place in the diorama. She felt that she owed him that much at least.

Dottie had made a quick detour on her way home too. This time to Riverbank Cottage in nearby Tollthorpe, the home of her most recent hit. Her recce had been planned right down to the final second as time was of the essence, she had to put everything into place before Gwilym's body was found and identified. Within hours his cottage would be locked down and forensics would be crawling all over it, so Barney Mutton's tooth, Danny Rook's battered iPhone, Rutter's fake TAG watch and Dana's earring, the one Dottie had quickly pocketed before her body had become a crime scene, had been stuffed into Gwilym's underpants drawer.

She smiled as the plump ginger cat she had hastily shoved into the cat carrier on her way out of Riverbank Cottage, sauntered into the room and lay down in front of her fire, spreading himself out like a melting orange Smartie. After the planting of evidence, the welfare, comfort and future of Mingus the Terrible had been a priority for Dottie. She couldn't bear to leave him, not knowing what would happen to him, so he had rather reluctantly, judging by the deep scratches on her arms, come to live with her and Wick.

Wick arched his back and rubbed himself against the side of the chair, his soft mewling alerting her to his presence. She stretched out her hand and tickled him under the chin, sensing his discomfort with her latest acquisition. Dottie had very little time for most humans, their deceitful ways, greed and common cruelties were always high on the list of traits the world could do without, but animals were a different matter. They gave unconditional love and loyalty, asking for nothing in return but a full belly, shelter and comfort.

'Oh come on now, Wick, you'll be friends in no time...'

She watched him tentatively approach Mingus, hesitating momentarily before he flopped down beside him. Dottie smiled and opened the journal at the page she had marked to read once more before she would send it on its way. She had to reinforce the justification for her recent actions at Abbey Towers.

Sunday 27th June 1976

I hate this place. I hate the name they've given me but if I say my old one, they beat me and it hurts so bad.

I'm not allowed to cry.

It's not fair, I'll get them back even if it takes me until I die.

I just want to be me again and to be with my mum.

I am William

William

William

William

William

William...

The name was written with a precise and careful hand, over and over again. As though it was the only way he could remember it, to prove he existed. Dottie turned to the next marked page. She had already digested every entry and every single word; some parts had made her heart ache, some had hardened her resolve, and others had terrified her as his life was played out on the pages. Day by day, week by week, he had slowly spiralled into the abyss, the madness taking him.

William George Bennett had been the little boy they had not expected to survive the horrors of Abbey Towers that fateful Halloween night in 1973. But he had. And whilst the bodies of his parents were barely cold, he had been spirited away by the church to save face and shame. He had then been thrust into a new nightmare, one of faith-affiliated hospitals and orphanages under a new name, where physical punishment and emotional abuse were standard practice as they erased the little boy he had once been.

Dottie felt a fleeting touch of sadness and a surge of anger as to how unjust and cruel the world could be.

That little boy had grown up to become the monster they had named Gwilym Benedict-Hughes, created and shaped by the actions of others, and upon his return, nurtured and finally destroyed by Black Abbey Towers and its ghosts. His final breath had been taken by her own hand, a decision that held no choice, no alternative, and no other outcome. Just a deep sense of regret.

She had recognised him the first day she had walked on set, and within days her secret was no longer her own and it was no longer safely kept. Gwilym was about to publicly claim and destroy what was his, something Dottie could not allow. Her dalliance with the then eighteen-year-old boy had been fun and daring, often making her breathless with his wild ways that matched hers. They had both been care-home children, failed and beaten by a pitiful and cruel system, and in turn had gone on to fail themselves. But not now.

'I made it right in the end, though, didn't I?' she whispered to herself as her eyes sparkled with tears. 'You're at peace now, my dear boy, and our precious secret is safe...'

Dottie closed the journal and placed it in a padded jiffy bag before carefully addressing the front with a black Sharpie pen. She peeled off the latex gloves she had been wearing and picked up the gilt-edged resurrection book that had been the ascendancy of evil over good for Gwilym and those before him. She had been reluctant to remove it from the vault at Abbey Towers, but the fear that it would once again fall into the wrong hands had made the decision for her. She stoked the fire and threw on more logs from the inglenook. As the flames flickered and rose higher and higher, she tossed the black book into the glowing embers.

The flames sparked and burnt blue before settling to a fiery orange that swallowed up the cover. She watched the flames spread across to the spine where they finally devoured each page, the words within slowly being eaten and erased for all eternity.

'Consummatum est... Diabolo fuge. Diabolo fuge...' her lips murmured, over and over until she was satisfied that only ashes remained.

THE MURDER BOARD

The double doors to the incident room at Winterbridge police station were working overtime. No sooner had they swung open and closed again, the pattern was repeated. The comings and goings of Andy's team was exhausting to watch. Everyone had been brought in, leave had been cancelled, and it was all hands to the pump.

Andy, with the full backing of Pru, had cut short his paternity leave. He counted his blessings that he had such an understanding partner who always had his back. He would make it up to her again as soon as he could.

He had just returned from the initial walk-through of the scene at Abbey Towers and was now in the process of rear-ranging his incident board, ready to update Murdoch Holmes. 'So, here's our suspect...' he pinned a photograph of Gwilym Benedict-Hughes in the middle. Lamb, Rook, Clapton and Rutter's photographs were angled around it, arrows all pointing towards Gwilym. 'What the boys have recovered from his home address links him to all three murders and the assault, along with this,' he pointed to a photograph of a gold-hooped earring that had trace evidence of blood next to a ruler for comparison on size. 'Dana Simon was missing an earring when she was found, so we're pretty confident this is hers, which I'm sure forensics will confirm on the DNA.' Satisfied his team were tasked and forensics were on top of everything, he welcomed the mug of tea that Lucy offered him.

'He's got to have been one sick cookie to do what he's done.' She sat down next to him, barely taking her eyes off the photograph of Gwilym. 'He'd actually posed poor Alice in a chair, Sarge; it was like something out of a horror film. He'd kept her like a macabre doll.'

'He was sick, Luce. By early accounts he was trying to sacrifice Fiona as part of a resurrection ritual. The others, well...' he scratched his head in frustration, '...we'll just have to spend time trying to find any links and why he chose them.' He pinned Dana Simon's publicity photo underneath Gwilym's and added another arrow. Alice's photograph, the one they had used for her missing reports, joined her side by side. 'We now know who murdered them all, but not why.' He stood back to check the progress of his handiwork. 'And what we also don't know is who in turn shot and killed him.' He stabbed his finger on the photo of Gwilym. 'With a Glock 17 no less!'

'They've recovered the festering bones of Calduggan Wraithe and taken them to the mortuary to confirm they are definitely his and not a more recent victim.' Lucy initialled a report and slipped it into a folder. 'I still can't believe he actually made it out alive from the fire but then popped his clogs in the basement. He's been lying there for over a hundred years and nobody knew.' She angled an evidence bag ready for cataloguing. The small figure inside that they had recovered from the diorama would still need to be processed. She carefully initialled the label, and tongue sticking out deep in thought she scribbled 'LH/2 Diorama Female floral dress'. 'This one is much more detailed than all the others, and the way it was placed in the kitchen of the diorama, it was a proper family scene with the little apple pie and the blue striped jug of custard. A lot of thought went into this one – a terrible shock of ginger hair on it, though.' She tipped her head, scrutinising it from every angle whilst comparing it to the photographs forensic had taken before it had been recovered. 'This meant something, didn't it?'

'Probably, but what, I have no idea. Nothing is adding up.' Andy stood in front of the board again, his mind working ten to the dozen. The arrows all matched, they all went in the right direction so why wasn't he feeling it?

Jack Finnegan lumbered across the room, a large cheese batch rammed in his mouth to keep both his hands free for his files and a coffee. He used Andy's desk as a midway coffee station. Plonking his mug down, he took a bite of the wholemeal batch and dropped it on Andy's desk. Grated cheddar tumbled out from between the two cobs.

Andy flicked the offending bits of cheese onto the floor. 'When you've finished filling your gob, Jack, can you task someone to follow up on the ballistic report once the post-mortem for Benedict-Hughes has been completed? Bob has confirmed it'll take place later this afternoon.'

'Will do. By the way, this was left downstairs for you.' Jack rummaged through his files until he found what he was looking for. He handed him a jiffy bag. Andy's name in bold black letters were neatly printed across the front.

Through habit, Andy felt the outline of the contents with his fingers, like a child would with a present at Christmas. 'It's a book!'

'No shit, Sherlock...' Jack guffawed loudly and then just as quickly went quiet. He pulled each side of his mouth down in contrition. 'Sorry, boss, no offence meant,' he mumbled to Detective Inspector Murdoch Holmes who had chosen that exact same moment to walk up behind him.

Murdoch, who was more than used to his squad taking the

proverbial out of his name, dismissively waved his hand. 'None taken, Jack. What have you got there, Andy?'

'As long as it's not a Ladybird book on breastfeeding; we've already got that one.' His eyes twinkled as he laughed, a welcome jest in the heaviness their office was currently enveloped in.

They watched as Andy slipped his hand inside the bag and pulled out a battered and frayed red-leather journal. The label on the front, the edges curled and peeling, announced its owner. He flicked through the pages. 'It's a sort of diary, dating back to the seventies,' he checked the jiffy bag for any sender details and in their absence, he shook the bag to see if anything else would drop out. 'I am William George Bennett...' he read out the label on the front in a whispered tone, an automatic response to something he uncannily felt he should pay reverence to. He checked the last pages of the book, comparing the writing which had matured with age as the years had progressed. He leant back in his chair, journal in one hand, his mug of tea in the other as he skimmed the words, rapidly flicking the pages. 'Dear God...' he gasped.

Concerned, Lucy looked over his shoulder, aware from his body language that this seemingly innocuous postal delivery had just had a profound effect on him. 'What is it?'

Andy shook his head in disbelief. 'If I've read this correctly, our suspect isn't who we think he is...'

THE CEREMONY

TWO MONTHS LATER

*P*ru carefully adjusted Andy's tie, not because it actually needed doing; it was more a show of love and support. She smiled as she watched him fussing over Phoebe. He tucked the pink blanket around her, gently swept her hair from her forehead and planted a soft kiss on her cheek.

'I don't know how I should feel about you fawning over another woman, Mr Barnes,' she teased. 'Sweet Miss P here seems to have you totally wrapped around her little finger.'

'As it should be,' he laughed, 'I just can't stop looking at her, she's simply perfect – like her mummy.' Andy was pleased that he had quickly redeemed himself, although he knew Pru wouldn't have his adoration of their daughter any other way. He shrugged his arm into his suit jacket, buttoned it up and took to the mirror to check his appearance. 'What do you think?'

Pru stood behind him and encircled his waist with her arms. 'Handsome as ever, my soon to be commended Delectable Detective. You should be very proud of your achievement, I know I am.'

Andy turned to face her. 'I *am* proud. It's just I wish my mum and dad could have been here to see me; they would have been over the moon.' He paused deep in thought. 'And I sometimes wish the ones that were responsible for bringing me into this world could share this and other special moments too.' Andy had never felt unwanted or unloved, even when he had been told about his adoption. His life had been full of happiness, laughter and more love than he could ever have imagined. He hadn't really been abandoned; he had been given up so he could have a better life. The letter that had accompanied his papers, gifted to him on his fourteenth birthday, had been one full of love, regret and trying to do the right thing. He could recite the final words from memory, forever etched.

And so, my beautiful son, until we meet again, keep looking for the brightest star in the sky each night. It will be the one that will hold all my love for you...
Mummy x

Phoebe gave a little snuffle. It was perfect timing to remind him of the here and now rather than the past. He quickly changed the subject. 'I've been thinking, not that it would change what our team achieved and what a great result it was, but it really just fell into place didn't it?'

Pru pressed her index finger on his lips. 'Shush, you're trying to talk yourself out of something you've more than earned. A commendation for an incredibly difficult investigation that saw a serial killer put to rights and several high-profile crimes solved.'

'He died, Pru, and that's not justice for all the victims and their families, is it? He should have been put on trial, they should have had their day in court, stood and looked him in the eye.' He adjusted his tie for the second time in as many minutes. 'And it took the murders of our suspects to solve those crimes. I just don't feel we should take all the credit, particularly as I'm not even sure they were all linked.' His deep-rooted sense of fairness and moral compass were really giving his conscience a hammering.

'Gwilym, or should I say William Bennett, was as mad as a fish. He would never have stood trial, you know that. He would have been committed, and where's the justice in that?' She handed him his coat. 'You did good, don't knock yourself down.'

'I know, but it was the other murders, Danny Rook and Barney Lamb, those ones. It just didn't feel right marking them down to William, even with all the evidence that linked him, he was hardly moral vigilante material, was he?' The itch was there again, right at the back of his head. It used to be called a 'copper's nose', and it was a trait that never left you. 'I can get the Dana murder, that was just simply to stop her from burning down what he considered was his sanctuary, to stop her from ruining his plans.' The journal had been a work of art when it had come down to their investigation to tie up loose ends. William had committed everything in the smallest detail to that book, his thoughts, his intentions and his reasons. 'Alice was a practice thrill kill, Clapton was in the wrong place, at the wrong time, but there's absolutely nothing on Lamb, Rook and Rutter, not a mention, nothing. Don't you think that's strange from a man who literally documented everything? And to top it all off, William's murder is still active, no forensics, no clues, no witnesses, just a ballistics report for a Glock 17 and a 9mm bullet. Not your average everyday murder weapon.' He went quiet, contemplating the events of the past few months.

It had been a nightmare piecing everything together initially, and the one thing that had left him baffled was the diorama and the figures that William had so cleverly crafted. The journal only referred to him 'putting mum back where she belonged', hence the redheaded figure in the blue dress placed in the miniature kitchen. Archives had confirmed Peggy Bennett was indeed the possessor of fiery red tresses. He could only surmise that everything else had been a game, tormenting the police with what

William believed was his superiority since he had taken on the persona of the Death Collector.

Pru finished sorting out the baby bag. She checked the number of nappies she had already packed and decided, based on Phoebe's recent performances, a few more thrown in wouldn't go amiss. 'How much more of a confession do you want, Detective Sergeant Barnes?' she gave him a playful punch on the arm. 'He even admitted to his plan to kill someone in a sacrificial ritual to bring back the dead mother his father murdered in 1973! Now if you ask me that's just plain weird, not to mention a little bit crazy, particularly if you include that figure he did of her for the kitchen scene.' She popped her eyes to prove her point. 'I know it's sad what happened to him when he was a child, but that doesn't justify what he did.'

The mere mention of the sacrificial ritual of resurrection made Andy shudder and smirk simultaneously. 'Talking about resurrections, how much longer?' He gave Pru a saucy wink, which prompted her to retaliate by sticking her tongue out.

'You'll have to catch me first…' She laughed. 'Come on, let's get a move on, we've got an awards ceremony to attend. I said we'd meet Bree and Mark in the pre-drinks reception room so we don't want to keep them waiting, and I'd like to get there before this little one decides to fill another nappy.'

Andy saluted her. 'Yes, ma'am…'

EPILOGUE

$\mathcal{D}$ottie checked her reflection in the restroom mirror, pleased that for once she actually looked quite feminine, although she did feel slightly 'Dick Emery-ish' in the court shoes she had donned for the occasion. Years of body-building had given her thigh muscles a Welsh rugby player would have been proud to have, which in turn made walking with any sort of grace in a pair of heels particularly difficult. The invitation from Murdoch lay on the vanity unit, ready to give her entry to the conference hall. She silently mouthed the words.

Winterbridge Constabulary Commendation Ceremony: Police Headquarters

She ran her finger down the list until she found the name she was looking for. A wistful smile touched her lips.

'Okay, Dorothy May Barker, assassin for hire, stunt coordinator, advisor and righter of wrongs, this is it. This is what you've been waiting for. You go, girl!' She teased a curl of hair that had flopped over her right eye back into place.

'Sorry, sorry – emergency coming through...' The pretty

woman with chestnut curls, vivid green eyes and a small infant in her arms, backed into the rest room. She was almost swamped by the large baby bag she had slung over her shoulder; disposable nappies poked from the side pocket; and a familiar aroma wafted in with her. She gave Dottie an apologetic grin. 'I'm so sorry, parent and baby is engaged, and little miss here has had a bit of a poonami.' She dropped the bag onto the vanity counter.

'Here let me help you.' Dottie had intended to open the bag and set everything up that would be needed for a nappy change as a way of assistance, but instead Pru handed her the baby.

'This is Phoebe, say hello to the lovely lady who is our extra pair of hands in a crisis.' Pru gave a gentle giggle before she began to busy herself putting out the changing mat, popping the baby wipes at the ready and spreading out a new nappy, all whilst regaling Dottie with the excitement of her husband being presented with a special award.

Dottie knew exactly who this stunning woman was. She had researched her and watched her from afar. Prunella Barnes had been one of her more enjoyable and fulfilling intelligence gathering forays. But this was something she had never envisaged. Dottie now had a perfect end to her story. She gazed longingly at Phoebe, taking in every little detail, consigning it to memory. The irony was not lost on her, this tiny infant, all that embodied innocence and hope for the future, in the arms of a woman who revelled in murder and retribution.

'Thank you so much, I'm so sorry I didn't get your name.' Pru took Phoebe from her and proceeded to deftly change her nappy. 'I really appreciate your help.'

Jolted out of her reverie, Dottie quickly responded. 'It's Dorothy my dear, Dorothy Barker.'

Pru thrust out her hand, then frantically inspected it to ensure nothing untoward from Phoebe had adhered to her fingers, before offering it again. 'Well, it's lovely to meet you, Dorothy.'

'Call me Dottie, that's what my friends do...' Dottie accepted her warm greeting. Her heart skipped a beat; this had been more than she could ever have wished for.

Another brief moment in time and one to treasure for eternity.

∾

The auditorium was standing room only as Dottie made her way to her reserved aisle seat. In all her years, throughout all of the dangerous missions she had undertaken, sanctioned or otherwise, she had never felt such excitement, trepidation or, dare she say it for fear it could be snatched away from her, an overwhelming sense of elation. This was a mission that she had spent over forty years waiting for. Forty years of regret, forty years of sadness, and forty years of trying to discover if the choice she had been forced to make then, had been the right one. She had asked very little of fate, but to share this brief moment before she would slip away unnoticed.

'And now we have the Chief Constable's Commendation which has been awarded to...'

Dottie held her breath waiting for the announcement, a glow of something she had never experienced before filling her completely. For a woman for whom death was a constant companion and where emotion had always feared to tread, she found herself swallowing hard, trying to dislodge the painful lump that had caught in her throat. Her heart ached as tears pricked her eyes. She vainly fought to keep hold of them, determined not to draw attention to herself, just as she always did. She was after all, Dottie the Invisible, the persona she needed for the game she was in. To slip in and out without being noticed, without being identified. She was an inglorious presence in a world that fought hard to value life above everything else.

She took a deep breath to steady herself, the small identity band she had taken from her memory box clutched tightly in her hand, as his name was read out.

'… Detective Sergeant Andrew Barnes.'

She watched Andy walk with confidence down the aisle to the stage, the applause filling the vast auditorium from wall to ceiling. It was a precious moment that she had stolen from Gwilym, but it had been a choice she would never regret. For Gwilym had not earned the right to be part of this cherished life she was watching unfold, nor to hold the privilege of being called 'father'.

Andy momentarily paused, standing right beside her, unaware of her presence. If she reached out, her fingers could almost touch his, just as she had on the day he was born. His tiny hand in hers, a brief moment in time before they tore him away from her, leaving her vulnerable and alone with only the guilt she had now carried for over forty years, and a severed name tag that simply said, 'Baby Blue'.

He had been the brightest star that had broken her heart.

'My perfect boy,' she whispered as she finally allowed the tears to fall.

'My son…'

**The absent are never without fault,
nor the present without excuse…
— Benjamin Franklin**

THE END

ALSO BY GINA KIRKHAM

ACKNOWLEDGEMENTS

I usually start with 'I never quite know where to start with acknowledgements' and then rattle on for eternity – and to be honest, after several previous attempts for my other books, there's sadly still no sign of improvement!

I am always so very grateful for the smallest of things, as much as the biggest of things, in my life.

To the wonderful ladies of The Women's Institute. Without you there would be no Kitty, Ethel or Clarissa, and no tales to tell. Your kindness, generosity and fabulous sense of humour became the inspiration for my characters. I loved your excitement and enthusiasm to be included, and hopefully I have created them just as you asked, like you, full of mischief, a little bit naughty and so much larger than life. Thank you for inviting me to speak at your meetings, and thank you for all you selflessly do for others.

For Loulou Brown my brilliant editor. It has been a pleasure to work with you again and to get another chapter of *Murders* into shape. You made the whole process so simple, straightforward and stress free, and, best of all, you 'get' me, my humour and my style of writing. Here's to being together again in the future. A very special thank you for Tara Lyons at Bloodhound Books. Tara, you are an absolute dream to work with; not only did I gain a fabulous Senior Editorial & Production Manager when I signed with Bloodhound, I also gained a beautiful friend… and someone who always embraces my quirky off-the-wall emails with such good humour!

A heartfelt final 'thank you' to Betsy and Fred, the founders of

Bloodhound Books, who have now moved on to exciting adventures with their new venture *Globescribe*. Thank you for once again taking a chance on this quirky old trout. It has been an honour to work with you, I'll miss you both, but I know Bloodhound has been left in the hands of an amazing team to continue your fantastic work.

I was delighted to be asked to participate in the **Children in Read** charity book auction again last year. Paddy Heron and his team from CiR do an amazing job and work so hard. They have raised a staggering sum over the years from their auctions. The winning bid for a dedicated, signed copy of *Murders at the Harmony Hollows Resort* and to have a character named after them in book five of the series, *Murders at The Black Abbey Towers,* was Mark Joynson. So, say hello once again to 'Mighty Marko' who has travelled over from *Harmony Hollows* to star in *Black Abbey Towers* as their film production chaperone to the fading stars, and just a little bit of eye candy for the Meddlesome Quartet!

Huge hugs and a thank you to Josephine Bilton, Anne Untisz and Charlotte Shaw who so very kindly agreed to be my go-to's for a first draft read-through to ensure I was on the right track with the storyline, and that I hadn't made too many blunders before sending it in! I don't know what I'd do without you! To Jools Smith for her fantastic input on up-to-date MISPER protocol, and Andy McLannahan for his invaluable expertise and advice on film production; I had absolutely no idea so much goes on behind the scenes of a film set.

No acknowledgement would be complete without mentioning fellow authors, Luca Veste and Dave Jackson. Thank you for your support, kindness and laughter over the years; some of my best (and funniest) moments have been with you both.

For my Auntie Josie, or 'HRH' as she is better known by her sons Del & JJ, carry on making those amazing memories at Casa Josefina - and I'll expect an invite to your 'wedding' with Alfonso!

Once again (I have to mention him as I truly am the doting

elder sister), to my very handsome, debonair brother, Andy Dawson – for no other reason than him being handsome, debonair and, of course, my brother. To my sister Claire: you are so far away but you will always be in my heart. To my daughter, Emma, and my gorgeous grandchildren, Olivia, Annie and Arthur. You are my sunshine, you make me smile every day, and I'm so very blessed to have you in my life and to be part of yours.

Last but definitely not least, a massive thank you to my handsome and very funny hubby, John. The love of my life, my bodyguard, chauffeur and human SatNav. The man who makes me laugh every single day (and frequently thinks of murder too). He has endured hours of torment as my muse and 'go to' for ideas for this book and my previous ones. He rolls his eyes and groans, but still continues reluctantly to participate in the most bizarre acts all in the name of research – well, at least that's what I tell him it's for! Without his love and support there would be no stories to tell – and I'd still be driving around various parts of the UK, panic-stricken and lost.

I hope I haven't missed anyone out, but knowing me and my scatterbrained head-thoughts, I probably have. I'm so sorry if you haven't appeared here because of my forgetfulness and mislaid notes, but please know there is a humongous 'thank you' in my heart for you.

Gina x

A NOTE FROM THE PUBLISHER

Thank you for reading this book. If you enjoyed it please do consider leaving a review on Amazon to help others find it too.

We hate typos. All of our books have been rigorously edited and proofread, but sometimes mistakes do slip through. If you have spotted a typo, please do let us know and we can get it amended within hours.

info@bloodhoundbooks.com